W9-BLQ-052

B & T

Glenwood Public Library
109 N. Vine St.
Glenwood, IA 51534

10/2021

THE
ATTIC ON
QUEEN STREET

ALSO BY KAREN WHITE

The Color of Light
Pieces of the Heart
Learning to Breathe
The Memory of Water
The Lost Hours
Falling Home
On Folly Beach
The Beach Trees
Sea Change
After the Rain
The Time Between
A Long Time Gone
The Sound of Glass
Flight Patterns
Spinning the Moon
The Night the Lights Went Out
Dreams of Falling
The Last Night in London

Cowritten with Beatriz Williams and Lauren Willig

The Forgotten Room
The Glass Ocean
All the Ways We Said Goodbye

The Tradd Street Series

The House on Tradd Street
The Girl on Legare Street
The Strangers on Montagu Street
Return to Tradd Street
The Guests on South Battery
The Christmas Spirits on Tradd Street

THE
ATTIC ON
QUEEN STREET

KAREN WHITE

Berkley

New York

November 9, 2021 B+T

BERKLEY
An imprint of Penguin Random House LLC
penguinrandomhouse.com

Copyright © 2021 by Harley House Books, LLC
Penguin Random House supports copyright. Copyright fuels creativity, encourages diverse
voices, promotes free speech, and creates a vibrant culture. Thank you for buying an authorized
edition of this book and for complying with copyright laws by not reproducing, scanning, or
distributing any part of it in any form without permission. You are supporting writers and
allowing Penguin Random House to continue to publish books for every reader.

BERKLEY and the BERKLEY & B colophon are registered trademarks of
Penguin Random House LLC.

Library of Congress Cataloging-in-Publication Data

Names: White, Karen (Karen S.), author.
Title: The attic on Queen Street / Karen White.
Description: New York : Berkley, [2021] | Series: Tradd Street ; 7
Identifiers: LCCN 2021017488 (print) | LCCN 2021017489 (ebook) |
ISBN 9780451475251 (hardcover) | ISBN 9780698193024 (ebook)
Subjects: LCSH: Paranormal fiction. | GSAFD: Suspense fiction. | Ghost stories.
Classification: LCC PS3623.H5776 A93 2021 (print) |
LCC PS3623.H5776 (ebook) | DDC 813/.6--dc23
LC record available at https://lccn.loc.gov/2021017488
LC ebook record available at https://lccn.loc.gov/2021017489

Printed in the United States of America
1 3 5 7 9 10 8 6 4 2

This is a work of fiction. Names, characters, places, and incidents either are the product of
the author's imagination or are used fictitiously, and any resemblance to actual persons,
living or dead, business establishments, events, or locales is entirely coincidental.

For Claire and Rich Kobylt and family.
Better than coleslaw.

THE
ATTIC ON
QUEEN STREET

CHAPTER 1

Snow in Charleston is as magical as it is rare, the icy white dusting on palm trees and church steeples, ancient statues and wrought iron fences transforming the Holy City into an enchanting snow globe. Snowmen sprouted like weeds in lawns and parks, and snow angels spread their wings on every flat spot of ground as children and adults alike ran outside to play in an exotic frosty playground.

For nearly three days after the record-breaking snowstorm as the temperature began to rise, patches of white clung desperately to every surface, gradually shrinking as the world thawed, leaving only trickling eaves and slushy puddles as a reminder that they had ever been there at all.

I watched it all from inside my house on Tradd Street, my heart seemingly as frozen as the icy stalactites dripping from the Pineapple Fountain in Waterfront Park. In less than a week's time, my life had flipped itself upside down as if it had decided to accept the wintry invitation to glide on the ice without benefit of skates. Or any kind of padding that might soften the inevitable fall.

I had somehow managed to go from being a very happily married mother of three to being a seemingly single mother with an estranged husband and a marriage as precarious as the melting ice. And all because

I had made the simple mistake of breaking my promise to trust Jack enough to share everything with him. To be a team in all things.

Despite what everyone seemed to think, it wasn't entirely my fault. Jack—a bestselling author of true-crime mysteries—and I had been working to solve the mystery of where a Revolutionary War treasure was hidden, before Jack's nemesis, self-proclaimed author and all-around jerk Marc Longo, discovered it first. Marc had managed to steal Jack's book idea about the disappearance of Louisa Gibbes, who'd once lived in our house on Tradd Street and been murdered by Marc's ancestor Joseph Longo. Marc not only made the book an international bestseller but also scored a major movie deal. And then he somehow managed to manipulate us into allowing the movie to be filmed in our house. For Jack's sake, I couldn't let Marc win again.

It wasn't my fault that Jack had had a bad case of the flu at the same time I'd figured out that the treasure was buried in the cemetery at Gallen Hall Plantation—owned by Marc Longo's brother, Anthony—and that I hadn't had time for Jack to get better. It wasn't my fault that Marc and Anthony had anticipated my solving the mystery and were waiting for me to point the way to the hidden treasure. Nor was it my fault that my half sister, Jayne, had told Jack what I was up to and that he had then insisted on going to the cemetery. And it was definitely not my fault that he had happened to step on an old grave full of crumbling coffins that collapsed under him, nearly burying him alive.

As far as I could tell, my only mistake was believing that Jack would be so happy that I'd found the treasure that he'd forgive me for everything else. But, as I'd discovered, hindsight is always twenty-twenty, and it turns out that asking for forgiveness is not necessarily easier than asking for permission.

I'd rushed through the snow-covered landscape of my Charleston neighborhood to tell Jack that I was sorry, that I'd made a mistake and wouldn't let it happen again, and found him packing his bags. His response had been telling me good-bye, followed by a decisive snap of the front door as it closed in my face.

For three weeks I didn't leave the house, not wanting to be absent when Jack decided to return. Friends and family came and went in various attempts to rouse me, to try to coax me outside with promises of doughnuts and coffee—neither of which seemed appealing to me anymore.

Christmas passed almost as a nonevent. My stepdaughter, Nola, had outdone herself by going against her own dietary preferences and making my favorite gluten- and carb-filled desserts and other dishes that I'd done my best to pretend to eat. She and my twenty-one-month-old twins, JJ—for Jack Junior—and Sarah, saved the entire holiday by being the only bright spots of joy.

Their nanny, Jayne, had bundled them up to take them to Jack's parents' house, where they would celebrate Christmas for the second time on the same day. Nola and the twins hadn't seemed to be nearly as upset as I had been at the prospect of their opening more gifts without me there. Gifts that no doubt had been wrapped haphazardly instead of their every corner being measured for preciseness and each dab of tape being exactly the same size since apparently only their mother knew how important those kinds of things were.

I'd even showered and washed my hair, with the dim hope that Jack would come himself to collect them, but then had had to bravely kiss the children good-bye. My three dogs—General Lee, Porgy, and Bess—had whined and snuffled, brightening my mood until I realized that they were upset not on my behalf but because they'd wanted to go, too.

Even after Christmas, when everyone was returning to work, my job as a Realtor with Henderson House Realty didn't entice me enough to put on clothes and make my way to my office on Broad Street. It was slow this time of year anyway, and our receptionist, Jolly, promised to call me with anything important. Besides being a meticulous record keeper and notetaker (something I appreciated more than most), she was also a self-professed psychic whose predictions were either wildly inaccurate or eerily spot-on. She'd called only once, to let me know definitively—according to her—that ghosts didn't leave footprints in the snow. I hadn't had the heart to tell her that she was wrong.

Now, almost three weeks into the New Year, I stood at one of the tall dining room windows that overlooked our Loutrel Briggs garden, which had been lovingly restored by my father. All of his painstaking work had been drastically undone by the previous spring's torrential rainstorms, which had revealed an ancient cistern and exposed more than just old bricks.

If my entire demeanor and outlook on life hadn't been as dark and empty as the bottom of the cistern, I'd probably have been hoping that the last of the restless spirits that had been awakened by its sudden exposure had quit the premises. After all, they were partially responsible for Jack's leaving. But only partially. The rest of the blame lay elsewhere, although Jack and I apparently had opposing opinions as to exactly where.

Pressing my forehead against the cold glass of the window, I watched with disinterest as small indentations began to appear in a line around what remained of the snow atop the blue tarp, protected from the sun by the ancient oak tree. The occasional bare peak of blue canvas made me think of the protruding elbows of frozen swimmers.

I blinked, recognizing the clear marks of the heel and toe of a small booted foot creating a path through the garden. I straightened when I realized the footprints had stopped directly in front of the window where I stood.

"Mellie?"

I jumped, something I rarely did, and spun around with my hand on my throat. For most of my forty-one years, I'd been visited by the dearly departed, but I'd always found them more annoying than frightening. Especially the ones who seemed to enjoy appearing behind me in mirrors or materializing on stair landings before rudely shoving me. At some point, I would need to have a discussion with them about manners.

Jayne stood behind me, holding a bag that smelled suspiciously like doughnuts. In her other hand she held a mug from the kitchen, with steam rising from the surface, its light brown color telling me that she'd added just the right amount of cream. We'd known each other for only about a year, but long enough to know we both liked our coffee with lots of cream and even more sugar, that she was more athletic than I was, that she hated the dark for the same reason I did, and that we'd both inherited from our mother the ability to communicate with the dead. She was looking beyond me toward the garden and the single set of footprints.

"Who is that?" she asked quietly, as if not wanting to alert whoever or whatever it was that we were there. But she was too late. The hairs on the back of my neck and along my arms were already standing at attention. I suddenly recalled the most recent column written by *Post and Courier* journalist Suzy Dorf.

. . . the cistern excavation at the former Vanderhorst residence on Tradd Street is still in progress, but an unnamed source has told me that there are more secrets hidden there, and there are bets going on in certain parts of our society on whether the owners of the house will be residing together in the home by the time the last treasure is revealed.

I deliberately turned my back to the window. "I have no idea, and no intention of finding out. I'm done with all that."

"But what about your friend Veronica? You promised to help her find out who murdered her sister. We're supposed to work together, remember? Not to mention that Veronica's counting on you. Especially now that her husband is pressing to sell their family home. Adrienne's still there—you've felt her presence. And we both know that if they move out, you'll lose the best chance of finding her killer."

I stared back at her for a moment before nodding slowly. "And I imagine that you won't let me forget about it anytime soon."

"Nope." She stood next to me and pressed her forehead against the window to peer into the garden. "Are they almost done with the excavation? Dad's garden is practically destroyed. Although between you and me, I think the prospect of starting all over again excites him. I think we should limit the number of gardening classes he attends. His enthusiasm is getting out of control."

I nodded, no longer on the defensive when she referred to my father as "Dad." She was born after my parents divorced, after our mother had reconnected with an old beau. Jayne's identity and the fact that she hadn't died at birth, as our mother had been told, had been only recently confirmed after she'd unexpectedly inherited a house on South Battery and we'd had to work alongside our mother to combat the angry ghost of her father's wife.

Having been only recently reconciled with my estranged mother and father, I'd had difficulty accepting a new sibling, who'd been immediately embraced by both parents. Despite my initial misgivings, I'd come to accept and love the new addition to my family and was secretly thrilled to have a sister who shared more with me than just DNA.

"Sophie keeps telling me that they're close to being done. I'm not going to tell her about the footsteps because I want that cistern filled in and forgotten."

Jayne turned to face me. Instead of rebuking me, she widened her eyes as she took a closer look at me. "Have you been raiding Sophie's closet?"

Dr. Sophie Wallen-Arasi was—against all reason—my best friend. A professor of historic preservation at the College of Charleston, she was mismatched tie-dye to my crisp linen suits with matching handbags, Birkenstocks to my Louboutins, and real Christmas greenery versus hassle-free plastic garlands, because she liked to make things more difficult than they should be. I liked to think that we complemented each other, rounding off any sharp edges of our personalities. She'd guided me through the extensive and never-ending renovations on my historic house, which I'd unwillingly inherited—along with a dog, General Lee, and Mrs. Houlihan the housekeeper. All the while, I had kept up a running commentary about her bizarre clothing choices in the hope that one day she might actually look in a mirror and fix things.

I looked down at my baggy sweatpants and moth-eaten cardigan sweater with an unidentified food stain on the sleeve, and felt my eyes well with tears. I'd found them in a dark corner of the closet where Jack had dropped and forgotten them. Besides our children, they were the only things of his he'd left behind.

As if to stave off more tears, Jayne held up the bag and mug with a hopeful smile. "I brought you doughnuts from Glazed. And made you coffee just the way you like it." She moved closer so I could feel the steam from the coffee. "Since Mrs. Houlihan is still on vacation, I helped myself."

My mouth would usually have started watering at the mere mention of my favorite doughnut shop, but all I could muster was a soft grumble in my stomach. I couldn't remember the last time I'd eaten.

I took the mug while she set the bag on the dining room table and eyed the shriveled oranges and the dead pine boughs regurgitating brown needles on the glossy wood surface. The centerpiece relic was from a Christmas dinner fund-raiser the night of the big snow when Jack had nearly been buried alive. A sudden flash of anger pushed away a little of my despondency. I accepted that I had perhaps broken our trust agreement by venturing out on my own. But I also couldn't stop thinking that if Jack had just stayed in bed to recover from the flu like he'd been told, he wouldn't have been in the snow-covered cemetery that night or fallen into a collapsed grave.

"It's almost the end of January, Melanie. Would you like me to help you take down the Christmas decorations?"

She indicated the drooping Christmas tree in the corner. The sad ornaments huddled at the bottom, where they'd slid off of bare branches next to puckered oranges in various stages of decay like victims of a massacre in which indifference had been the only weapon.

I shrugged. "Sure." Ignoring the doughnuts, I took a sip of coffee, barely tasting it. I wrapped my fingers around the mug, appreciating its warmth, but paused as I raised it to my lips for a second sip. "Why are you here? Sarah and JJ are with Jack today."

Jayne sighed. "Besides the fact that I shouldn't need a reason to visit my sister or to bring sustenance since Mrs. Houlihan is away, I am bringing a message."

"A message?" I didn't bother to hide the hopefulness in my voice; one of the best things about having a sister was the absence of the need for pretense.

She gave me a consoling smile. "From Rebecca. She and Marc would like to meet with you and Jack about the filming. She considered asking you herself, but with Marc and Jack involved, she figured she'd need me as a go-between. She mentioned it's hard to clean blood off of these antique rugs."

I raised my eyebrows. Rebecca was our distant cousin as well as Jack's onetime girlfriend and my sometime nemesis. She'd married Marc Longo, whose main talent appeared to be using his far-reaching influence to ruin Jack's writing career.

I closed my eyes and shook my head. "No. That's not going to happen. We don't need the money anymore, not since we found the rubies in the cemetery." I didn't add *the night Jack was nearly killed* because I didn't need to. Everyone remembered that night not only because of Jack's near-death experience but also because Marc got dragged feetfirst into a mausoleum and his hair turned solid white.

I continued. "Our lawyers have already been in touch with the film production company with a generous cash-settlement offer to get them to change filming locations. We had to remind them that we were forced into agreeing only because we were trying to avoid a lawsuit after Nola's car accident with Marc and that creepy producer, Harvey Beckner. But now, because of the rubies, we're not that desperate. There is absolutely nothing Marc can say to make us change our minds."

"Marc is aware. But Rebecca says there's more to it. She suggested meeting at your office at a time that works for both you and Jack."

"Both of us?" I didn't care how pitiful my voice sounded or how my firm insistence on not having a film crew anywhere near my house had been quickly replaced with thoughts of what I would wear to the meeting if Jack was there and how I should probably wash my hair. "He agreed?"

"He hasn't agreed yet. They thought it best that you ask him and then let them know."

My excitement dimmed. "Oh. I'll try. That's the only thing I can promise. Although I think we'd have a better chance of another big snow in Charleston than of Jack agreeing to sit down with me, not to mention with Marc and Rebecca."

"All right. I'll let Rebecca know." She squatted and picked up two of the oranges, the spiked cloves that I had so painstakingly applied in precise rows now looking more like crooked pimples on shrunken heads. "Why don't I start clearing away all of the rotten fruit and dried greenery? It's a fire hazard, you know."

I didn't answer, distracted by the sound of Nola's guitar coming from her room. My stepdaughter had inherited her musical ability from her late mother and had already found success writing jingles for commercials, as well as a few hit songs for pop heartthrob Jimmy Gordon.

Breaking a dry spell that had run in tandem with Jack's own during our recent crisis involving three restless Revolutionary War–era spirits and the upcoming filming scheduled to begin after the holidays, her parents' current woes had apparently added fuel to her creative fire. The melancholy strains of her guitar were now a constant soundtrack to my life.

It didn't help that the lyrics were as dismal as the melodies, but Nola's music was important to her, so I didn't ask her to stop, although I had started shoving earplugs in my ears after I heard the first words to her latest effort: "My shriveled heart, all black and cold, yet still it beats, until I'm old . . ." I had to keep reminding myself that Nola had chosen to stay with me when Jack moved out, a show of affection and solidarity I appreciated, although she insisted she wasn't choosing sides. But after listening to her music, I couldn't help but wonder if she'd stayed as a way to punish me for being so completely stupid where her father was concerned.

I heard Nola's bedroom door open and the sound of three sets of paws, one set slower than the others, scampering down the hallway toward the steps. Even General Lee had deserted my bed and now chose to sleep in Nola's room in a canine form of reproach. Although I kept reminding myself that I didn't like dogs, his desertion hurt almost as much as Jack's.

As Jayne retreated to the kitchen to retrieve a garbage bag, I shuffled into the foyer to watch Nola descend the stairs, each step causing dead pine needles to cascade to the floor from the banister garland. The plastic pomegranates and other contraband that I had snuck in behind

Sophie's historically authentic eye remained full and ripe amid the desiccated wreckage of the garland. I wanted to take a picture to prove to Sophie that I'd been right about how plastic had a place among my Christmas decor, but even that righteous victory felt hollow.

Nola's long dark hair fell forward as she devoted all of her concentration to her seemingly physically attached phone, her thumbs flying over the screen as she descended the stairs with the three dogs running circles around her ankles.

"Could you at least hold the banister with one hand? That's really not safe."

She continued her descent as if she hadn't heard me, her thumbs pausing only when she reached the bottom. She looked up at me with Jack's piercing blue eyes—all three of my children were clones of their father, as if their mothers had merely been holding cells between conception and birth—and smiled her father's smile, which always caught me off guard. "Did you say something? I was texting Lindsey and Alston about seeing a movie later."

I opened my mouth to repeat myself, but then thought better of it. If I'd learned anything about handling teenage girls in the three years since Nola had come to live with us, it was that choosing which battles to fight was the difference between domestic tranquility and living with a ticking time bomb. Nola was generally easygoing, except when someone mentioned her lack of a driver's license, questioned her devotion to being vegan, or asked her where she wanted to go for college.

Instead I bent to scratch three sets of fluffy ears. "Shouldn't you be in school?" I was rewarded with soft licks from little pink tongues, the show of affection bringing tears of gratitude to my eyes. Not that they were any substitute for Jack, but at this point I'd take it.

I could tell Nola was fighting the urge to roll her eyes. Ever since Jack had left, she'd been keeping the eye-rolling to a minimum, apparently to stop my ego from completing its downhill slide. "It's Saturday. Today's the campus tour at the College of Charleston, remember?"

I was fairly certain she hadn't mentioned it to me, as I'd already checked my phone and desk calendars and they were both empty. And

I would have remembered it. The whole college question had become a sensitive issue, which she faced with quiet stoicism as she left the house to attend her SAT prep class or college fairs—all done without Jack or me. She didn't want any "undue influence," which was ridiculous, really. Jack and I had both attended the University of South Carolina—Jack on a football scholarship—and we only wanted her to find the school where she'd fit in best. Just because Jack had season tickets to watch the Gamecocks and wore cardinal and gold for most of the fall didn't necessarily mean he wanted her to attend his alma mater. Not that he'd have objected. We'd at least achieved her agreement to allow us to visit colleges with her, as long as we remained silent.

"Actually, I don't."

Her eyes moved to the dogs as she studiously avoided my gaze. "Yeah, well, Dad's taking me."

"Oh, okay," I said, feeling more than just a little hurt. I'd envisioned the three of us doing the college hunt together, me with my spreadsheet carefully noting the pros and cons of each institution of higher learning in which Nola expressed an interest. I managed a smile that might have been more wobble than actual smile. "I can print out my spreadsheet for you to take with you if you like. I'll be happy to type in everything later."

Her eyes met mine and I ignored the look of pity in them. I wondered if I resembled General Lee when he sat by the table begging for scraps.

Nola's face brightened. "You know, Dad didn't say that you *couldn't* come. I mean, if you want to."

The old Mellie would have shouted *Yes!* But that was the old Mellie. After all my false starts and stops at becoming a better edition of myself, I was now working on Mellie Version 107 or so.

Before I could say no, Nola interrupted me. "I'd like you to be there." She crossed her arms and rolled her eyes so that her meaning couldn't be interpreted that she *needed* me there. "I mean, if you aren't busy or anything. You *are* my parents, and I know Alston's and Lindsey's parents are all going. So it would be weird if you didn't."

I tried to keep the excitement from my voice, so I sounded as low-key as Nola. "Well, in that case, I should go. I need to talk to your dad anyway, so I can kill two birds with one stone."

She picked up Porgy and narrowed her eyes. "Is that an old-people saying? Or do you have something against birds?"

Jayne entered the foyer, interrupting my own eye roll. She carried a stuffed plastic garbage bag over her shoulder like Santa Claus, awkward knobs and the stray twig protruding from the plastic. "Hi, Nola," she said, dumping the bag on the floor between us. "You ready for your college tour today?"

I glanced at my stepdaughter, who shrugged. "She knows only because she was here yesterday when Alston and Lindsey and I were talking about it. We may have discussed your spreadsheet."

I glared at my sister.

Nola tugged on my sleeve. "Why don't you go have breakfast? I bought you Froot Loops. Plenty of processed sugar and empty calories, just the way you like them."

I was oddly touched. Nola was usually on a stealth mission to restrict my diet to cardboard and sawdust disguised as health food.

"Thank you. But I'm going to run upstairs to shower and get dressed since we have that college tour. Jayne brought doughnuts, too, but I'll save those for later."

Nola's phone pinged. "The tour isn't until one o'clock. You have three hours," Nola said as her thumbs flew over her phone screen.

I considered her with open admiration. I could barely type one letter at a time when fully focused on texting.

Jayne's eyebrows rose as her gaze scanned me from head to toe. "It might take her that long."

"Ha," I said, turning to head up the stairs.

"Oh, wait," Nola said, calling me back.

I turned and watched her pull something out of the large pocket of her plaid pajama bottoms. "Did you put this on my nightstand?"

Jayne inhaled sharply. I squinted and took a tentative step forward to see better, Jayne's reaction making me glad for once of the vanity that kept me from admitting I needed to wear glasses. "What is it?"

Nola held her hand closer so I could see better, and I immediately wished she hadn't. An iron coffin-shaped box filled her outstretched hand, a small round window at the top showing the sallow pixie face of a small doll-like figure inside. Its eyes were black ink-drawn dots with a red circle to indicate an open mouth caught at the moment of surprise. Bold, raised letters on the lid read: *LISTEN TO YOUR MOTHER.*

"It opens, too," Nola said.

I lifted a hand to stop her, but she'd already flicked up a clasp on the side of the box to reveal a small porcelain doll, its pale arms crossed over its chest. The tiny white body lay upon what appeared to be a bed of antique buttons made of pewter and mother-of-pearl.

Jayne kept her distance—she was eight years younger than me, with apparently better vision. "I think that might be one of the most hideous and horrifying things I've ever seen. And I've seen a lot."

"Worse than the Edison Doll in your attic?" Nola asked, referring to an antique talking doll with the unnerving habit of appearing unexpectedly.

"I'd say it's a tie. And this was on your nightstand?"

"Yeah. I thought Mellie gave it to me."

My eyes met Jayne's in mutual understanding, both of us recalling the footprints in the snow. We looked at Nola. "I've never seen it before, and I certainly wouldn't have put it in your room." If I had seen it before, I would have burned it or thrown it into the Cooper River. I was a big believer in ignoring the obvious and pretending bad things didn't exist. Until they undeniably did.

"Maybe Ginny could hold it and see if it speaks to her?" Nola suggested.

"No!" Jayne and I shouted simultaneously.

Ginette Prioleau, our mother, had been blessed—or cursed, depending on which one of her daughters you asked—with the ability to channel spirits by holding objects. It was one of the reasons why she wore gloves all year long. But her strength would have been zapped from her for weeks, sending her to bed. I imagined Jayne was thinking the same thing: that not involving our mother would be for the best not only for her physical health but for our peace of mind.

I reluctantly took the doll in its little coffin from Nola, gingerly clasping it with my thumb and forefinger as if it were a dead palmetto bug. "It's old, so chances are, Sophie will know what it is. Or at least know why it was put in your room. Maybe Meghan found it in the cistern and brought it upstairs when you weren't here and you're just noticing it now." Meghan Black was one of Sophie's graduate students who'd been helping to excavate the cistern.

"Probs," Nola said, nodding along with Jayne and me as if we were all in agreement that what I'd just said wasn't something with which to fertilize the garden.

I quickly placed the box and its unnerving contents in the small chest in the entranceway, hearing the buttons shift like crawling insects as I closed the drawer. "Thanks for the doughnuts and coffee, Jayne. I'll see you when you bring the twins back."

"Just promise me that you'll eat at least one doughnut."

"I promise that I'll try. And even have a spoonful of Froot Loops. I need my fruit."

"You do know there's no actual fruit in that whole box, right?" Nola asked.

I shrugged, then listened to the chiming of the old grandfather clock from the parlor. "I'd better hurry—I've got only two and a half hours to get ready."

I ignored Nola's eye roll as I hurried past her. But as I headed up the stairs, I paused, seeing in my mind's eye the hideous face of the coffin doll and Suzy Dorf's article, one line seeming to flash in my brain with neon lights: *an unnamed source has told me that there are more secrets hidden there.* Who could that be? And how could they know what secrets might still be waiting to be unearthed? I clenched the handrail, then gritted my teeth with determination as I continued to climb the stairs. I didn't care. The Ark of the Covenant could have been hiding in my back garden and I simply wouldn't have cared.

I'd promised to help my friend Veronica find out who had killed her sister, Adrienne, more than twenty years ago. But then I was done. Besides the emotional well-being of our children during our separation, there was only one thing I cared about. Getting Jack back. The restless dead and their footsteps in the snow would have to find someone else to haunt.

CHAPTER 2

Lindsey's parents, Veronica and Michael, picked us up in their SUV. It wasn't a long walk to the College of Charleston campus—a positive or negative, depending on who was asked—but the streets were still slushy.

Alston sat in the rear third row with Lindsey, so Nola and I slid into the middle row. After greeting everyone, I asked, "Where are Cecily and Cal?"

"Daddy's sick, so my mom's staying home with him." Alston grinned. "We figured with you and your spreadsheet, they won't miss anything."

I barely heard her, as I was too busy trying to think of a casual way to ask about Jack, something that made me seem interested without sounding pathetic. I focused on buckling my seat belt while Veronica turned around from the front seat. As if reading my mind, she said, "Jack's meeting us there." She smiled reassuringly and patted my knee before facing forward again.

"It's good to see you, Melanie," Michael said, glancing at me from the driver's seat. "I wasn't aware this was a dress-up event, or I would have worn my Sunday best, too."

I looked down as if to remind myself what I'd put on fifteen minutes before. "Oh, this?" I said, referring to the slim-fitting red cashmere dress with a low scoop neckline and matching jacket. "It's just an old thing I pulled from the back of my closet. Nothing fancy."

Nola snorted, no doubt recalling the piles of discarded outfits strewn around my bedroom with sleeves akimbo like plague victims.

"How are you?" I asked, trying to redirect the conversation. I was also trying to be pleasant. I was friends with his wife, Veronica, but I'd never felt the warm and fuzzies with Michael. Probably due to the fact that he was adamantly opposed to his wife's so-called obsession with her sister's murder. He claimed it had reached an unhealthy level, and he was now leading the process of putting their old Victorian house on Queen Street up for sale so they could all move on. The house had been Veronica and Adrienne's childhood home, and it remained full of memories and relics of the two sisters. And the spirit of one of them who wasn't ready to head into the light.

Michael pulled out onto Tradd Street. "Doing well. Just tired of all the workmen your friend Sophie keeps sending to fix things in the house that I wasn't even aware were broken. If she weren't a respected professional and your friend, I'd say she was purposely trying to delay us putting the house on the market."

I saw Veronica's shoulders stiffen, because we both knew that was exactly what Sophie was trying to do—delay the sale until I'd figured out why Adrienne was still there and what she needed to tell us about what had happened to her.

"Sophie's very methodical. I mean, look at me. I've been renovating my house on Tradd Street since I inherited it. Doing it right takes time." I almost bit my tongue, having many times during the restoration process admitted that the house would make a spectacular bonfire.

"That's not helping, Melanie," he said, offering a conciliatory grin in the rearview mirror.

I smiled back, but I knew it lacked sincerity.

We found parking after circling for a solid ten minutes, and I found myself wishing Jack were with us if only because he had the magic touch with downtown Charleston parking. He had only to drive down a street and a parking spot would magically appear exactly where he needed it.

Just the thought of Jack made me teary-eyed and I turned my face toward the window so nobody would see. It was ridiculous, really. I was a mother of three and a successful professional woman. I'd even faced some very scary ghosts and lived to tell about it. I had no reason to believe that I couldn't get through Jack's departure with grace, dignity, and the courage to believe that our separation was temporary. And with the sure knowledge that I could figure out how to get him back. Yet I still woke up each day with the urge to stay in bed, curl into a ball, and cry until Jack took pity on me and returned to me.

We left the car, then walked down George Street toward Porter's Lodge. The small Classical Revival building resembled a Roman triumphal arch and served as the actual entrance to the campus, according to the thorough research I'd done online the night before. It sat at the bottom of the bucolic Cistern Yard and in front of the stately and columned Randolph Hall, site of the spring graduation ceremony that involved white dresses, long-stemmed red roses, and white dinner jackets with red rose boutonnieres instead of caps and gowns. Alston had been talking nonstop about it during the entire car ride, making me wonder if she'd thought about what she'd have to actually study and achieve at the college before she got to that point.

I strolled casually, trying not to think about seeing Jack for the first time in almost four weeks. Or that I hadn't a clue as to what I was supposed to say to him. If I could have traded in my ability to talk to the dead for knowing how to talk to Jack instead, I would have. Although I still couldn't convince myself that I could have done things any differently. And maybe, as a niggling thought kept reminding me, that was the crux of the problem.

Nola walked ahead of the group and turned left into the middle arch, disappearing from view. I hurried after her, thinking she might have spotted Jack, but stopped when I saw her standing under one of the many ancient live oaks scattered across the Cistern Yard, staring down at her phone.

Fighting back my disappointment, I turned to wait for the rest of the group but instead found myself facing Jack. He stood three feet away, nonchalantly leaning against a tree as if seeing his estranged wife was something he did on a regular basis. Despite my instinct to step forward and throw my arms around him, I held myself back, aware of the approaching group and the certainty that Jack wouldn't welcome an embrace from me. I don't think I could have stood the rejection.

"Red?" he asked in greeting, his eyes not giving anything away. I hoped he was remembering how he liked me in red and how a particular red dress had been instrumental in conceiving the twins.

It took me a moment to find a reply that didn't sound pitiful or anything like begging. Both had been tried and had equally failed, so I needed to move on. I swallowed. "I hoped it would keep me warm." I gave an exaggerated shiver.

A corner of his mouth lifted and my heart did that little squeezing thing it usually did when I was near him. "It's almost seventy degrees, Mellie. You're the only person I know who thinks seventy is freezing."

He pushed away from the tree and took a step toward me. "You're looking well."

While I silently congratulated myself for making the extra effort in getting dressed, which included shaving my legs and plucking eyebrows most werewolves would have envied, I waited for him to say more. *I missed you. I can't live without you. I want to come back.*

When his expression began to change into one of concern at my silence, I blurted out, "You're wearing a blue shirt."

Either I was having a stroke or Jayne's awkwardness around attractive men had somehow managed to attach itself to me. His eyes widened.

"Dad!" Nola shouted as she jogged toward us before allowing herself to be embraced by her father. She stepped back quickly to show everyone that she was too sophisticated for hugs while I wished I could exchange an entire commission to trade places.

After greetings and handshakes, we turned as a group to look up at Porter's Lodge, taking in its triple arches and Doric columns. Greek letters stood out in bas-relief—a term I'd learned from Sophie—across the top of the middle arch.

I dug into my handbag for my carefully inscribed notes tucked next to my printed spreadsheet, but before I could open them, Jack said, "'Know thyself.'"

"I didn't know you knew Greek," I said.

Cool blue eyes settled on me. "There's a lot you don't know about me, Mellie." He paused, then leaned closer. "You're not the only one who knows how to Google." He began to walk past me but paused to look back, a partial grin on his face. "I'm glad you thought to bring a spreadsheet. With Nola's list of about twenty colleges, we need something to keep it all straight."

Motionless, I stared at him, wondering if he'd just said something nice to me and if I should ask him to repeat it to be sure. He stared back at me without moving, as if waiting for something to happen, then indicated the departing group with a nod.

"Oh," I said, feeling like the dorky girl in high school being asked to join the popular lunch table.

We walked a bit behind everyone, with Nola occasionally glancing at us over her shoulder.

"Your cast is gone," I pointed out, trying to make conversation, then immediately regretting my choice of topic.

"Yeah. It is. Nice to have that particular reminder removed." He shoved his hands into his pockets. "We need to talk."

My heart jumped. "I'm so relieved to hear you say that. I completely agree. There's so much we left unsaid." I hushed my inner caution and instead reminded myself that Jack had just complimented me. As if that meant anything at all. "I miss the children when they're not with me," I blurted out. "And I know they want us together, too. I've kept your chest of drawers and your side of the closet empty, so it shouldn't—"

"About Marc and his movie," he said, cutting me off.

"Oh. Right." I tried to hide my disappointment and forced my thoughts onto another track. I swallowed. "Jayne came to see me this morning to tell me that Rebecca and Marc want to set up a meeting with us. He's aware of the deal offered via our lawyer."

"I know. I ran into Rich Kobylt at the hardware store yesterday," he said, referring to the plumber/handyman we'd been keeping fully employed since I'd first inherited the house on Tradd Street. Reliable and a hard worker, he also had the dubious distinction of possessing a sixth sense. "He's been doing some work for Marc and Rebecca and overheard Rebecca's conversation with Jayne. He thought we should know. He also felt the need to tell me that we shouldn't let Marc within a football field's length of our house."

I raised my eyebrows, distracted by the use of the word "our" before "house." If he still considered it ours, then according to my own calculations, all was not lost.

"I couldn't believe it," Jack said.

"That they want to meet with us?"

"No, that Rich Kobylt would offer his opinion like he's a member of the family."

"Well, he almost is. He's been practically living in the house as long as I have, and he was the one who convinced Nola not to dye her hair blue, remember."

Jack raised his eyebrow. "Yeah, I remember."

"Jayne said they want to meet at my office—on neutral ground. We pick the day and time."

"There's no need for a meeting, Mellie. We have the funds to fight this in a court of law if we have to. We have the funds now. The only reason I'd want to meet with Marc is to tell him where he can put his movie, and I can do that over the phone."

"But don't you think at least one of us should meet with them, see what they have to say?"

"No, I don't." His eyes narrowed. "Unless you're planning on meeting with them anyway?"

I considered evading his question, then remembered that was what Mellie Version 106 would have done. I lifted my chin. "I might as well. I figure it's time to go into the office anyway. It's been a while."

I thought I saw a flicker of compassion in his eyes, but it quickly vanished. "Do what you want, but I won't be there." He ran up the steps to the admissions building, where we'd start the tour with a formal presentation. He stopped at the top to hold the door open for me, allowing me to swallow the lump in my throat and regain my composure. As I passed by him, he touched my arm and I stopped, my heart hopeful but my head resigned.

"We do need to talk. About us. I just need a little more time. I'm still so angry with you that I can barely think straight. I never thought that I could want someone as much as I want you, while at the same time never wanting to see you again. Every time I look at you, I can't help but remember how you betrayed my trust. It's a hard thing to get over."

I took a deep breath. "You still want me?"

He dipped his head and chuckled. "Oh, Mellie. You certainly have a way of hearing only what you want to hear. Yes, I still want you. But it's just not that easy."

I wanted to tell him that it was, but he was pressing his hand against my back, guiding me toward the large room where he made sure he was seated between Veronica and Nola so there was no place for me next to him.

Following the presentation, we were led around the campus by an undergraduate student named Alex who was tall and dark and handsome and had Alston and Lindsey giggling and flirting like they weren't the smart, competent young women I knew them to be.

Nola was more circumspect since Cooper, Alston's elder brother and a senior cadet at the Citadel, would be moving to California to pursue a career in aeronautical engineering following graduation in May. They hadn't technically been dating—mostly because of the age difference—but they really were great together. Cooper had even helped us solve a puzzle surrounding the cistern, and Jack liked him. Except Nola was still in high school and Cooper was ready to make his mark on the world. She'd cried for two whole days before rousing herself enough to watch with me the DVD collection of Hallmark Christmas movies she'd given me.

I don't know if it was my comforting presence or her inability to take another happy ending that roused her enough to get dressed and leave the house again. Maybe a brokenhearted person just needed to be with another brokenhearted person to recognize that wallowing in self-pity wasn't going to help. At least it had worked for her. I had remained on the couch and finished watching the entire collection, but that hadn't helped, either.

When Alex announced that part of the tour included one of the dorms, Jack said, "I think we can skip that since we've already decided on which dorm you'll live in if you end up coming here."

"'We'?" Nola stressed.

"Yes, 'we.' The people who will be paying your tuition. Which are the only opinions that matter."

I slid a glance at him, wondering if he'd been including me in the "we," but decided by his expression and Nola's that this wasn't the best time to ask.

"But what if I don't like it?"

"Doesn't matter. It's the only all-female dorm. So you can stay there. Or live at home. Your choice."

Nola's expression was that of a teenager being sent to a convent in Siberia. She stopped walking, crossed her arms. "That's not fair!"

Jack kept walking. "Sure it is. I've given you two really great options. Do you know how many people would give anything to live in a historic Charleston home?"

Nola rolled her eyes as Alston and Lindsey joined us. "If it's got three-occupancy bedrooms so the three of us could be together, I'd be fine with that," Alston said.

"Which dorm is it?" Lindsey asked, opening the folder we'd each been given at the presentation.

"Buist Rivers," Jack said with enthusiasm.

"Ugh," Nola said. "It's so *old*. And it's the only dorm on the entire campus with a hall bathroom. No, thank you."

I pulled out my spreadsheet. "It's really not that old, Nola. It was built in 1963, but it's been heavily renovated since then."

Nola wrinkled her nose. "Like I said. *Old*. I might as well live at home."

"As I mentioned, that could be arranged," Jack said as we stopped at the perimeter of the tour group gathering in front of the brick-and-glass Stern Student Center.

Alex began to talk about the "awesome" food choices on campus. Even his mention of vegan selections didn't erase Nola's frown.

Veronica approached and put her arm around Nola. "You'll get wrinkles if you keep frowning like that," she said lightly, her gaze meeting mine over Nola's shoulder. "What's wrong?"

I shrugged. "Jack has 'opinions' about Nola's living arrangements."

Nola gave an exaggerated sigh. "If I decide on the College of Charleston, then I have the option of either living in the only all-girls dorm or living at home."

Veronica stilled, her smile slipping. "Which dorm is that?"

"Buist Rivers. It's *ancient*. The Kelly House apartments are newer and *so* much nicer. And they're pink." She glared at the back of Jack's head. "But Dad doesn't seem to care what *I* want."

Nola slunk away to stand with Lindsey and Alston closer to the front, near Alex. The faint scent of Vanilla Musk teased my nostrils, letting me know why Veronica's mood had abruptly changed.

"Was that Adrienne's dorm?" I asked quietly. It was the perfume her sister had worn, a guaranteed tell that Adrienne was near.

Veronica nodded. "Room 210. Her body was discovered in a janitor's closet on the same floor."

"Why don't we skip it, then?" I suggested.

"I don't think it's the dorm on the tour, but I was hoping we could get inside anyway. Adrienne might want to show you something."

"I really don't—"

"What are you two whispering about?" Michael leaned in between us. "Are you finding conflicting data on Melanie's spreadsheet? Maybe a column's too wide?"

Veronica turned to look at her husband without smiling. "No, Michael. We were discussing Buist Rivers dorm."

His eyes widened in question.

"Adrienne's dorm," Veronica explained.

"Right," he said before sighing heavily and looking down at his feet. "Is it on the tour? Because we don't have to go inside."

"No, it's not." Veronica paused. "But I do want to see if Melanie and I can get into the dorm to look around. I bet we could find someone to let us in."

I was surprised to see the resignation in Michael's expression instead of the anger or antagonism I'd been expecting. All of our past conversations on the subject of finding out what had happened to Adrienne had ended badly. Maybe the mere fact that Veronica had finally agreed to sell the family house was the olive branch he'd needed. Or the water on the fire. The flames might have been out, but I was pretty sure I could still feel the steam.

"Fine," he said. "But you two are on your own. I want no part in any of that mumbo jumbo, Melanie. Whether you really can talk to dead people or just pretend, I don't care. Do what you have to do and rejoin the tour. I'm staying with Jack and the girls."

He began to walk away, then briefly turned back to look at Veronica before shaking his head and leaving. I searched for Jack, easily catching sight of him because he and Michael were the tallest people in the group. He stood behind Nola, but was watching me with raised eyebrows.

"Can you let Jack know, Michael?"

He nodded without looking back while Veronica and I headed toward Adrienne's old dorm, the scent of Vanilla Musk growing heavier the closer we got.

"Do you smell that?" I asked.

Veronica shook her head. "Is it her perfume? I used to smell it a lot after she died, but not so much anymore."

I nodded, then looked up at the brown stucco building. "This is really ugly. I wouldn't want to live here, either."

I turned to Veronica to get her reaction, but she was staring at the glass front doors, her head tilted to the side. "It's changed a lot since I was here . . . the last time."

"When was that?"

Her eyes met mine. "When I came to pack up her things after . . . afterward. I thought I'd have to do it alone because my parents couldn't face it, but Michael came to help. I couldn't have done it without him."

"Too bad it's locked," I said, tugging on the handle, ready to turn away.

Just then, two students approached, both laden with backpacks, too focused on their conversation to pay attention to us. One of the girls swiped an ID card and they both entered. Before the door could close, Veronica reached forward and held it open for me.

I hesitated as she stood by the open door. "I know this is a hard thing for you, Melanie. And I hate asking you now, while you're dealing with so much. But I feel an urgency that I've never felt before. Adrienne is running out of time." She paused, an odd expression crossing her face. "I can't let her down again."

Before I could ask her what she meant, another resident approached the door with her ID in hand. Veronica and I stepped into the lobby and held the door for her before letting the door close behind us.

The Vanilla Musk scent here nearly choked me, and I found myself gagging as if it had been poured down my throat and squirted up my nostrils. Veronica grabbed a clean tissue from her purse and handed it to me. "Are you all right?"

I held up my hand and nodded. "In a minute."

I pointed to my purse and she scrambled to open it and pull out the small bottle of water I always carried with me. Her eyes widened as she noticed my just-in-case kit that included a small can of WD-40, a container of hand sanitizer, a Mace spritzer, and a pair of pliers, among other necessities. Without a word she twisted off the bottle cap and handed me the water.

"Thank you," I said after I had downed half of the bottle. "It was . . ."

"Adrienne?"

I nodded. "I think she was trying to get my attention." I glanced around the deserted lobby filled with sterile furniture and fluorescent lights. "It worked."

I stood still, waiting for the Vanilla Musk scent to dissipate. "Do you hear that?"

"Hear what?"

"That music?"

Veronica shook her head. "No. But we're in a college dorm, so it wouldn't be that unusual, would it?"

"No, but it's an old song. Not something the kids today would listen to. Nola would rather shave her head."

"Do you think it's Adrienne?"

"I don't know. But I think I'm supposed to find out where it's coming from." I walked to the elevator and pushed the button. "Room 210?"

Veronica nodded, her face gone pale.

"You can stay here if you like. I doubt I can get into the room, so it shouldn't take long."

"I'm fine. Really. It looks so different from . . . before."

The door opened and we stepped into the elevator. "It's been renovated, remember. So it won't be the same."

We stepped out onto the second floor and Veronica turned right. I followed her although I didn't have to. The sound of the music grew louder as we walked, the scent of Adrienne's perfume returning. We stopped at the same time in front of a white-painted door, the number 210 in black on the wall beside it, the door covered with pictures of sorority mascots and Greek letters. The names of the occupants were printed in pretty calligraphy on laminated cardboard stock on either side of the door.

Veronica wore a wobbly smile. "It's just like when Adrienne was here. Just different names."

The song was now playing at such a high decibel level that I was sure Veronica was able to hear it. I'd begun to ask her when the door was flung open and the music stopped abruptly.

The young woman—either Jessica or Rachel, according to the signs—stepped back with surprise that quickly turned to alarm. She removed headphones from her ears, the tinny beat of a rap song continuing to play. I stared at the headphones, realizing that whatever the woman was listening to definitely wasn't the music I'd heard.

"Can I help you?" she asked.

Veronica stepped forward. "We knew someone who used to live in this room. We were just hoping to get a look inside. . . ."

Jessica/Rachel stared at us before shaking her head. "How did you get in here? I'm calling security." She stepped inside the room, opening the door enough for me to glance inside to see the two narrow bunk beds with matching colorful quilts on either side of the tiny space before the door slammed in our faces.

"Let's go," Veronica said, tugging on my arm as we walked quickly back down the hallway to the elevators. She paused in front of a door and twisted the knob. "It's locked. But this is where they found her. Do you sense anything?"

I closed my eyes but heard nothing. I shook my head. "Sorry."

When the elevator door opened downstairs, we hurried across the lobby toward the exit, looking over our shoulders for campus security. As we reached the safety of the walkway outside, Veronica asked, "Was Adrienne there?"

"Oh, yeah. She was definitely there. I could smell her perfume. I finally remembered the name of that song I kept hearing, and now I can't get it out of my head. It's one of those earworm songs that, once you hear it, replays over and over so you can't forget it no matter how much you want to. It's an old one—early eighties, I think. My freshman-year roommate was obsessed with eighties music and especially that one song and would play it over and over."

"What was the song?"

"'O Superman.'"

She stopped suddenly, her face noticeably paler. "By Laurie Anderson?"

"You've heard of it? How?"

"That was the CD that was in Adrienne's Discman when they found her. We could never figure out why, though. She absolutely hated that song."

"That's strange," I said.

"That she hated the song?"

"No—everybody hates that song. I meant that it's strange that not only was it in her Discman, but she would use that song to lure me upstairs to her dorm room. It must mean something."

We rejoined the rest of the group, my heart doing its usual flip as I spotted Jack, then immediately falling when I remembered that nothing was settled between us, and he would not be returning home with me.

He walked us to the Farrells' SUV and waited for Nola to get in. I held back, having no rehearsed words but needing to say something. "Jack . . ."

He looked at me with those eyes and it was all I could do not to throw my arms around him. I realized I was leaning toward him because he gently pressed his hands against my shoulders to steady me. "Yes, Mellie?"

"You left a shelf full of sweatpants and sweatshirts in the closet. So I unfolded everything, made it messy, and tore off the shelf label I made."

His lips quirked, and I saw a hint of the old sparkle in his eyes. "Well, that's progress. Congratulations." He leaned past me to say good-bye to the other occupants of the van, then stepped back. "Good-bye, Mellie," he said with a brief smile before turning around and walking away. I'd begun to hate those words.

I climbed into the SUV and sat down, aware of something behind my back as I buckled my seat belt. I reached behind me and pulled out a red heart-shaped pillow. I didn't need to examine it to know it was Adrienne's with the small careful stitches and ruffled edge. I'd found it in the box of Adrienne's belongings in Veronica's attic. The pillow had the odd habit of showing up unexpectedly, regardless of where it had last been placed. I looked up to find Veronica watching, but thankfully Michael was focused on pulling the SUV out onto the street. She raised her eyebrows in question.

"Later," I mouthed, then placed the pillow in my handbag.

I stared out the window the remainder of the short ride home, with something Veronica had said while we were at the dorm echoing inside my head. *I can't let her down again.*

I'd have to ask her what she meant. After I got home and locked myself in the bathroom, where I could cry without Nola hearing me. And after I started a new spreadsheet, one to help me navigate a problem for which I didn't have a clue where to start.

CHAPTER 3

I sat at the kitchen table with my laptop open to a new blank spread-sheet under the header MELANIE V. 107. One hundred seven was only a guess—the real number was probably much higher—but admitting that my false starts at becoming a better version of myself had reached at least three digits was as far as I was prepared to go right now.

The days of the week sat at the top of each column, but only one row description had been filled in. Get dressed. The number one had been typed under Thursday, today. The curser had been blinking to the left of the second row now for almost thirty minutes.

I took another sip of coffee and winced. Mrs. Houlihan and her superior coffee-making skills would return on Monday. I put down my mug and reluctantly raised my hands before forcing them to type Exercise. Jayne had been calling me daily to start running with her again, but despite how I currently felt, I didn't hate myself enough to drag myself out of bed before dawn, throw on something that wouldn't keep me warm enough, and then run.

But it was supposed to be good for me. And it was something I could do with my sister. And it got me outside of the house so I wouldn't focus on how empty it was. All things the new Mellie needed to embrace to become a better version of herself. Except I imagined I could get the same benefits having a conversation with Jayne over coffee and doughnuts.

Sadly, she didn't share my assessment. Jayne told me to pick Monday or Tuesday to resume our running, which was a lot like choosing which day you'd like to be guillotined.

Nola walked into the kitchen, dragging her backpack, the three dogs bounding in behind her and racing to their bowls, which I'd filled the night before. She would never be a morning person and I'd already made a mental note that when I helped her schedule her classes for her first year in college, no classes would start before ten. I couldn't allow myself to believe that she wouldn't need my help in organizing her life when she started college. Things were hard enough for me as it was.

She stopped short when she spotted me. "You're wearing real clothes for the second day in a row and your hair is clean. Who are you and what have you done to Melanie?"

"Very funny. I've decided it's time to go back to work. I've even showered."

"Good for you," she said without a hint of sarcasm. "What are you working on?" She indicated the laptop.

Before I could close the lid, she moved to stand behind my chair. "Just a little mental health worksheet. Trying to be my best self and all that," I said, parroting what Jayne and Sophie had been trying to drill into me. "Attempting to discover what's missing."

Nola glanced over my shoulder. "Wow, Melanie. 'Get dressed' and 'exercise.' Careful—you don't want to aim too high."

I sent her a withering glance. "Jayne said to start small, with manageable goals."

She opened the fridge and pulled out a bottle of thick greenish juice and took a swig. I didn't remind her that in this house we used glasses, because nobody in their right mind would want to drink any of her concoction anyway. "Then go ahead and add 'breathe' to the list. And 'reorganize something that's already been organized ten times.'"

"Aren't you going to be late for school?"

She flung open the pantry door and took out a breakfast bar. She peeled off the paper of what looked to be a small dirt brick and took a bite. "Mrs. Ravenel is doing car pool again and she's always late, so I've got a good ten to fifteen minutes." She indicated the laptop again with her chin. "Does that have anything to do with my dad?"

I had to remind myself that not only was she just sixteen going on seventeen, but that Jack was her father. "Sort of," I admitted.

She slid into a chair across the table from me and I tried not to gag at the smell of the dirt bar she seemed to be enjoying. "You know, Melanie, I don't think that whether or not you exercise or get dressed matters to Dad. He loves you—warts and all. He even thinks it's pretty cool that you talk to dead people and that Sarah seems to have inherited it from you." She chewed thoughtfully. "I think the issue isn't reorganizing his desk drawer without asking or labeling his closet shelves. It's more that even though you're married, you still think like you're on your own. That he's not your partner in all things. That you're so afraid of being told no that instead of discussing it, you go off and do your own thing regardless of the consequences."

I looked at her, ready to argue that she was wrong, because what I did had never been meant to result in subterfuge or outright lying; my motivation had been to protect Jack and others I loved. But I couldn't find the right words to refute what she'd just said. Maybe I just needed more coffee.

Instead, I said, "Did you come up with that on your own?"

She shook her head as she slid out her chair and stood. "Nope. I overheard a conversation between Dad and my grandparents. That's pretty much verbatim." She smiled, then took another bite of her breakfast bar.

"Are you working after school today? I can pick you up and drive you home so your grandfather doesn't have to."

She'd been helping my in-laws for a few hours each week at Trenholm Antiques since the previous summer with managing the website, working the cash register, and learning about the business and antiques. Ever since she'd been given an antique doll house—not the best choice, as we'd learned—Nola had been morbidly fascinated with anything that had been owned by people who no longer walked the earth.

I, of course, didn't share this fascination, but as soon as Jack agreed that she was old enough for a part-time job, Nola had begun working for her grandparents and seemed to enjoy it almost as much as she enjoyed writing music. At least until recently, when a new hire, apparently a bossy and arrogant—according to Nola—man, had been brought on to help with the heavy lifting as well as to help manage the store. My in-laws had decided to travel more, scouting for antiques across the globe while at the same time being the tourists they'd never allowed themselves to be. They insisted they weren't ready for retirement, so this would be the best of both worlds.

I wasn't sure if Nola's issue was with taking direction from a stranger in a place where she'd been allowed free rein ever since she'd arrived in Charleston or something else entirely. I hadn't mentioned it to Amelia, hoping Nola's disgruntlement would settle itself without parental intervention.

Nola sighed. "Not until Saturday. Lord Voldemort decided it would be more productive if I worked only weekends."

I wanted to ask her more, but her attention was distracted by the window behind me that faced the wrecked garden. "Dr. Wallen-Arasi is here. And . . . oh, crap."

I closed my laptop and stood, wondering at her reaction. I reached the door before Sophie could knock and excite the dogs, and I opened it so she and her companion could enter the kitchen. The chilly bite of early-morning air hit me and I slammed the door shut as quickly as possible.

"Good morning," Sophie said cheerfully as she unwrapped a rainbow-striped knit scarf from around her neck. It matched the footie socks she wore with her Birkenstocks and the beanie cap on her head. I didn't ask for her coat because I hadn't had enough coffee yet to face whatever outfit was hiding beneath it.

"I brought someone I'd like you to meet because I think you're going to be seeing quite a lot of him going forward."

I dragged my eyes away from the footie socks to look at her companion for the first time. He was young—just a little older than Nola—and very tall, at least six foot three, with blond hair that was probably light brown when not in the sun, and café au lait–colored eyes. His suntanned face and hands told me that he spent a lot of time outside.

"Beau, this is my friend Melanie Trenholm I've been telling you about."

"Beau Ryan," he said, extending his hand. "It's nice to finally meet you, ma'am."

If I couldn't tell from his accent that he was Southern, the "ma'am" would have been a dead giveaway. He had a nice, firm grasp, which I appreciated, but the "ma'am" thing needed to be dropped immediately or I'd feel the need to learn how to knit.

"It's nice to meet you, too, Beau. But please, call me Melanie."

"Yes, ma'am," he said with a bright smile, showing even white teeth.

I squeezed his hand a little harder than necessary before stepping back. "And this is my stepdaughter, Nola."

Nola stayed where she was, regarding the newcomer with narrowed eyes that made her look even more like Jack. Crossing her arms to make it clear she wasn't going to be shaking any hands, she said, "We've met. He's the new guy working at Trenholm Antiques."

I mouthed the words "Lord Voldemort," then looked back at Beau. From Nola's descriptions of the new hire, I'd pictured a balding, paunchy, and middle-aged imbecile who couldn't tell the difference between Chippendale and IKEA.

"Beau is in his second year at the American College of the Building Arts pursuing a bachelor of applied science in blacksmithing," Sophie explained. "I think he's perfect for replacing the missing sections of your iron fence, so I wanted him to meet you and your dad."

Sophie had already given me a guesstimate of the cost to replace the broken fencing and gate that encircled our property, and my only response had been maniacal laughter that I hoped had conveyed the word "no." As in I didn't care if the fence was broken or missing or had disappeared completely. I had one child going to college and another two who hadn't even started preschool yet. I wasn't about to spend their education money or inheritance on an iron fence. I'd even started going online to search for alternative fencing options that resembled iron but at a price that didn't make me feel faint, none of which I was fairly certain would pass Sophie's approval. Not that it was needed since she wasn't the one paying the bills.

"Beau's already started drawing up plans. Hopefully he will be able to make it one of his school projects to replace the missing parts or, if necessary, replace the entire thing."

I opened my mouth to say something but could only wobble my chin. I was busy doing the mental calculations of how many houses I'd need to sell so that we could still put food on the table without selling a single ruby. "Well, then, I guess I'd better get back to work. It's been a pleasure meeting you, Beau. I'll be sure to have a chat with my father. I don't think the work is going to be as extensive as you might think. . . ."

"Oh, trust me, ma'am. I've gone over every inch of the entire fence and there's a lot of damage. I'm thinking it would be best to replace the whole thing."

Nola slung her backpack over her shoulder. "I hope he knows more about iron fencing than he knows about antiques." She said this almost under her breath and directed at me, but loudly enough for everyone to hear.

Beau gave her a patient smile. "Actually, my family has owned an antiques store on Royal Street in New Orleans for almost a century—it's pretty famous in the antiques world. We have a fully restored 1910 Muller carousel horse in the window, the last one of its kind in existence, and people come from all over just to see it. I took my first steps by pulling up on a Georgian breakfront full of Sèvres porcelain and toddling over to a hand-carved Victorian birdcage without breaking anything."

"How cute," Nola said, her tone saying otherwise. "I've never been to New Orleans, so I wouldn't know."

He frowned. "Funny—because people refer to New Orleans as 'NOLA.' I thought maybe you had a connection."

"Oh, I do," she said, a slow grin spreading on her face.

I gave her a look that told her she should stop there, but she pretended not to notice.

"My real name is Emmaline Amelia, but my mom called me Nola because that's where I was conceived, in a cheap hotel room in the French Quarter." She turned to Sophie. "By the way, I found something in my room yesterday. We think maybe Meghan Black found it in the cistern, but I haven't seen her, so I'm just guessing. Do you have a minute to take a look?"

"Sure—would love to," Sophie said, lowering eyebrows that had risen to meet her hairline as Nola spoke.

Nola dropped her backpack and rushed from the room as I called after her, "Hurry! I'm sure Mrs. Ravenel will be here soon."

"I love her like a daughter, but I'm her stepmother," I said to Beau, hoping to clarify that I hadn't conceived anyone in a cheap hotel room in New Orleans.

"Yes, ma'am. I understand."

I gritted my teeth at the "ma'am" thing, but I let it pass. There was something endearing and sincere about his smile, and I wondered if Nola had noticed that, too.

I heard the hall chest drawer slam shut, and a moment later, Nola hurried back into the kitchen, clutching the small iron coffin. She placed it on the kitchen table in front of Sophie.

"It's a Frozen Charlotte," Beau said immediately, looking over Sophie's shoulder. "What does it say on the top?"

"'Listen to your mother,'" Nola said. "Obviously designed by a mother." She rolled her eyes.

"I've heard of Frozen Charlottes," Sophie said. "But I've never seen one in person."

Beau reached down and picked it up. "Does it open?"

Nola nodded, then used her finger to flick open the latch. "It reminds me of that scary clown in *It*. Worst movie ever."

Beau examined the doll without touching it. "*Best* movie ever. Nobody will ever look at a stray red balloon the same way ever again."

"That doesn't make it a great movie," Nola said with disdain. "So, what's a Frozen Charlotte?"

"They originated during the Victorian era and were called Frozen Charlottes—or Charlies, for male dolls," Beau said. "They were made in response to a popular song, 'Fair Charlotte,' which was based on an earlier poem, 'A Corpse Going to a Ball.'" He grimaced. "It was a cautionary tale for children—especially young ladies—about the dangers of vanity and not listening to your parents. That's what the words on top of the little coffin are for. The dolls were made of porcelain—which is why this one is still in perfect condition—and very cheap to buy, which added to their popularity. They were even baked into birthday cakes at one point. Not all of them had their own coffins, though, so this one is special."

"Sounds uplifting and perfect for children," Nola said.

"Those crazy Victorians." Beau grinned. "They were also fond of postmortem photographs of loved ones and making jewelry out of a deceased person's hair."

"You sure it's Victorian?" Sophie asked.

"Yeah, definitely," Beau said, handing her the coffin.

"So it probably didn't come from the cistern," I said. "Everything we've pulled out of it has been middle to late eighteenth century."

"But what's the significance of the buttons?" Sophie asked, reaching inside to pick up a mother-of-pearl button layered with painted tulips.

Beau studied it closely. "You've got me on that one. I can call my grandmother—she'll probably know. She actually has a collection of Frozen Charlottes."

"Of course she does," Nola muttered just as a car horn sounded from outside. "That's Mrs. Ravenel," she said as she scooped up her backpack again.

"See you Saturday at the store," Beau said. "The front display windows need to be cleaned. We're expecting that shipment of Italian crystal serve ware that Amelia wants to put there."

I saw Nola's jaw working as she ground her teeth, just like Jack's did when he was trying to pretend that he wasn't annoyed. Without another word, she left. We waited a moment before hearing the front door slam behind her.

Beau turned his smile on me. "Nice girl. A little sensitive at times, but a nice girl. Speaking of sensitive—"

Sophie interrupted him. "Not yet, Beau. I haven't had a chance to say anything to Melanie yet."

The hairs on the back of my neck began to dance, alerting me to two things at once: I wasn't going to like what Sophie was supposed to have told me, and it was no longer just the three of us in the kitchen.

"Say what?" I asked.

Beau held up his hands. "Sorry. I don't want to jump the gun or anything. But when I first came to Charleston, I read Marc Longo's book, *Lust, Greed, and Murder in the Holy City*. I'm sure you're aware that you're mentioned in the book along with his allegations about how you can talk to ghosts."

I flicked a glance at Sophie, understanding now what she'd meant when she'd introduced me to Beau as the friend she'd been telling him about. If only laser eye daggers were a thing, Sophie would have been putting out small fires now peppering her hideous scarf. Or for real punishment I'd make her wear a solid navy one without even a hint of fringe.

Returning my attention to Beau, I said, "I wouldn't know, because I haven't read it."

A brief smile graced his face as if in acknowledgment that I'd avoided answering the unasked question.

Beau continued. "I met Dr. Wallen-Arasi at a Charleston Library Society lecture about Philip Simmons and I mentioned my podcast to her. She told me that you were friends."

I sent Sophie a look meant to emphasize the word "were." "Your 'podcast'?"

"Yes, ma'am. I host a paranormal podcast about real ghost stories. It's just a hobby, something I started a couple of years ago because it's something I'm interested in."

"I have no idea what a 'podcast' is, but if it has 'paranormal' in the description, I probably don't need to hear any more."

"Sure—I get it. Dr. Wallen-Arasi warned me. I was just hoping . . ." He shook his head. "Never mind." He straightened, smiled. "So, I'll find out if my grandmother knows anything about the buttons, and I'll work on an estimate for the fencing. You'll probably see me out here taking pictures and measuring, but I promise not to disturb you."

"Sounds great. Thank you, Beau. And do keep an open mind when you're thinking about the fence. There are many more materials, many a lot less costly than iron, that would work and still look nice."

He and Sophie wore matching expressions, something I imagined people facing an approaching tsunami might wear.

"Yes, ma'am."

I walked toward the back door and held it open. "It was a pleasure meeting you. I'll talk to you later, Sophie." I smiled at her but I was sure I saw the fear in her eyes. "And, Beau?"

"Yes, ma'am?"

"If you call me ma'am one more time, you might find yourself a subject of your own podcast."

He grinned, and I couldn't be angry with him. Jack's grin seemed to have the same effect on me. "Yes, ma—Melanie."

From the corner of my eye, I saw something move. We all turned to see the Frozen Charlotte in her coffin standing up on the counter by the refrigerator instead of on the table where we'd left her.

"I didn't see anything," Beau said.

I faced Beau, who was staring directly at the startlingly mobile tiny coffin. "Me, neither," I agreed. He looked at me for a moment before turning quickly away and leaving me wondering how much Sophie had told him. And why.

I shut the door behind them, then leaned against it and closed my eyes and wondered, for about the millionth time, what had happened to my once-uneventful and orderly life.

CHAPTER 4

I parked my car behind Henderson House Realty, feeling dispirited at the sight of two other cars. In my pre-Jack days, before parents, sister, and children were a part of my world, my job had been my life. I was always on the top of the sales leader board, and I'd prided myself on being the first person to arrive in the office. Until now.

I recognized fellow Realtor Catherine Jimenez's silver minivan and our receptionist Jolly Thompson's pale blue Camry. I touched the hood of Catherine's minivan as I passed. The engine had already cooled. I apparently needed to wake up even earlier if I was to claim my spot on the leader board again.

It wasn't that I resented the new additions to my life. I treasured each and every one of them and wouldn't trade a single moment I'd spent with my new family. But the last month had taught me that my ego and my confidence were as firm as warm Jell-O. My job was the one thing I knew I was good at. Maybe even great at. More than that, it bolstered me enough to handle the other failures in my life.

I pulled open the door, and put my finger to my lips before Jolly could speak and alert Catherine that I was there. It's not that I didn't like

Catherine, because it was impossible not to. She was warm, kind, enthusiastic about everything, and very energetic. She also brought me an endless supply of home-baked goodies, which I appreciated, since I was denied them at home.

But I found Catherine exhausting. She had four children, as was evidenced by all the sports and school stickers on the rear of her minivan and all the framed photos on her desk and scattered around her office like confetti. She'd retired from her job in the tech world to stay home with the kids and had only recently received her Realtor's license. I'd felt sorry for her at first, wondering where she'd find the time to be an effective Realtor, but that was before she'd started making big sales and attracting lucrative listings.

It had taken her only two months to install her name firmly at the top of the board, while mine lingered near the bottom until it had finally fallen off completely sometime in December. I no longer felt sorry for Catherine and did my best to avoid her, or at least stay out of her way so I wouldn't get run over. She reminded me of a hurricane, sucking up all the air in a room and then swirling it around before you realized what had happened.

It also didn't help that she was the consummate mother and community volunteer, achieving more in her day with four kids and a flourishing career and no nanny than I did. It was depressing and demoralizing and I could take her only in small doses, and only after I'd had enough coffee to keep me on my toes.

Jolly shook her head in disapproval (since she—and everyone else— adored Catherine), her dragonfly earrings shimmying from her earlobes. She slid over a small stack of pink message notes clipped together by date. We had an automated system for messages, but Jolly understood that I preferred mine in paper form, and she'd instinctively known that I liked them organized in date order. It's why I'd voted for a generous Christmas bonus for her.

I nodded in thanks and began to tiptoe back to my office, thankful to hear Catherine talking on the phone.

"Did you forget someone outside?" Jolly whispered loudly.

"What?" I swung around to look through the glass door of the office.

Jolly stood staring out at the street with a frown on her face. "There was a woman there—she was walking right behind you, but she didn't come inside." She settled her eyes on me. "She seemed . . . wet. Like she'd just been caught in a storm."

I moved toward the door and opened it, looking up and down Broad Street, but besides a passing jogger, there was no one close enough to have just been in front of our building. And definitely nobody wet. I looked up at a clear blue sky with thin and wispy white clouds. But when I glanced down on the sidewalk, the unmistakable wet footprints of a woman with about my shoe size could be seen coming from around the corner, but no footprints appeared to be returning. They'd simply stopped at the front door.

Ignoring the tingling at the back of my neck, I reentered the lobby, shaking my head. "Not sure what you might have seen, but there's nobody there."

I smiled brightly as I passed her, ignoring the questioning look in her eyes as I said a silent prayer that she wouldn't go outside and see the footprints. Keeping my voice just above a whisper, I said, "I've got Mr. and Mrs. Longo here for a meeting at nine o'clock. Please send them right in. And don't offer them coffee—I don't want them staying longer than they need to."

Jolly gave me a thumbs-up, her green eyes serious behind the dark frames of her glasses.

I'd opened my office door halfway when I heard Catherine call my name. "Melanie! So glad you're back in the office. We've missed you around here." She winked at the receptionist. "Hope you don't mind that Jolly spilled the beans. She wanted to make sure you had a warm welcome back."

I looked into Catherine's wide blue eyes, her blond hair expertly styled without a strand out of place. She smiled like the majorette she'd once been at Georgia Tech, her customary fit and flare dress showing off still-enviable legs.

"Oh, thank you. It's good to be back."

She held up a Tupperware container. "We had a family bake-a-thon last night—something Javier and I like to do with the kids. We made pralines, and since I know how much you love sweets, I brought you some."

Despite feeling guilty that I'd been avoiding her, I accepted the Tupperware. "Thanks, Catherine. That's very kind of you."

She smiled. "It was our pleasure. Now, if you'll excuse me, I've got six showings today and a closing, ballet and soccer practice, plus a DAR meeting. Busy day!"

I nodded as she said good-bye, creating a draft in her wake as she headed out toward the lobby and exit.

I had just settled myself at my desk when my office door opened. I looked up in surprise, my mouth open as I tried to think of an appropriate response between passing out from happiness and pretending to be calm and collected.

"Good morning, Mellie," Jack said, closing the door behind him with his foot. He held two large coffees from Ruth's Bakery, one with a tall clear plastic bubble on top to accommodate all of the whipped cream. "I thought you might like some coffee."

He placed both cups on my desk while he shrugged out of his leather jacket—a gift from me our first Christmas together—before sitting casually in a chair on the other side of my desk.

I quickly closed my mouth, then tried to think of something nonchalant to say without giving away the acceleration of my heart rate or the sudden dryness in my mouth.

"Thank you," I managed. I picked up my cup and pried off the top, lowering my face to taste the cream if only so I'd stop staring at him like a drowning person might eye a floating stick. When I'd recovered enough of my composure, I straightened and said, "Why are you here?"

He took a sip of his coffee. "Aren't you meeting with Marc and Rebecca this morning?"

"Yes, but I thought you said you weren't interested in attending."

He paused, his eyes drifting to my mouth and making my insides do funny things.

"I did, but then thought better of it. You shouldn't have to face them on your own. Marc and Rebecca need to see a united front."

I felt my stomach and heart switch places. "I didn't think you cared."

"Of course I care," he said softly. He leaned back in his chair. "And you have a bad habit of agreeing to things that aren't in our best interests when left to your own devices." His gaze remained on my mouth as he lifted his index finger to his lips and wiped at something invisible.

The movement distracted me from absorbing the impact of his words. He flicked at something on his lips again, his gaze moving between my eyes and my mouth. "Mellie," he said, leaning forward again, his hand outstretched.

Yes, my mind and heart whispered in unison. But, thankfully, not my mouth. Instead, he swiped his finger along the side of my mouth, revealing a glob of whipped cream on the tip of his finger. He immediately wiped it on the napkin wrapped around his cup, erasing the stray thought of me licking it off his finger.

"Oh, thanks," I said, leaning back in my chair. "For the record, I have never said or done anything with the intent of hurting you."

"I know. But your intent isn't the problem. It's the outcome. You skip right from intent to action without considering the collateral damage. It makes you a very difficult person to be married to and to live with. It's like I always feel as if I have to sleep with one eye open."

I heard every word he said, but I couldn't seem to make them stick together and make sense. Maybe I'd lived alone and independently for too long. I remembered in fifth grade getting a note from my teacher to bring home to my father. *Doesn't play well with others.* Maybe that was what Jack meant.

"Is it my labeling gun? I can get rid of it if that would help."

Jack sighed heavily as he rubbed his hand over the stubble on his chin, the sound of it achingly familiar. "Oh, Mellie . . ."

A sharp rap on the door made him stop. The door opened and Marc and Rebecca stood in the doorway, a flustered Jolly behind them.

"I'm sorry, Melanie—they didn't want to wait for me to announce them."

"That's all right, Jolly . . ." was all I could get out before my words were smothered by Rebecca's embrace.

My cousin was dressed head to toe in mauve—her new shade to avoid her usual bright pink, which she thought appeared too startling next to Marc's new hair color—including mauve boots and a matching hair ribbon. The Empire waist of her maternity dress was topped by another mauve bow. Luckily her dog, Pucci, General Lee's paramour and the mother of Porgy and Bess, wasn't with her. They usually wore matching outfits and I just didn't think I could take it this morning.

"How are you?" she said with an exaggerated frown. Simultaneously discovering that she was pregnant and that Marc had a girlfriend hadn't dimmed her perkiness or her commitment to her marriage. While I might have found that admirable in some people, in this case I found it beyond comprehension.

Jack stood and faced Marc, shoving his hands in his pockets. "Good to see you're out and about, Matt," Jack said, deliberately using the wrong name, as he'd been doing since the two adversaries had first met. "Not sure I'm on board with the new hair thing, but we won't be seeing each other often enough for that to matter."

This was the first time I'd seen Marc since that night in the cemetery when his hair had inexplicably turned white. Well, maybe not inexplicably. He'd been dragged by unseen hands into a mausoleum, after all. The experience had made him a softer and gentler version of himself, according to Rebecca, but I had a strong suspicion that it wasn't a permanent transition. The Marc Longo I knew had a piece of coal for a heart and it would take more than a serious fright to turn him into something resembling a human being.

The white hair distracted me for a moment, making me forget that he was about my age and not a feeble old gentleman. He was our enemy, and I had to keep reminding myself that regardless of what he looked like or what Rebecca said about him changing, he was still the same Marc Longo I knew. And that Marc Longo was neither friend nor family.

Marc smirked, although it did seem to have less smarminess than I'd seen in the past. "How's the writing, Jack?"

If there was one thing I'd learned since knowing Jack, it was that the worst thing to ask a writer was how the writing was going. It brought up feelings of inadequacy, doubt, and sheer panic. Jack's face remained calm, although I recognized the tic in his cheek. "It's going great—thanks for asking."

Jack walked across the room and dragged a chair back to my desk, placing it next to the one he'd just vacated. "Let's go ahead and get this started so I can get on with more pleasant tasks. Like waxing my chest."

I sat down again behind my desk while Jack waited for Rebecca and Marc to sit down across from me. Jack perched himself on the corner of the desk and smiled. "I'll just stay here in case Matt tries to steal a pencil or something and I need to tackle him. He's got sticky fingers."

Marc shook his head, looking more annoyed than hurt. "Look, I came here to make a truce. In case your head has been buried in the sand and so you aren't aware, the filming is going to happen whether or not you want it to. Harvey Beckner and the other producers won't back down. You signed a contract and unless you want to be sued for everything you own, I'd suggest you honor it."

Jack nodded pleasantly, the tic in his cheek stronger. "So, if I don't have a choice, why are we having this meeting? I do believe our lawyers made our position very clear. If we have to settle this in court, we're prepared to do that. There is no reason for us to meet face-to-face. It causes me intestinal distress just to be in the same room with you, and that's something I'd rather avoid."

Rebecca folded her hands primly in her lap. "Marc and I decided to call this meeting because we're family. And because we're family, we believe that we can continue with the filming in a mutually beneficial way. You'd avoid the necessity of emptying your bank account and selling a single ruby to fund an unnecessary and ill-advised lawsuit, and Marc gets his movie made. We want this all to go as smoothly as possible so the film people can get in and out quickly and you and your family aren't inconvenienced more than you have to be. We want to work together, not be adversaries. Because we *are* family."

Jack picked up my pencil cup and began replacing each pen and pencil in an upside-down position. It made me squirm, and I had to sit on my hands so I wouldn't yank the cup out of his hand and put everything back the way it was meant to go.

He continued to smile. "I might believe that, Rebecca, if your husband and I didn't have such a long history. And if he didn't have the reputation of being a liar and a thief."

Marc started to stand, his hands in fists, but Rebecca pressed her hand on his leg. "No need to make this physical. We are all adults. Why don't we discuss this in a rational manner?"

"Just as soon as you tell us why you're really here. If Harvey is hell-bent on us honoring our contract, there's no need for us to talk. It's in the lawyers' hands." Jack placed the cup back on my desk with the contents all askew while he stood. "Otherwise, I'm leaving."

Rebecca looked at her husband with raised eyebrows.

"Fine," Marc said, although his expression was that of a man who suddenly realized his underwear was too tight. He took a deep breath. "It's . . . important that this movie happens and that there are no lawsuits or complications that might impede or delay its filming and release."

"The movie based on my book, which you stole from me." Jack began walking toward the door. "I've already heard enough. Maybe I can schedule a colonoscopy today, too. Anything to make my day brighter."

Just as Jack reached the door, Rebecca jumped up. "We need a loan."

Jack stopped, and remained completely still for a moment. Slowly he turned around with an expression I'd seen only once before, when he'd been lying at the bottom of an open grave staring up at me.

He wiggled a finger in his ear. "I'm sorry. I'm sure I didn't hear that right. Or I've been suddenly thrown into an alternate universe. Because nowhere in the real world would you two even *consider* asking us for anything, not after everything you've done to harm me and my family.

Either you hit your head harder on those mausoleum steps than you originally thought, or you are as incredibly stupid as I've always known."

Marc stood and began zipping up his coat. "Come on, Rebecca. I told you this wouldn't work."

She held up her hand to him, her expression fierce, before turning her attention to me. "Yes, it will, because Melanie is family." She cupped her hands over her belly. "And because our baby will be Melanie's god-daughter."

The old Melanie, who'd never had a best friend or been picked for teams in playground kickball or been a bridesmaid, did a small silent cheer while the rest of me moved my horrified gaze between Rebecca, Jack, and Marc.

"Oh, come on," Jack said. "Do you really think Melanie would fall for the 'we're family' card?"

When I didn't say anything, he focused his attention on me. "Mellie? Right?"

As much as I hated being manipulated by Rebecca, she was my cousin, and she'd even had moments when she'd been a friend to me and shared the psychic dreams she'd had in an effort to help me. I couldn't just turn my back on her.

"Look, why don't we all sit back down and hear them out?" I indicated the chairs in front of my desk.

Jack sent me a cautioning look. "I'll stand," he said as Marc and Rebecca reluctantly took seats again, "just in case I have the urge to lose my breakfast."

I gave him one of my looks usually reserved for a whining toddler or a sullen teenager. "Rebecca, why don't you tell us what's going on? But I'm not going to pretend that everything Jack has said isn't true, so do your best to stick to the truth."

Marc sat in stony silence while Rebecca sat up with her hands cupped demurely over her barely there baby bump. She was only at the end of her first trimester, and I remembered looking like I was on the verge of delivery by the end of my first month.

Rebecca cleared her throat. "Marc—I mean, we—have had a few investments fail in the last few months through no fault of our own."

Jack let out a huff and I sent him a warning glance.

Rebecca lowered her eyes. "And I'm sure you've heard about Anthony's lawsuit against us, suing for his share of their grandfather's estate." She paused. "He's claiming that Marc cheated Anthony in regards to the winery and other property."

Jack and I looked at each other. We hadn't known about Marc's brother suing him. After discovering that Anthony's romancing Jayne had been instigated by Marc to spy on our treasure-hunting efforts, we'd wanted nothing to do with him. Although it was no small surprise that Anthony had finally stood up for himself where Marc was concerned and fought back.

"As a result, we have a bit of a . . . cash-flow problem. We know that you're in a stronger financial position now with the discovery of the rubies, and we'd like to discuss a loan. We just need the movie to come in on time and under budget and do well in theaters. Marc's agent said that if it does, he can expect a huge deal for his next book."

Jack looked around with raised eyebrows, as though waiting to hear an announcer tell him that he'd been punked. Finally, he said, "You do know that to sell a book you need to deliver original material, right? I'm not going to let you steal your next idea. Not that it matters. You're not only wasting our time, but you've apparently lost all touch with reality." He took a step toward the door.

Marc's words stopped him. "I can give you back your career. When the movie wraps, I'll come clean on all the misinformation that may have inadvertently soiled your image and reputation, along with those of your previous editor and agent."

I knew that was as close as he would ever come to admitting to throwing a wrench into Jack's career. To paying people to accuse Jack's editor of improprieties, and monetarily assisting with Jack's agent's early retirement, essentially orphaning him. We would never know in full what else Marc had done, but he had taken advantage of Jack's precarious position with his publisher after Jack's book about our Tradd Street house had been canceled because of Marc's thievery. It was supposed to be Jack's salvation book, the project meant to resurrect his career following the dismal failure of his previous release and the public debunking of its subject matter. Instead of Jack's book riding the bestseller lists, doors had suddenly slammed in his face, stalling his career indefinitely. For a man whose identity was so closely linked to his career, it had been like suffering a slow death.

Jack calmly faced Marc, his eyes narrowed and his face showing the same look of disbelief the twins exhibited when I tried to hide a piece of broccoli in a muffin.

"'Inadvertently.'" Jack repeated the word with heavy sarcasm. I wondered if I was the only person who'd seen the flash of interest in his eyes.

"More or less," Marc said, not bothering to look even the slightest bit apologetic. "Regardless of the reason, I know that your current editor is barely off of training wheels, has never read your books, and wants Kim Kardashian to blurb your next book. And you don't have an agent to tell your editor where to shove those ideas because no agent worth a grain of salt is returning your phone calls."

Jack gave a little laugh, but the tic in his cheek was now pulsing like a jackhammer. He casually leaned back against my desk and crossed one leg over the other. "And you could fix that?"

"I can."

Rebecca cleared her throat. "There's one more thing, isn't there, Marc?"

Marc wore the look of a man sitting in a dentist's chair. He nodded. Swallowed. "Yes. We're prepared to give you twenty-five percent of our net earnings from the movie."

Jack raised his eyebrows. "If I loan you money."

"Yes."

"And we step back and allow the film crew to come into our home without any interference."

"Yes."

"Make it fifty percent. Of gross."

"That's . . ." Marc began, but was cut off by a sharp look from Rebecca. "Thirty-five," Marc countered.

"Fifty or we're walking. It's not negotiable."

Marc nodded, his lips pressed together tightly, making them nearly as white as his hair.

Jack looked at me briefly, then turned back to Marc. "I'm not convinced that trusting you is in our best interest. My first instinct is to run. But my wife, for reasons I don't understand, considers you and Rebecca family." He was silent for a long moment, his eyes not leaving mine. "Melanie and I will need to discuss this together."

My heart did a flip-flop at the word "wife."

"And if we somehow lose our good sense and agree, we'll need a few concessions to be made. One—the filming is restricted to the bottom floor of the house and the garden since that's where most of the action takes place. Harvey can use a soundstage elsewhere for the rest. That's not negotiable. Mellie and my children do not need to have their lives disrupted. I know the contract allows for hotel accommodations for the duration of the filming that, as previously agreed, is not to last one day longer than eight weeks. This is our home. We're not leaving. Don't even try to talk us out of it—that's a nonstarter.

"Two—and again this is a major 'if'—if we decide to do this, we'll want our lawyer to draw up the contract with all the provisions of the loan, including an inflated interest rate that will increase with each week the principal isn't repaid in full past the term of the loan. And three"— he grinned—"the party or parties responsible for a breach in contract will have to fulfill their part of the agreement without the wronged party being held responsible for theirs."

"I'm not sure if Harvey—" Marc began.

"Of course," Rebecca said, cutting him off. "Marc will settle the terms with Harvey. Harvey has a lot riding on this production and is as eager to get started as Marc, so he'll want to agree. And we'll also allow your lawyer to work out the details. After you and Melanie have had a chance to discuss it, of course." She stood and approached me with her arms outstretched. She clasped both of my hands in hers. "I'm so glad we're family."

Jack pulled himself away from the desk and moved to put himself out of Rebecca's arm range. "I think I'm going to subscribe to ancestry.com to confirm that."

Rebecca laughed. "Because I'm so petite and blond and Melanie . . . isn't? Oh, don't be silly. We're from Charleston. Our family tree is practically tattooed on our chests the moment we're born." She sobered. "Not that we have tattoos, of course."

"Of course not," Jack said, his eyes frosty.

Jack and I escorted Marc and Rebecca to the door. "We'll be in touch," I said as they moved into the corridor.

"How soon?" Marc asked, a note of panic detectable in his voice.

"Good-bye," Jack said in response, shutting the door firmly in Marc's face.

There was a long silence from the other side of the door and then the sound of slow footsteps retreating down the hallway.

I looked at Jack, realizing my nose was almost touching his chin. He didn't step back and I couldn't move at all.

"So, what do you think?" he asked, his voice low. I thought it also sounded sultry, but that could have been just my wishful thinking.

I cleared my throat a couple of times and swallowed. "I think you agreed to think about it too easily. It's nice that you would consider my feelings about helping family, but you and I both know my feelings don't extend to Marc. Which makes *me* think you're working on your own plan."

He smiled lazily. "You know that saying about keeping your friends close and your enemies closer? Let's just say that I see an opportunity here that Marc isn't aware of. I just might finally have a chance to beat him at his own game." He looked at his watch. "And I'll tell you all about it later. Right now I've got to run."

"Chest waxing?"

Jack chuckled. "Not exactly. Yvonne Craig needs my help moving boxes for her garage sale," he said, referring to the octogenarian and long-term research librarian. His gaze turned serious. "If we agree, it will mean having a film crew in the house while you're living in it. But there's no way we can allow Marc free run of our house."

I nodded, my eyes trying not to focus on his mouth. "I know."

"And more bumps in the night from all the extra activity."

"Yes. But you'll at least get paid for *your* story. There's some justice there, don't you think? Even if it's only fifty percent and not the one hundred percent that you deserve. But it's something. And we won't have to spend the children's education funds on a lawsuit." My voice sounded almost as husky as his.

His eyes drifted down to my lips, and I found myself leaning forward, my eyes closing, my heart racing, a brief worry that I might still have whipped cream on my face.

Jack's hands gently gripped my arms, my puckered lips touching only empty air.

"Are you all right, Mellie? It looked like you were about to fall."

"Sorry." I stepped back, flustered.

His eyes darkened, reassuring me that he'd felt the pull, too. He zipped up his jacket and headed for the door. "Thanks, Mellie. We'll talk later, all right? And as soon as you and I agree on terms, I'm going to give Harvey Beckner exactly one week to agree or the deal's off. He already took care of the necessary permits back in December, so there's no reason why he can't begin filming as soon as the ink's dry on the contract."

"Sounds good." I forced a smile, watching him walk out the door and close it behind him. I still hadn't moved when he opened it again.

"Mellie?"

"Yes?"

"That was almost kiss number what?" he said, referring to the running joke we'd had before we were married.

"I don't remember." I straightened. "Maybe we can start over. Make it almost kiss number one."

He smiled sadly. "I'll have to think about it. I don't really believe in do-overs." He shut the door behind him again, and I listened as his footsteps faded down the corridor.

I stared at the closed door for a long time before I sat at my desk again and emptied out my pencil cup, rearranging all of the pencils and pens by size and color. My concerns over how quickly Jack had agreed to consider Marc's proposal were overtaken by the replay in my head of Jack's words when he'd referred to me as his wife, reassuring me that despite everything, he hadn't forgotten.

CHAPTER 5

A week later, I found myself driving down Queen Street, more than half an hour early for a house showing nearby. Catherine Jimenez had shown pity on me and handed me the client since she was overwhelmed with business. I was too grateful to lie and say I was too busy juggling enough of my own clients to accept her castoffs.

I slowed the car in front of Veronica's house after I made a last-minute decision to stop. A clutter of construction vehicles prevented me from parking nearby, and I had to walk two blocks back to Veronica's yellow Victorian. As I walked, I smiled to myself as I took in all the noise and commotion of construction, happy to acknowledge that at least one of my plans was actually working.

The sound of a circular saw greeted me as I neared, the noise almost as gratifying as the pile of reclaimed wood in the small front yard. Sophie had mandated that no new wood was to be used in replacing any termite-ridden cornices or floorboards, extending the time frame of the renovations considerably. Hopefully until I had heard everything Adrienne needed to tell me and the mystery of her death had been solved.

As I approached the short driveway, I recognized my mother-in-law's green Jaguar. The trunk was open and the impeccably groomed Amelia in a royal blue bouclé Chanel suit and matching heels was leaning inside it, pulling out what appeared to be stacks of catalogs.

I rushed toward her. "Let me help you," I said.

"Oh, Melanie. So good to see you," she said, and kissed me on both cheeks before handing me a heavy stack. Amelia leaned back in and took out another pile, managing to balance it in one arm while she pushed the close button for the trunk. "Would you mind helping me bring these inside?"

"Of course not. I've got a little bit of time before my next appointment, so I figured I'd stop by to see Veronica about . . ." I'd almost said "Adrienne," but stopped. Because she was my mother's best friend and Jack's mother, chances were she knew about my "special gift," but neither one of us had ever acknowledged it. She instinctively understood that I found it easier to relate to people when I could pretend that I was normal. "About her new home search," I finished.

We began walking toward the front steps. I glanced down at the stack in my arms. "What are these for?"

"Those are recent antique furniture auction catalogs. Veronica has asked for my help in estimating the value of the furniture in her house. Because they're downsizing, it's not likely they'll find a home for everything in their new space. It's good you're here, then, since we might want to include some pieces with the sale of the house. Anything left over, I may take on consignment for our store."

"I guess it's never too early to think ahead," I said, juggling my stack so I could ring the doorbell. "Veronica wants to wait until this one is put on the market, and then I'll help her and Michael find a new home."

"Which, according to Veronica, could take a very long time." Amelia winked at me and I smiled.

She tilted her head, studying me as if I were a Meissen figurine with a glaring chip. "You look tired," she said, giving me a sympathetic look. "This whole separation thing . . ." She shook her head. "I'm not taking sides here—I've been married long enough to know that I shouldn't. But I do hope that you and Jack figure this out soon. The children miss you when you're not together, and I can't even imagine how much you miss them when they're not with you. Not to mention how much Jack misses seeing Nola every day."

I could only nod, knowing that if I tried to speak, I'd probably cry. I missed JJ and Sarah every moment they weren't with me. Just as I missed entering the nursery together with Jack first thing in the morning and having our special time with them before our days started, before phone calls and chatter and car pool.

The circular saw began whirring again, obliterating all other sound as well as the need for me to respond as the door opened and Veronica ushered us inside, but not before I caught the telltale scent of Vanilla Musk perfume.

"Hello, Amelia, and what a nice surprise, Melanie."

"I hope you don't mind me just stopping by."

"Of course not," Veronica said, shutting the door behind us.

I barely recognized the usually dark foyer and staircase because of the paper runners covering the steps and the white sheets thrown over all the heavy Victorian furnishings. The house smelled of sawdust and paint, the occasional hammering punctuating the steady hum of the circular saw outside.

"It's better in here," Veronica said, leading us into the library.

Shelves of books lined the walls behind a dark burgundy leather chesterfield sofa and a matching armchair; an ancient rolltop desk was tucked into the circular window that I recognized from the tower outside. She slid a pair of pocket doors closed and we took a collective breath in the relative silence.

Veronica smiled apologetically as she helped us unload our burdens onto a library table, its legs on small wheels. "I've asked Sophie to leave this room for last," Veronica explained, "so that we have an escape from all the construction." She sent me a worried glance. "Michael's about ready to lose his mind. I don't know how much more of this he can take before he decides to just sell it as is."

She indicated the sofa. "Why don't you two have a seat, and I'll go finish with the tea tray? Lindsey made some of her grandmother's famous cheese straws and I have to say they're better than anything I could buy in a store."

Veronica left the room just as a familiar tingling began on the back of my neck, along with a gentle tug on the sleeve of my dress, the scent of Vanilla Musk wafting around me.

Amelia picked up a catalog, then put it down again, taking a deep breath as she did so. "Melanie, dear," she said as she faced me. "You know I love you like a daughter, so you must know that I have only your best interests at heart. Which means I feel compelled to tell you that I think this idea of you and Jack allowing filming in your house while you're living there all alone with Nola and the two babies isn't safe."

"Really, Amelia. It's fine. Part of the deal is that hotel rooms are available for us if we choose. And the option will remain for the duration of the filming. Since the crew is allowed only downstairs in certain rooms and the upstairs is off-limits, I know we can hold on to our privacy. It's just that I don't want to disrupt the children's lives any more than we have to—especially right now—and Jack and I just aren't comfortable with Marc having the unchecked freedom to dig through our personal effects. I'm sure I'll be fine. . . ."

As if she hadn't heard me, she said, "Your parents think so, too. They were over last night for supper. We all agreed that it isn't an ideal situation, and spent most of the evening trying to come up with a workable solution."

"And nobody thought to call me and ask what I thought?"

She regarded me with surprise, as if this was the first time someone had considered my opinion. "Well, no. I suppose it's because we know you have bigger worries right now."

"Yes, but . . ."

Amelia patted my hand. "I know. You are certainly capable of taking care of yourself and your children. It's just that as parents and grandparents we can't stop ourselves from worrying."

"Yes, but . . ."

"Unfortunately, James and I don't have the room, or we'd love to have you. Your parents offered for you and the children to move in with them, but we didn't think taking the children and Nola away from everything that was familiar to them would be a good solution, either. So we put our heads together and came up with a solution that we all thought worked best."

I leaned back, considering her with narrowed eyes. I'd never seen this manipulative side of Amelia Trenholm before, maybe because it was usually disguised by a kind smile and a Chanel suit. But she *was* Jack's mother. "And?"

"We thought it best that Jack move back in. In the guest room, of course. And just until the filming is done. Or until you're reconciled." She smiled hopefully.

I'd be lying if I said the thought of Jack moving back in—regardless of the reason—didn't do interesting things to my heart rate. I might even have started a mental list of all the things I needed to do—starting with shaving my legs—before he got there. Then I realized that there was one missing component to this plan, and I sank back against the sofa.

"Jack will never agree. He'll find another solution that doesn't involve him living under the same roof with me."

A smile that could be described only as devious graced her face. She reached over and patted my hand again. "Leave that to us."

The memory of Jack leaving me in the foyer of our house, the door shutting in my face, flashed across my brain. "Trust me. Jack isn't ready. And he's about as bullheaded as they come. He could never be talked into doing something unless he really wanted to. And he definitely doesn't want to live with me right now."

The pocket door slid open again, the sound of construction amplified for a moment before Veronica entered, balancing a tray with one hand, then closing the door with the other.

"Well, technically, it won't be *with* you. And don't look a gift horse in the mouth," Amelia added quietly as she stood to help Veronica with the tray.

The knot that had begun forming in my stomach when Amelia first mentioned Jack returning home solidified at the sight of the cheese straws and iced tea. I looked at my watch, grateful I didn't have to lie.

"Veronica, I have a showing, so I can't stay. I just dropped by so I could go up to the attic again, see what else I might find. You'd mentioned that Adrienne had a Discman. Was that in the box with all of her belongings?"

Veronica's brows knitted. "I suppose it should have been, but I don't remember seeing it when I went through Adrienne's box with Detective Riley. I could have missed it, though. I had to look away a few times. Too many memories." She waved her hand in front of her face as if to stop tears. "I haven't been up there since. But you're welcome to go take another look."

The tugging on the back of my dress became more insistent. "Thank you." I walked toward the pocket doors Veronica had just closed. Turning back to Amelia, I almost said *Good luck*. But instead I just waved and let myself out into the foyer, knowing she would need a miracle and a bulldozer to get Jack Trenholm to budge.

The pressure of a pair of hands pushing me up the stairs continued up all three flights to the attic, the door helpfully opening on its own when I reached it. I turned around to see if there'd been any witnesses, and was relieved when I didn't see anyone.

I closed the door behind me, then stood inside the gloomy space. Nothing appeared to have been moved since I'd last been up there. A dusty glass hurricane lamp with a thick red Christmas candle inside sat on one of the thick windowsills. The draped shapes of furniture still lurked against the walls, keeping company with children's playthings, including a Raggedy Ann doll. I thought I saw something move in the black bead eyes, and turned around to see if it had been a reflection. But nothing was there except for the lingering scent of Adrienne's perfume.

The dirty stained glass windows cast a watery rainbow across the attic's gloom, giving it the impression of being underwater, the dust motes like tiny air bubbles floating to the surface. I held my breath for a moment, listening to the stillness that wasn't exactly still. More like an anticipatory cessation of movement waiting for something to happen. Slowly, I exhaled with the certainty that I wasn't alone.

"Adrienne?"

I waited for a sign: a sound, an unexpected movement of the child's rocking chair that waited in a corner. An apparition, even. But that was the thing with Adrienne's spirit. It was as if she was waiting in anticipation of something happening. She seemed to reserve her energy, saving it for times when she felt it necessary to be unleashed. Or whenever she needed to show me something, I thought as I remembered the red pillow and the sudden appearance of Adrienne's gold necklace with the Omega Chi charm with the space for a missing letter. Again and again I apparently kept misunderstanding what the clues were supposed to tell me.

I knelt beside the cardboard box containing Adrienne's belongings from her dorm room, all four flaps lying open, the curls of dried packing tape on the floor next to the box just like I'd left them. I recognized the sorority scrapbook, the stack of photographs and invitations to various campus events, the USC Gamecocks baseball hat.

I picked up the hat, curious as to why it was there. It didn't appear as if it had ever been worn, making me wonder if it had been a gift from Veronica, who'd attended USC. I placed it on the floor and began emptying out the box, looking for the Discman and anything that might give me some idea of what had happened to Adrienne.

Piles of freshman-year mementos soon began to form next to the box: maroon-and-gold pom-poms, a stack of multicolored plastic drinking cups with various occasions marked in peeling paint on the outside. I shook out and refolded about half a dozen College of Charleston and Omega Chi sweatshirts before pulling out a pile of twice as many T-shirts.

A search through the shirts yielded a yearbook tucked between them. I pulled it out and held the spine up to the light of the stained glass window: *The Comet.* The sprawl of dozens of signatures and well-wishes, with lots of hearts, X's and O's, decorated the inside of the front and back covers. I opened the book wide and shook it to see if anything would fall out. When nothing did, I placed it on the floor. Everything in this box had already been examined and reexamined by the Charleston police, as well as more recently by Detective Thomas Riley, who'd been assigned to work cold cases. I hadn't really expected to find anything new. I was simply waiting for Adrienne to tell me if we'd missed something important.

A dried-rose wrist corsage rained small flakes as I pulled it from the box. I'm not sure why, but I held it to my nose as if to capture something of the night it had been a part of and the girl who'd worn it. But all I could detect was the faint scent of Vanilla Musk. And decay.

I placed it on top of the growing pile and returned my attention to the box. I could now see the cardboard bottom, littered with loose plastic beads from a ball of tangled and broken Mardi Gras necklaces in yellow, green, and purple.

I reached back into Adrienne's box and pulled out a stack of old magazines, an issue of *Seventeen* on top with a photo of actress Claire Danes wearing a denim jacket, and a teaser title at the top: *When your friends turn against you.*

Lifting the pile of magazines out of the nearly empty box revealed an old headset with disintegrating foam earpieces. I placed the magazines on the floor and returned to the headset, following its connection wire under a pile of scarves. A wave of excitement passed through me when I spotted a Discman in bright pink. A strong scent of Adrienne's perfume wafted past as I pulled it from the box, feeling as if I'd just opened a time capsule.

Swirls of white powder clustered in clumps over most of the player, presumably fingerprint dust. I'd never owned a Discman, but even though this device was foreign to me, it wasn't hard to figure out that the oozing orange leaking from the battery compartment on the back meant that the batteries had never been removed. And that if I pressed the OPEN button, the top would lift up.

I stared inside the empty cavity, the fingerprint dust generously applied here, too. The absence of a disc made me wonder if the police had taken out the Laurie Anderson CD that Veronica had mentioned and kept it as evidence.

Being careful not to touch the battery acid, I placed the Discman back inside the box and then returned everything else on top of it, trying to leave it exactly as I'd found it. I stood, wiping dust off of my knees.

"Okay, Adrienne. I didn't find anything. What did you want me to see?"

I wasn't expecting a response, but I'd hoped at least for some kind of sign. She'd gently pushed me up the stairs, so something had to be up here that she wanted me to see. I waited a moment. Exasperated, I said, "Fine," then headed for the door.

I turned the handle, but it didn't budge. I tried several more times, but it still wouldn't turn. I wiped my hand on my skirt and tried again. Nothing. The door wasn't locked; it felt more like someone was holding the handle from the other side.

"Come on, Adrienne!" I banged on the door. "I've got to go. Please let me out."

I tried again, but still nothing. Turning around, I leaned back against the door, suddenly aware of the tinny sound of music through what sounded like distant headphones. I returned to the box and emptied everything out again, the music getting louder as I got closer to the bottom. I moved faster when I recognized the lyrics to "O Superman" spoken through a vocoder.

As soon as I'd uncovered the Discman, the music suddenly stopped.

"Okay," I said as I carefully lifted the Discman out and then replaced the rest of the contents of the box. "Can I please leave now?"

I turned toward the door with trepidation. An odd ripple in the stale air blew a chill against my skin. Reaching out, I twisted the doorknob. Nothing.

I glanced at my watch. "Adrienne, I have to go. Please let me out." I somehow managed to keep the panic from my voice as I found myself wishing that I'd brought my cell phone with me instead of leaving it inside my purse in the library. I gave the doorknob another twist, just in case.

I turned around again, my gaze settling on the yearbook lying on the floor next to the box. I was fairly certain that I'd put it back in the box, but I wasn't going to argue. I picked it up and stacked the Discman on top of it. "Is this what you wanted me to have?"

To test my theory, I twisted the doorknob. To my relief, it turned easily, allowing me to pull the door open. I stood at the top of the steps, oddly suspended as if held in place by two separate forces. An icy breath blew against the back of my neck as indecipherable words growled in the empty air by my ear. A hard shove sent me tumbling forward, the suddenness of it freezing my brain and making me unable to control my arms and legs.

With a force as abrupt as the one that had sent me hurtling forward, my unchecked fall was halted by unseen hands before I reached the bottom, still cradling the CD player and yearbook against my chest.

"You all right?" A workman wearing a paint-splattered T-shirt and jeans looked at me and then up at the attic door, which had slammed after I'd reached the bottom of the steps.

"I am. Thank you," I said, forcing my voice to remain steady. "Just being clumsy."

He dragged his gaze from the door to me and nodded. "If you say so." He backed away from the steps all the way to the paint bucket at the end of the hallway without turning around.

I ran down the steps to the foyer, the CD player and the yearbook clutched tightly in my arms, and I felt a gentle pressure on my back hurrying me along. It wasn't until I was back in my car driving to my appointment that I began to shake, my brain slowly unraveling what had just happened, translating the growl into words. Remembering them as the ones my mother had said when she'd held Adrienne's broken necklace, which Veronica and Thomas had found in the box and I now wore around my neck: *You don't want to know the truth.*

I pressed my foot to the accelerator, eager to be anywhere I wasn't alone.

CHAPTER 6

Early Monday evening I sat at the kitchen table working on my personal-growth spreadsheet while Nola sat next to me doing homework. Sarah and JJ sat in their high chairs playing with Cheerios, alternating between eating and throwing them. Nola and I had separate work spaces in the house, but after Mrs. Houlihan's return, we'd both gravitated to the kitchen to be near the housekeeper as she prepared supper. We hadn't planned it, but it was clear neither one of us wanted to be left to our own rudimentary culinary devices ever again. Being near Mrs. Houlihan meant she couldn't escape through the back door. Even the dogs appeared attached to her heels, no doubt as excited to see her as they were about the possibility of dropped food scraps.

"Is it just the two of you for dinner tonight?" Mrs. Houlihan asked, wearing an aggrieved expression, her hands on her considerable hips. She wasn't used to anyone invading her domain while she was working.

"Just us," I said, smiling brightly. "But we're starving. Could definitely eat enough for two."

"Or three." Nola nodded enthusiastically. It was important Mrs. Houlihan felt needed.

Mrs. Houlihan smiled tenderly at the twins as she gave them fresh

Cheerios from the box, her expression returning to a grimace as she began to fill a pot with water.

The doorbell rang. Nola lifted her head, her gaze meeting mine. The doorbell, despite being fully functional according to Rich Kobylt, appeared to work only when it was someone we wanted to see, which was why Rebecca was usually left outside on the front piazza.

I rubbed my quadriceps under the table, trying not to wince. "You're going to have to get that. My legs hurt too much to stand." As promised, I'd gone running with Jayne twice, and I was already regretting my decision. I looked back at my spreadsheet where I'd added two more row titles: Be Nice to Rebecca (Plan Baby Shower) and Get House Ready for Filming (Call Greco).

Nola stood and glanced over my shoulder. "Really, Melanie? You have to remind yourself to be nice to Rebecca? I mean, I know it's a challenge, but still . . ." She grabbed an apple from the fruit bowl in the middle of the table and took a bite, heading out of the kitchen to answer the door. "Can't wait to see Greco again," she called back.

She'd already passed through the swinging door before I could remind her not to talk with food in her mouth.

Mrs. Houlihan opened the refrigerator door and let out a sharp cry.

I bolted out of my chair, my legs screaming in protest. "What's wrong?" I asked as I hobbled toward her.

She turned around, her outstretched hand clutching a small object. "I'm going to have to have a word with Nola about frightening me with this . . . thing. This morning I found it in the middle of the floor. I just about had a heart attack."

I didn't have to look to see what the object was. The Frozen Charlotte in her coffin had gone missing the previous day and I knew it was futile to hope that it had disappeared forever.

I took it from the housekeeper's hand, the iron icy cold to the touch. "I'm so sorry, Mrs. Houlihan. I'll talk to Nola." I limped back to my chair and shoved it in my briefcase. If Mrs. Houlihan knew about half of the odd happenings in the house, she would have given her notice long before now.

A Cheerio pinged the side of my head. I swiveled toward the children in their high chairs, eager to identify the culprit. Both cherubic faces lit up, their chubby arms reaching past me toward whoever had just walked into the kitchen.

Even without their reaction, the static electricity that suddenly began to buzz around me would have been enough to inform me that Jack had entered the room.

"Mr. Jack!" Mrs. Houlihan opened her arms, her entire body shaking with excitement.

"Mrs. Houlihan," he said with the same level of enthusiasm and proceeded to wrap his arms around her in what could only be described as a bear hug. Despite Mrs. Houlihan's considerable cooking skills, I'd never felt a moment's jealousy toward her. Until now.

As Jack moved toward the children to shower them with hugs and kisses, I spent the time rearranging myself in my chair to appear only mildly interested and not at all excited about Jack's presence, and I focused on my computer screen without seeing it.

"I think Version 107 is an optimistic guess, but I gave up counting long ago." Jack's voice came from right next to my ear, where he was leaning over to read my screen. I jumped, my chair rebelling by sliding out from under me.

Two strong hands that I felt all the way to my heart kept me from falling while the chair crashed to the floor, startling the babies and the dogs into silence until JJ started laughing.

Jack slowly released his grip on me and picked up the chair. "Maybe 'treat furniture with respect' should be at the top of the list."

My mouth might have opened and closed like a dying fish's, but despite all of my years in sales, I couldn't find a single word to say. I could only hope that the wild flipping of my heart couldn't be detected beneath my dress.

"Jack," I finally managed. I reached behind me to lean casually against the table but misjudged the distance and instead did an odd flapping motion with my arm.

Half of his mouth turned up. "Hello, Mellie."

I took a deep breath, ordering my body to calm down. "What are you doing here?" I slid my desk calendar toward me. "Did I mess up the visitation schedule?" I almost added *As if* but remembered that I was trying to be more mature.

"Dad's brought a suitcase!" Nola said.

"Wait. What?" I remembered the conversation I'd had with Amelia and then dismissed because there was no way Jack could be coerced into moving back under the same roof as me. Yet here he was. I resisted the impulse to poke him with a fork to make sure he was real. "Nobody told me . . ."

Jack crossed his arms. "Mother said she had mentioned that it would be a good idea if I remained here for the duration of the filming and that you hadn't objected. The film crew is scheduled to arrive Wednesday to begin setting up, so I wanted to be here before they arrived and help prepare the house for the onslaught."

I tried to lean back again, forgetting that I wasn't close enough to the table, and did the weird arm-flopping thing again. "Yes, but you didn't call to let me know." I worked hard to mask my enthusiasm as an accusation.

"I didn't want to give myself time to change my mind. And I didn't think you'd say no."

"Does this mean Marc is holding up his end of the arrangement?"

"Yep." He patted his satchel. "He's signed all of the papers and I've got them right here for us to go over and sign to make our agreement official. Not that I trust him, of course. But he's not getting a ruby from us until he's met all terms first."

Mrs. Houlihan interrupted. "Will you be staying for dinner?" she asked, already reaching for the box of whole wheat pasta noodles.

Jack looked at me. "It's up to Mellie."

I pretended to think. "Well, if you think it's for the best, then you should stay." Both of us acted as if the decision was mine.

"I'll set the table," Nola said, making everyone, including the twins, turn toward her. Usually she disappeared when she sensed Mrs. Houlihan making dinner and was unable to hear us when we called her to come help, her hearing suddenly sharp when it was time to eat.

"I just put clean sheets on the bed, Mr. Jack, and I'll make sure there are fresh towels for you in the master bathroom."

I tried not to look overly hopeful and occupied myself with saving my spreadsheet in three different ways, so I was able to hide my disappointment at Jack's answer.

"Actually, Mrs. Houlihan, I'll be staying in the guest room. I know where the sheets are and I'm quite capable of making the bed myself."

"And I'll be sure to lock my door," Jack said at the same time I said, "And I'll be sure to lock my door." Except only one of us meant it.

I don't think I imagined the *hrumph* uttered under Mrs. Houlihan's breath as she turned back to the stove.

Nola had just reentered the kitchen when the doorbell rang again. "I guess you want me to get that," she said, sounding as if she carried the weight of the world on her narrow shoulders.

"Only if you want to get fed tonight," Jack suggested.

With a heavy sigh, Nola headed out of the kitchen again. After a few moments, she returned with Beau Ryan behind her, a pleasant smile on his face. Nola wore an annoyed expression and her cheeks appeared sunburned. Jack and Beau stared at each other, waiting for Nola to say something, but she seemed unusually flustered.

Finally, Beau reached out a hand for Jack to shake and introduced himself. "You must be Nola's dad. It's a pleasure to finally meet you, Mr. Trenholm."

"Likewise," Jack said, giving Beau's hand an extra shake. I thought I saw Beau wince. "What can we do for you?"

"Actually, I came to see Melanie. I told her I'd find out about something that may have come from the cistern out back."

"'May have'?" Jack asked.

"We think so," I said. "Nola found this in her room." I retrieved the Frozen Charlotte in her little coffin from my briefcase and placed it on the table before opening the lid. "And she's lying in a bed of antique buttons."

For the first time, the scent of smoke wafted from the coffin, strong enough to make me cough. "Does anybody else smell that?" Blank expressions met mine around the table.

Sarah let out a piercing shriek from her high chair, her gaze focused on the tiny doll in its coffin, my daughter's little arms and legs straining to escape. Jack scooped her up and she clung to him, her face buried in his neck. JJ remained oblivious, busily attempting to pick up loose Cheerios from his tray with his nose, his ever-present whisk clutched in one tiny fist. For some reason, he had chosen it as his comfort item since he was an infant.

Mrs. Houlihan turned from the stove to face us, an avenging wooden spoon held in her hand, red sauce staining the edge. "And I found that . . . that *thing* in the refrigerator. That wasn't very nice, Nola."

Nola glanced at me with wide eyes and I quickly shook my head. She turned a repentant face toward the housekeeper. "I'm so sorry, Mrs. Houlihan. I won't do it again."

Beau watched Nola carefully as she spoke, a speculative expression on his face.

"I'd appreciate that." Mrs. Houlihan turned to me. "One more for dinner?"

"Yes," I said.

"No," Nola said at the same time.

Jack raised an eyebrow, his assessing gaze moving between Nola and Beau.

"Unless you have other plans?" I said.

As if unaware of the hostile gaze being beamed at him from Nola, he said, "Only if it's no trouble, I'd love to. It's been a while since I've had a home-cooked meal. Lots of ramen noodles and pepperoni pizza. And my specialty macaroni and cheese with sliced hot dogs."

"So you're not vegan?" Jack asked, his expression thawing.

"No, sir. I like food I can taste. I have nothing against vegetables, but give me some crawfish and andouille sausage to go with them. Or a juicy steak or hamburger—or both." He patted his flat stomach as my own growled loudly.

I turned to Nola. "Would you please put another place setting on the dining room table for Beau?"

With yet another heavy sigh, she pulled out silverware from the drawer, and slammed it harder than necessary before retreating to the dining room.

"You said you had something for me?" I reminded Beau.

"Yes." Beau reached into his backpack and pulled out a sandwich-sized Tupperware container. "Sorry it took me a while to get back to you—I had a project due for school, and then I had to wait for my grandmother to send me this." He placed the container on the table and Jack and I gathered around to watch Beau pull open the lid.

The box was filled with loose old buttons of various sizes, designs, and materials. Thin strips of what appeared to be dehydrated leather straps lay at the bottom of the container, shriveled like dead earthworms on a summer sidewalk.

Nola returned, making sure she stayed on our side of the table instead of standing next to Beau. She studied the contents of the box for a moment, then said, "It looks like the buttons used to be strung together on strings or leather straps."

"Very good," Beau said, his eyes lighting on Nola.

Her cheeks flushed. "Just a guess, but those little bits of old leather here and at the bottom of Charlotte's coffin kind of gave it away."

Nola reached inside and plucked out a brass button with a fleur-de-lis etching on top, rolling it between her callused fingers.

"You play guitar?" Beau asked.

Nola's cheeks reddened again. "A little."

I shared a sidewise glance with Jack at Nola's grand understatement.

"Me, too," Beau said. "I love the sound of an acoustic guitar, probably because I remember my mother playing to me when I was really little. She used to make up her own songs."

"My mother did, too," Nola said softly, her eyes focused on the button between her fingers.

Jack and I reached for her at the same time, our arms encircling Nola in an awkward group hug. Knowing Nola's tolerance of parental affection was limited, Jack and I moved away after a moment, although the places where Jack had touched me still smoldered.

"So," Nola said as she tossed the button back into the box, "why were these with the Frozen Charlotte doll?"

Beau scratched the back of his head. "We're not really sure. Mimi—that's my grandmother—also collects charm strings, and she believes that might be what those buttons in the coffin are from. She's just not sure why they'd be together, although the Victorian time period is the same for both."

"Charm strings?" Jack asked, his finger flicking through the buttons.

"Yeah. It was a thing girls did back in the eighteen sixties. They would sew or string buttons on a piece of fabric or a leather strip. When they added the thousandth button, that's when they would supposedly meet the man they would marry." Beau chuckled. "I guess before Tik-Tok and Instagram, girls had a lot of time on their hands."

"Girls?" Nola crossed her arms.

"Boys, too," he quickly added. "Mimi has a whole section in the back room of the store with anthropomorphic taxidermy and diatom arrangements to prove that guys also had weird ways of keeping busy. She actually has an entire rabbit school and a cat wedding complete with preacher and pulpit. And a nice collection of diatom arrangements using butterfly wings and insect legs. Pretty cool, huh? You should check it out online—I handle their website and those pages get the most hits."

Nola wrinkled her nose. "Did you get your weirdness from your grandmother, or is it something that runs in your entire family?'

Beau considered her with somber eyes. "I wouldn't know. My parents disappeared during Hurricane Katrina, trying to find my little sister. I was only five years old, so I don't remember very much about them."

Nola clenched her eyes shut. "I'm . . . I'm so sorry. I didn't . . ." She stopped, knowing that any apology wouldn't be adequate.

"I'm curious, Beau," Jack said. "I knew a Dr. Beauregard Ryan from New Orleans when I was with the Army. He patched me up once in Afghanistan. Any relation?"

Something flashed behind Beau's eyes, but he didn't flinch. "Yes, sir. My father."

Jack nodded, his expression giving nothing away. "And you don't know what happened to your mother or father after Katrina?"

Beau paused. "No, sir."

There was a moment of silence as we all realized Beau wasn't going to add anything else. The silence that fell was mercifully broken by the binging of a text on Beau's cell phone. He slid it from his pocket and looked at the screen.

"Sorry—thanks for the invitation to stay for dinner, but I have to go. My podcast partner is having technical issues with some of the equipment and I need to see if I can fix the problem before we record tonight."

"No worries," I said. "Hopefully we can do it another time soon."

He nodded. "And thank you, Mrs. Houlihan. It sure smells good—sorry to be missing it." Beau stuck out a hand to Jack. "It was nice meeting you, sir."

"Likewise," Jack said, his expression level.

"Beau," I said, "since you're calling me Melanie, I think you should call him Jack."

"Actually, 'sir' is fine. Or 'Mr. Trenholm.'" Jack smiled.

"Yes, sir," Beau said, nonplussed, as he put the container back into his backpack.

Something made me hug Beau. Maybe it was what he'd said about his parents and sister. Or maybe I just recognized the same lost expression Nola had worn when she'd first shown up at my front door.

"Thank you for bringing the buttons and talking to your grandmother about everything. I really appreciate it."

"You're welcome." Beau turned toward Nola, who was now juggling Sarah on her hip. "See you later. I won't be in on Sunday, so I'll leave a list of things for you on my desk. The back room really needs a good dusting and mopping. It aggravates my allergies every time I have to walk back there."

I placed a calming hand on Nola's arm to keep her silent. "Thanks, Beau. I hope to see you again soon."

I wasn't about to suggest that Nola walk him to the door, so I escorted him out, and waited until he'd reached the end of the piazza before I closed the door.

When I turned around, I saw Jack with his suitcase at the bottom of the stairs. "I thought I'd go ahead and unpack before supper."

"I guess you know where the guest room is."

"I do." Jack lifted his suitcase and began climbing the stairs.

I watched him for a moment before I blurted, "The Frozen Charlotte has a friend who left footprints in the snow that stopped at the dining room window. And wet footprints followed me to work, and I have no idea where they came from, but I don't think it's the same person because they're different sizes. I also took a Discman and a yearbook that belonged to Veronica's sister from her attic to see if I can figure out anything more about Adrienne's murder. I'm also pretty sure that there's another spirit up in the attic with Adrienne who doesn't want me there. At lunch today I bought a really beautiful skirt at the Finicky Filly that wasn't on sale but it's a classic and well-made, and I'll have it forever, so that justified the price. Plus it matches the new shoes I bought at Charleston Shoe Company, which I went into only because it was practically across the street from Buxton Books. I'd popped in only to get a copy of Marc's book so I'd understand what was being filmed in my house, but ended up buying a few other books because Sophie says I need to read more than just the real estate ads in the paper."

Jack tilted his head, his eyes narrowed in confusion, his lips twitching as if he was trying to hold back laughter. Or unable to think of something to say.

"You said you wanted me to tell you everything. So I am."

"Well, then, that's a start." He resumed his ascent.

The smell of burning I'd first detected when we'd opened the Frozen Charlotte coffin filled my nostrils again, and I had a desperate need for fresh air. I moved out onto the piazza to feel the cool breeze, breathing in deeply to capture the sweet scent of the Carolina jessamine vines creeping up the piazza, unfazed by the cool February evening.

I was beyond happy that Jack was back. In the guest room, but better than in a separate house. My conversation with Amelia kept playing out in my head, as did my argument that he'd never be coerced. Which meant that regardless of the reasons he'd given his mother or me, Jack had come back because *he'd* wanted to.

A small ball of heat sparked to life somewhere in my chest, giving me the first ray of hope I'd had since Jack had left me.

I turned to go back inside, the porch light reflecting what looked like puddles on the floorboards despite the fact that it hadn't rained in several days. I leaned over to see better, then jerked back. Puddles in the shape of footprints led across the piazza from the steps, then stopped decisively at the front door, waiting to be let inside.

CHAPTER 7

I awoke to the scent of roses. Half asleep, I pressed my face into the warm body lying in bed next to me. Reveling in the knowledge that I wasn't alone in the bed, I pressed myself closer and began rubbing my nose on his back. And a thick coat of fur. My eyes shot open, and I was horrified to see in the glow of Jack's bedside clock the small sleeping form of General Lee, who'd apparently forgiven me enough to return to my bed. I rolled over onto my back and breathed in deeply, the heady scent of the roses calming me, and helping me to forget that Jack slept just down the hallway. My eyelids drooped as I began to drift into sleep, content in the knowledge that my family was at last under the same roof again.

I bolted upright, my gaze shifting to the video child monitor on my nightstand, on which the motionless forms of JJ and Sarah could be detected behind the rails of their cribs. The smell of roses could mean only one thing: Louisa Vanderhorst had returned. The spirit of the young mother who'd once been buried in our garden fountain wasn't one to stick around for fun. She always had a purpose, appearing almost as an omen of something about to happen. The anticipation of which was always softened by the reassurance that she'd returned to protect the children until the danger had passed.

Shivering as I slid out of bed, I put on my fluffy bathrobe and matching slippers, both Christmas gifts from Nola. The door opened and I took a step forward before I paused. The key was still in the lock, but I hadn't turned it. I distinctly remembered locking it the night before—if only because I'd heard Jack turning the key in his own lock.

I stepped out onto the carpeted hallway runner, my slippers silent as I made my way to the nursery, the scent of roses growing stronger. I stopped abruptly outside the room, the hallway night-light illuminating a six-inch gap between frame and door. I gave the door a gentle shove and it groaned its disapproval, the sound amplified like a brass band in the quiet house.

A waft of rose-scented air greeted me as I stood on the threshold. I tiptoed over to JJ's crib to check on him, and drew back when I saw that his blanket was carefully tucked around him, his whisk poking above the edge. I imagined the handle firmly clutched in his pudgy yet surprisingly strong little hand. Someone had covered him recently. JJ's record for keeping his blanket on him was pushing five minutes and he'd been put to bed a good six hours before.

"Louisa?" I whispered.

"Not quite," came a masculine voice from a corner of the room.

My heart thudded. Not because I was scared, but because it was Jack. I turned toward the corner where Jack sat rocking a bundled Sarah on his shoulder.

"Louisa's here," I said softly.

"I know. I heard Sarah babbling to someone while I was standing out in the hallway. And the temperature in here is about five degrees colder than the rest of the house." I felt his eyes on me. "Are you worried?"

I shook my head. Maybe it was the dark room lit only by a nightlight and the lack of sleep that made me blurt out something that sounded remarkably like the new Mellie. "No," I said, "because you're here. Since I've met you, I've never doubted that we can face anything as long as we work through it together." I almost added *Until now.*

He held my gaze, but if he'd been about to say anything, the moment was lost when Sarah lifted her head, then twisted to reach for me. "Mama."

Jack relinquished his hold and I gathered our daughter in her blanket and sat down with her in the adjacent rocker. All was silent except for the gentle creaks of the rocking chairs and Sarah's rhythmic thumb sucking.

Jack broke the silence. "It's a good thing I already packed up my office and moved it to the apartment—less to get out of the way for the film crew."

"Why would they go into your office? The contract stipulates containing the filming to the foyer, parlor, dining room, and garden."

"All true. But I wouldn't put it past Marc or Harvey to get nosy. Speaking of which, how far are you on packing up the silver? I don't want anyone to think they can take souvenirs."

I rubbed my chin gently against Sarah's baby-fine hair. "It took longer than I thought because I decided it would be a good time to polish it all. And re-sort and label the velvet drawers. It makes a lot more sense to store them horizontally than vertically, I found." I couldn't keep the pride from my voice. "Sophie and Chad are coming tomorrow and will take most of the really valuable stuff to store at their house."

"Good," he said, a smile in his voice. "I'd like to take most of the original paintings from the walls, but Harvey wants them left there—for 'authenticity.'" Jack snorted softly. "As if there's anything authentic in Marc's book to begin with. But Sterling Zerbe hired a company to take an inventory just in case anything's lost or damaged."

I nodded, glad to know that our lawyer, Mr. Zerbe, was in charge and ahead of the game. "I just hope we can keep disturbances to a minimum so they're out of here sooner rather than later. Although dead people aren't really good at listening or keeping to a schedule. I made a spreadsheet that lists the filming schedule with nonworking hours highlighted. It's on the bulletin board in the kitchen so any restless spirits hanging around can see it."

I felt his gaze on me. "You didn't really . . ."

I laughed to cover my embarrassment. "Of course not. That would be ridiculous." I made a mental note to remove the spreadsheet from the bulletin board first thing.

He coughed quietly, but it sounded more like a strangled laugh. "Your dad said he can stop by tomorrow and start disguising the cistern and removing the yellow caution tape. I suggested the two of you draw straws. The loser has to let Sophie know that the excavation has to wait until the filming is done."

I groaned. I'd been on the receiving end of Sophie's vengeful side more often than I wanted to admit. I was still getting letters from PETA since Sophie sent them photos of my dogs dressed up at Christmas. "Or maybe I can ask Meghan. I need to call her anyway and ask her if she knows anything about the Frozen Charlotte."

We continued to rock in silence, unwilling to leave and unaware of the passing of the hour until I heard the muted chime of the grandfather clock downstairs. Sarah went slack in my arms, meaning she was in a deep sleep and it was the optimum time for returning her to her crib. Knowing I couldn't delay any longer, I stood, and Jack stood, too, taking the sleeping baby from my arms. His arms were longer than mine, so he had a greater chance of not waking her when placing her back in her crib.

I looked over at JJ, whose blanket had been kicked off and who lay in his usual starfish position on his back, his arms and legs splayed, his whisk clutched in his right hand like a lightsaber in Luke Skywalker's. As Jack gently lowered Sarah into her crib, I covered JJ again with his blanket, even managing to rearrange a few of his stuffed animals before Jack straightened.

We stood at the foot of the cribs watching our sleeping children, the scent of roses still strong. "I miss this," I said.

"Me, too."

For some reason, his words stung. Maybe because I'd held out too much hope that once he realized how much he'd lost, that would be enough to bring him back.

I swallowed, the sound loud in the quiet room. "Do you think you'll ever forgive me?"

He lifted his gaze to meet mine. "I already have. But that was the easy part."

"The easy part?"

Jack nodded. "Your intent wasn't to harm, so forgiving you was never the problem."

"It wasn't?"

"No. The problem is that I just don't think I can make myself that vulnerable again by trusting you completely. I'm not a cat with nine lives, Mellie. I have three children and I want to live long enough to see them grow up. And I mean as a live person."

I almost laughed. Any other couple having this conversation wouldn't have had to qualify. But there was the problem. I knew how to make him forgive me. I just had no idea how to make him trust me because I still wasn't convinced that a lack of trust had been at fault.

"Do you . . ." He paused.

"Do I what?"

Jack took a deep breath. "Until I know what's going on with my career, I'm going to take a pause on my current manuscript. Especially considering all the commotion happening in the house for the next few weeks. So I was wondering . . ." He stopped.

"Yes?" I said, trying to sound casual.

"I was wondering if I could help you and Veronica find out what happened to Adrienne. And anything else—like why that hideous doll was in Nola's room. It will be a good distraction from . . . everything. I've been told I'm pretty good at puzzles."

"By whom?" I asked. "And Desmarae doesn't count."

Desmarae was the adolescent editor who'd replaced Jack's seasoned editor, who'd been suddenly terminated, leaving Jack orphaned at the publishing house and at the mercy of a new editor who knew nothing about Jack's books. Jack often accused Desmarae of still reading picture books.

"Of course not. She doesn't read my books, remember?"

"Right." I pretended to think. "Well, since you do have some free time, you might as well. It couldn't hurt, right?"

"Unless we have to investigate a cemetery."

I couldn't tell if he was being sarcastic.

"Fine. After we get the house situated for the film crew, I'll fill you in."

His white teeth flashed in the darkness as he smiled at me. Putting his hand on the small of my back, he led me out into the hallway, where we stood facing each other like awkward teenagers on their first date, unsure of how to say good-bye.

"You're the only woman I know who looks beautiful in a fluffy robe and slippers and with bed head."

"Really?"

"Yeah. Not that I've seen many, but you're definitely the most beautiful."

I stared at him in the dim hallway for longer than I should have, until I found myself leaning toward him, my eyes drifting closed.

"Good night, Mellie."

His words jerked me back, my eyes flying open as I tried to pretend that nothing had happened. "Good night, Jack."

I abruptly turned before I did something the old Mellie would have done, and began walking toward my room. I'd reached the door when Jack spoke.

"I do, you know." Jack's voice sounded low and gravelly.

I stopped. Turned around. "You do what?"

"Believe we can get through anything. As long as we work through it together."

I told myself he was talking about more than solving the mysteries of Adrienne's murder and the Frozen Charlotte. The hopeful part of me couldn't help but believe that he might also be referring to us.

"Good. I'm glad we're on the same page."

I could hear the smile in his voice when he spoke again. "And if I believed in do-overs, that would have been almost kiss number two."

I watched as he turned and began walking toward the guest room. I closed my bedroom door behind me, not bothering to lock it, then crawled under the now-chilly covers. I settled myself against General

Lee's warm body, trying not to convey to him that he was a poor second. I lay awake for nearly an hour, my mind playing my conversation with Jack over and over before, as I finally dozed off, settling on something he'd said, wondering what Jack had been doing standing in the hallway in the middle of the night.

CHAPTER 8

The following morning, I stood with my mother watching my father and Jack stretch out a new tarp over the cistern in the first step toward disguising the deep gash in the back garden. The next step involved rolling out fake grass on top of it, along with an entire plastic garden that Harvey's set designer, Lori Cole, had promised would look just like the real thing on film.

I checked my watch, not wanting to be too late getting to the office, knowing that Catherine would have made six sales by the time I got there if I was five minutes late. Inside, Sophie, her husband, Chad, and Meghan Black had been conscripted into helping us move boxes into Sophie and Chad's vintage VW van. They had all insisted they didn't need my assistance or the helpful diagram showing how each box should be situated inside the van. They'd even refused my offer to help move the boxes into Sophie and Chad's spare bedroom.

I'd started to insist when Jayne pulled me away to get my suggestion on what the twins should wear and if the baby Birkenstocks (birthday gifts from Sophie and Chad) should be pulled from the back of the closet since their daughter, Blue Skye, had arrived with her parents for a play-date. I was happy to intervene, and when I returned from the nursery,

Sophie said they were almost done and that I didn't need to check the van for accuracy.

Even though a morning chill lingered in the air, my father straightened to wipe sweat from his forehead with his sleeve.

My mother sighed next to me. "As much as it hurt your father to see all of his hard work erased when the cistern caved in, he's looking forward to getting started rebuilding it. I honestly don't think I've seen him this excited since he discovered the original Loutrel Briggs garden design in the archives."

"I know. He and Jayne have been threatening to get me involved in the reconstruction as soon as the filming is done. Assuming Sophie says we can."

I felt my mother's gaze on me. "You do realize that you're the homeowner, right?"

"Have you ever had Sophie mad at you? Trust me. It's easier to go along with her. Mostly because she's usually right. But if you ever tell her I said that, I will never speak to you again."

She laughed softly, the corners of her green eyes creasing. Although in her sixties, she could easily have passed as my sister. She remained slender but with curves in the right places, and still carried the poise of the opera singer she had once been. Despite being estranged from me for most of my life, she had become an integral part of it and I couldn't imagine my life without her. "When do the stars get here? I can't wait to meet them." She sounded like a giddy schoolgirl.

"I don't know. As of last week, Harvey and Marc were still working on script changes and changing the filming schedule. Harvey is blaming it on us because of all the delays last December. He said the changes are meant to keep the project on budget, but I have no idea how and they don't find it necessary to keep us informed."

My mother frowned. "I told Rebecca to let Marc know that I'm happy to open my house for the stars to stay in. We're so close by. I haven't heard back."

"You probably won't. I think Marc would like all access restricted, especially from anyone related to Jack. They've temporarily converted our carriage house to dressing rooms and with strict orders that no one is allowed to go near them."

She sighed, reaching up a gloved hand to tuck a stray hair behind my ear. "How did it go with Jack last night?"

"Fine. And no, we're not 'together' together." I took a deep breath, still feeling the sting of Jack's words. "He said he's already forgiven me."

"But that's never been the problem, has it?"

I looked at her, realizing I shouldn't have been surprised. Although her sense of touch connected her to the spirit world, her ability to read my thoughts was simply due to a heightened maternal acumen. "No. It's the trust issue."

She turned to look back toward my father. If I'd thought she'd give me guidance on what I should do, I'd have been wrong. "You'll figure it out, Mellie. Love really does always find a way."

I wanted to tell her that she might be wrong, that Jack and I might still love each other but that wasn't a guarantee we'd stay together.

"Hello?"

We both turned to the garden path that led from the front of the house, where the tall form of Detective Thomas Riley appeared. He wore his usual beige raincoat, a detective's nod to a uniform, and he was in need of a hair trim. Although, if pressed, I'd admit it made him look even more ruggedly handsome than usual.

He waved to Jack and my father before turning to us.

"Good morning," my mother said, and kissed him on each cheek. "It's been too long. Did you come to see Jayne?"

A flash of pink suffused his cheeks. He and Jayne had become an item right after she'd moved to Charleston because she'd inherited her house on South Battery—along with a rather nasty spirit. Then an argument and Anthony Longo had come between them, ending the relationship. But, my mother and I agreed, not permanently.

"No, I'm afraid not," he said. "I came to see Melanie." He pulled out his phone and looked at the screen. "Her text came in around three thirty this morning, which I think accounts for the garbled bits, but after I translated it, I think it said that she wanted to see me."

I looked at the screen, trying not to squint and glad I wasn't wearing my glasses so I couldn't see all the typos. "Yes—sorry. Sometimes when I can't sleep and I think of something, I go ahead and type a text so I don't forget. I usually wait until morning to hit SEND, but I might have been half asleep. I hope it didn't wake you."

"No worries. I was up anyway. And I was in the neighborhood this morning and decided to drop by. What did you need to see me about?"

"It's about the cold case you were working on—Adrienne Hall."

"I was surprised when Veronica mentioned you were helping her with that."

Detective Riley had reason to be surprised. His argument with Jayne had been about her desire to go public with her own abilities, to advertise about helping people, the exact opposite of what I wanted to do with my own "gift." Even our mother had been on board. But the detective had been staunchly against it, saying he'd agree only if she'd go incognito. He wasn't eager to make Jayne a target. I couldn't say I disagreed.

"Yes. But just this once. I promised her because she's my friend, and I really want to help her. Then I'm done." I held up a finger while I looked around. "Does anybody else hear that?"

"Hear what?" my mother asked, tilting her head.

"That song. It sounds very tinny—like it's coming from someone's headphones."

"That's funny," my mother said. "I don't hear the music, but my feet want to tap out a steady beat."

My eyes widened with realization. "Hang on one second and let me go get what I wanted to show you."

I dashed inside to the kitchen, where Jayne was feeding the twins while Mrs. Houlihan stood at the stove, accidentally dropping bacon bits onto the floor for the three dogs.

"Mother wants to see you," I said to Jayne. "She's out in the back garden. I have to run upstairs and get something. Mrs. Houlihan, could you please finish feeding the twins?"

"Of course," she said, beaming at JJ and Sarah.

I kissed the tops of their heads—barely missing a clump of scrambled eggs mixed in with JJ's thick hair—then ran upstairs to retrieve the Discman and the yearbook. When I returned to the garden, Jayne stood awkwardly in front of Thomas while attempting to form a comprehensible sentence. Growing up in the foster system and being a career nanny had not taught her how to relax or hold a conversation with the opposite sex.

"You're standing here. With shoes," she managed to say to Thomas before shooting me an accusatory glance.

"I am," Thomas said with a grin. "It's good to see you again, Jayne. It's been a while. Are you and Anthony . . . ?" He didn't appear able to finish the question.

"He's a man," Jayne offered.

"They're not," I interjected. "Not after we found out he'd been lying to us and secretly working with Marc. Not that it worked out for either of them." I gave a short laugh. "Jayne gave him a very nice shiner, although he deserved much more. Didn't you, Jayne?"

She nodded, resembling a bobblehead more than a sane woman. I'd hoped that her former familiarity with Thomas meant she wouldn't have to go through the awkward phase with him again. Apparently, I'd been wrong to. To distract them both, I held up the yearbook and the CD player, then walked over to the small wrought iron café table that had once sat in the now-obliterated garden. It currently rested on wobbly legs on the brick patio, causing me to hesitate before carefully putting the book and the Discman on top of it.

"I know you already saw these, Thomas. They were in Adrienne's box in Veronica's attic. It's where you found the charm necklace." My fingers reached automatically for the chain I now wore all the time. I'd tried leaving it in my jewelry box, but it would keep appearing wherever I happened to be. I thought I'd save Adrienne the trouble by just keeping it around my neck.

Thomas picked up the CD player. "I did. I even had this redusted for fingerprints. But by then it had been handled so many times, it made any of the results irrelevant."

Jayne picked up the yearbook and opened the front cover, displaying the autographs and drawings of Adrienne's friends. "Were you able to find all of these people to interview?"

Thomas nodded. "Those we could identify. There were a few with nicknames that we couldn't trace to anyone. We asked those we could find and we were able to identify a few more, but there were still a few we couldn't. The fact that she was killed at the end of the school year meant Adrienne's yearbook had a lot of autographs in it and we had great hopes it would offer at least one clue we could use. Sadly, no new leads there. Basically, we're back to where we started. Unless . . ." He looked pointedly at me.

"Unless Adrienne can tell me more. That's why I brought these." I paused, something I always did so I could do a mental check of those present to ensure I didn't say anything alarming to the uninitiated. "She told me to."

Thomas's brow furrowed as he flipped the CD player over. "She did?"

"Well, not in so many words. But she more or less showed me."

He nodded absently, turning the machine over again, then hitting the OPEN button. His eyes met mine. "Where's the CD?"

"That's what I wanted to ask you. Was there one inside when you went up in the attic with Veronica?"

He shook his head. "No. But on the original police report, it listed a CD in the player."

"Was it a Laurie Anderson album?" I asked.

He frowned for a moment. "Yeah, I think so. I'll double-check, but I'm sure that was the artist. I remember it because I had to ask who she was."

"She was famous for her one-hit wonder in the early eighties, 'O Superman,'" Jayne said. She spoke slowly, focusing on each word. We were definitely back at ground zero.

"I've never heard of it," Thomas said.

"No one has," we said in unison.

"But once you have, you're not likely to forget it. It's like after food poisoning when every time you smell a particular food you have flashbacks of the nausea. It's really awful while at the same time unforgettable." I shook my head, trying to clear it of the steady beat that had wormed its way inside.

"There's something more," I added. "It wasn't just Adrienne in the attic. There was another spirit up there. Someone not happy to see me. Someone who's quite insistent that I don't want to know the truth."

My mother grabbed my arm, squeezing tightly. "It's the same thing from before."

I nodded, both of us remembering the menacing words forced from her mouth when she'd clutched the charm necklace in her hand. "Yes. Whoever it was wants me to go away. I think that's why I rarely see Adrienne and just feel her presence."

"She's saving her energy," Jayne said quietly, "so she can protect you."

I took the yearbook from Jayne, studying the signatures and well-wishes written in multicolored ink, a time stamp in the life of a young woman whose existence seemed suspended in the past, tethered to this world by an unanswered question. For the first time since Veronica had asked for my help, I understood. Not inside my head, where I normally comprehended what was happening around me in both this world and the next, but in the deepest part of my heart, where I held the love of Jack and my children.

I rubbed my finger over a drawing of a swan. "I'm assuming swans are the Omega Chi mascot?"

"Yes," Thomas said. "Most of the signatures in here were from her sorority. We interviewed every member back when the murder happened, and again recently when we reopened the case. Again, no leads. Same with Adrienne's boyfriend and his fraternity brothers. Nothing. Maybe Adrienne was randomly selected by a stranger. At this point, we know only that she died from a blow to the head with a blunt instrument that was never identified or discovered, her body found in a supply closet three days later."

"Why did it take so long for them to find that poor girl's body?" my mother asked, her eyes moist, as she was perhaps thinking of Jayne and me.

"Her roommate had gone home for the weekend and didn't return until Monday morning. It wasn't until later that evening when Adrienne still hadn't turned up that the authorities were called. By then the perpetrator had had plenty of time to cover his tracks."

The sudden sensation of fingers pressing against my throat made me gasp for air, my own fingers ineffectually trying to pull away invisible hands.

"What's going on?" Thomas darted behind me, looking for my assailant

"Stop it!" Jayne and Ginette shouted in unison.

We are stronger together. I imagined hearing the chant we used when facing a common adversary.

Immediately, the pressure on my throat disappeared, leaving me gagging. I sat down hard on the wrought iron bench, and took a deep gulp of my now-cold coffee. I looked up in time to see my father and Jack peering in our direction. My mother followed my gaze and waved at them. They paused for a moment before waving back and resuming placing a roll of fake grass across the cistern.

"What was that?" Thomas asked. He leaned closer, his finger gently touching a spot on my neck. "You've got welts like fingers going around your neck."

I rubbed my throat. "I don't know. Are you sure Adrienne wasn't strangled?"

"Positive. I've seen the autopsy photos. It was definitely a blow to the head."

A strong gust of icy wind blew past us, bringing with it the pungent scent of Vanilla Musk. My mother, Jayne, and I all exchanged glances.

"She's here," I said.

"Then who was strangled?" Jayne asked, gently cupping my face and turning it side to side, studying my neck.

Thomas pulled out his phone and snapped a few photos. "Strangulation isn't uncommon in cases I've worked on, but no connection to this particular case."

Before Jayne and I realized what she was doing, our mother had removed her gloves and picked up the pink Discman in her bare hands. She sat down heavily on the bench beside me, her mouth open in shock.

"Mother?" Jayne tried to pry the CD player from our mother's hands, but she wouldn't let go.

We watched in helpless horror as our mother's eyes rolled back in her head, her skin blanched a deathly white, the red lipstick on her mouth resembling bloody slashes from a knife. Instinctively, Jayne and I stepped in front of her, blocking the view from the cistern. We knew what to expect, and my father didn't need to witness it.

A growl, pulled from some deep, dark place, rumbled in our mother's chest and up her throat until it exploded from her mouth like sewage.

"YOU. WILL. BE. SORRY."

She began to shake, her knuckles bulging under the skin as she gripped the CD player, her staring eyes like black holes in her skull.

Jayne and I reached for the Discman at the same time, the shaking stopping as soon as both of our hands had touched it. Our mother's hands fell to her sides as her head slumped forward. Thomas grabbed her to keep her from slipping to the ground, kneeling next to her and gently rubbing her hand.

"I'm fine. I'm fine," she managed, her words sliding sideways out of her mouth, her eyes searching until they settled on me. "That . . . machine," she managed. "It's important."

"Let's get you inside . . ." Thomas began.

Mother held up her hand. "In a minute. This is . . . important." She swallowed, then turned to Thomas. "Take that machine. Look at it again. There's something that was . . . missed. They . . . don't want you . . . to see."

"Who's 'they'?" I asked.

She shook her head. "I don't . . . know. They wouldn't let me see."

My gaze met Jayne's, my throat smarting as I spoke. "Still on board?" I asked.

Her smile didn't completely hide her worry. "Stronger together, remember?"

I nodded as we each squeezed one of our mother's hands. We stood together, carefully pulling her to her feet. "I'm taking you home and putting you to bed. Jayne can make up something to tell Dad."

Thomas picked up the Discman and the yearbook. "I'm taking these both to see what we might have missed. I'll be in touch." After being assured that Ginette was going to be fine, he said his good-byes and left, Jayne's gaze following him until he'd rounded the corner of the house.

As I watched him leave, something soft hit me on the side of the head. We all looked down, spotting the red heart-shaped pillow with the ruffled edge that had once belonged to a young woman who'd been dead for over twenty years.

CHAPTER 9

I brought my order outside to the small red table in front of the Queen Street Grocery, my stomach grumbling at the scent of my Nutella crepe smothered in powdered sugar and whipped cream. I'd opted for the side of fruit to quash any guilt. It wasn't my preferred doughnut for breakfast, but anything from the Queen Street Grocery was a worthy substitution.

A young waitress wearing a College of Charleston T-shirt brought out my large cappuccino with an extra helping of steamed milk foam on top. I resisted the impulse to lick it, instead leaning forward and closing my eyes, breathing in deeply and enjoying the moment. Despite it being February, the temperature was almost balmy with a rare treat for Charleston—low humidity. I sat back in my chair, intent on allowing myself to be momentarily happy. My family was under the same roof, I was ready to finalize my first sale in over four months, and I was about to eat real breakfast food without the disapproving glances of Sophie or Nola.

"Mrs. Trenholm?"

My eyes shot open to see Meghan Black standing next to my table, wearing an adorable pink swing coat with a large bow at the shoulder, black leggings, and riding boots. I'd seen the entire outfit in the front window of the Finicky Filly. Either Meghan had found another source of income, or her mother still loved dressing her little girl.

"I'm meeting Mrs. Farrell." I hadn't meant it to come out as a shout or to sound like I was apologizing.

"Okay . . ." Meghan said slowly.

"I'm sorry," I said. "I thought Sophie or Nola sent you."

When her look of confusion didn't clear, I said, "Have a seat. I think my friend is running a bit late." Which was understandable, considering the construction commotion at Veronica's house. I'd set up the breakfast meeting so I could tell her about the episode in my back garden the previous day.

"Thank you," she said, sitting down and hanging her black-and-white polka-dot Kate Spade backpack on the back of her chair. "I'll just stay a minute."

I took a sip of my cappuccino, and was careful to wipe off any foam from my mouth. "Thanks for your help in packing up our valuables. We really appreciate it. I'm glad to see you today, because there was something I needed to ask you and I didn't get the opportunity the other day with everyone being so busy."

She smiled patiently as she flicked her phone to silent mode and placed it facedown on the table—something I greatly appreciated.

"It's about a Frozen Charlotte doll inside a little coffin we found in Nola's bedroom. We weren't sure how it ended up there, so we were thinking you might have left it or at least know how it got there."

"A Frozen Charlotte and coffin?" Her eyebrows formed a V over her nose. "In Nola's room?"

I nodded. "She found it on her nightstand and has no idea how it got there."

"No idea?" Meghan stared at me with round, questioning eyes.

"No idea," I repeated. "We were thinking you might have found it in the cistern and then brought it inside to show us."

She slowly shook her head. "I know what a Frozen Charlotte is, but I haven't found one in your cistern. And if I had, I would have given it to Dr. Wallen-Arasi first. Except . . ." She stopped, her large brown eyes settling on me for a moment before she quickly looked away.

"Except?"

She pointed at my crepe. "Is that a Nutella crepe? They're so good here, aren't they?"

"Except?" I repeated, not wanting to get sidetracked.

Meghan laced her fingers together and rested them on top of the table. "I don't think it came from your cistern."

"No?"

She shook her head. "The last section that we were working on before we had to stop was turning up lots of artifacts from a time period that was much later than the Revolutionary period, where everything else seemed to date from."

"But that doesn't make sense, does it? The more recent stuff should be on top, right?"

"Right. Which is why we had to go back and do some research on the property abutting the rear of yours." She smiled sheepishly. "Dr. Wallen-Arasi didn't want to mention any of this to you yet because of everything else going on in your house right now. She said it would be better to tell you when she had some answers."

"She did, did she?" I sat back casually in my chair. "But I'm here now, and you've got me interested. So what did you find?"

Meghan looked at me skeptically. "Are you sure you want to hear this?"

"Very."

She looked relieved and not just a little excited to be sharing her discovery with anyone interested in hearing it. "Well, it looks like another structure existed behind your house next to the cistern. We went back to the original plots and saw what looks to be a kitchen house. Apparently, it was burned to the ground during the great fire of 1861 and a lot of debris from the house either fell or was put into the cistern."

I took a bite of my crepe and had to pause for a moment while I forced myself to swallow, the food suddenly tasting like ash. "The great fire of 1861? It sounds vaguely familiar." That was a lie, but I didn't want to admit that I'd read romance novels during most of my history classes at the various Army base schools wherever my father and I had lived.

"Yes. A lot of people attribute the damage visible in post–Civil War photos to the Union Army's bombardment, but that didn't start until 1863. The great fire was in December of 1861—the origins of it are unclear. What we do know is that fourteen houses on Queen Street were blown up to create a fire block."

Meghan shuddered, as if the destruction of historic properties was a fate she couldn't even imagine. "That one action did save a couple of hospitals, the medical college, and the Roman Catholic orphan house, but still." She shuddered again. "By noon the next day the fire had cleared the peninsula and was starting to peter out. The city market and most of Meeting, the north side of Queen, most of Broad, and this side of Tradd Street were devastated. It's really a miracle your house didn't burn down, too." She looked at me with excitement. "I can show you pictures."

I feigned enthusiasm. "Maybe later." The phantom smell of burning wood drifted past me, reminding me of the scent that had wafted up when I'd opened the Frozen Charlotte's tiny coffin. I sipped my coffee, trying to erase the sooty taste in the back of my throat. Recalling the small footprints in the snow, I asked nervously, "When you say 'debris,' do you mean things like bricks?"

She nodded, but her eyes had shifted to my plate. "Um, sure. We definitely found bricks."

"And . . . ?" I held my breath.

She fidgeted in her chair, which wasn't at all like the Meghan Black I knew. "Well, yes, and bits of china and old chicken bones and trash like in the rest of the cistern. But we're also finding more . . . personal things."

"'Personal things,'" I repeated. "Like what?"

She glanced up at the sky as if reading a list, counting off things on her pink-tipped fingers. "Like an old doll with a porcelain head. A silver vanity set and a pair of nearly new boots made for a young girl. Also a training corset meant to be worn by an adolescent girl." She frowned, her gaze meeting mine again.

I pushed my plate away, my appetite having vanished. "It almost sounds like things a person might be buried with."

"It does, doesn't it?" she said, her expression making it obvious that this idea wasn't new. With forced lightness, she continued. "It could have been a family burial ground associated with a house that stood behind yours and that burned in the fire, but the good news is that we haven't found any human bones. Although we did find a nearly intact skeleton of a small dog—but lots of people bury their dogs in the backyard, so that's not so surprising. As to the possibility of a human grave site, when the property lines were redrawn after the Vanderhorsts acquired the property behind theirs following the fire, they might have moved the body to a cemetery but left behind any items that might have been placed in a coffin at burial."

I regarded her with curiosity. "The body? So there *was* a grave?"

"Well, assuming it *is* a grave site—and we don't know for sure—it looks as if there was only the single one."

She'd grabbed a napkin and was in the process of shredding it into tiny pieces.

"Was there anything else that Sophie didn't want to tell me yet?"

Meghan's shoulders sagged with relief. "Do you promise not to tell her how you know?"

"She'll know whether I tell her or not, but let's not forget it's my house we're discussing."

"Right," she said, nodding once. "So, we also found a headstone."

An icy rivulet of fear traced the length of my spine, making me shiver. I pulled my sweater tighter. "A headstone?"

"Yeah. Marble. Which is the worst material, just about, for headstones in this climate. The lettering on it is so shallow that it's unreadable except for part of the first name. We think it starts with the letter E but the second letter is unclear—might be an M, or a U, or an N. It's really anybody's guess."

A memory of footprints in the snow flashed through my head. Another icy shiver ran through me. "'E,'" I repeated. "Was there anything else?"

She scratched her chin, then lifted her finger. "Oh, and a large collection of buttons."

My eyebrows shot up. "Like how large? Tens? One hundred?"

"I'd say hundreds. And since everything else appeared to be Victorian, I immediately thought they might have been from—"

"A charm string," I finished for her.

She smiled. "Exactly. Have you seen one before?"

"Not a complete one. But I know what they are."

Meghan looked at her watch and then stood. "I'm sorry—I've got to get to class. It was nice seeing you. And if there's anything else . . ." She gave me a worried look.

"Don't worry—I won't get you in trouble. But I will talk with Sophie. I'm curious as to whom all the stuff belonged to."

"Me, too. We haven't gotten that far into the research yet." She smiled. "I'll see you later." She took a few steps and then abruptly turned around. "I've been meaning to ask—was that Beau Ryan at your house the other night? I was riding my bike down Tradd Street and I could have sworn I saw him leaving your house."

I looked at her with surprise. "Yes, actually. It was. How do you know Beau?"

She didn't answer right away. Finally, she said, "We dated for a few months last year. I even went to visit his family in New Orleans during a week off from school."

"Must have been serious, then."

Meghan shrugged. "He's a great guy, and I really liked him. It's just . . ." She stopped.

I kept silent, willing her to go on.

"It's just, his family is sort of . . . strange. Don't get me wrong. His grandparents were warm and welcoming, and they have this beautiful Italianate Revival house in the Garden District, on Prytania. It's been in Beau's family since the early eighteen forties. Absolutely gorgeous and filled with old family antiques."

"Sounds lovely—except for the 'old' part," I said lightly, but I was already bracing for what she was about to say.

"Oh, it is. But . . ." She bit her lip. "It had very odd vibes, you know? Like your house on Tradd. But . . . darker. Beau said I was free to explore—I mean, who could resist all that gorgeous old house with all of its nooks and crannies?"

I almost raised my hand, but didn't want to interrupt her.

"But there were two doors that were kept locked, and when I asked Beau about them, he just said his grandmother kept those rooms locked because they were crammed with overflow from the attic. Which I understand, but why lock the doors?"

"Well, they certainly wouldn't be the first elderly eccentric couple living in a spooky old house, would they?" I said, even managing a little laugh.

"No, I suppose not. They also own an antique store in the Quarter." She swallowed. "But I don't think antiques is all they sell there."

My eyebrows shot up. "What do you mean?"

"I shouldn't be telling you all this. I'm not a gossiping kind of person, but when I saw you with Beau . . ."

I made a motion of zipping my lips. "I promise you that this stays with me. Although I might share it with Jack," I added hastily. "But he can also be trusted."

She seemed to consider this for a moment before continuing. "So I don't think it's drugs or weapons, if that's what you're wondering. No evidence of that, but if you met Mr. and Mrs. Ryan you'd understand. But that back room, well, lots of weird stuff there. Tons and tons of old books and other things I couldn't identify. I was only in there once because Beau let me in, but it was also kept locked all the time. And lots of people would come in the main entrance and walk straight to the back, and I don't think they were there to shop for antiques."

I nodded, remembering what Beau had said about his grandmother's Frozen Charlotte collection. "Beau said he does their website and he has some of the stuff on there."

"Trust me, what's on the website is a small fraction of what's in there. And those creepy dolls aren't the worst of it." She glanced at her watch again. "Sorry—I really do have to run. It was good talking to you. It's like having another mom when I'm away from home." With a smile, she left.

I wanted to shout after her that I was barely past forty and not nearly old enough to be her mother, but I couldn't find the energy. I sat back in my chair, my appetite completely gone, my mind running in so many directions, I wondered if Jayne would allow me to include it in my daily exercise goal. I stared down the street and spotted Veronica walking toward me and I waved, then picked up my phone to text Jack. A glimmer of excitement coursed through me as I contemplated working with Jack again, no longer having to come up with an excuse to see him.

I opened the screen, then stopped when I saw that I had a waiting text with a phone number I didn't recognize with a local 843 area code. I clicked on the message and my throat tightened as I read the words in all caps, almost hearing them shouted in my ear.

SHE DESERVED IT

CHAPTER 10

When I returned home from work later that afternoon, I almost drove past number 55 because of the large box truck blocking my driveway, and the people scurrying around the front yard and piazza like ants at a picnic, dragging thick ropelike cords through the open front door.

A red Ferrari squatted behind the truck, its rear half jutting into the street. Despite the City of Charleston permit sign that had suddenly sprung up at the end of my driveway, I hoped a diligent parking officer would see the car and slap a ticket on the windshield. I had no doubt to whom the sports car belonged.

I stopped my car and checked two of my calendars to make sure it wasn't street-sweeping day, then pulled into a spot at the curb. My residential parking decal would allow me to avoid the nuisance of a ticket, but that was one piece of information I wasn't going to share with Harvey Beckner.

I'd spent my entire lunch hour speed-reading *Lust, Greed, and Murder in the Holy City* and my face still burned. If I looked in a mirror, I was sure I'd find that my eyelashes had been singed. And though I'd left my copy of the book available for Jack to read or at least skim through after he'd moved back in, he was still too wounded to read even as far as the acknowledgments page. The few details Jack knew about Marc's book had come from Jack's editor, Desmarae, who'd told Jack it was the best book she'd ever read. Just one of the many reasons Jack had been so eager to make a deal with Marc and find a new publisher. He was struggling to finish the book still under contract while declining suggestions by Desmarae to turn it into a graphic novel and appear shirtless on the back cover. I doubted that John Grisham or Stephen King had ever had to field the same suggestions. And to have his editor suggest that Marc's book was one of the best books she'd ever read was like her rubbing salt into the wound.

I could only hope that we still had time to change the most highly inaccurate and insulting elements of the screenplay before this nightmare became fully realized on the big screen. Although I had the strong suspicion that doing that would be like holding back a hurricane with my pinkie.

I walked toward the house, my steps slowing as I neared the commotion. Every light in the house had been turned on, and as I got closer, the lights all brightened in unison before going completely dark. I stopped. A man cursed as someone ran down the piazza steps, then stopped as the house was flooded with light again. It seemed, I thought, as if the house had just winked. Or sent out a warning.

"We don't have to stay here, you know."

I swung around to see Jack standing beside me. Despite it being only late afternoooon, the winter sky had already deepened into purple, making it difficult for me to distinguish real people from shadows. Or worse. Which was why dusk had always been my least favorite time of day regardless of the season.

I waited for him to place his arm around me and pull me close until I remembered that he wouldn't. And why. I watched the small patch of grass on the side of the house get flattened by dozens of booted feet and winced. "This is what we wanted, right?" We had agreed to stay in the house during all of this because Jayne said it would be best for the children, to avoid removing them from their structure and routine.

A familiar tic twitched in Jack's jaw. "Yeah, but after we negotiated everything into what we assumed was a workable situation, I had no idea that limiting the filming to three rooms and converting our carriage house to dressing rooms would still require all . . . this."

"Neither did I. But would you really trust Harvey enough to give him free run of the house without supervision?"

Jack didn't hesitate. "Nope." He turned to survey the house, his lips pressed together.

"How long have they been here?" I asked.

"I don't know—I just got here. I was inside only long enough to see Mrs. Houlihan chasing a member of the crew out of her kitchen with a soup ladle, shout at Nola to remain upstairs with Jayne and the twins, and tell someone who appeared to be in charge that they needed to put a cloth on the dining room table before they placed the crew's dinner on it or she'd give Sophie their direct number."

"So, about the film . . ." I started, determined to push back my first impulse of going directly to Harvey and demanding changes. I wanted to spare Jack more mental anguish but made the effort to upgrade to the new Melanie, no matter how tempted I was to ignore the problem in the hope it would all go away. I cleared my throat and tried again. "So, about the film . . ." I started again.

"She's a beauty, isn't she?"

The sound of Harvey's flat, nasal voice was like a needle scratching across a record. We turned to see Harvey walking from the piazza steps toward us. He wore tight black jeans, a white T-shirt, and designer high-tops. A sweater was draped over his shoulders, its sleeves tight in a knot on his chest. His face didn't glow in the darkness like everyone else's, so I assumed he had a tan beneath his spiky bleached blond hair. He looked like a cross between an eighties New Wave band member and an ad for J.Crew.

"Yes, she is," Jack said, draping his arm around me and pulling me close.

I kept a casual smile on my face if only to prove to myself that I could act like an intelligent, mature woman when in close proximity to Jack, who had just said something nice about me—even though it was in jest.

Harvey stopped in front of us, a disdainful look on his face. "I meant the car. I had it sent from California so I'd have the freedom to drive myself." He frowned. "Since your daughter nearly killed me, I've had lots of trust issues with other people driving me. I hope that little menace of yours is off the streets."

Jack's muscles tensed. He started to take a step forward but I held him back. Reminding myself that we needed to be nice, I refrained from poking Harvey in the chest while I spoke. "If you're referring to Nola, you scared and intimidated her so much after the accident that she swears she's never getting behind the wheel of another car as long as she lives."

"I'm sure the world is thankful," Harvey said dismissively. "So," he said, looking over at the piazza and the steady stream of people moving lights and wires and boxes from the truck to the front door, "is this what you expected?"

Jack frowned. "Actually, no. I assumed it would be a little more . . . contained."

Harvey rolled his eyes. "It is. But even though your ridiculous contract demands we limit the filming to just three main areas, we still need a crew and lights and a way to generate electricity so this pile of lumber doesn't go up like a bonfire. The option of staying in a hotel is still on the table, you know."

Jack and I exchanged glances as a young woman approached with a clipboard for Harvey. After giving it a cursory glance, he signed it and returned to our conversation. I didn't like the smile on Harvey's face, and when I glanced at Jack, I could tell that he didn't, either.

"Those 'technical difficulties' last December," Harvey said, making air quotes with his fingers, "cost me and the other producers a lot of time and money. We don't like to lose money. So we've had to make drastic changes to keep us on schedule and budget."

Jack's hand, still resting on my shoulder, squeezed me and I had a sinking feeling that whatever Harvey was about to tell us we wouldn't like. "What sort of drastic changes?" Jack asked, an "I can play nice" smile sitting uncomfortably on his face.

"For starters, we're going to begin with the contemporary story frame so that we've worked out all the kinks before the big stars arrive to film the historic parts with Robert and Louisa Vanderhorst and Joseph Longo. The costuming alone will cost us a fortune, so we've had to do a little editing."

I felt Jack flinch. Marc's book had already strayed so far from reality that it hardly resembled the story it was based on. And Jack didn't know the half of it. "What kind of editing?" Jack asked, his mouth barely moving so it could stay in a smile.

"We've hired younger unknowns to portray the two of you. We figured our younger audience would want actors they could relate to, and their lower pay grade helps my bottom line."

"What about Katherine Heigl and Rob Lowe?" I asked. Despite my refusing to allow myself to be starstruck, the fact that two Hollywood stars would be gracing my home had definitely gone to my head.

"They'll be here eventually. That's why we want to start filming the contemporary parts of the movie first to get any technical kinks worked out." He looked pointedly at me, then turned his attention to Jack. "Now that you have skin in the game, we're hoping everything here goes smoothly and finishes in a timely manner without any of the earlier 'technical difficulties.'" He again made air quotes.

"That's the drastic change?" Jack asked, some of the tension leaving his body. "Saving money isn't drastic. I'd imagine for a movie production it would be necessary."

Harvey grinned, the newly fallen darkness an appropriate backdrop for his white capped teeth. "I wasn't done. We're also adding more sex—lots of sex. Sex sells, and it's all about the bottom line."

I felt a little queasy. I'd read the book and that had been explicit enough. I wondered if Harvey might be after an R rating. Or worse. I figured now was as good a time as any to appeal to his better nature. Or, since he apparently lacked one, his sense of honor and decency. I imagined my own thoughts sending me eye rolls.

I took a deep breath and said, "You know, Harvey, in real life, Louisa Vanderhorst and Joseph Longo didn't have an affair like Marc's book alludes to. Louisa and her husband were madly in love. She wouldn't have betrayed him or abandoned their son."

His grin didn't fade. "Like I said, sex sells—"

"But this isn't a sexy story," Jack interrupted. "It would take a person completely lacking in intelligence and vision to think it is." Jack's Mr. Nice Guy smile had melded into something almost menacing.

I put my hand on his arm. I didn't know Harvey Beckner very well, but I was pretty sure he wasn't the kind of guy who enjoyed having his artistic abilities insulted. Especially by someone whose talents he clearly viewed as inferior.

I cleared my throat and forced a smile. "I'm glad we're having a chance to talk before the filming begins, Harvey. I read Marc's book, and I have to say, I found not only the historical inaccuracies of the story off-putting, but also the crazy lives of John and Margot Trellis. People will know that's meant to be us and might even believe that we have wild sex parties and séances in our home."

Jack took a step forward, and I squeezed his arm in warning. I continued. "Please remember that we have a teenager and two toddlers living here. I think the story of Louisa's murder and how Jack and I found the Confederate diamonds is much more compelling than salacious fiction. I'm sure if you let Jack look at the screenplay, he'd be able to—"

Jack pulled me back. "That's enough, Mellie. I can fight my own battles." He was still smiling, but his muscles tensed beneath my hand.

Harvey casually crossed his arms. "I'm guessing Jack hasn't read the book, then."

I looked at Jack to apologize or to warn him or to make sure he knew we were together in this. Although, I admitted to myself, if I'd had Marc's book in my hand, I would have hit Jack with it. He should have read it months before. We both should have. But it was too late now.

"No, I haven't," Jack said. "For my own personal reading, I prefer books that are written above the fourth-grade level."

Harvey made a noise that was probably his version of a laugh. It was hard to tell from watching his face because of all the Botox. I imagined the devil making the same sound each time he captured another soul. "Yes, well, it's too late for objections to the script. You should have thought about that before you rushed to sign the contract. Regardless, your opinion doesn't matter. Although you're welcome to mention it to the new director, I have a feeling he'll tell you the same thing."

"New director?" Jack said.

"Yeah." Harvey's grin broadened. "That's the other drastic change. It took some doing, but I finally convinced the other producers that we could save a bunch of money by hiring another director. Someone with less experience but who was already familiar with the story."

I didn't need to look at Jack to know we'd reached the same conclusion. I'd felt rather than heard his intake of breath, the chill night air pulsating between us like a living thing. As if it'd been summoned, a large black Escalade pulled up to the curb, the heavy beat of rap music vibrating the windows until the driver turned off the ignition and opened the driver's door. Marc Longo, his shock of white hair stark against the now-dark night sky, walked toward us, his wide smile scaring me more than any ghostly specter.

He stopped in front of us, casually tossing his car keys in his hand. "Jack and Melanie. Like the new car? I figured, with Nola out on the road, I needed to drive something substantial. I'm assuming Harvey has already given you the good news."

If I wasn't already familiar with his cocky swagger and abnormally white hair, I might not have recognized Marc. He'd always dressed in conservative yet stylish Italian suits or crisp linen pants and Gucci loafers. And he preferred opera music on his car stereo—at least, he had when we'd dated. But this edition of Marc Longo was nearly unrecognizable. Yet still, apparently, insufferable. The fact that this wasn't the version he'd shown us during our discussions in my office or with our lawyers sent tidal waves of anxiety through me.

Marc lowered his spiky-haired head as he placed his keys in a cross-body man bag that looked identical to the one Harvey sported across his own chest. Something twinkled on Marc's left earlobe as it caught the house's lights, and even without my glasses I could tell that Marc now wore an earring. Maybe two. I wanted to look at Jack to gauge his re-action, but I was too mesmerized by the train wreck I was about to witness to move.

"Hello, Matt. Perfect timing. Billy Idol just called and he wants his hair back." Jack's gaze flicked down to Marc's neon green pants and matching muscle shirt, a black leather jacket with multiple zippers tossed casually over one shoulder. "You look like Billy Idol's love child with a Troll doll. Please go inside and change so I can take you seriously."

An almost imperceptible movement shifted Marc's smile, nudging it toward sinister. "Always the jokester, aren't you, Jack? Hasn't gotten you very far in life, has it?"

I stepped back to stand next to Jack, to show solidarity. He took my hand, his touch burning my palm. I remained calm, but inside I was on fire. I could almost hear his teeth clenching, his jaw popping.

Jack shrugged. "I wouldn't say that. I've hit the bestseller lists and won several writing awards for books I actually wrote all by myself."

I wasn't sure if it was my eyesight or if Marc blinked, but suddenly his eyes darkened, the lights from the house no longer reflected in them, as if he'd flipped a switch. Jack must have seen it, too, because he squeezed my hand.

"Who cares? My book is being made into a major motion picture, and not only did I write the script, but I'm getting to direct it, too. You probably didn't know that I was a film major in college. I actually have a few short films I made my senior year, as well as a documentary about alligator breeding that almost won an award."

"You're right. I didn't. And I will admit to being surprised. I didn't think you'd gone beyond the eighth grade."

Marc's nostrils flared. "Just make sure that you stay out of the way of the crew and actors—unless you want to volunteer to fetch coffee or toilet paper."

"I'd love to be responsible for personally bringing you your coffee and toilet paper." Jack's affable grin hid all the devious possibilities I was sure were running through his fertile mind.

Harvey began walking toward the piazza. "Come on, Marc. Let's stop wasting time with these two. We've got a lot of work to do before tomorrow."

It was clear that Marc wasn't happy to let Jack have the last word, but after several false starts, he followed Harvey into the house.

Jack stared after them, not moving, and he continued to hold my hand, his grip tight. We stood that way in silence for a long moment before he finally spoke. "In all of the years I've been sober, I have never wanted a drink more than I want one right now."

He looked at me and I was reminded of Marc's eyes, of how the light in them had disappeared. But Jack's weren't menacing, just empty. Crew members continued to rush past us. I tugged on Jack's hand and led him into the blissfully empty side garden, where Nevin Vanderhorst's swing dangled from the ancient oak tree. It was where I'd spotted Louisa on my first visit to the house, when I'd been hoping to get the listing so I could sell it. Instead, Nevin Vanderhorst had died and left me his property. For the first time in a long while, I wondered if I would have been better off never crossing the threshold at all.

I led Jack to a bench, where he sat and immediately put his head in his hands. His voice was muffled when he spoke. "How could I have been so stupid?"

"This isn't your fault, Jack. Sure, we should have both been better informed, but with everything that happened in December, and then Marc offering you a way to clear your name and save face by offering you a percentage of earnings—for the story *you* created, no less—we both wanted to believe that our luck had finally changed."

"But I *knew* better than to trust him. I knew better. And I still allowed him to get the better of me."

"*We* knew better," I corrected him. "We'll fix it. We always figure things out, don't we? If we put our heads together."

He looked at me, his eyes in shadow. "This has nothing to do with you, Mellie."

I jerked back. "What?"

He stood and began to pace. "I'm sorry. I didn't mean it that way. It's just that . . . with us being separated, I'm forcing myself to think of us not as a team. To see how that fits."

I stood, rubbing my arms for warmth as a chilly breeze rustled through the Spanish moss above us and spun the old swing. "And?"

Jack stared at me for a long moment, then gently took my face in his hands, my whole body warming from that single touch. "I've been failing miserably."

I didn't close my eyes this time, wanting to see Jack's face as he leaned toward me. The air hummed around us like an exposed wire as we stared at each other in the garden, near the spot where we'd said our wedding vows. Despite the world screaming around us and the walls of our lives apparently crumbling along the periphery, there was still *us*. I knew it. But as I waited for Jack to close the distance, I wasn't sure that Jack did.

He dropped his hands. Took a step back. "That would be a mistake. Because it won't solve anything."

The old Melanie, always poking at the surface of the thin veneer of the new Melanie I was trying to be, would have argued that he was wrong. That we'd already survived so much because we'd done it together. But the annoying new Melanie clamped her hand over the old Mellie's mouth, understanding—finally—that Jack had to reach his own conclusion without any coercion. His conviction was one of the things I loved about him. And the reason why we'd gotten married. He simply never gave up.

Although there were times—like this—when I wanted to throw myself at him and erase all doubts that we were meant to be together and deal with the consequences later. I pushed aside the memory of the twins' conception, which had been exactly that.

Jack rubbed his hands through his hair. "I'll figure this out, although I have a feeling there's not a damned thing I can do."

I flinched at his use of "I'll" instead of "we'll." I pushed the hurt aside, determined to think about it later. "Don't say that," I said. "You have a knack for solving puzzles."

A corner of his mouth lifted for a brief moment. "Which makes it even more inconceivable that I could be duped so easily. If I could—" He stopped suddenly, looked at me.

"If you could what?"

He shook his head. "Nothing." He glanced back at the house, still lit up like a national monument. "I can't bear to go in there right now and see their gloating faces. I'm going to drive around for a bit—give myself some time to think. I'll be back in time to tuck the twins in and to shout at Nola to turn down her music."

"I'll let them know."

He nodded and waved while I stood without moving, watching him. He paused and turned. "That was number three," he said, then resumed following the path. I stared after him until the garden gate slammed shut.

An overpowering scent of roses enveloped me, wrapping me in thoughts of summer although it was still February. A gentle creaking sound murmured behind me, and I held my breath, waiting. I wasn't afraid. I remembered the sound from the first time I'd visited 55 Tradd Street, which seemed now like a thousand years ago.

I turned to see the swing moving back and forth, too high and steady to be from the wind. It reminded me of the last time I'd seen Louisa's spirit. It had been right after I'd done what Nevin Vanderhorst had asked: I'd solved the mystery of his mother's disappearance and cleared her name. She'd been standing beneath this tree and pushing her young son, both long gone. And although I'd smelled her roses often in the intervening years, I hadn't seen her again. I didn't expect to now.

But there was something different tonight. I always sensed her around the children during times of turmoil. Yet I was in the garden alone, the scent of her signature flower pressing down on me like a mother's hands. I squinted into the back corner of the garden, trying to see in the dim light cast by the house.

"Louisa?" The single word traveled stealthily across the still garden.

The creaking of the swing continued, a confirmation of sorts. She was trying to tell me something with her presence—something that had nothing to do with the children.

I heard the back door open and shut, the sound of two men arguing while moving toward the cistern, dropping f-bombs more profusely than palmetto bugs laid their eggs. I didn't turn around, recognizing Harvey's and Marc's voices and resenting them for disturbing the quiet of my garden.

The swing spun in a sudden circle, twisting and twisting until the ropes were coiled tight like a snake waiting to strike. I waited with held breath while the swing was let go by unseen hands, bumping drunkenly into the trunk of the tree as it unfurled. I watched it until it had straightened, its movements accountable only to the gentle breeze.

I looked toward the arguing men, finally understanding what Louisa was trying to tell me. This house had become part of the family I had gathered under its roof. Just as it had once been for Louisa. It was our job to protect it and the people living in it. I had never considered my "gift" to be anything more than an annoyance, but for the first time, I was beginning to see the possibilities.

I took a deep breath, the air full of fragrance, and considered all of my promises to Jack and my dedication to being a better me. But Jack had left to go think, to figure something out by himself. I didn't resent that. Hadn't he on more than one occasion said two minds were better than one? Couldn't we fix our shared problem with two different approaches? We could work together but separately. This was our family and our home we were fighting for from our different corners. The outcome was the only thing that mattered, not the means.

I looked up into the branches of the tree that Louisa had once stood under while pushing her little boy in his swing. "Thank you," I whispered into the night air as the leaves rustled in the breeze like tiny clapping hands.

I strode across the garden toward the house, pulling back my shoulders as I prepared for battle. Goose bumps tickled the back of my neck, making me pause as I neared the now-covered cistern. Someone—or something—was watching me from the shadows. It didn't seem menacing, just . . . curious. I remembered the footprints in the snow and what Meghan Black had found in the dirt near the cistern. How she'd thought it might have come from a grave.

I didn't turn my head, not willing to acknowledge—or engage with—whatever it was. I had no doubt that I'd be forced to deal with it at some point, but not now. I had more pressing problems I needed to deal with. Like saving my marriage and restoring peace and tranquility to our family home and all who lived within its ancient and troubled walls. And wreak havoc on Marc Longo for all of the pain and suffering he'd caused Jack and me. Yes, we'd signed a contract. But he wasn't the only one who could play dirty.

I began walking forward again, not sure if the feeling of gentle hands pushing me forward was just a figment of my imagination.

CHAPTER 11

I sat curled up in the chaise longue in the guest room, waiting for Jack. I was tempted to lie down on his empty bed, but I didn't want to give either one of us any ideas. To stay awake I'd been listening to Beau Ryan's podcast on my iPhone. With the titillating title *Bumps in the Night and Other Improbabilities*, it had done its job of keeping me awake, but not because I'd been scared. I closed my screen and sat in the dark, the room lit only by the night-light from the hall, my thoughts moving between my worry over Jack and what I'd been listening to.

I was still shaking with agitation when I heard the grandfather clock downstairs chime three times, followed by the sound of footsteps on the stairs announcing Jack's return. My shoulders and neck softened with relief as I listened to Jack climb the steps, following his progress. I'd memorized each creak in the relatively short time I'd lived in the house. I wondered if that meant we were truly bonded now, like a mother recognizing her baby's cries in a room full of crying babies.

His footsteps stopped at the top of the stairs as if he was considering which way he should turn. Eventually his slow tread headed toward the guest room. He paused in the doorway, his tall, lean form backlit by the hallway night-light. "Mellie?"

I hadn't said anything or moved; I had even held my breath. But he'd known I was here. Even he couldn't deny the pull that existed between us, the parts of him and the parts of me that were incomplete without those of the other. Like two puzzle pieces with slots and grooves in all the right places.

I listened as his hand brushed the wall in search of the light switch. The room flooded with light as the two bedside lamps and the ancient porcelain ceiling fixture flicked on. Jack's eyes settled on me huddled in the chaise, his expression difficult to read.

"Jack." I wanted to stand and throw my arms around him but managed to remain seated. Instead, I said with an impressively calm voice, "Where have you been? I was worried."

I was pinioned by his steady blue gaze, making me forget my own question.

"Sorry. I would have called, but I thought you'd be asleep by now and I didn't want to wake you." Jack closed the door behind him, then shrugged out of his jacket, the scent of leather and crisp winter air clinging to him. He dropped the jacket on the desk chair, and my hands instinctively clenched. I resisted the impulse to jump up and hang it properly.

As if he could read my mind, he said, "I'll get it later." He sat down on the edge of the bed, leaning forward with his elbows on his knees, his hands clasped. "I've been driving around, burning gas. I went as far as Gallen Hall and parked in front of the cemetery for a little while. Don't worry. All was quiet. No Revolutionary War soldiers or bodies hanging from trees. And all holes have been filled in."

"Well, that's a relief." I tried to hide the uncertainty in my voice. "I'm surprised you went back. Especially since you don't believe in do-overs." I gave a little laugh that sounded false even to me.

"I don't. Trust me, I wouldn't want to relive that scene in the cemetery. I just . . ." He shrugged. "It's almost as if my car drove there on its own. It's like it knew I needed some quiet time. The house is for sale. Did you know? I wonder if Anthony needs the money for the lawsuit against his brother."

"Wouldn't surprise me. I doubt Anthony will allow Marc to push him around again. I would like to hope that Anthony's learned his lesson."

We regarded each other in silence. Jack wanted to say something but appeared as reluctant to speak as I was, although most likely for a different reason. I'd missed our nightly conversations in bed, and this was the next best thing. I wasn't eager for it to end. It had been hard for me the last couple of months to fall asleep without him beside me, his voice the last thing I'd hear.

My eyes must have been slowly drifting closed, because when Jack finally spoke, I startled, my eyelids flying open. "Were you waiting up so you could sniff my breath?" His tone was only partially joking.

"Of course not." The old Mellie would have stopped there, happy to put the unpleasantness behind her and move forward with happier topics. Instead, I found myself asking, "Why? Were you tempted?"

He nodded, his eyes not leaving my face. "I was. It's why my first stop was to see your dad." Jack had been my dad's AA sponsor and this was the second time Dad had returned the favor.

"And you're feeling better now?"

"Much. I did a lot of thinking while driving around. I forced myself to come to terms with what Marc has done. I figure I can put up with him for a little longer. We both have reason to want the film to be a success now, so I guess I just need to grin and bear it. We both will."

He smiled at the thought of Marc being as miserable as he was. "The best news is that I came up with a pretty exciting plot idea. I'll mull it over some more, jot down some notes, but I'm raring to go on the new project as soon as it's a little better formed. It's the first time in a long while I've been this excited."

"That's wonderful," I said. "What's it about?"

He shook his head. "I don't want to talk about it. Not yet. Probably not for a while. I need to let it get past the seedling stage before I can share it."

"I understand," I said, even though I didn't. I was still his wife, after all. And he'd always shared his story ideas with me before. It left me wondering what was so different about this one. But writers, I'd come to understand, were a weird bunch, with so many idiosyncrasies that I'd given up trying to make sense of them all.

He kicked off his shoes and pulled his legs up onto the bed. He laced his fingers behind his head and leaned against the pillows like I remembered. I recalled how I'd crawl into bed and rest my head on his chest, listening to it rumble as he spoke, and how sometimes his hands would drift down to rest on my shoulders or hips and then . . .

"Mellie?"

I jerked back, realizing he'd been speaking while I'd been staring at his chest. "I'm sorry—what did you say?"

"I was asking why you were waiting up for me. You could have just texted me or left a note. I'm assuming you would have called if it had been an emergency."

"I know. But I didn't think you'd be this late. And then I started listening to Beau's podcast and lost track of the time." I sat up straight, agitated all over again. "Have you listened to it?"

"His podcast? No. Should I?"

"I think so. Especially if someone like that is working for your parents and is in close proximity to Nola."

Jack sat up and put his feet on the floor. "Why? Is he a Satanist?" His eyes widened as a new horror occurred to him. "Or a Communist? Not that there's much difference, but still not someone we want Nola hanging around with."

I shook my head. "I wish. It's much worse."

"Worse?"

I nodded. "The whole purpose of his podcast is to debunk ghost stories and expose fraudulent psychics."

He stared at me, blinking once. "I think I'm missing something here."

"Don't you see? He read Marc's book and that's how he found out about me—and is probably why he sought out Trenholm Antiques for employment. It's all like some big . . . plan or something."

"A big plan for what? Sounds like you'd applaud someone who shines a light on those who might trivialize others like you who have a real gift."

"More like a goiter on my neck, but whatever. It just seems like someone with an unspoken agenda shouldn't be invited into our lives so easily." I closed my eyes and shook my head. "God only knows what Nola might have inadvertently told him about me and Jayne and our mother without her even knowing Beau was taking notes."

Jack stood. "Now, Mellie, his family owns an antiques store in New Orleans, so it would make sense that he'd look for a job in one here in Charleston. I think it's just a happy coincidence that my parents happen to be related to you."

Our eyes met. "Except there's no such thing as coincidence," we said in unison. It had been Jack's mantra before we'd met, and it had become mine, too, in the ensuing years. Mostly because it was always true.

"We need to talk to your parents. Maybe they should fire him or make sure he and Nola aren't scheduled to work at the same time. . . ."

Jack stepped forward and put a finger to my lips. "Before we jump to conclusions, why don't we have a talk with Beau, see what he has to say?" He dropped his hand and I resisted the impulse to lick my lips. He continued. "Regardless, I doubt you have anything to worry about. You've never advertised your psychic abilities. All the spirits you've dealt with since I've known you have found you and not the other way around. If he wanted to make a podcast episode about you, I'd suspect it would be a very short one." He gave me a lopsided grin. "Unless he wanted to discuss your methods of organizing your life. That could fill a year's worth of episodes. Maybe more."

I stood to face him. "Sure. You can laugh now. But if Beau does want to go that route, I might become the next Marie Kondo and never have to worry about money again for the rest of our lives."

Jack chuckled. "Well, let's mention that to Beau when we have our little chat." He squinted, studying me closely. "You have an eyelash getting ready to drop into your eye. Hang on a sec—don't move."

He stepped closer and I could feel his warm breath on my face, heat-ing my entire body. "Look up." One hand held the back of my head while he gently removed the offending eyelash.

"Got it," he said, but he didn't step back, nor did he remove the hand that was cupping my head. "I think you're good to go."

I stayed where I was, blinking several times in the hope that another eyelash would shake loose. "Are you sure?" I closed my eyes, enjoying the sensation of being so near him again. I leaned closer.

"Mellie?"

My eyes jerked open. "Yes?"

"Is there anything else you needed to tell me? It's late."

"Oh, right." I stepped back. "I wanted to let you know that I made an appointment to see Yvonne Craig tomorrow morning at ten. In case you wanted to come, too." I tried not to sound too hopeful. "I asked her to find out what she could about the property beside the cistern. I'll fill you in tomorrow, but we may have found a grave near the cistern."

Jack didn't blink. "Because this wouldn't be our house if there wasn't at least one skeleton buried somewhere. I can't even pretend to be surprised." He looked up at the ceiling. "I do believe that my calendar is completely empty, so I'm available." He yawned, covering his mouth with his hand because he'd been raised by Amelia Trenholm. "Anything else?"

"Last thing—promise. I received an odd text yesterday. From an 843 area code, so it's local—but not a number I recognized."

"What was the message?"

"'You will be sorry.' All shouty caps."

"'Shouty caps'?" Jack failed to suppress a grin. "I don't think that's what it's actually called."

"Of course it is. If I'd just said 'all caps,' that could signify someone forgot to take off the caps lock. But by saying 'shouty caps,' you know they were intentional and that the words were meant to be shouted at you. There's a big difference."

Jack faked a serious face. "All right, then. Maybe I'll use that in my next book." He pulled his phone from his back pocket and opened the screen. "What was the number?"

"I already did a Google search," I said proudly. "I didn't get any hits."

"Good thinking." His eyes were warm as he spoke, making me more pleased with myself than the simple task of Googling warranted. "But let me have it anyway. Maybe it's someone I know with an unlisted phone number."

My spine stiffened. "But why would—"

"I'm just hypothesizing, Mellie. I have a long history of interviewing people for my books who prefer to keep under the public radar. Not that they'd have a reason to text you or have your number. I still have to check. And I promise I'm not having some sordid affair."

"I didn't say you were."

"You didn't have to. I seem to have acquired the uncanny ability to follow your thinking as it jumps from conjecture to conclusion without pausing in the middle. I think it might be a self-preservation instinct from my prehistoric ancestors."

I narrowed my eyes. "Too bad you haven't moved farther along the evolutionary path. I guess I should be glad that the father of my children can stand upright."

"And here I was thinking that you actually liked some of my more animallike behavior."

My face flushed as I recalled exactly *how much* I liked it; then I reached for my phone to avoid looking at him. I read out the number while Jack typed it into his phone, his mouth definitely wearing a smirk.

He shook his head. "Not someone in my contact list. We should—"

"Tell Detective Riley," I finished for him. "I already did. He said he'd let me know what he finds."

Jack sent me his trademark blood-swooshing grin. "Well done, Mellie. Beauty *and* brains. I knew there was a reason I married you."

He'd meant his words to be lighthearted, but the unasked question sat heavily in my chest. *But not enough reason to stay with me?*

I took a step toward the door, as eager to leave as I was to stay. "I guess we should both go to bed." I frowned, my tired brain replaying what I'd just said out loud. "Separately, I mean. With you here. And me there. In our beds. But not together." I *really* needed to stop hanging around Jayne so much.

"Good night, Mellie."

I backed up toward the door, pausing as my hand touched the doorknob. As tired as I was, I was still reluctant to leave. Being with Jack, even without touching, made me happy. I had the fleeting thought that I should ask him if I could sleep in the chaise longue just so I could know he was near. Instead, I found myself focusing on the ancient porcelain ceiling fixture.

"I'm going to call Greco. He did such a great job redecorating Nola's bedroom, I'd like him to work on the guest room for one of the twins. At some point they're not going to want to share a room anymore. Jayne says that if we do it sooner rather than later, it won't be as stressful on JJ and Sarah."

"Sounds good. But can it wait?"

"Oh. Sure. We can talk about it tomorrow."

"No, I meant I'm still sleeping in here. I'd rather not have Greco start until I'm gone."

His words stung. I hadn't thought about him leaving. I'd been so happy that he was at least under the same roof that I hadn't considered that it might be temporary. I assumed Jack hadn't considered it temporary, either.

"Oh, sure." I smiled to hide the thickness in my throat. I turned and twisted the knob. "Good night, Jack," I managed as I stepped out into the hallway.

A piercing scream from behind Nola's closed bedroom door ripped the quiet night. I sprinted toward her room, Jack right behind me. To my surprise, the door opened on its own, and we panted in the doorway, fumbling for the light switch. The ceiling fixture flashed on with a glaring light before exploding with a shattering *pop*.

"I'm okay," Nola said into the darkness. She flicked on her bedside lamp, illuminating her sitting straight up against her pillows, only the black of her Brad Paisley T-shirt separating her deathly white face from the pale sheets. "Someone was in here—next to my bed."

Jack went into special ops mode, looking under her bed and in her closet. He disappeared into her bathroom and I heard the rings of the shower curtain being whipped aside.

The scent of smoke slipped past us, drawing me toward the window overlooking the cistern and back garden. All was in blackness, yet I could detect shifting away from the house a shadow darker than the night.

Jack returned and we sat down on the edge of Nola's bed. "I'm guessing your visitor wasn't an intruder." He met my eyes briefly.

I picked up Nola's ice-cold hand. "It was a girl," Nola said. "About my age—maybe a little younger, like fifteen or sixteen. And she was wearing old-fashioned clothes."

Jack frowned. "You screamed. Did she hurt you?"

Nola shook her head. "No. She just . . . startled me. I was sleeping and I felt this . . . this . . . icy hand on my arm. Like someone trying to wake me. And when I opened my eyes, I could see that there was someone standing next to my bed." She swallowed. "She didn't make me feel scared. She was . . . sad. And I think she wanted to tell me something." She looked at Jack and then back at me. "I screamed because I turned on the flashlight on my phone so I could see better. And that's when I saw her face." Her hand began to shake in mine and I squeezed it tighter.

Nola's voice was just louder than a whisper. "Her face. It was . . . it was *melted*. And . . ." She swallowed again. "Her eyes were missing, or maybe . . . maybe they'd just been absorbed into her melted skin."

She started to cry and I gathered her to me while I gently patted her back the way JJ and Sarah liked when they needed to be soothed. "We're going to see Yvonne tomorrow to find out what's going on, all right?"

She nodded against my chest.

"Would you like me to stay here with you tonight? Or to come to my room? I promise not to tell your friends."

She lifted her head, wiping her eyes with the heels of her hands, a hint of a smile on her lips. "No. But thanks. I'll probably read for a bit and fall asleep with the light on."

"You're not scared?" Jack asked.

Nola shook her head. "She didn't mean to scare me—I could tell. It was just . . . a feeling. She wanted me to know she was there. I'm sure of that. I think she was trying to tell me something. She's not here to scare me."

I pushed her dark hair from her forehead. "All right. But you know where I am if you change your mind. The night-light's on in the hall, but if you need to turn on the hall light, go ahead. I figure since your scream didn't wake up the twins, a bit of light in the hallway won't, either." I stood and fluffed the pillows behind her while Jack fetched a glass of water from her bathroom. I stepped forward, then leaned down to kiss her forehead. "Good night, Nola."

Something hard on the floor pushed against the thin sole of my slipper. I moved my foot aside to see a silver button winking at me from the tight weave of the rug. When I bent down to retrieve it, I spotted four more buttons in a row right behind it. I collected all the buttons and placed them on my outstretched palm.

"Maybe those are from her charm string," Nola said. "She'd be about the right age."

I nodded, thinking about the headstone and the other items Meghan had mentioned. "Hopefully Yvonne can shed a little more light on all of this when we see her tomorrow."

We said good night and headed for the door. Jack paused. "Do you want me to leave this open?"

For a moment I thought Nola might refuse, but she didn't. "Just an inch. Or two." She frowned. "Where are Porgy and Bess? They jumped off the bed when I screamed."

"I spotted them under the bed. They looked happy there," Jack said.

I returned to the bed and knelt to look underneath. The two fluff balls lay next to each other, their dark round eyes looking out at me as they each chewed on one of General Lee's soup bones, saved especially for him by Mrs. Houlihan. I knew better than to reach under the bed to separate them from their treats. As sweet as they were, threatening their food source could have meant a lost finger. Or two.

Jack helped pull me up, my knees cracking as I straightened and faced Nola. "Did you give the dogs a bone?"

"No. Why?"

"Well, someone did. Someone who must like dogs."

Nola leaned back against her pillows. "That's a relief. I told you I wasn't scared. Anyone who likes dogs can't be that bad, right?"

Jack coughed, probably recalling the repeated antidog declarations I'd been making ever since I'd inherited General Lee.

"Good night, Nola," I said again, then followed Jack into the hallway. I watched him partially close the door. "Should I get a ruler? She said one to two inches."

"Um, no. I don't think that's necessary."

I began backing up, eager to avoid another awkward moment. "Good night, Jack. I'll see you in the morning."

"Good night, Mellie."

I headed down the hallway and didn't turn around to see him watching until I'd closed my bedroom door behind me.

I placed the buttons on my nightstand and crawled into bed, grateful for the warm spot General Lee had created. I lay awake for a long time, staring up at the ceiling, listening to General Lee lick parts of himself that I preferred he keep private. When my phone binged, I flipped it over and opened the screen to find a text from Jack.

AK#4

It took a moment for my sleeping brain to understand. I replaced my phone on my nightstand and curled back under the covers, eventually falling asleep with a smile still on my lips.

CHAPTER 12

I awoke the following morning to loud banging coming from the front door. I jerked upright, dislodging an annoyed General Lee, who'd been comfortably sleeping on the top of my head. After fumbling for my glasses, I slid them on and blinked at the two alarm clocks placed strategically across the room. Five past six. I was still processing this when the banging sounded again.

I threw myself from the bed, dragging half of the covers with me as I stumbled to keep from falling. General Lee grumbled as I struggled into my bathrobe and slippers before running toward the stairs. I almost collided with a shirtless Jack in the hallway as another *boom boom* came from the door and Sarah let out a screech. I knew it was Sarah because JJ could have slept through a tornado.

"I'll see who's at the door while you go to Sarah," Jack said as he headed down the stairs. It was only Sarah's wails that pulled my attention away from Jack's bare torso and sent me running toward the nursery.

Sarah stood at the side of her crib with fat tears running from her big blue eyes and down her chubby cheeks. She wore a piteous expression often seen on the Precious Moments figurines that Rebecca liked to collect for reasons I couldn't understand. "Mama," she said, lifting her arms toward me. Her sobs immediately subsided as I held her close and she buried her face in my neck.

I patted her back as I walked over to JJ's crib, where he was still sleeping peacefully with his whisk. Another bang sounded on the door, leaving me wondering what was taking Jack so long to answer it. I hurried from the nursery with Sarah in my arms and went downstairs.

We found him in the vestibule, attempting to open the door. I peered through the sidelights and spotted an annoyed Marc Longo with an even more annoyed Harvey Beckner standing behind him. Beyond them on the driveway adjacent to the piazza stood various crew members next to their vans. I placed my hand over Sarah's exposed ear so she couldn't hear the curses coming from Marc and Harvey.

"I don't know what the problem is," Jack said, his biceps flexing as he tugged on the doorknob, then attempted to turn it left and right. Nothing budged.

Jack shouted for the men to head toward the back door, miming with his hands to go around the corner. If I hadn't been enjoying watching him move without his shirt, I might have told him that I doubted the back door would open, either.

An even louder *boom* shook the door, and we stood back. I anxiously glanced at the Tiffany glass sidelights and fan window over the door, fearing Sophie's wrath if she found a single crack in the glass or a dent in the solid wood door.

I'd opened my mouth to shout at them to stop when Sarah lifted her head from my shoulder, turned toward the door, and pointed at it with a soggy index finger. A word that sounded something like "open" tumbled from her mouth.

The doorknob turned and the door opened suddenly, causing both Harvey and Marc to stumble inside, accompanied by more choice words. Jack barred them from entering the foyer while I gently squeezed our daughter's pudgy leg in thanks.

Jack stood in front of the men like an avenging angel. "Before I ask you what you're doing here before the agreed-upon start time of eight o'clock, I have to insist that you watch your language while you're on my property. I don't want to have to wash your mouths out with soap."

Harvey told Jack what he could do with himself and then tried to brush past him, but Jack couldn't be budged. "I've been looking forward to spending time with you guys, but not until eight. Why are you here?"

Harvey smirked. "Because the contract says we can't start *filming* until eight. But we can't start filming unless we've got everything set up."

"Is that so?" Jack asked, his outstretched arms still barring the way. "I'll have to go over the fine print in the contract. If you're right, I would appreciate you not banging on the door. I've got two babies and a teenager in the house, and if they're cranky, we're all going to be cranky."

"Not my problem. I suggest you give me a key so I don't have to bang on the door. Your doorbell is broken."

"No, it's not," Jack said. "It just doesn't like you."

"Very funny, Jack," Marc said, stepping back to press the doorbell. Nothing happened.

With a straight face, Jack turned to me. "Melanie, why don't you have Sarah show these men how to press a doorbell?"

"I don't have time for this," Harvey said, trying to slip past Jack's arm again and failing. "If you don't let me through—"

His words were cut off by the sound of the doorbell as Sarah gleefully pressed the button again and again as she giggled her baby belly laugh.

"Good girl," I said, kissing her cheek.

"Just give me a damned key," Harvey demanded.

"No. You can arrive at six if you like, but this door won't be opened until eight. Because I'm a nice guy and we're already awake, I'll let you come in. But today only. And I don't care what time you show up. The house isn't going to let you in a minute before eight." He made an exaggerated show of looking at his watch. "It's now twenty past six. Time's a-wasting."

The two men glared at each other. Finally, Harvey spun around and stepped closer to the door. Beckoning to the crew waiting outside, he said, "All's clear. Come on in."

The crew remained frozen in the driveway, looking up at the house, focused on something on the second floor.

Harvey let out a string of expletives more or less telling the crew to hurry up and get to work. Their heads moved in unison, first to Harvey, then switching to the upstairs window, and then to one another before returning their gazes to Harvey and starting all over again.

Harvey stood in the doorway with his hands clenched and his face red under his tan, giving it the appearance of an inflamed cyst about to pop. "You have exactly one minute to get inside or you're all fired!"

Nola, fully dressed in her school uniform, appeared from inside one of the vans, carrying what looked like a can of beer. She immediately put it down when she saw Jack.

"Hi, Dad!" She smiled brightly as she stepped out of the van, her smile fading as she followed the gazes of the crew. With a look of relief, she said, "Oh, don't be scared. That's just Louisa, the nice ghost. Most of the time, anyway. She's not the one you need to be worried about." She glanced at Harvey before addressing the crew again. "And you're not who she's upset with, so you *should* be fine."

The crew huddled together, mumbling something we couldn't decipher, their gazes traveling from the apoplectic Harvey back to the upstairs window.

Marc stepped out onto the porch. "He's serious. Get in here now or consider yourselves fired."

With looks of resignation, the crew gathered their equipment and marched up the piazza steps, then through the front door.

Marc waited a moment for everyone to pass before pulling Jack aside. "Look, Jack. We're family, remember?"

"Are we really, Matt? Cain and Abel were family, too, and look how that worked out."

Marc's lips thinned in an attempt to keep smiling. "We want the same thing, right?"

Jack looked surprised. "I had no idea you also wished you'd disappear and never be found. Who knew?"

Through gritted teeth, Marc said, "I meant, we both want this to be over so that we can get paid and you can get your career back on track. Seems to me it would be to your advantage if you helped things go more smoothly. Just give me a key and the alarm code and I'll make sure everyone keeps the noise to a minimum until eight o'clock. All right?"

Jack pretended to consider his answer. "You know, I think I'd rather sew my head to the carpet. But thanks for the suggestion."

Marc dropped all pretense of affability. "Fine. But tell your wife to make those ghosts back off. I had to hire a whole different crew because the original one was too spooked to return after all the little electrical problems and other issues they experienced in December. We can't let that happen again."

"I'm not sure what you're referring to, but if you have an issue with Melanie, I'd suggest you speak with her directly. She doesn't need me to tell you where you can shove your opinions."

I sent a warning look at Jack just as Sarah sent a smelly and especially loud explosion into her diaper. She usually did that only for Rebecca, but I supposed she considered Marc an extension of his wife. I wished she knew how to high-five.

"I need to go take care of this. And as far as me having any control over any assumed paranormal elements in this house, I don't. It's an old house, and old houses are almost always haunted. Deal with it."

I headed toward the stairs, trailing a path of stinkiness while Sarah remained oblivious, thanks to the uberexpensive (and well worth it) disposable diapers I put on the children at night. The cloth diapers Sophie had sent were kept neatly folded in a drawer in the back of the nursery closet. Jack's voice followed me as I slowly climbed the stairs, pausing midway so I could listen.

"I know what you're doing, Marc. Why you want a key. And I'm not going to give it to you. You can't get it through your thick skull that there is no more treasure hidden in our house. No more hidden diamonds. I'm guessing you must have read the article in that online treasure-seekers blog last month about the Hope Diamond, or you wouldn't be breathing down my neck for the key. Well, don't hold your breath." He paused as if considering. "Or better yet, please do. Right now I've got to go talk to my daughter." He stepped past Marc out onto the piazza, his bare feet stomping onto the wood floor.

Sarah squirmed in my arms, starting to fuss. To my relief, Jayne entered the foyer from the kitchen. "Good morning!" she said, running up the stairs to greet us. She pulled back, putting her finger under her nose. "I'm hoping the smell's coming from Sarah."

"Funny," I said, handing the baby to her. "I'd help you, but I have to go play referee right now. JJ's still sleeping." I headed down the stairs.

"Don't you want to get dressed first? Or at least brush your hair?"

I didn't even pause. "After three skeletons removed from the property and the unending construction work, the neighbors won't even notice."

I dodged crew members to grab a throw from the sofa in the front parlor before catching up with Jack. He stood at the curb in a wide stance with his hands on his hips, just like park rangers advised that one do if confronted by a bear or another dangerous animal. I blinked in confusion until I realized that Nola wasn't alone. I placed the throw over Jack's shoulders, but I wasn't sure he noticed.

"What are you doing here so early?" he asked Beau, who looked rather calm, considering the circumstances.

Before Beau could answer, Jack's gaze moved to Nola. "And why are you up and dressed for school already?"

"I have to be at school early with Lindsey and Alston to set up our science project. And Beau is here because I needed him to buy beer since he looks twenty-one and has a fake ID."

"That's not helping."

Beau stepped forward. "Actually, sir, the beer's not for her. It's for the film crew."

Jack crossed his arms, the tic in his jaw starting. "Is that right?"

"Dad!" Nola stepped in front of Jack, and I was struck again by their nearly identical profiles with the same stubborn chin. "I gave them each a copy of one of your books with a can of beer." She lowered her voice. "I overheard you and Melanie talking about how the filming needs to go smoothly, and I thought I'd do my part. Everyone knows that sometimes you have to put a fatter worm on the hook to get the fish to bite."

Jack dropped his arms, his face softening as he studied his daughter. "Thanks, Nola. I had no idea that you knew how to fish."

She slid a glance toward Beau. Looking embarrassed, she said, "It was his idea. And I figured it couldn't hurt."

It was at the moment that Jack noticed the motorcycle at the curb, a large knapsack sitting on the ground next to it. "Is that yours?"

"It is now. It used to be my dad's back in the day. It was stored at my grandparents' mountain house during Katrina, so it wasn't destroyed."

Jack didn't say anything as he stepped closer to the motorcycle. "A vintage Harley Shovelhead. Nice bike. 'Seventy-five?"

"'Seventy-seven. I know that only because it was the year my mom was born. I was told that my dad had to do a lot of searching until he found one from the right year. Did a complete nut-and-bolt restoration."

Jack walked around the bike, pretending to study it, although I could tell he was busy figuring out his next move. Without looking at Beau, he said, "I remember your dad. He fixed me up after a skirmish in Nangarhar. Good surgeon. He had a higher survival rate than most."

Beau watched Jack, his face expressionless.

Jack straightened. "For some reason the Afghanis wouldn't let him near them. Never understood why."

Beau didn't flinch or blink. He simply stared back at Jack, almost daring him to ask the unspoken question. As I waited for one of them to make a move, I was distracted by the sudden formation of a translucent cloud hovering over the wide leather seat of the motorcycle. No one else seemed to notice it, and it disappeared completely when Jack finally spoke.

"Nola, why don't you go inside and have your breakfast? Use the kitchen door, please."

"But, Dad—"

"Go." He didn't shout.

We were left alone, facing Beau, feeling oddly disadvantaged, standing in our pajamas and a couch throw.

Beau broke the awkward silence. "I need to get to class. I'm sorry if

I shouldn't have brought the beer. It seemed like a good cause." He moved toward the motorcycle.

"Does Nola know the purpose of your podcast?" Jack asked, an edge to his voice.

Beau slung the knapsack on his back, then kicked up the side stand before straddling the Harley. "I have no idea. We've never discussed it. I'm here today only because I overheard her talking with Amelia about that Marc guy and the filming. Other than that, we've kept our conversations limited to the store and work."

I stepped forward. "I listened to several episodes last night. So we're curious, Beau, about your motives for seeking employment at Trenholm Antiques. Jack and I can't help but think that you read Marc's book and took what he wrote about me as fact. Then you looked for a way to insinuate yourself into our family so you could observe me at close range."

A foul odor drifted up from the front of my robe, but I didn't look down. I had a good idea of what it was and made a mental note to reexamine my choice of diaper brands.

Beau grinned, altering his face from merely good-looking to movie-star handsome. I'd have to ask Nola if she'd ever noticed. Or maybe not, judging by the narrowed-eye scrutiny with which Jack was now regarding him.

"Think what you want, but I needed a job and I'm familiar with antiques. It was a no-brainer. And Trenholm isn't an unusual name in South Carolina, so it wasn't a natural conclusion that you were related."

"So it was a coincidence?" Jack asked.

Our mantra rang inside my head: *There's no such thing as coincidence.*

"Sure," Beau said, priming the kick start a few times before giving it a solid pump. A loud rumble erupted from the engine, making it impossible to continue our conversation, which I'm sure was *not* a coincidence.

I shouted over the noise, "You should wear a helmet, you know. Dr. Wallen-Arasi calls motorcyclists who don't 'organ donors.'"

He didn't seem to hear me, his attention drawn to the asphalt by the side of the Harley where a set of isolated wet footprints had stopped. Light brown eyes fixed on mine briefly before Beau glanced at his wristwatch—a real one. "I have to get to class now. Good-bye, Mr. and Mrs. Trenholm."

He slid on a pair of aviator sunglasses and, with a rev of the engine, pulled out into the street, the rumble of the engine following him like a restless ghost. The thought made me look down at the street, but the footprints were gone.

"It's not a coincidence, is it?"

Jack shook his head, his gaze following the bike as it disappeared down Tradd Street. "Nope. And if he thinks my daughter will ever ride on that thing, he's got another think coming."

I remembered photographs, which Amelia had shown me, of Jack in his younger years on or standing near a similar motorcycle. More often than not with some beautiful woman on the seat behind him. I judiciously refrained from commenting.

I shivered in the cold and Jack put his arm around me. I needed to remember to wear fewer sweaters than I needed so this would keep happening. We were approaching the piazza steps as I attempted to remember something Beau had said at our first meeting.

"Do you recall what Beau said about his parents?"

"About how they disappeared during Hurricane Katrina? He said they were trying to save his baby sister. Why?"

I chewed on my lip. "Because I keep seeing wet footprints—a woman's. I just saw them again next to Beau's motorcycle. And I'm pretty sure he saw them, too."

Jack raised his eyebrows. "Can't be a coincidence, can it?"

"Is it ever?"

He kept his arm around me as we neared the front door, stopping as all the lights in the house flickered and then shut off. Even the generator was silenced. An irate scream and a stream of choice words from Harvey Beckner followed two crew members as they ran out of the door toward one of the trucks parked in the drive.

"Is that Louisa?"

I shrugged, avoiding his eyes. "Who knows? It's an old house, re-member. It's bound to have electrical problems."

As if on cue, a Hard Rock Foundations truck pulled up to the curb in front of the house.

"Marc must have called Rich Kobylt," Jack said. "I need my coffee before I can handle a glimpse of his rear end this early in the morning."

He reversed our direction, guiding us through the garden toward the back door, while I felt grateful for a reprieve that had nothing to do with our handyman. The generator buzzed on and then off again, and I whis-pered a silent thanks to Louisa.

CHAPTER 13

After dressing, I headed toward the garage for my car, belatedly remembering it was parked on the street somewhere between Legare and Logan. I wound my way through the line of vehicles in the driveway, thankful for the blue sky and balmy temperatures that made parking outside tolerable. If the filming was still going on once the weather warmed up, we'd have to figure out an alternate parking situation, so I wouldn't melt walking to my car or self-combust getting inside it.

I had made it only to the street when I heard Jack calling my name. I turned as he jogged to catch up.

"I thought we had our meeting with Yvonne this morning," he said.

"That's where I'm heading. My car's down this way."

Jack looked confused. "I thought we were going together."

It was my turn to be confused. "We're meeting with Yvonne together, but I didn't . . . I mean, well . . . I thought you'd rather we get there separately. Since we're, um, separated."

"I think we can manage a short trip together without getting on each other's nerves, don't you? Besides, we both have great parking spots on the street and I don't want to lose them by moving the cars. It's a beautiful day and we have time, so why don't we walk?"

I glanced at my watch and then double-checked the time on my phone. "All right. I promise to do my best not to get on your nerves." I began walking quickly toward King Street. I could at least window-shop to distract myself from Jack's words and to stop myself from asking what he'd meant about *getting on each other's nerves.*

Jack's long strides easily caught him up to me. He gently took hold of my arm, bringing me to a stop. We faced each other, his hand still on my arm. "I'm sorry. That came out the wrong way." He looked up at the sky, shook his head. "Heaven knows my nerves are the least of my problems. They all seem to leap to attention whenever you're near. It makes it very hard to concentrate, which I need to do to figure us out. *All* of us. Our problems are certainly not physical."

I briefly closed my eyes and took a deep breath, trying to put words to my frustration like my string of therapists had been trying to tell me to do for years. "Really, Jack? What is there to figure out? We love each other. We have a family together. I made a mistake. You've already forgiven me. Can't we just move on?"

He took my head in his hands, pressing his forehead against mine. "I wish I could. It's just not that easy."

I wanted to tell him that it was, that we were both fumbling with the intricacies of being married despite being two different kinds of people but loving each other anyway. At least according to my mother, with whom I happened to agree. But I held on to my words, knowing they would bounce off of him. I had met brick walls that were more pliable than Jack Trenholm. And if I had learned anything in the short time we'd been married, it was that he had to reach his own conclusions. That was something I'd figured out myself, without the help of my mother.

I stepped back, needing space between us so I could think clearly. "Come on. You know how I hate being late." He walked behind me until we reached Meeting Street, where he fell into step beside me. My phone buzzed and I glanced down to see if it was Detective Riley. Despite having the largest text size available, I still had trouble reading it while walking.

"Anything I can help with?" Jack asked.

I almost said no, but I was eager to find out if Detective Riley had had any luck with discovering who'd texted me from the unknown number. I sighed. "If you wouldn't mind." I handed Jack my phone.

After a moment, Jack relayed, "Thomas says he's got a lot of info to share, but he's unavailable today, working on another case, and wants to know if we can meet with him tonight."

He handed me the phone. "I'm free."

"Me, too."

We stopped at the light at the corner of Broad and Meeting streets, my gaze moving toward the imposing edifice of St. Michael's, where a bride in a nineteen forties–style wedding gown stood under the portico between two giant columns. Her arm rested in the crook of the arm of a man wearing what looked like a World War II Navy uniform. They were smiling at each other, making me smile, too. Until the man turned to look at me and I saw that half of his face was missing.

"Are you all right?" Jack took my arm and began leading me across Broad Street.

I nodded, watching as a man on his cell phone walked through the bridal couple. "Yes. I'm fine."

"Are you sure? You don't look fine. Anything I can do?"

We'd reached the opposite side of the street and I paused to look over my shoulder toward the wedding couple being showered with a barrage of white petals that turned scarlet as they fell. "Nothing. Nothing that can be fixed right now." Because no matter how many times it happened, I could never get used to the sheer number of restless spirits who could see me coming and invade my life when I wasn't paying attention. I shuddered to think of what would happen if I agreed with Jayne to let our combined lights shine.

"Would you like me to respond to Thomas?"

I faced Jack, trying to recall what we'd been talking about.

He held up my phone. "A meeting—tonight."

"Right." We crossed Meeting Street and began walking toward King Street, turning right at Berlin's. I gave a passing glance at the store window, trying not to remember the red dress my mother had bought there and I'd worn to my fortieth-birthday celebration. The same dress Jack and I held responsible for the happy existence of the twins. It hung in the back of my closet, too snug for me now, but holding more memories than an entire photo album.

I continued. "I think it would be best to meet somewhere besides the house because of the film crew being there, not to mention Marc and Harvey. I'm sure Marc is up to something, and I'd prefer it if he didn't know what we were doing. I know they're supposed to be done by six, but who knows?"

I paused in front of the big front window of Buxton Books, reminding myself that I needed to read more and that Sophie's birthday was coming up. I made a mental note to return and shop. "Why don't you tell him to meet us at six thirty for dinner? He can pick the restaurant, and we'll make the reservation. I'll invite Jayne, too, since I'm sure she'll want to be kept up-to-date."

"Right. And because three is an odd number for dinner."

"Exactly," I said, avoiding his eyes.

I had no desire to be told that my romantic instincts weren't the best and some might even say were completely off base. After all, I'd once dated Marc Longo and had considered his brother, Anthony, a great match for Jayne. Both matches had been abysmal failures, but surely I'd learned something from the experience. Surely.

When we turned off King to meander through the back streets to reach the Addlestone Library on the College of Charleston campus, Jack brought up the subject I'd been anticipating.

"Nola said she'd like to apply to UCLA. She said if she wants to pursue songwriting, that would be a good school. And it would be taking her back to her roots. She was raised in Los Angeles for the first thirteen years of her life, after all."

I nodded. "She also mentioned schools in New York and Ohio, for majors other than songwriting. And recently she mentioned Sewanee and Tulane. Personally, I think if she's not sure about her major, she should start at USC or the College of Charleston and then transfer if she needs to when she figures out what she wants."

"Me, too," Jack said.

"What?"

"I'm not ready to say good-bye, either. And I cringe at the thought of her being so far away from home. I can't believe I didn't know she existed for so long and how in such a short time she's become such a huge part of my life."

"Yep. Mine, too." I used my knuckle to wipe away an embarrassing drop of moisture. I felt Jack looking at me and said, "Allergies."

"Winter allergies are the worst." He took my hand and squeezed it, then let it go.

I cleared my throat. "I overheard what you said to Marc about a recent blog post. Something about the Confederate diamonds?"

Jack shoved his hands in his pockets, something he did when he paced his office while deep in thought. "Yeah. Apparently, some treasure hunter with a big online presence—known only by his blogger name Blackbeard—said he'd dug up something about the diamonds not being the only part of the treasure given to the Confederacy by the Sultan of Brunei. Some connection to the Hope Diamond."

"And people took it seriously?"

"When there is the potential for a hidden and valuable treasure, people pay attention. Sort of like how the mention of a new rose variety gets your dad's gardening group all salivating. Except with treasure hunting, there's real money involved, so it becomes very competitive. And sometimes dirty."

"Which is why Marc follows those kinds of blogs. But it's not true, right? We found all of the diamonds in the clock. There can't be more, or we would have heard about them by now."

Jack shrugged. "Anything's possible, I guess. There was a recent article in *USA Today* about the Hope Diamond being sent from the Smithsonian Museum of Natural History to Harry Winston's in New York for cleaning and minor restoration work. A reader of mine e-mailed the article to me because it mentioned the history of the diamond, and various conspiracies including a possible connection to the Confederate diamonds. The reader knew I'd been working on a book about the diamonds, so he thought I might be interested. Apparently, he doesn't know about Marc's book."

"And I hope you didn't tell him. I'd hate to think Marc got a penny of royalties because of you."

"I'd rather glue my lips together." He took my arm and moved us both to the edge of the sidewalk as two girls wearing College of Charleston sweatshirts passed us in single file, both of them talking while tapping furiously on their phones without tripping or looking up. Resuming our walk, I said, "Wasn't the Hope Diamond once owned by Marie Antoinette?"

"Not by her personally, but it was owned by the French royal family until they were beheaded. It's why legend says it's cursed. Nothing like having one's head removed to start a nasty rumor."

"I bet. So, what does the Hope Diamond have in common with the Confederate diamonds? I'm assuming it has to be pretty plausible to get treasure bloggers all in a tizzy."

Jack sent me an odd look. "You really want to know?"

"Sure. If Marc's going to start digging again, I should probably know why."

"Sounds fair. Well, when the French treasury was looted during their revolution, the French Blue—as the Hope Diamond was known then—was stolen and disappeared for twenty years. It originally weighed about sixty-seven carats, but when it showed up again two decades later, it was only about forty-four carats. It was rumored that it had been cut in half, but no one is sure what happened to the other half—until an obscure photograph of the Sultan of Brunei wearing what looks like a replica of the French Blue was unearthed. The stone hung from a neck ribbon in the same setting as King Louis XIV once wore. Even without verification, the photograph was included in that *USA Today* article. It got lots of tongues wagging on all the treasure-hunting forums."

While he'd been talking, Jack had kept his hands in his pockets, his gaze focused on the sidewalk in front of us, his brows knitted in deep concentration. It was the same look he had when immersed in his plotting.

"Was this the story idea you weren't ready to tell me?"

He started and stopped several times, never quite managing to get the words out.

"You're still not ready to talk about it." I wasn't quite able to hide the hurt in my voice.

"Pretty much."

Before I could remind him that we always discussed his books at every stage in the process, I was distracted by Jack putting his hand on my lower back to steer me around a group of tourists walking abreast on the sidewalk, oblivious to other pedestrians. I loved the solid warmth of his palm, the heat wrapping me like a coat. When he dropped his hand, I almost asked him to put it back before I remembered that we were separated. Even though we were still living in the same house. And still loved each other.

I thought again about bringing up the subject of going to visit a marriage counselor but swallowed back the words. I wasn't eager to repeat the experiences I'd had when I was younger, seeking counseling to deal with my mother's abandonment. There had been something about the process of opening my mind and digging deep that made me particularly vulnerable to troubled souls looking for a way in. I kept switching counselors each time one suggested medication to quiet the voices I heard inside my head, until I finally gave up therapy altogether.

I also fostered a secret fear that a therapist might tell Jack and me that we were incompatible and should make the separation permanent. Which is why when my mother or Jayne brought up the subject, I reverted to the old Mellie and sidestepped the subject entirely.

We took a right on Coming Street, our conversation paused as we dodged more pedestrian traffic before reaching the impressive and glaringly new Addlestone Library, where the South Carolina Historical Society Archives were now housed. After climbing the steps, we walked through the library in hushed silence, heading up to the third-floor reading room.

We found Yvonne Craig sitting behind her computer at the reference desk. She was wearing a pretty yellow sweater draped elegantly over her shoulders, her beautiful white hair combed back in a glossy bun. In my mind, I still pictured her in the old Fireproof Building on Chalmers, where the archives were housed before they'd been moved, along with Yvonne, to the new library on the College of Charleston's campus.

Despite her years, Yvonne stood quickly, letting her glasses dangle from the chain around her neck. She walked toward us, wearing a bright smile apparently meant for both of us, but I knew it was aimed mostly at Jack. It had taken me a while to stop being jealous of the octogenarian's close relationship with my husband, but I had eventually learned to accept it.

She raised each cheek to Jack to be kissed and then did the same to me before stepping back to adjust the yellow cardigan on her shoulders.

"Correct me if I'm wrong, Yvonne, but when we first met, I seem to remember you used a cane."

"I certainly did—horrible arthritis, you know. Jack suggested yoga and it has changed my life. Keeps me flexible. And Zumba. You should really try it sometime."

Despite still wearing my coat, I shivered. I wasn't sure if the interior's chilliness was for the preservation of old archives or because the brittle volumes and papers contained within the archives' walls were accompanied by their creators. I looked around us stealthily, the unmistakable sense of being watched brushing the back of my neck. Though I'd experienced the same sensation before on my many visits to the archives, this was the first time it seemed there was intent in the interest and not simply passive curiosity.

I shivered again and Jack casually draped an arm around my shoulders, making me realize that being spied on by an unknown spirit had its benefits, too.

Yvonne looked at me closely, her pink-painted lips pursed in thought. "Is everything all right? You look . . . tired." Her face brightened. "Are you . . . ?"

Before she could finish her sentence, both Jack and I said in unison, "No." We said it loudly enough that several heads turned in our direction.

Avoiding looking at Jack, I said, "I'm fine. Just not sleeping well."

"I'm sorry to hear that," she said, sending a sidelong glance at Jack before leading us to one of the long wooden tables where neatly stacked folders and books sat waiting. There were many reasons to love Yvonne Craig, but her sense of organization was right up there at the top of the list. We must have shared a common ancestor—not an uncommon reality among Charleston's older families.

Jack pulled out a chair for Yvonne at the head of the table in front of the stack, then another one next to her for me before sitting down across from me.

Leaning toward Jack, she whispered, "Is this for a new book?"

"No," I said at the same time Jack answered, "Maybe."

I sent him a piercing look, which he avoided by sliding the first book off the stack and opening it. "So, what have you discovered?"

"Oh, lots of interesting things, as usual." She gave Jack a coquettish grin, then patted my hand. "Don't worry, Melanie. I have my own beau now, so Jack is safe."

I remembered the handsome older gentleman she'd brought to the Holiday Shop and Stroll at the Francis Marion Hotel in December. "I'm so happy to hear you and Harold Chalmers are still stepping out together."

A small V appeared in the smooth skin between her brows. "Isn't it called 'hooking up' these days? I'm around all these young college students now, so I'm trying to get with the lingo."

My surprised eyes met Jack's. "Um, I'm not sure that's the correct term—" I began.

"Well, look at this," Jack interrupted as he opened the leather-bound book in front of him that had been tabbed with a place marker. "Is this the land plat for our house?" He slid the book toward the middle of the table so the three of us could get a better view.

I ignored the little jump in the pit of my stomach when he said the words "our house" and leaned closer. "I don't see the cistern or any outbuildings. But a plat should include all structures on a property, right?"

Yvette smiled at us as if we were her star pupils as she placed another plat on top of the first. "That would be correct. As you can see in this one from 1848, when the house was built, the lot contained several dependencies, including an outdoor kitchen and henhouse." She pointed to small rectangles on the pages with pink-tipped fingers. "The cistern was added a bit later, which is why it's not shown on this plat."

She flipped back to the original page. "This plat was made in 1944, at the time the land at the back half of the original property on Tradd Street was sold and Ford Alley created behind it and the two houses on the alley were built." She tapped her finger on the outline of one of the outbuildings on the page, then slid her finger next to it. "This is where your cistern is, correct? By 1944 it had been filled in, which is why it doesn't appear here. But it makes sense that the cistern would have been next to the kitchen house."

"What happened to the outbuildings?" Jack asked.

"According to what I could find in the archives regarding your house, it seems it sustained some damage during the fire of 1861 and then again during the earthquake of 1886. I imagine the dependencies were probably damaged or destroyed by either event, and at some point it was decided not to rebuild those. My guess would be that the kitchen would have been incorporated into the main house when that occurred."

"Fire?" I said, my nostrils flaring at the remembered scent emanating from the Frozen Charlotte. "Were there any casualties?"

"If there is a casualty list, I have yet to discover it. Surely there were casualties—over five hundred forty-five acres were burned, after all. Those were turbulent times, with the war going on. Considering how devastating it was, there's a sad lack of documentation about the fire. And don't forget the earthquake of 1886. Almost every single structure in the city was damaged, and most had to be rebuilt or demolished."

Jack leaned closer to study the plat. "Is there any chance this was a cemetery at some point?"

Yvonne shook her head. "Not really. The Vanderhorst mausoleum is in Magnolia Cemetery, as you know. Of course, any graves discovered could predate the house, with no connection to the Vanderhorsts."

"Perhaps." I reached into my purse and pulled out the plastic baggie filled with the buttons we'd found in Nola's room that morning. I opened it and let the buttons spill out onto the table. "We found these near the cistern, in what we think might have been a grave. They might have been part of a charm string."

"You found them in a grave?" Yvonne asked, picking up a mother-of-pearl button and placing her glasses on the end of her nose to examine it.

Jack and I glanced at each other for a moment before I replied. "More or less. Along with other items that definitely point to the Victorian era. But no skeletal remains. Well, except for those of a dog, but that might not be connected."

Yvonne lowered her glasses on their chain again. "Then why do you think it was a grave?"

"Because the excavators also found a headstone. The only thing legible was the letter E. No other grave markers have been found to indicate this might have been a cemetery, but they could have all disappeared when the land behind the house was excavated in 1945 prior to building the houses on Ford Alley."

Yvonne frowned in concentration. "I'll need to double-check, but if my memory serves me right, there was an Emily Vanderhorst born in the 1830s. I seem to recall she married an Englishman before the war and lived the rest of her life in London. I'll see if I can find her grave, but I'm confident she was buried in England."

"Any other ideas?" I asked.

"Well," Yvonne continued, "the Victorian era was between 1837 and 1901. So perhaps the headstone belonged to a victim of the fire or the earthquake, and with the chaos ensuing from both catastrophic events, the family interred the person temporarily."

"It was fire," I said definitively, making Yvonne send me a questioning look. "Just a guess," I added.

Her eyes settled on me briefly before returning to the plat. "So whatever was in that grave might not have had any connection to the cistern at all."

I nodded. "If a victim from either of those events was buried in the ruins of the destroyed outbuildings, over time with the flooding and other erosion factors, any remains or artifacts might have mingled with those from the cistern."

"Very true." Her eyes sparkled with excitement. "Looks like we have more research to do! Jack, you already have the Vanderhorst family tree, so go back and see if there are any other people with names—possibly female, but let's look for both—that begin with E who might have died in 1861 or 1886."

I opened my mouth to tell her it was definitely the fire, but she held me back with a stern look. "As a research librarian, it is my job to cover all angles. The earthquake spawned several fires, so it wouldn't be inconceivable that citizens fell victim to fire. Besides, it makes the research so much more fun."

"'Fun,'" I repeated. "Right."

Jack pulled out Yvonne's chair and helped her adjust the yellow cardigan draped over her shoulders as she stood. She picked up a folder from the table and handed it to him. "I made copies of the plats as well as a few old newspaper articles about the fire and the earthquake. Even if they're not useful, I know you'll find them informative."

"Thanks, as always, Yvonne. You're the best." She beamed as Jack took her hands and kissed each cheek. "You let me know if Harold isn't treating you like the queen you are, you hear? I can set him straight."

"Oh, no worries there," she said, her cheeks pinkening. "But I'll be sure to let you know."

I slid my own chair back and stood. As I bent to kiss Yvonne's cheek, she grabbed hold of my hands, her warm eyes settling on mine. "We don't always marry someone we can live with. We marry someone we can't live without." She lifted her cheek, whispering into my ear as I kissed her, "He'll come around. Don't you worry."

I pulled back, taking my time removing my purse off the back of my chair and adjusting it on my shoulder so I could blink back the dust particles that had apparently gathered in my eyes.

After leaving the library, Jack paused at the bottom of the steps. "Are you heading to the office now?"

I made a show of glancing at my watch and then my phone to double-check. "Yes. I don't have an appointment until one o'clock but I've always got paperwork and listings to go through." I waited for him to invite me to lunch, feeling like the nerdy schoolgirl I'd once been.

"All right. I'm going to run back to my apartment to pick up all of my Vanderhorst notes. Then I'm headed back to the house to keep an eye on Marc and Harvey. Hopefully they'll be busy, so I can get some work done."

"Sounds like a solid plan," I said with forced enthusiasm.

"Thomas picked the Grocery for dinner tonight. What time do you want to head over? I'll be happy to drive."

My heart did a little flip until I remembered that we'd probably be driving with Jayne. "Six fifteen? It's a quick drive and there's a free parking lot next to the restaurant."

I waited to see if he'd give me a platonic kiss on the cheek, like the one he'd given Yvonne. Instead he just smiled, said good-bye, then left.

As I turned toward Broad Street and Henderson House Realty, my phone beeped. I looked at it eagerly, hoping Jack had changed his mind and was asking me to lunch. I sighed when I realized the text was from the nosy reporter and my sometime nemesis, Suzy Dorf. I hesitated a moment, wondering if I should delete it without reading it first. But that was something the old Melanie would have done. I stopped walking and squinted at the screen, reading the entire message twice, wishing immediately that I hadn't chosen that moment to be the more mature version of myself.

Don't forget—u o me interview. Have u heard new info about ur diamonds? need to discuss w/u

I cleared the screen and resumed walking. I'd been avoiding her for over a month. A few more weeks wouldn't make a difference, and if I planned on calling her in a few weeks, that meant I wasn't pretending she'd go away like the old Mellie used to do. I just couldn't deal with her right now on top of everything else.

Instead, I texted my mother, asking if she was free to babysit the twins tonight since Jayne and I were going out. Nola would be at Lindsey's, studying for a test, so I texted her, too, asking if she needed us to bring her home after our dinner.

I felt someone watching me from across the street where my favorite shoe store, Bob Ellis, had once been for over sixty years. The building was still there—a boutique hotel now with retail space—but it hurt too much to see it and remember the happy times I'd had there, experiencing retail therapy. But my attention was drawn to a woman standing on the corner in front of the building, watching me.

She seemed familiar, and I waited for her to call out to me or wave, but she simply stood where she was. I needed my glasses to see her better. I thought she might be an old client of mine and I didn't want to appear rude. But when I'd pulled out my glasses from my purse and glanced up again, the woman was gone. I looked up and down King Street, curious as to where she could have gone in the few seconds it had taken me to open my purse. I crossed the street to the spot where she'd been standing, wondering if she'd entered the hotel. I peered through the large glass doors and again up and down King Street. When I felt the pinpricks on the back of my neck, I looked down on the sidewalk, already knowing I'd see the droplets of water created by rivulets from soaking hair and two wet footprints disappearing around the corner.

CHAPTER 14

The first thing I noticed when entering the Grocery restaurant was the wall of pickle jars spotlit above the open kitchen and accessed by a rolling ladder. They had been arranged neatly and chromatically left to right, from dark red cherry peppers to pale green tomatoes. I knew without taking my first bite that this would be my new favorite restaurant.

"Have you been here before?" Jayne asked as Jack gave our name to the young woman standing at the front of the restaurant to greet us.

"No. It was Thomas's suggestion."

"Figures. He's such a foodie."

I turned to look at her. "Thomas? Detective Thomas Riley? I thought he was more a doughnut-and-beer kind of guy."

Jayne sent me a withering glance. "Why? Because he's a detective?"

"It wasn't meant as an insult. Some of us happen to consider doughnuts a delicacy."

She shook her head in exasperation, then returned to her perusal of tables and their occupants. "When we were dating, he always took me to the most innovative restaurants. Knew how to pair the right wine and everything. One of his sisters is a chef in New Orleans—trained under

Emeril himself. Growing up, she tested out all of her recipes on Thomas since he was the youngest and didn't know any better."

"Right this way." We began following the hostess around tables, Jack's hand on my back. Jayne's sharp intake of breath was enough to alert me that we were nearing our table and that Thomas was already there.

"Take a deep breath and speak slowly," I said quietly. Jayne nodded in acknowledgment, and the look on her face was similar to the one JJ made when we announced it was bath time.

Thomas stood and Jayne smiled at him as he pushed in her chair, the smile remaining firmly fixed on her face as Jack seated me and we all accepted menus.

"It's good to see you again, Jayne," Thomas said, unfolding his napkin and placing it in his lap. "I didn't know you'd be here, but I'm glad you are."

Jayne sent me a look of reproach.

"Sorry—I must have forgotten," I said, fiddling with my own napkin. "I just thought, considering the subject matter of what we'd be discussing, Jayne should be part of it. So should Veronica, but it's her wedding anniversary and she and Michael had other plans." I didn't add that I didn't want Michael involved. Even though we'd declared a kind of truce, his doubts about my ability to find answers and his impatience to be done with the investigation into Adrienne's death were too distracting. I'd tell Veronica everything later and leave it up to her what she'd choose to share with her husband.

Jack nudged my foot under the table at my blatant lie about forgetting to tell Thomas about Jayne, but I ignored him. "So," I said brightly, "I can't wait to hear everything, Thomas. But first—can we order? I'm starving." I opened my menu, noting how it was divided into produce, seafood, and meat, and my heart fell as I studied all of the healthy options. I had second thoughts about this being my new favorite restaurant. Until I spotted the dessert portion and my mood was immediately restored.

"It's been a while since I've been here," Jack admitted. "What do you recommend?"

"Everything," Thomas said. "The chef, Kevin Johnson, is well known for doing amazing things with vegetables, but there's really nothing bad on the menu." Thomas opened his own menu and glanced at it. "I'd suggest sharing a few starters—as long as one of them is the fried oysters. And I would highly recommend the wood-fired whole fish for the table for our main."

"Sounds good to me." Jack tilted his head in my direction. "But Mellie doesn't like to share her food. Trust me, I've got scars from puncture wounds on the tops of my hands to prove it."

I glared at Jack, knowing only half of his statement was fictional, then looked over at Jayne. She continued to smile and nod like a bobblehead. I lifted my foot under the table to give her a quick yet solid kick to make her stop.

Thomas grunted, then leaned down to rub his leg.

"Sorry." I smiled. "Just crossing my legs." I turned to my sister. "Does sharing some starters and then fish for the table sound good to you?"

She nodded twice.

"Fine," I said. "Let's do that. But I'd like my own order of the oysters, and can I go ahead and order the peanut butter bar for dessert? I'd hate for them to run out before we finish our dinner."

I felt three sets of eyes on me as I carefully slid my menu away to show that my decisions had been made. "I'm starving," I said again.

Thomas ordered wine for the table—sparkling water with lime for Jack—and after several attempts, Jayne was able to join in the small talk until the main course arrived and the waiter left us.

Jack put down his water glass and turned to Thomas. "Were you able to find out anything about who sent that text to Mellie?"

"I was." Thomas took a bite of his wreckfish, and closed his eyes while he chewed slowly. After swallowing he continued. "But it wasn't as helpful as I'd hoped."

"What do you mean?" Jayne took her time enunciating each word, just as we'd practiced.

"The phone number was last assigned to a public pay phone that was in the lobby of Buist Rivers dorm. It's not there anymore, and the number hasn't been reassigned."

"A pay phone? But you can't send a text from a pay phone."

"Nor can you send a text from a phone that's not there anymore," Thomas added.

"That's the dorm Adrienne lived in and where her body was found," I clarified for Jack's benefit.

"Was her roommate ever a suspect?" Jack asked.

"No." Thomas took a sip of his wine. "She was at her parents' house in Atlanta for the weekend. Her alibi is solid. She lives in Summerville now, so I took a little drive to interview her. Just to see if there might be anything she hadn't thought important before and didn't mention."

"And?" Jayne managed the one-syllable word perfectly.

"She confirmed again that Adrienne hadn't been fighting with her boyfriend. That she had lots of friends and no known enemies. But she did bring up something that wasn't in the police reports from the time of the murder."

The three of us leaned forward in unison.

"She might not have been fighting with her boyfriend, but the roommate seems to remember Adrienne arguing on the phone a few times the week of her death."

"With whom?" Jack asked, his hands flat on the table.

I stared at his left hand. He wasn't wearing the gold wedding band I'd placed on his finger on our wedding day. I wasn't sure if this was new or if he hadn't been wearing it for months and I had simply refused to notice. It wouldn't be the first time I had been deliberately oblivious. I took a long sip from my wineglass, hoping it would help soothe the hurt that had begun to radiate throughout my body.

"Her sister," Thomas said, his voice dragging me back to the conversation.

"Veronica?" Jayne asked, having mastered the one-word question.

Thomas nodded. "Yes. Lynda—the roommate—said that it seemed

that Adrienne needed to tell Veronica something important, but she didn't want to tell her over the phone. Each conversation was the same, with Adrienne telling Veronica she needed to see her to tell her in person and Veronica saying if she couldn't tell her over the phone, then it would have to wait until the weekend because Veronica was on a work deadline and she couldn't get away to meet with her."

Jack tapped his fingers on the table, something he always did while thinking, except now that I'd noticed the absence of his wedding ring, it seemed to me he was stretching his fingers to see how it felt for the third finger to be bare. "Did they ever get to meet?" he asked.

Thomas shook his head. "No. Adrienne was killed that Friday. Veronica never saw her alive again."

Something Veronica had said flashed through my brain. *I can't let her down again.* I took a large bite of fish and chewed slowly so I could think. Veronica was my friend, and I wasn't willing to give up any confidences before I'd had a chance to speak with her first.

"That's awful." Jayne put her fork down on her plate and sat back, pressing both hands against her heart. Now that she was focused on a subject of discussion instead of Thomas, she was able to speak normally. "No wonder she's so desperate to find out who killed Adrienne. She probably feels responsible."

I took another gulp of my wine as Jack continued his bare-finger drumming on the table. It took all of my self-control not to smack his fingers down with my hand.

After we'd finished and the dishes were cleared, Jack asked, "Anything new on the yearbook and CD player?"

"Oh, yes," Thomas said, watching as our waiter placed my peanut butter bar in front of me.

No one else had ordered dessert. I held my knife and fork for everyone to see so that they'd take Jack's earlier warning seriously.

Thomas continued. "That's why I wanted to meet in person instead of doing this over the phone. I hoped Veronica would be here. She didn't answer her cell phone, and when I called the house phone, Michael answered. I gave him the message that I had new information and to have Veronica call me. But she didn't."

I hesitated a moment before putting the first bite of dessert into my mouth so I could answer. "She's having a date night with Michael, so that must be why."

He nodded. "Must be. I'll try again tomorrow. I also need to ask her about Adrienne's involvement with the sailing team. Her name isn't on the roster, but I'm pretty sure she's pictured with the team in the yearbook. If she was a part of the team, that could be a whole new source of people I should talk to. Assuming it's her, that is. It doesn't appear that any team members were interviewed after the murder."

"Well, that's certainly something new to go on," Jack said while glancing at my dessert plate. I moved it an inch closer to me.

Thomas continued. "We also found a new fingerprint on the CD player. I had the whole thing redusted, although with all of the new handling, I had doubts that we'd find anything useful. But I figured if we were going to reopen this case, we didn't want to leave any stone unturned."

"And?" Jayne asked.

Thomas looked at her and grinned. "And I was right. There is a single and very clear thumbprint on the inside of the lid. Not where a person would usually touch, which is probably why it was overlooked. I compared it to all of the other fingerprints discovered on the first go-round and it's definitely a new one. I'm having it run through AFIS now to see if it shows up. If the person has ever been fingerprinted, we should get a hit."

Jack stopped his drumming so he could pick up his cup of decaffeinated coffee—his version of dessert. "Do you remember whose fingerprints were identified originally?"

Thomas nodded. "Yep—Adrienne, of course; her roommate, Lynda, who liked to borrow the Discman; and also Adrienne's boyfriend, Chris Kelly. He would sometimes hang out in their room, listening to music while Adrienne was in class. As I said, Lynda had a solid alibi, and so did Chris."

I watched as Jayne took a deep, calming breath. "What about the CD—the one with 'O Superman' on it? Did you find it?"

"It's on the inventory list, but it hasn't been located. It could have been misplaced. Or it could have been taken."

"Or it was intentionally destroyed as an act of mercy," I said.

"I've never heard of it," Jack said as he lowered his cup to the saucer.

"Consider yourself lucky."

I looked up in surprise at Michael, who stood behind my chair. Jack stood and extended his hand. "Michael—good to see you. Is Veronica with you?"

"She had to go powder her nose. It's our anniversary, so we're painting the town. We just had drinks at the Ordinary, and now we're ready for dinner." He looked pointedly at Thomas and then at the remains of our dinner. "Was this business or pleasure?"

"Oh, a little of both," Jack said vaguely. "We'd invite you to join us, but we're just finishing up."

"That's a shame." Michael turned his attention to me. "I need to talk with Melanie. About coming up with a timeline for listing our house. It's like the renovations will never end."

I slid back my chair, stood, and placed my napkin on the seat. "Just call Jolly at my office and we'll set up a meeting. I have all my sales data there. I believe I have some openings at the end of the week. Now, if you'll please excuse me."

"Me, too," Jayne said as she pushed back her chair.

Jack remained standing and Thomas stood as we left the table to find the ladies' room. As we walked, Jayne nudged me with her elbow. "Are you thinking the same thing I am?"

"If you're thinking this is the perfect opportunity to get Veronica alone, then yes."

We found Veronica applying lipstick at the sink, our eyes meeting in the mirror. Smiling, she turned around. "This is a nice surprise," she said, putting her lipstick in her clutch and snapping it shut.

"It is," I agreed. "We were just finishing our meal and Michael came over to say hello. He wants to set up an appointment with me to discuss speeding up the selling process. I promise to come up with a few road-blocks I can mention at the meeting, but I want you to come up with a few issues, too. I think we've found a couple more clues to move us forward on the investigation into Adrienne's death, but we need more time."

Veronica's eyes widened with interest. "What have you found out?"

"It was actually Thomas," Jayne said, comfortable with her words now, although her cheeks pinkened when she said Thomas's name. "He found a new fingerprint on the inside of the lid of the Discman, so that's hopeful. He also thinks he spotted her in a photo with the sailing team, but she wasn't on the team list printed beneath the photo."

Veronica was silent for a moment. "I'd almost forgotten. Adrienne wasn't on the team. But she had a lot of good friends who were—it was coed, so both boys and girls. She loved to sail and would drag Mom and Dad and me to every regatta to watch, but she wasn't a sailor. Our family never had that kind of money. Instead she sort of became the unofficial team manager."

A toilet flushed and a woman came out of one of the stalls. We waited for her to wash her hands and leave before we continued.

"You need to let Thomas know," I said. "He couldn't find any interviews with any of the sailing team members in Adrienne's file. There could be new information there."

Veronica nodded, her face brightening with hope. "I'll call him tomorrow. I can't talk with him tonight. . . ."

Jayne held up her hand. "We know. That's fine."

"Thank you." Veronica tucked her clutch under her arm, preparing to leave.

"One more thing," I said. "When we were at Adrienne's dorm, you said something to me that I've been meaning to ask you about."

She closed her eyes for a quick breath, then met my gaze directly. "I said I didn't want to let her down again."

I nodded. "What did you mean?"

After a brief pause, she said, "In the days leading up to her death, she called me several times, asking me to meet her because she had something important to tell me."

"And you didn't go because you had a work deadline," Jayne offered softly.

At Veronica's startled look, I said, "Thomas told us. He interviewed Adrienne's roommate, Lynda."

Veronica nodded. "She said she had something important to tell me, but that it needed to be face-to-face."

"And you have no idea what that was about?" I asked.

Veronica shook her head. "None whatsoever. She was always a little prone to drama, so I didn't think it was as urgent as she made it out to be."

"It's not your fault," Jayne said calmly, putting her arm around Veronica. "You had no idea. The only fault is with the person who killed her. Not hers, and not yours. We're here to make sure we find the person responsible and make sure whoever it is faces justice."

I looked at my sister with a new appreciation. I was good with the spreadsheets and the logical progression of a puzzle, but Jayne's first instincts were all about the personal repercussions. It wasn't that I didn't understand the emotional aspects of losing a loved one; it was just that I hadn't been raised with open emotions or the ability to express them. I'd simply had to take a crash course in the last few years since Jack, Nola, and my parents had joined my life. I was still suffering from the whiplash of being shoved from my isolated life to navigating the current one of family and other people's emotional wants and needs.

I cleared my throat. "I want to go back to your attic and ask Adrienne questions. When is a good day when you know Michael won't be there?"

"I'll let you know. Maybe we can do it after our meeting? Michael will be eager to return to the office. He hates being pulled away in the middle of his workday."

"Sounds good—just call me."

Jayne hugged Veronica. "You go on and enjoy your dinner, all right? And happy anniversary."

Veronica smiled and said her good-byes. I was about to suggest to Jayne that we might as well use the facilities while we were there when the lock was unlatched on one of the stalls, and the door opened.

"Melanie—what a nice surprise!" Suzy Dorf said pertly as she approached the sink and began washing her hands the way a surgeon would, scrubbing between her fingers and around the tops. It fit her personality, which suited her journalist profession: thorough, detailed, and intrusive. I found it as impressive as I found it annoying. Especially when her tunnel vision was trained on me.

"Suzy, how nice to see you." I grabbed Jayne's elbow. "Would love to stay and chat, but we were both leaving . . ."

Suzy faced me as she dried her hands. "Did you not get my texts? I've sent about a dozen in the last week."

"Did you? I've been so busy, it's possible I might have missed—"

"You owe me an interview, remember? You promised—before all that business with the Gallen Hall cemetery. That's old news now, so instead I'm asking for an exclusive regarding the new treasure hunt that's buzzing around the Internet right now."

"An exclusive . . . ?"

"Interview. The one we're going to schedule right now while we both have our phones so that there're no missed texts."

"I don't . . ." I stopped. Recalled the moment I stood in the back garden and felt Louisa's presence. Felt her subtle reminder of the priority of family. Remembered Jack going off to think on his own and my conviction that Jack and I worked great together. Even if that meant that we sometimes had to work separately, because we had always shared the same end goal.

I met Suzy's gaze. "Okay."

"Okay?" She didn't bother to hide her surprise.

"Yes. As long as it's anonymous." I held up my hand, anticipating her objection. "I'll let you use my name eventually—but right now I need your help in eradicating an infestation of unwanted pests currently invading my house. And having a little fun tormenting a particular director."

Suzy smiled and I remembered that she had reason to intensely dislike Marc, too. But then her lips pursed. "As appealing as that sounds, I don't really think that I can print just anything—"

"But you already have. Let's see. . . ." I closed my eyes, then quoted verbatim from the article she'd printed in the *Post and Courier* that I'd read so many times I'd memorized it. "'. . . the cistern excavation at the former Vanderhorst residence on Tradd Street is still in progress, but an unnamed source has told me that there are more secrets hidden there, and there are bets going on in certain parts of our society on whether the owners of the house will be residing together in the house by the time the last treasure is revealed.'"

I smiled. "And anybody who reads your column knows that you're not averse to using anonymous sources—as long as it sells papers."

Suzy reached into her purse and pulled out her phone. "I'm free on Monday morning. Shall I meet you at your office?"

"No. How about Washington Square? I really don't want my husband or anyone else seeing us together. The park is usually deserted at eight o'clock." I pulled out my phone from my tiny purse and frowned. "Actually, I also need my desk calendar. Could you please e-mail and text the details to me? And call the receptionist at my office, Jolly, too, just in case. That's the best way."

Suzy tapped the information into her phone. "All righty, then. I'll look forward to it. I hope I'm not being premature when I say it's about time."

We said our good-byes, and she left the bathroom looking very pleased with herself.

"What was that about?" Jayne asked.

I put my hand on the door handle and pulled it open. "Come on—we need to get back before the men think we've fallen in."

Jayne followed me out into the restaurant. "Melanie." Her voice held a warning note. "Are you sure you know what you're doing?"

"Don't I always?"

"Do you really want me to answer that?"

I sailed past the other tables toward ours, pretending I hadn't heard her. The men stood as we approached and we left the restaurant as a group. When Thomas suggested he drop Jayne off at her house to save us a trip, I immediately said it was a great idea and shut down all of Jayne's arguments.

Yet even as Jack drove us home, I imagined I could feel my sister's gaze boring into the back of my head. Or maybe that was the old and new versions of Melanie playing tug-of-war with my conscience.

CHAPTER 15

The following Monday, I sat cross-legged on the floor of my closet, the blue light of my laptop screen illuminating the hems of the dresses hanging above it. It was nearly four o'clock in the morning, and I'd been awake for almost two hours. Naturally, that meant I should reorganize my shoes and redo the inventory worksheet by season. I also had a couple of new additions that I'd found still in their Shoes on King shopping bag that I had hidden from Jack, forgetting that he hadn't been in our closet since he'd packed up his clothes in December.

I stretched my hands over my head, my joints snapping and crackling like a bowl of Rice Krispies, and recalled which thoughts had been keeping me awake. Most of them had been centered around my upcoming chat with Suzy and how I wasn't planning on telling Jack about it. Regardless of what Jayne thought, I did know what I was doing. I was solving a problem to benefit our family by doing what I knew how to do best without distracting Jack from doing what he did best. I accepted that he wouldn't like it. I'd simply realized that I had no other options.

My wee hours' woolgathering had also lingered on the absence of Jack's wedding ring. I'd considered that what I was attempting to do was a way to get back at him, to show him that I, too, could be independent, able to use my own resources. A lingering thought reminded me that that might have been the root of the problems we were experiencing now, but I brushed that aside to look at later. Because no matter how I tried to examine the situation, I saw the answer to all of our problems as putting Jack's career back on track. Discrediting Marc Longo was simply a bonus. Whether we worked together or separately, we would pursue the same goal as a team.

Still wide-awake, I flipped over to my Melanie Improvement spreadsheet, startled to realize I hadn't added anything since **Be Nice to Rebecca (Plan Baby Shower)**. I'd forgotten all about the baby shower, and Rebecca hadn't called me, so my hope was she'd realized that with the filming I already had too much going on. I almost laughed out loud.

I closed out the worksheet, prepared to close the lid of my computer and try to sleep. I paused with my hand on the lid. The beautiful faces of my children and Jack stared out at me from the computer's desktop wallpaper, a reminder of everything we had lost. Or maybe we had just misplaced it. Everyone wore mismatched outfits, and the dogs were naked despite all of my efforts to coordinate our Christmas card photo, but everyone looked so happy. Tears stung the backs of my eyes as I remembered that day and wished I could go back. Not, I realized with surprise, to do things differently. I simply wished we could all be happy and together again.

Accepting that sleep was no longer a possibility, I hit the Google icon. I took a deep breath and began typing, eager to distract myself with a search for the anonymous blogger and online presence known as Blackbeard. I remembered to filter out terms like "Pirate" and "Edward Teach" and prepared myself for several hours of chasing down links, but was surprised by the short list of results. Either Blackbeard was new to the treasure-hunting forums, or the identity was newly created.

There was nothing nefarious about having different identities online. Yvonne Craig had been the one to suggest using another name to protect my privacy when I'd first begun researching the history of my house. Only she, Jack, and Nola knew that DonutGirl was really ace Realtor Melanie Middleton. Yvonne was Batgirl, although she'd never explained why and I was a little afraid to ask.

Every Google hit was from a treasure-hunting forum, blog, or You-Tube channel. All of the flagged comments were listed under stories about the Hope Diamond and the supposed existence and whereabouts of the other half of it. I gritted my teeth at the mention of Jack and me and our house in relation to the Confederate diamonds as well as links to buy Marc's book online. Mr. (or Ms.—it was impossible to know) Blackbeard asked intelligent questions and seemed genuinely interested in the history of the diamonds and even hypothesized about the credibility of the rumors surrounding the Sultan of Brunei.

My phone binged with a text from Yvonne. U up?

I almost laughed, imagining the elegant older lady texting in slang. We had first bonded over our mutual admiration of Jack Trenholm, but had recently discovered that we were both early risers. Or, in my case, late to bed due to stress-induced insomnia.

Yes.

Three dots appeared as she typed and I turned my attention back to my laptop while I waited. The phone binged again, but this time when I looked, dread seeped through me. It was the anonymous number from before, the number assigned to a nonexistent pay phone in the lobby of the College of Charleston residence hall where Adrienne had once lived. And died.

I hesitated, my thumb hovering over the screen, my mouth dry. I wanted to erase the message without reading. Pretend I hadn't seen it. But that was something the old Melanie would have done. The old Melanie I wished I could still be at times. Like now. Before I could talk myself out of it, I opened the text to read.

IT HURTS IT HURTS IT HURTS

I stared at the screen. Texting with a ghost was a first for me, and while I was wondering if I should text back, another message appeared in a green bubble.

SHE DESERVED IT

With a shaking finger, I tapped each letter slowly. WHO?

My phone rang in my hand and I jumped, sending my phone skidding across the wood floor. General Lee gave a sleepy *woof* of complaint from the bed as I grappled for the phone to look at the screen. To my relief I saw it was Yvonne calling and slid my thumb to answer it.

"Hello?"

"Melanie, are you all right? You sound out of breath."

"Fine," I lied, my whole body vibrating with the heavy thumping of my heart. "I dropped my phone and had to find it—sorry."

"No worries. I just had some information for you and I figured it was easier to call than to text. I know how you dislike reading on your phone. You really should try and enlarge the text size."

"I have," I muttered, unwilling to share that Nola had compared my text size to that used on Jumbotrons.

"Yes, well . . . Is Jack awake? You could put him on speaker and I can tell you both what I've found. It's about that grave we were talking about."

"He, uh, he's sound asleep and I don't want to wake him. Go ahead and tell me and I'll fill him in when he awakens."

"Or I could call back later."

"No. Please. I couldn't stand the suspense and I'd never get to sleep."

She laughed. "Do you know if Jack has had a chance to study the Vanderhorst family tree yet?"

"Yes. He had time for only a cursory glance, but he didn't find any Vanderhorsts—male or female—who died in 1861 or 1886 with the first initial of their name an E except for Emily, and we already discounted her. He said he'd dig a little deeper when he has the chance later tomorrow. His files are stored . . . off-site. Because of the filming going on around here, he wanted to keep them in a safe place."

"Ah, very smart. I don't trust that Marc Longo. He called and left a message at the reference desk here asking for an appointment. I told the other reference librarian that I would handle it." I imagined I could see her impish grin.

When she didn't say anything, I realized she was waiting for me to go first. "So, Yvonne, did you find anything?"

"Oh, yes!"

I pictured Yvonne with her breath held, waiting for me to prompt her, and for a moment I considered telling her I'd changed my mind and decided that I could wait. Instead, I said, "Since it's four in the morning and we're both on the phone, you might as well tell me what you found, don't you think?"

I heard a slow exhalation of breath. "All right, then. Do you recall the name Captain John Vanderhorst?"

My fingers tapped impatiently on my drawn-up knees. "Yes. He was the man responsible for hiding the diamonds in the grandfather clock. He was killed in battle in 1863."

"Very good!" I pictured her clapping her hands at my stellar recall. "I found a picture of a painting of him wearing his cavalry captain's uniform—he was quite the handsome man. The painting belongs to the Charleston Museum, but it is no longer on display. You and Jack might want to try to acquire it since I believe it belongs in the house. . . ."

"I'll put it on my to-do list. What else did you discover?"

"Well, since I couldn't find any Vanderhorsts who fit our parameters, I spread my search a bit and began looking for the names of nonfamily people associated with the property around the time of the fire and the earthquake."

When she didn't say anything, I prompted, "And did you find anything?" Someone really needed to talk with Yvonne about her need for drama when relaying information.

"I did! During the time of the great fire in 1861, the Vanderhorsts had a cook. Well, they had other servants, too, but I thought because of the headstone's proximity to the kitchen house, this would be the best place to start. . . ."

"And did her name begin with E?" I interrupted.

"No, it didn't. Her name was Lucille. Her parents were enslaved and Lucille's mother was the cook at the Vanderhorsts' Magnolia Ridge Plantation. In 1847 Lucille was brought from Magnolia to work as the cook in the Tradd Street house, and John Vanderhorst manumitted Lucille and her parents a year later. I can't find a birth date for Lucille, but from what I can gather with very sparse information, she would have been around eighteen or nineteen when she moved to Charleston."

I bit back my impatience. "So who was E?"

"I'm getting to that." She cleared her throat. "Lucille apparently had a husband at Magnolia."

"And his name started with an E?"

"No. It didn't. But when Lucille was brought to Charleston, her husband was left at Magnolia."

"That's terrible."

"Agreed. But that's not all." She didn't continue, and I imagined her holding her breath again, eyes sparkling as she tortured me, waiting for me to prompt her.

"And why is that, Yvonne?"

"Well, records for nonfamily members are scarce, but I did a little more digging into the Vanderhorst family archives, and you'll never believe what I found! I think I was very clever to think of—"

"Yvonne," I said, not caring if she could tell I was speaking through gritted teeth.

"Yes, sorry. It's just so exciting when I find that elusive morsel! So, I knew I wouldn't find anything in the genealogy records, so I did the next best thing and looked for the household records. It's always amazing what one can find in old grocery lists and haberdashery invoices—"

"And what did you find?" I asked, cutting her off, my patience long gone.

"Invoices for baby supplies. A carriage, a cradle, feeding bottles—that sort of thing."

"Well, that makes sense. John had a son, William."

"Very good, Melanie! But William wasn't born until 1860. These invoices dated from 1847—a good thirteen years earlier. Even more revealing is what I found on an invoice for a draper's shop on Market Street."

I sighed heavily into the phone, feeling too tired to guess. "And what was that, Yvonne?"

"Two yards of pink muslin and two strands of pale pink silk ribbon."

I thought of Rebecca. "So someone liked to wear pink."

"One would think—until you remember the styles of the period and how two yards of fabric wouldn't make a complete dress for an adult woman."

I sat up, flipping through the details in the filing drawer I called my brain. "So there was a baby girl born sometime in 1847?"

"Exactly! And not a Vanderhorst baby or she'd appear in the family tree. Not to mention how the family already owned an heirloom cradle and wouldn't need a new one. Plus the items weren't purchased at the most fashionable shops, nor were they of the best quality."

"So Lucille may have been pregnant when she left her husband at Magnolia and came to work as the cook at Tradd Street?"

"Yes!" Yvonne shouted in triumph.

"And she had a baby girl with a name beginning with the letter E!"

"I was wondering when you were going to get there," Yvonne said with reproach. "Guess how I found out the name."

"Can you just tell me the name and save the story for later?"

Ignoring me, she said, "There was a small invoice that I almost missed—from a haberdashery shop. It was for an embroidered name to be put on a pink muslin blanket. Apparently, the person ordering the embroidery must not have been of the class of young women who were taught how to embroider practically from the cradle."

I stretched my legs out in the closet and tilted my head back so that I could stare at the ceiling. "Fascinating," I said, my voice flat. "So what was the baby's name?"

After a dramatic pause, Yvonne said, "Evangeline. Which, coincidentally or not, is the name of the famous Longfellow poem published the same year."

I frowned, flipping through my brain file again. "Doesn't sound like the sort of name an uneducated enslaved person would be familiar with to name her daughter."

"No, it doesn't. Sadly, that's the last I could find of her. I'll keep looking, though. But if that was her original grave site, then your guess that she died in the fire of 1861 instead of during the earthquake of 1886 would mean she would have been a young woman of around fourteen when she died."

"The right age for someone who would have a charm string," I said.

I startled at the sound of a door opening in the outside hallway. Whispering into my phone, I said, "Yvonne—I have to go. I need to check on the children."

"Yes, dear. You give those sweet babies a kiss for me. And Jack, too."

I pressed END, then stood, hearing my knees crack, and waited for the rest of my body to adjust to being forced to stand. General Lee snored gently on his back in the middle of the bed, his paws in the air in surrender. After glancing at the children on the monitor, sleeping peacefully in their cribs, I tiptoed toward my bedroom door and pressed my ear against the cool wood surface. Holding my breath, I listened.

It took me a moment to identify that I was hearing the slap of bare feet running down the hallway, accompanied by the slower gait of another person—another person with the tap of heels and the clang of jewelry. The hair rose on the back of my neck, but I wasn't afraid. Slowly, I opened my bedroom door and peered out into the night-light-lit hallway.

I smelled roses, pungent enough that if I closed my eyes, I could have imagined I was standing in the rose garden in May. I stepped into the hallway, feeling the now-familiar sensation of my bare feet pressing against a loose button. I stooped to pick it up, pausing as I looked down the hallway at the night-light's reflection on a dozen more buttons lined up in a row like stepping-stones.

Being careful to avoid treading on them, I followed them down the hallway to where they stopped, directly in front of Nola's open bedroom door. My chest tightened as I peered inside. The bed was empty, her covers pulled to the floor. I knelt to peer beneath the bed, alarmed to see that Porgy and Bess were gone, too.

Turning back to the doorway, I caught a glimpse of an unusual object on the nightstand, a black and ominous shadow in the shape of a small coffin. I gave an involuntary shudder as I moved past it, quickly crossing the hallway and then shivering in the chill of the old house as I descended the stairs.

The telltale jingle of collars from the front parlor guided me in that direction. I stopped abruptly, nearly colliding with a hard and naked chest that smelled like Jack. He placed his hands on my shoulders and gently turned me toward the clock.

In the glow of the pale predawn light through the windows, I spotted Porgy and Bess first. They were rolling around on the floor in their usual puppy play, but there was something different about it. Something odd. I squinted in the dim light, eventually realizing that there were three dogs. I recalled leaving General Lee snoring on my bed upstairs, so I squinted harder, trying to determine where the interloper had come from. I hoped against hope that it wasn't Rebecca's dog, Pucci, knowing that would mean Rebecca couldn't be far away.

Goose bumps rippled my skin. I stepped closer to Jack for his body warmth, then followed his gaze toward Nola. She stood in front of the clock, her hands on her hips, her head tilted as if in question.

"Nola?" Jack said softly. "Is everything all right?"

A puff of condensation rose from his mouth when he spoke, confirming that we were definitely not alone. The hairs on the back of my neck stood at attention, my eyes failing to find anything lurking in the dark corners.

"She brought me here," Nola whispered back.

"'She'?" Jack asked.

"The girl. The one with the melted face. She came back."

I shivered, then gave a casual glance behind us. "I can't see her."

Nola shook her head without turning around. "Her mama said not to let anyone see her face."

I shared a quick look with Jack. "Because of her burns?"

Nola shrugged. "She didn't say. She brought her dog this time."

Porgy and Bess bounded in front of us, only the muted outline of a tail of the third dog still visible.

"His name is Otis."

Jack and I stepped forward to stand on either side of Nola. "You can hear her?" I whispered.

Nola nodded. "Well, sort of. It's like . . . talking in a dream. You don't see the lips move or anything, but you hear the words inside your head, you know?"

"Yes, I do," I said. "She must be a very strong spirit to be able to communicate with you. Most people who aren't . . . sensitive . . . usually can't hear them, which is why there are so many ghost sightings but rarely stories of the ghosts actually speaking."

"Beau uses EVP recorders with his investigations. Maybe I should ask him."

"No," Jack and I said simultaneously.

"Do you even know what an EVP recorder is?" I asked him.

"No. But I don't think Nola needs to be asking Beau about it. He rides a motorcycle. She doesn't need to be asking Beau about anything."

"Didn't you have a motorcycle in your distant youth?"

"Yep."

I let that pass for now, saving it for a longer conversation later. "'EVP' means 'electronic voice phenomenon.' For ghost hunters who need help communicating with spirits. Basically, for amateurs." I returned my attention to Nola. "Did she tell you what her name is?"

Nola shook her head. "No. She just said that she doesn't like the bad man." She let out a heavy sigh, finally turning to face us. "Why do you think she brought me down here?"

I opened the glass door covering the clockface as if I could find the answer there. It looked the same as it had the first day I'd seen it, when visiting Nevin Vanderhorst. "I don't know. We recovered all of the diamonds. Believe me—we went through every part of this clock, so we'd know if we'd missed anything. It's just a clock now."

"Hmm." Nola frowned. "Remember how the first time I saw the girl I said that I thought she was trying to warn me? I've just been staring at the clock, trying to figure it out. She left as soon as Dad entered the room."

"Sorry," Jack said. "Maybe she'll give us another chance. Right now why don't you take the dogs back upstairs and try to get a little more sleep? Tomorrow's a school day. Or should I say today is a school day?"

Nola answered with a wide yawn. "Sure. But if you see her, please tell her to stop putting the Frozen Charlotte in my room. It's creepy."

We watched as she picked up the two small dogs and left the room; then Jack and I listened to her tread up the creaking stairs.

"I wonder what that was all about," I said, turning to look at Jack.

He had an odd expression on his face.

"Is something wrong?"

"No. It's just . . ." He brushed his hands over his cheeks, the raspy sound of his palms against his unshaven beard like a haunting memory.

"It's just what?"

"I'd forgotten what you look like first thing in the morning. With your hair like that. And your face . . ."

I didn't move as he lifted his hand and stroked the side of my face. "I've missed it," he said.

"Me, too."

He dropped his hand and we stared at each other in the growing light, listening to the incessant ticking of the clock, daring each other to make the first move.

"I've missed everything about you, Jack." Before I could stop myself, I leaned forward to kiss him, but at the last moment, I turned my head and pressed my lips against his cheek instead. I was playing with fire—the fire that always smoldered between us, waiting for ignition. A fire I had to keep banked for now. I pulled away and ran from the room, running up the steps as fast as I could so I wouldn't change my mind.

"Was that almost kiss number five?" he called out softly.

I paused halfway up. "If it wasn't on the lips, then it doesn't count."

I ran the rest of the way up the stairs and into my bedroom, closed the door behind me, then leaned against it to catch my breath. I heard the grandfather clock chime the half hour as my gaze traveled to the bed. My breath sat suspended in the middle of an inhale at the sight of the neat little pile of buttons on my pillow, right next to the Frozen Charlotte sleeping inside her tiny iron coffin.

CHAPTER 16

I stood in front of the coffee machine in the kitchen, my bleary eyes staring it down to make it go faster, my fingers tapping impatiently on the counter. I hadn't been able to go back to sleep the previous night, my toes continually bumping into loose buttons at the foot of the bed. Several times I'd gone to the door, wanting to go to Jack to talk to him about what the buttons might mean and who the "bad man" could be. My mind immediately jumped to Marc or Harvey, but we already knew they were bad. I just worried that we were missing something.

I told myself I just wanted to talk with Jack, discuss why the girl was trying to warn Nola and about what. Yet I never turned the doorknob, knowing that I had ulterior motives for going to Jack's room in the middle of the night. *I'd forgotten what you look like first thing in the morning. . . . I've missed it.* The expression in his eyes as he'd said that was the primary reason I'd been unable to succumb to sleep.

Exhausted but still unable to sleep, I'd showered and dressed, then written Jack a long e-mail explaining everything I'd discussed with Yvonne and, not wanting to wake him with a bing on his phone, scheduled it for a delayed send so that he wouldn't receive it until my meeting with Suzy Dorf was over. He usually stayed up late to work and, like JJ, he was a grouch if awakened too early.

Squinting at the tiny numbers of the clock on the coffee machine, I gave up and looked at my phone. I had exactly thirty minutes to get out of the house before the film crew and actors arrived. For the first couple of days after the filming started, I'd waited to go into work so I could see them in action. Despite everything, I was a little in awe that a piece of Hollywood was in my parlor. I didn't recognize the ridiculously young actors portraying Jack and me—although Nola did and was trying very hard not to appear starstruck—which took away some of the excitement. By the second day of watching Marc's overblown self-importance and smirk every time he caught Jack or me looking in his direction, I'd had enough. Although Jack said he could handle staying in the house to work and to keep an eye on Marc, I avoided the house as much as I could while the crew was there. There were a few night scenes to be filmed, already negotiated by the lawyers and on our calendars, and I was still deciding if I'd remain and stew in my room while they filmed, or decamp with the children to my parents' house.

At the sound of tapping on the back door, I jerked, knocking my hand into my ceramic mug and sending it sliding toward the edge of the counter. I closed my eyes, waiting for the crash, not wanting to witness the death of my favorite mug. It had been a gift for my first Mother's Day from Jack and had the tiny handprints of JJ and Sarah in blue and pink, respectively, glazed onto the sides. When nothing happened, I opened my eyes again. The mug sat suspended precariously on the counter's edge like an Olympic diver.

I snatched it up. "Come in," I called out while I filled the mug with coffee and a healthy pour of cream as my mother entered the kitchen.

"Good morning, Mellie," she said as she hugged me, then kissed each cheek. Pulling back, she examined me more closely. "You look tired." She raised a suggestive eyebrow.

"No, Mother. That's not why."

She unwound her silk Hermès scarf from her neck and unbuttoned her coat. "You can't blame a mother for wanting her daughter to be happy. And you and Jack make each other happy. Most of the time."

"Well, someone needs to tell that to Jack." I frowned. "What are you doing here?"

"Jayne has a dentist appointment this morning, so I'm going to watch the children. Jack said he would, but I know he's deep into the research phase for his next book and Jayne and I didn't want to break his momentum. And it's not like I don't look for every opportunity to see the little munchkins."

"Jack's busy researching?"

"Amelia told me," she explained. "I assumed you knew."

I shook my head. "He said he's not ready to discuss the new book project with me yet."

"I'm sorry. That must have hurt your feelings." She narrowed her eyes. "So why aren't you acting hurt?"

"I'm not?"

The word "munchkins" reminded me that I hadn't had breakfast yet. Eager for a distraction, I placed my mug on the table, then opened the pantry door and pulled out a box of instant grits—an item guaranteed to sit on a shelf unopened in perpetuity. No self-identified Southerner would ever desecrate grits by getting them from a box. Reaching into the box, I pulled out a grease-stained bag from Glazed Gourmet Donuts, closing my eyes as I sniffed the doughy and sugary greatness contained inside. I replaced the empty box in the pantry and closed the door.

"No. What are you up to, Mellie?"

I kept myself busy getting two plates from the cabinet. Manners dictated that I offer one to my mother even though I knew she'd say no.

But instead she hung her coat on the back of a kitchen chair, sat down, then primly folded her hands on top of the table. "Thank you, Mellie."

I stifled a small stab of resentment at sharing my doughnuts as I placed all of them—except for the chocolate caramel cheesecake one, which I kept in the bag—on a serving plate, which I placed in the middle of the table. "Would you like me to make you some tea?" I asked.

As if she could see my legs shaking in anticipation, she shook her head. "Just water, dear. From the tap is fine."

I managed to sit down and offer Mother the tongs first, and lamented only the loss of a plain glazed doughnut as she put it on her plate. I placed a choco-nana nut doughnut on my plate before putting a forkful into my mouth. I chewed slowly, my eyes on the clock as I gauged how much time I had before Nola would descend and catch me.

"Aren't these the best?" I asked after swallowing my bite with a mouthful of cream-filled coffee.

"You didn't answer my question, Mellie. Remember, despite missing out on a lot of years together, I'm still your mother."

My next bite stuck in my throat. I'd been a stepmother and mother for only a short time, yet I always seemed to feel the pull of a gossamer thread that connected me to my three children—a connection that went from my heart to theirs. Always joyous and sometimes painful, it was certainly more accurate and more attuned than any other sixth sense.

"I'm sure I don't know—"

"Mellie," she said with the same tone of voice I used on JJ when he tried to ride General Lee like a horse.

I put my fork down. "Louisa helped me have a bit of an epiphany in the garden the other night." I took a deep breath, waiting for her to interrupt. Preparing my defense. When she didn't interrupt, I pressed on. "Jack's strength is figuring out puzzles and writing about them. My strength is being able to talk to dead people. There's no reason why we can't work together—but separately—to solve our problems. Even Jack would agree that we're a pretty formidable team when we both use our assets to figure things out."

I waited for my mother to speak, my appetite for doughnuts miraculously evaporating. Momentarily, anyway.

"Good for you, Mellie."

I'd already opened my mouth to defend myself but ended up stuttering something unintelligible instead. After several tries, I managed, "What?"

"The meek and groveling Mellie isn't the real you. She's an impostor whose existence was necessary for a while as you grappled with what happened and tried to figure out how to deal with the fallout."

I stared at her. Then blinked. Twice. "Who are you and what have you done to my mother?"

She reached across the table and placed her hand on mine. "I owe you an apology. We all do. Just because you approach problems differently from the way we might doesn't make you wrong. Certainly, sometimes you act before you think, but your motivation is never to cause harm. You love strongly and fiercely, and your independent streak should be admired."

I squeezed her hand. "Are you dying?"

She jerked back with surprise. "Hopefully not for a long time. Why would you ask?"

"Then why are you saying all this?"

"Because I miss the Mellie you are. My warrior daughter who has had to fight for everything in her life and managed to become a strong, determined, and successful woman, not to mention an incredible mother."

She sat back in her chair. "Most important, you have a forgiving heart. You forgave your father and me for the incredible pain we inflicted on you in your childhood and have even opened your life to include us and share your children with us." My mother regarded me. "Mellie, you weren't made to tiptoe through life. I'm glad you're working on a plan to see your way out of the situation you are in right now. I'd probably feel better if you talked it out with someone—and you know I'm always available—but I'm not going to tell you what to do. You're a smart woman. I trust you to do the right thing."

I warmed under her gaze. "And if Jack doesn't agree with my methods?"

"Then he's not half the man I've always thought him to be." She paused. "And not the type of husband you need—one who sees what he perceives as flaws but loves you anyway."

I smiled weakly. "Jack said that once. He may have called them quirks, but I think that's what he meant."

Mother squeezed my hand. "Well, then, that's a good sign."

A Valkyrie-like shriek sounded from upstairs, startling my mother. "What was that?"

"That's new. It's the sound JJ makes when he wakes up and finds Whisk on the floor. Sometimes Louisa puts it back in his crib, but she must have been busy doing something else."

"Then I'd better go reunite him with Whisk." She grinned. "I suppose I shouldn't be surprised that one of your children has a kitchen utensil as a comfort item."

"And another one who can see dead people," I added.

We both stood, and my mother wrapped me in a tight embrace. Despite her petite frame, she gave fierce bear hugs. They were some of the happier memories of my childhood. I closed my eyes, reveling in the sanctuary I'd rediscovered within my mother's arms. And feeling confident that what I'd decided to do was the right thing because it came with my mother's support and understanding.

"Mellie?"

"Um?"

"Can you just promise me one thing?"

I nodded, my eyes still closed.

"Whatever it is that you're planning, please think it through. And for heaven's sake, stay out of cemeteries."

The crisp morning air signaled another beautifully clear and moderate Charleston winter day. I decided to walk to Washington Square for my meeting with Suzy Dorf, the exercise my olive branch to Jayne for skipping our morning run. And in reparation for bringing a doughnut.

I walked through the wrought iron gates of the park that faced Broad Street, eager to find a bench and use the fifteen minutes before our meeting to eat my second doughnut and drink my coffee in peace. But as I strolled down the brick walkway in the direction of the miniature replica of the Washington Monument in the center of the park, my heart fell at the sight of the pert and perky form of Suzy Dorf sitting on a bench beneath one of the matronly oak trees. A heavy swath of Spanish moss hung from a thick branch directly over her head, temporarily blocking me from her view.

I changed my direction and ducked behind the pedestal holding the statue of George Washington while I tried to decide whether to eat my doughnut there or risk finding another bench.

"Melanie—I'm over here!" Her unmistakable voice was as perky as the rest of her, and I stifled a groan as I straightened.

Pretending surprise, I waved and made my way toward Suzy. "Good morning," I said. "I never have a chance to read the plaques on these statues. So interesting."

Her look made it clear I wasn't fooling anyone. "Good morning, Melanie." She tilted her head. "To be honest, I didn't think you'd come."

I sat down next to her, noticing how her toes barely brushed the ground. "Really? Why is that?"

With raised eyebrows, she said, "Are you really asking me that? Maybe the constant avoidance of my phone calls made me think you didn't want to talk to me. Even though you owe me an interview."

"I know, I know. And I'm sorry. It's just that with three kids, a house, a job—"

"Stop." She held up her hand. "I know. And with Marc Longo practically living in your house and directing the film. I keep waiting to get the call to write about the homicide."

"Really, Suzy. Marc's pretty awful and underhanded, but I can't imagine him committing murder."

"It's not him that I'm worried about."

I raised an eyebrow. "Yes, well, even after he's dead, there's no guarantee that he won't bother me anymore. Assuming I'm able to talk to the dead."

Suzy turned a hard gaze on me. "Right. Assuming."

I didn't blink. "So, what did you want to talk to me about?"

She let out a long, satisfied sigh. "You have no idea how long I've waited for this. As I've mentioned before, and assuming that you are a conduit to the dead, I'd like to interview you about your abilities, as well as witness you"—she made a vague gesture with her hand—"doing your thing with ghosts. My goal is to write a series for the paper or put it in a book. Or both. I've already started on the book—about fascinating Charleston residents past and present—and as I've already told you, I think you'd be a pivotal figure because you can be the bridge between them."

I was careful not to give her any indication that I'd heard what she'd said or agreed to any of it. I bit my bottom lip, carefully considering my words. "You once told me that you're not a fan of Marc Longo. That he bankrupted your brother in a sour business deal."

Her gaze didn't stray from my face. "Yes. That's all correct. It's why I've helped you several times, despite your unwillingness to return my phone calls. He did more than bankrupt Kenny. He destroyed him. Kenny spent two years in a psychiatric institution and is still trying to put his life back together."

"I'm sorry to hear that." I looked down at my crumpled doughnut bag. "My 'abilities,' as you call them, aren't something I've ever wanted to advertise or even make use of. But that could change. Marc has backed us into a corner and I'm willing to do anything to get him out of our lives."

Suzy raised her pixielike chin. "I think we could work together. We have a common goal. I could help you send Marc running with his tail between his legs, and then I get to 'out' you in my book. The pen is mightier than the sword, right? I could really mess with Marc with just a few well-placed columns." She tilted her head. "Except I'm assuming that you've made some sort of devil's deal with Marc to allow him to film in your house, so sending him running might be complicated. And with all the online chatter about there being a missing half of the Hope Diamond that might be connected to your cache, I can only imagine that's the main reason why Marc has insinuated himself into your house, to have a closer look."

I returned her gaze, recalling how she'd once told me that she'd seen Jack in a bar, apparently bargaining with his demons before ordering a ginger ale. Despite our somewhat cantankerous relationship, her warning had been offered with concern instead of the malicious gloating I would have expected. Nor had she publicized what could have been a humiliation that Jack couldn't have afforded. Her kindness had surprised me, had even altered my perception of her, and was the main reason why I'd finally agreed to meet with her.

"Possibly," I said, my reluctance to admit the full extent of our deal due more to embarrassment at our gullibility than uncertainty as to whether or not to trust her. "We made the mistake of believing that Marc had changed along with his hair, and he and Rebecca appealed to us because we're 'family'—distantly and only by marriage, thank God."

"So what happened?" she asked gently. When I didn't respond right away, she said, "My brother tried to kill himself after Marc was through with him. It's taken him nearly five years to get his life back on track. Believe me when I say that I will do everything in my power to bring Marc Longo down to his knees." She shrugged. "Besides, I like you. I like your family and the way you've made the Vanderhorst house a home even though I know you're not a fan of old houses. Maybe it's your sense of doing the right thing that I admire. I know Nevin Vanderhorst would approve."

"You knew him?"

She smiled softly and nodded. "I met him only once or twice, but we were sort of pen pals. He wrote to me years ago about an error in an article I'd written. He was right, of course, and the way he criticized me was so gentlemanly that I wrote back to thank him. We continued to exchange letters over the years, pretty much until the day he died. And I know how much he adored his house and how happy it would make him to see you and your family growing and thriving in it." Her lips thinned. "Just as much as he'd dislike Marc Longo darkening your doorstep." She tilted her head. "So, what happened?"

I took a deep breath. "Marc threw a wrench into Jack's career. Not just by stealing Jack's book idea, which resulted in Jack's publisher canceling his book. Marc—who apparently has connections everywhere—spread lies and rumors about Jack and those he'd worked with so that

Jack's supporters in the publishing world were all gone. Marc promised Jack he would fix things if we allowed the filming, even promised to make introductions to several top literary agents. He also agreed to split his gross fifty-fifty with us. More than anything else, I think the lure of finally earning money for his own story idea is what made Jack cave and agree. But despite our due diligence, I'm convinced that this is just another lie Marc has told us, and he just wants to get inside the house to find treasure he believes might still be hidden there. I have no doubt that when this is over with, he will find a way to somehow weasel out of his promises and leave us right where we were. Except it will be worse because we will have allowed the filming of a movie based on a book that Marc stole from Jack. Not only that, but we both signed a contract stating that whoever breaks the contract loses everything."

"Assuming you're caught." Suzy gave me an impish grin. "And what does Jack think?"

I studied my hands, opening my left one, where my wedding and engagement rings winked the sun's reflection, reminding me of Jack's bare ring finger. "I'm on my own here. It's . . . complicated with Jack and me right now. I just know that I can't sit back and wait for the train to crash without trying to stop it first."

I looked up at the sound of her clapping. "Brava, Melanie. Brava." She grinned impishly again. "I think we have a lot in common, and I expect we'll enjoy working together."

I returned her smile, then quickly sobered. "My only hesitation is from wondering if I'm wrong about Marc. What if he has every intention of following through on his promise and I inadvertently take this opportunity away from Jack?"

"What does your gut instinct tell you?"

"That a palmetto bug can't change its wings."

"What?"

"Sorry—that's Charlestonese for 'a leopard can't change its spots.' My own regional adaptation."

Suzy nodded slowly. "Okay. I happen to agree with you regarding Marc. Once a low-down dirty liar, always a low-down dirty liar. He's greedy and dishonest and I could see him selling his own child if it might benefit him."

I refrained from voicing my thought that if the child Rebecca was currently carrying had the opportunity to be raised by different parents, it might not be a bad thing. "It looks like our thoughts have been running parallel to each other. I've been thinking of a way to stop the filming and to get Marc right where it hurts—his wallet and his ego. It would involve using my . . . 'abilities.' It would also involve your journalistic skills and bringing back your series on buried treasures in the Holy City."

Suzy leaned forward. "You're right. We have been having parallel thoughts—which is a very good thing. I'm eager to hear more and even more excited to get started."

I met her gaze. "Me, too. But I'm hesitant about getting started because the outcome will be the same—Jack's career will be permanently stalled whether or not Marc gets his movie filmed. Marc will probably make me the scapegoat so that Jack blames me."

Suzy surprised me by laughing. "Don't worry about that, Melanie. Trust me on this. Marc Longo isn't the only one with important connections in the publishing world. And Jack has many fans, me included."

"Why haven't you mentioned this before?"

"Maybe it's because you never return my phone calls or texts."

I blushed. "I'm sorry. It's just that—"

She held up her hand to stop me. "Water under the bridge. Now," she said, pulling out a pad of lined paper and a pencil, "we have work to do."

CHAPTER 17

I pushed open the door to the Normandy Farm Artisan Bakery on Broad Street, enjoying my favorite mixed aromas of baking bread and coffee. I had been forced to find another purveyor of sugary confections and whipped-cream-smothered coffee near my office after the sudden and recent closure of Ruth's Bakery. Ruth's rent had tripled and her daughters had sweetened the incentive to retire by buying her a small house on the same street where they and Ruth's grandchildren lived. Catherine Jimenez had been both the listing and selling agent—of course—so I'd been left not only without Ruth's sweet smile and delicious coffee and pastries waiting for me each morning, but with the dire necessity of finding a nearby replacement.

I found a table in the middle of the small dining area and sat down with my large coffee and ham and Gruyère croissant. I'd considered taking it the few doors down to my office and eating it at my desk, but I didn't want Catherine to see me sitting down or eating because I'd never seen her do either.

I had just taken my first bite of croissant when I heard the sound of a chair being dragged across the floor. Then I felt a bump as it collided with the leg of my table, spilling my coffee. With my mouth full, I looked up in annoyance, surprised—although no less annoyed—to see Michael Farrell sliding into the chair now placed next to me.

"Good morning, Melanie. I was just about to come see you at your office, but saw you come in here. I hope you don't mind."

It was a good thing my mouth was full or I would have told him that I did mind very much. He took my silence as acquiescence and settled back in his chair. After swallowing a sip of coffee, I made a big show of checking my wristwatch and my phone and then my two calendars. "I thought our meeting was in half an hour." I didn't make it sound like a question, because when it came to schedules, I was never wrong.

"I know. Veronica will join us at your office then. I just wanted to speak with you privately. She gets very . . . emotional . . . when we talk about Adrienne and selling the house, so I wanted the chance to cut to the chase before our official meeting."

"Emotional? Adrienne was her sister, who was murdered by some person who has never been brought to justice. Someone who is still out there more than two decades after Veronica and her parents buried Adrienne. The house that you are so eager to get rid of is Veronica's last connection to her dead sister. I think it's perfectly logical that she is emotional."

His lips thinned, so at least he looked chagrined. "Of course. I get that. But her emotions are clouding her judgment. I mean, this whole delay in putting the house on the market so it can be updated. I'm at the point where I don't care anymore. I'm tired of the sound of saws and hammers. We need to finish this endless renovation now, send the workers home, and list the house at whatever price you think is reasonable. I'm beyond caring if we don't get top dollar. We just need to move on."

I checked my temper, knowing that Veronica and I still needed to buy more time. Forcing a smile, I said, "Really, Michael—they're almost done. Sophie says it's a month—tops. And with the condition the house will be in when we put it on the market, I doubt it will last more than a day before multiple offers pour in. I have no doubt we'll get more than asking. It's always a hot market for historic Charleston real estate, especially for those properties that have already been renovated." I gave him the reassuring grin I used for all of my publicity photos.

He was already shaking his head, but I moved in for the kill. "In the meantime, I've got an entire list of homes back at the office to show you and Veronica. It will take some time to find the perfect one, because you will want it to be your forever home, right? So let's use this time wisely, and my bet would be that if we start looking now, we'll have two closings in one day—one and done."

He thought for a moment. "Has she . . . said anything to you?"

"Who—you mean Adrienne?"

He nodded, looking embarrassed. "Yeah. That's what you do, right?"

I straightened my shoulders. "Actually, I'm well-known for being a Realtor with teeth. I make things happen for my clients. You just need to trust me and my process."

I began rolling my half-eaten croissant in my napkin, preparing to end this conversation and get back to the office, but he put his hand on my arm, stopping me.

"So have you?"

I didn't bother asking him what he meant. "No, I haven't." Which was true. Adrienne never spoke directly to me. She would appear and sometimes push me in the right direction, but she'd never spoken to me. Because I was convinced she was saving her strength for something I hadn't yet figured out.

He dropped his hand. "If Adrienne . . . does talk to you, would you let me know first? Veronica is very fragile right now, and I want to make sure that I'm the one to couch it in terms I know she can handle."

I narrowed my eyes. "What do you think Adrienne has to say that might upset Veronica?"

He shook his head, his expression contrite. "I have no idea. I just . . ." His eyes appeared to moisten, and I felt myself softening toward him. "I love my wife. She's been through so much. When Lindsey graduates and Veronica is left alone all day, I don't know what that might do to her mental health. That's why I want to make this move now. So that we can start our new lives while Lindsey is still living with us to help smooth the transition for Veronica."

"I understand, Michael. I . . ."

He reached across the table and took my hand. It felt awkward, but I thought it might be more awkward to snatch my hand back, so I left it there. "But do you really?" His eyes held an unexpected anguish, and I felt myself softening toward him a little more. "Considering what's going on in your own marriage, I'm not so sure."

I pulled my hand back, my sympathy evaporating. "My personal life has nothing to do with my ability to do my best for my clients. Like I said, I'm asking for only one more month—a month to finish all of the renovations and for me to help you find your next house."

He looked at me, considering. "And you're sure it should be only a month?"

"Positive," I said, hoping I was right, resisting the impulse to cross my fingers behind my back.

Michael seemed to relax, his shoulders slumping slightly as he leaned back in his chair. "I just want this to be over."

I nodded. "How well did you know Adrienne?"

He shrugged. "Not very. She was Veronica's little sister. They were close, only three years apart. She was just a kid, really. She was the maid of honor in our wedding, and I saw her at family events, but that was pretty much the extent of my relationship with her. I helped move her into her dorm freshman year, and then again during the Christmas break."

"She moved? Why—roommate issues?"

He shook his head. "Same roommate. They just wanted a larger room and one opened up."

I sat up. "Were there any other guys you remember helping out with that?"

He was silent for a moment, then nodded and said, "Yeah, a couple of other guys. Her boyfriend—I don't remember his name—and a guy she knew from the sailing team, I think. He looked the type, you know? And I'm pretty sure it was the sailing team because she was obsessed with sailing." He gave a small laugh. "Which I always found kind of funny, because she wasn't a sailor herself. But she loved watching the sport."

"Do you remember his name?"

"Nah. He was tall and slim. Blond. Very tanned." He grinned ruefully. "But they all are, right?" He glanced at his watch. "We should get going."

"One more thing. The week Adrienne died, she was trying desperately to tell Veronica something that she didn't want to tell her over the phone. But they never had a chance for a face-to-face meeting. She died before they could talk. Do you have any idea what that was about?"

He leaned forward, elbows on the table. "Believe me. Veronica and I have gone over this a million times over the years, going over the possibilities, and nothing sticks. Which makes it even more devastating for Veronica that she didn't go see Adrienne. I don't think we'll ever know. Which is why it's time to move on. To start a new life and leave this . . . unknowing behind us. So please. Help us sell our house and find a new one as soon as possible." His next words caught in his throat. "I don't know how much longer this can go on."

"I get it," I said. "And I will find you a new house, one that you'll all love. I promise," I said, sliding back my chair.

Michael did the same, then stood. "I'll be sure and let you know if I think of anything."

He held out my chair, then placed his hand on my back as he escorted me out of the bakery, my skin burning beneath his palm as if crawling with dozens of fire ants.

Veronica drove us to her house on Queen Street following our meeting with Michael. I sent him back to work with a folder full of listings to go through (everything color coded and listed in order of the number of boxes checked for his wants). I gave Veronica a matching folder, but the order was different, as apparently her wants and needs didn't match Michael's. I was more than a little relieved that this anticipated additional delay because of their disparate requirements would not be of my own making.

I could hear the sawing and banging through the closed windows of the car as Veronica pulled onto the small parking pad in front of her house. As she parked, we both turned at the sound of a car pulling up behind us. I recognized Detective Riley as he exited the car, carrying what looked like Adrienne's yearbook, calling out a greeting that was quickly muted by the sound of a chain saw. Veronica motioned for him to follow us inside, where we sought refuge in the library again.

Sitting down next to me on the sofa, Thomas placed the yearbook on the coffee table. "Sorry to drop by unannounced, Veronica, but you're a hard person to reach. I think I've left about a dozen voice mails on your phone, and I've left a few messages on your landline answering machine."

"Yes, sorry. We usually delete the messages without listening to them since they're mostly sales calls, and I seem to have misplaced my cell phone. I don't want to replace it because I'm sure it will turn up at some point—I lose it about a dozen times a day just in my house!" She forced a little laugh. "I must have turned it off when at a client's house and the Find My Phone app doesn't seem to be working."

"No worries," Thomas said. "I actually dropped by Melanie's office first and the receptionist—the one with the dragonfly earrings—told me that Melanie had just left with you. She said you were headed here." He frowned. "She, uh— Jolly, is it?"

I nodded.

"Yes, Jolly. She's an interesting character, isn't she? She also told me that I had a white aura surrounding me and that she wanted to give me a crystal for protection." He raised his eyebrows. "She also said that a young girl—not a child, but more like a tween—was following me. Along with her dog."

"Really?" I said, a familiar chill tiptoeing down my spine. "Either her online classes on how to be a psychic are going better than I thought, or she's a very good guesser. We've experienced those same apparitions at the house. Although I don't have a clue about auras or crystals. You're on your own with that."

"Thanks." He frowned again. "I wasn't really giving much weight to what she was saying, but then Jolly said something else that was a little more concerning."

"And what was that?"

"That the apparition said that the girl was in danger. That she needed my help."

"The girl?" I repeated.

Thomas nodded. "At first I thought the apparition was talking about herself. But that doesn't make sense, does it? Wouldn't she refer to herself by name or at least a personal pronoun like 'me' or 'I'? Which got me thinking that it was another girl."

Veronica and I shared a glance. "Like Nola or her friends?" I suggested. "Unless Adrienne had a dog . . ."

Veronica shook her head. "Never. And she wasn't a young girl when she died."

"Yes, well, interviewing apparitions is Melanie's area of expertise," Thomas said. "It could mean absolutely nothing—considering the source. I just thought I'd mention it." He reached into his jacket pocket and pulled out his notepad and pencil. "So, I have some information about that fingerprint on the Discman. Although I'm disappointed it wasn't as informative as I'd hoped."

Afraid that I'd be forced to drag out every morsel of information like I had to do with Yvonne, I said, "Just tell us everything. Don't hold back."

I looked at Veronica, who nodded. "I can handle it."

Thomas referred to his notes. I pushed back a twinge of jealousy when he didn't whip out a pair of reading glasses.

"There was only one clear print that was lifted—a thumbprint. After putting it through the AFIS database, we were able to positively identify it as belonging to a Lauren Dempsey, a senior from Sarasota, Florida, at the college at the time of Adrienne's death. She was also on the sailing team. We have her prints in the system because she had a couple of DUIs while in college and a misdemeanor theft—stole a handful of lipstick tubes from Tellis Pharmacy on a dare, but Lauren was the only one charged. Does that name ring any bells?"

Veronica's face puckered in concentration before she slowly shook her head. "I don't think so. Do you have a picture of her?"

Thomas slid the yearbook toward him and opened it up to a book-marked page. He turned the book around so that Veronica could see and pointed at a class photo. "This is her senior picture." He waited a mo-ment for Veronica to study it, then turned to another bookmarked page. "And these are two group pictures of the sailing team—a formal one and a casual pose at an award ceremony. Lauren is the one standing next to the guy holding the trophy."

Veronica leaned closer, flipping between the two pages, finally paus-ing on the team photo. "She does look vaguely familiar. There were a few times when Adrienne invited us to post-regatta parties. Our parents usually begged off, but Michael and I would sometimes go, so we met pretty much the whole team. It's just been so long that I don't remember . . ." She stopped, her head tilted to the side. She picked up the yearbook and held it directly in front of her. "The dress she's wear-ing. That was Adrienne's."

"Are you sure?" Thomas stood to look over Veronica's shoulder.

She nodded. "I'm certain because I gave it to her. I'd worn it only a few times and, knowing she didn't have the funds for new clothes, I offered it to her. She altered it—gave it a ruffle hem and shortened the sleeves. Almost made me regret letting it go. But she was amazing with a needle and loved to sew. She'd planned to be a fashion designer." Ve-ronica's voice caught. "Yeah, this is definitely the same dress."

"Do you find it strange that she might have lent it to someone else to wear?"

Veronica sat down, cradling the yearbook against her chest. "No. Not at all. Adrienne was the most generous person I've ever known. If you told her you liked something she was wearing, she'd either let you wear it or offer to make one for you. Even if she and this Lauren Dempsey were only acquaintances from the sailing team, Adrienne would have loaned her a dress. Or her CD player."

I stood and reached for the yearbook. "Which one is Lauren?"

Thomas pointed to a tall woman with sun-bleached, almost white blond hair. She was slim, but her muscular arms, shown to advantage in the dress, revealed her hobby of hoisting sails. With her bright white smile gleaming against her tanned face, she could have been posing for a toothpaste ad.

"She's very pretty."

"If you like tall blondes," Thomas said without a glimmer of sarcasm.

Veronica and I both looked at him while I smiled to myself, picturing Jayne, who was tall but definitely not a blonde.

"Have you had a chance to interview her?" Veronica asked Thomas.

"Well, that's the thing. We were unable to locate Lauren, so I contacted her parents, who still live in Sarasota." He paused. "They haven't seen her since right before graduation. Apparently, Lauren left a note in her dorm room the day before she was to graduate, telling them that she needed some time alone and was going to backpack across the country for a year before settling down into her adult life. Most of her clothes and belongings had been packed up and removed from her room while her roommate wasn't there, so nobody knows where she went or if she went with anyone."

My chest felt heavy as I imagined how I'd feel if Nola ran off with just a note. "And her parents haven't seen her since? Surely they were suspicious that something wasn't right? I mean, was Lauren the type of person who'd just up and disappear?"

"Her mother said that Lauren had always had a bit of wanderlust, and she enjoyed hiking and the outdoors and had taken several trips overseas with friends. But never by herself and never without letting her parents know where she was. They called the police and reported Lauren missing, but without any evidence that she'd been abducted, and with the note saying she'd left of her own free will, there was nothing they could do."

"Those poor parents," I said. "And the note was in Lauren's handwriting?"

"According to the parents, yes. When the police closed the case, the Dempseys sold pretty much everything they owned and took out a second mortgage on their house to pay for private investigators. Every once in a while, they'll get a lead, but there's been no trace of Lauren."

"That's so heartbreaking," I said. "I'm wondering if Lauren and Adrienne were close friends and if Adrienne's murder affected her in a bigger way than she let on."

Thomas nodded. "I thought the same thing, but when I asked Lauren's parents, they didn't remember Lauren ever mentioning Adrienne. However, it was a long time ago, and Lauren was very popular and had lots of friends."

"Just like Adrienne," Veronica said softly.

"So there's been no contact at all?" I asked.

Thomas nodded. "Actually, there has been. Every once in a while, her parents receive a postcard from Lauren—always from a different location around the country—letting them know she's fine and that she'll come home when she's ready. And that she loves them."

"But it's been more than twenty years," Veronica said. "Are they sure the postcards are from Lauren?"

"They say they are, but I've asked them to send me the postcards as well as the note she left on the day she disappeared and some of her older handwriting samples. I'm going to have an expert analyze the handwriting to make sure they were all written by the same person." He paused. "I really hesitated to share this information with you. Lauren's thumbprint on the CD player only means she touched it at some point. Her disappearance could have absolutely nothing to do with Adrienne's death. It could just be a coincidence."

"Except there's no such thing as coincidence," I said, turning my head before belatedly remembering that Jack wasn't there.

The pungent aroma of Vanilla Musk suffused the room, but Veronica and Thomas didn't seem to notice. I casually looked around the room, but as usual I saw no sign of Adrienne. The hair on the back of my neck stood on end as I felt Adrienne move behind me in what seemed to be a protective gesture. The thought made my nerve endings tingle, all senses on alert as I tried to figure out what she was attempting to protect me *from*.

Thomas continued. "I also checked with the college. Lauren's transcripts have never been requested by any company where she might have sought employment."

"So, what does that mean?" Veronica asked.

"Well, if she had some kind of employment record, we could at least track her movements, see if they correspond to the letters her parents have been receiving over the years," Thomas explained. "We've run her Social Security number, and there haven't been any hits since her job at the college bookstore while she was in school here."

"Which means she's purposefully off the grid," Veronica said.

"Or dead." Neither Veronica nor Thomas looked at me when I spoke, their thoughts mirroring my own.

"I'll keep digging," Thomas said. "Either the fingerprint is our biggest lead or it means nothing at all. I'm afraid we won't know for sure unless we can locate Lauren and interview her."

I coughed, my throat suddenly tight. I tried to swallow and rubbed my neck the way I rubbed General Lee's when giving him one of his pills to make it go down. The sensation of invisible fingers encircling my neck brought me to my feet, coughing. A strong whiff of Vanilla Musk drifted past me as the choke hold abruptly disappeared, leaving me rubbing the skin, trying to erase the icy-cold impression of ten invisible fingers wrapped around my neck.

"Are you all right?" Veronica jumped up and came to my side.

"I think so. Could I have a glass of water?"

"Of course. I'll be right back."

She left the room, leaving Thomas and me alone. "Was it the same person who attacked you in your garden?" he asked.

"I have no idea—it could be. But it's definitely not Adrienne. She's trying to protect me from whoever has taken a pretty intense dislike to me."

Veronica entered, carrying a glass of water. I took it and drank it in big gulps, trying to erase the burning sensation inside my throat.

"Should we call Jayne?" Thomas asked.

Veronica and I both looked at him.

"Because I know you two do best when you work together," he quickly added.

"Right. I don't think that's necessary. But I'll let you fill her in. You still have her number?"

"It might still be in my phone." He didn't bother to look, and I was careful to hide my smile.

His phone rang, and after glancing at the screen, he excused himself and stepped out into the hallway to take the call. After a moment, he popped back in. "I have to go. I'll let you both know if I find out anything else."

We walked back out into the foyer, the saws in a temporary lull as the workmen worked in another part of the house, the smell of paint and pinewood hanging thick in the air.

Thomas stopped at the door. "Oh, before I forget: As I was leaving your office, one of your coworkers gave me a Tupperware container full of homemade brownies. She said she and her kids had made them for you, and when I told her I was looking for you, she asked me to give them to you when I found you. I didn't catch her name, but she was very well put together. Very energetic."

"Catherine Jimenez," I said. "She's amazing." I actually sounded like I meant it. "While she was baking, she probably also made two new sales." I hoped the bitterness didn't come through in my tone.

"Well, they're in my car if you'd like me to get them for you."

I waved my hand at him. "Oh, I wouldn't think of it," I said, trying to be the new version of Melanie while also knowing that those brownies were all I *would* be able to think about. "She brings me baked goods all the time, so enjoy."

"Thank you. I will."

He reached for the door handle just as a flash of red from the stairwell caught our attention. I spotted the object first and slowly climbed the stairs to the landing to hold it up for Veronica and Thomas. "It's Adrienne's pillow. It was in my bedroom last time I looked."

I put my hand on the banister to head back down the stairs, but my phone beeped with a text, making me pause. Tucking the pillow under my arm, I pulled out my phone and read the screen. The sensation of icy water dripping down my back made me shudder.

"It's from that number—the pay phone at Buist Rivers."

Thomas took a step forward. "What does it say?"

With a hesitant thumb, I clicked to open the text and read it out loud. "'Now you know what it feels like.'"

I looked up and met Veronica's gaze. Before I could say anything, a sudden shove from behind threw me against the wall, then sent me tumbling down the stairs headfirst. The last thing I remembered before blacking out was the tinny noise of distant music that sounded a lot like "O Superman."

CHAPTER 18

At the sound of tapping on my bedroom door, I quickly shut my laptop and slid it under the covers before calling out, "Come in."

The door opened and Jack appeared carrying a breakfast tray that contained a very large and steaming cup of coffee and, less exciting, a bowl of oatmeal. He was followed closely by Nola, wearing her Ashley Hall uniform and carrying a paper bag that smelled suspiciously like doughnuts. She clutched the bag to her chest as Jack settled the tray over my lap. He leaned over me, and I closed my eyes, anticipating at least a kiss on the forehead. Instead, I felt my laptop being slid out from beneath the covers. My eyes popped open to see Jack holding up my computer while sending me one of his signature raised-eyebrow looks of reproach.

Nola placed her bag on the far side of the tray. "You can have a doughnut only after you finish your oatmeal. And only one. Save the second one for later."

"Thank you," I said, adjusting myself so the tray didn't wobble and spill a single precious drop of coffee. "Really, I do appreciate it. But I'm totally fine. I blacked out for just a minute. There's no reason to be put on bed rest. . . ."

"Doctor's orders—just until tomorrow." Jack held up my laptop again. "And you're supposed to be resting."

I leaned back against my pillows in defeat. "Do you know how many more sales Catherine is making while I'm being held prisoner here? The only positive is that Jayne didn't drag me out for a run this morning." I pointed at the coffee. "I hope that's not decaf. You know what happened last time."

Nola shook her head. "Trust me, we learned our lesson. Keeping you fully caffeinated is for our protection."

"Seriously, though," I said to Jack, "I'm completely fine. You didn't need to send the film crew away."

Jack stuck a spoon into the oatmeal and rotated the handle in my direction. "Oh, they're still working. They're doing the scene where the skeletal remains are discovered in the fountain."

Nola sat down on the edge of my bed and plucked a blueberry from the top of my oatmeal before popping it into her mouth. "I hope Louisa's fine with that."

I kept my smile to myself. "Yeah. Me, too. And if she isn't, there's nothing I can do. I already warned Marc that I have no control over the unexplainable."

Nola took another blueberry. "I've invited Lindsey and Alston to come watch the filming after lacrosse practice. I promise we'll be quiet and not bother you."

"Please bother me—and bring the twins. Jayne allowed only a brief supervised visit this morning, but I say the more the merrier. I'm bored out of my mind. Anyway, you brought me doughnuts, so you're allowed to make as much noise as you'd like."

There was another tap on the door. I pulled up the high neck of my heavy flannel nightgown when I spotted Beau Ryan. He wore a sheepish grin and had a newspaper tucked under one arm while carrying a small and lumpy paper bag with his other. "Good morning." He looked uncertainly into the room, relaxing as he spotted Nola. "Nola told me to wait outside, but I brought something for Melanie. Before I could

ring the doorbell, the front door just opened. I called out. Nobody answered. I wasn't sure what to do, so I let myself in. You might need to
check that latch. Anyway, I was going to wait in the foyer, but the nice
lady told me I could go up. So I just followed the voices. I'm sorry if I'm
interrupting."

"Absolutely not," I said, eyeing the bag.

"You are," Jack said at the same time, his narrowed gaze focused on
Nola.

"He's joking," I said, motioning for Beau to come in.

He stood awkwardly by the side of the bed, then placed the newspaper on the breakfast tray. "I found today's paper on the hall table downstairs, so I brought it up. I figured you might need some reading material
while you're cooped up in bed."

"Thank you, Beau." I squinted at my bedside clock.

Jack slid it closer to me.

"It's seven fifteen." I thought for a moment about Beau's "nice lady"
comment. "I guess Mrs. Houlihan is early—she didn't say anything to
me yesterday when she left."

"That wasn't Mrs. Houlihan. The lady who let me in was much
younger and, um, smaller."

"Right." I felt Nola and Jack looking at me. "That must be her sister.
She comes to help Mrs. Houlihan sometimes." My gaze drifted to the
paper bag again.

"Oh, sorry!" Beau handed the bag to me. "Nola told me how much
you like boiled peanuts. The best are from the Rosebank Farms produce
stand, but they don't open until April. Still, these are pretty good." He
handed me the bag. "Opening the shells before eating should help pass
the time."

"That's so thoughtful. Thank you, Beau."

I waited for Beau to leave, but he held back. Jack crossed his arms and
turned to Nola. "How did you know Beau was coming this morning?"

"Because he's taking me to school." Nola plucked another blueberry
from my rapidly cooling oatmeal, and chewed it slowly as if unaware of
the gasoline she'd just poured on a smoldering fire.

Jack turned to Beau and in an icily calm voice said, "Absolutely not. My daughter isn't riding on the back of a motorcycle."

"No, sir. I brought my truck. It has seat belts and doors and every-thing." A hint of a smile touched his mouth and I hoped Jack hadn't noticed.

Nola jumped off the bed. "Dad! Beau's doing me a favor. Since Alston and Lindsey have their driver's permits, they're driving to school with their moms. But they're not allowed to have passengers, so I said I'd find another way to get to school."

"That's funny," Jack said, his voice humorless. "I don't remember you asking me to drive you."

Beau cleared his throat. "Well, sir, that's because I was in the store with Nola when she got the phone call from Alston, so I offered. I felt sorry for her, since she's not allowed to get her permit yet, and I figured I could help. I'm working on the broken sections of the iron fence today, so I had to drive here anyway."

Jack stared at him. "Because she's not allowed—"

"Dad!" Nola interrupted. "I don't have a permit because I don't *want* one," she emphasized. "It's so overrated." She rolled her eyes as Jack and I shared a glance.

"Well, I'm here now," Jack said, already heading toward the door. "I'll drive you."

I sat up, jostling the tray table. "Actually, I have a few things I need to discuss with you. I'm sure Beau is capable of driving Nola the two miles to school."

"Or I could walk," Nola said. "It's not that far. Especially since Beau offered only because he *pities* me."

Beau shrugged. "Fine with me. Although I just downloaded the entire new Vampire Weekend album and thought you might enjoy lis-tening to it. There are a couple of guitar riffs and lyrics that made me think of that song you were working on at the store instead of invento-rying the silver."

Nola paused, pretended to consider. Drew a deep breath. "Whatever. I guess I'll go with Beau." She headed to the door.

I reached out and tugged on her skirt, holding her back. "And?"

"Thank you," she said, barely loud enough to be heard.

"I'll be back shortly to start working on that fence," Beau said as he followed Nola out of the door.

"Take your time! With the fence, that is!" I called after him. I dreaded paying the bill when he was done. Even with the financial windfall from the rubies, we still might have to sell a child to afford the repairs and the twins' college tuitions.

Jack took a step toward the door, but I held him back. "She's fine, Jack. Really. And much safer than her being behind the wheel herself."

A tremor went through him. "True." His face brightened. "And if she never gets her license, she might be forced to live at home while she goes to college."

Jack sat on the side of the bed, then placed his hands on the pillow on either side of my face and examined me like a scientist studying a specimen under a microscope.

"What's wrong?" I asked.

"Yesterday, when Veronica called me to tell me she was taking you to the hospital, I . . ." He paused. "I thought the worst. I wouldn't believe that you were fine until I saw you myself." He sat back, his eyes still fixed on mine. "You drive me crazy, but I can't imagine my life without you."

A fissure of hope sprang up inside me. "Yvonne said that we don't marry someone we can live with, but someone we can't live without. For the record, I agree."

He leaned over me again, jostling the bed tray, and I tilted my chin in anticipation of the kiss I'd been waiting for. I held my breath. Closed my eyes. Then felt his forehead pressed against mine.

"I need more time, Mellie."

The small fissure fizzled out as I watched Jack pull away. I touched his arm and felt the familiar zing between us. *What about me?* The words that the new version of Melanie was trying to say got swatted away by the old Mellie, who refused to retreat. Because deep down, I was still that poor abandoned girl desperate for affection, afraid to say or do any-thing that might make Jack back away permanently.

I dropped my hand as he gave me one last, smoldering look, then stretched out on the bed in his usual spot and opened the newspaper.

"What are you doing?" I asked.

"Waiting for you to eat your breakfast so you can tell me what you wanted to talk about."

"Right," I said, then took a bite of lukewarm oatmeal, not bothering to hide my grimace. I took another bite, and washed it down with a large gulp of coffee. I picked up my spoon, then hesitated when I saw that Jack seemed absorbed in what he was reading.

I replaced the spoon in the bowl, then very slowly and carefully be-gan unrolling the doughnut bag. I had managed to open the top wide enough for my hand to fit inside when Jack sat up suddenly, letting out a small expletive.

"I just wanted a bite," I said.

He looked at me with confusion until he saw the opened bag. With a grimace, he folded up the newspaper so that whatever he'd been read-ing was on top and replaced my bowl on the tray with it. "Have you seen this?"

I quickly read the headline: HOPE DIAMOND OR HOPE-LESS TREASURE HUNT? My eyes swept to the byline. *Suzy Dorf.* I swallowed. "No, I haven't." Which was true. I hadn't actually *seen* the article.

He picked up the paper. "It looks like Ms. Dorf is resurrecting her Hidden Treasures in the Holy City series. I hope this wins the *Post and Courier* another Pulitzer. Listen to this."

Once again there is drama at a particular house on Tradd Street where a movie based on the fictionalized story of the disappearance of Louisa Vanderhorst in 1929 as interpreted by Marc Longo is being filmed. It is interesting to note that Longo is the descendant of Joseph Longo, the suspect held responsible for Mrs. Vanderhorst's death. A source who wishes to remain anonymous calls the novel and the resulting film "farb" ("far be it from reality")—which, for the uninitiated, is a term used by war reenactors for those participants who exhibit indifference to historical authenticity.

"This is going to make Marc insane." Jack didn't sound upset. "And listen to this."

Longo, a Charleston businessman, is neither a writer nor a director by profession, which makes this journalist pay attention to the rumors that a more accurate version of the historical events surrounding the Confederate diamonds once hidden inside the house on Tradd Street was purloined and eviscerated to make a more scintillating novel and subsequent spicy film treatment.

He read in silence for a moment. "Looks like Ms. Dorf has been following the treasure-hunting blogs. She mentions the Hope Diamond and the Sultan of Brunei rumors, and the growing consensus that the most valuable part of the treasure remains hidden." He cleared his throat.

It remains to be seen if the supposed hosts of spirits who purportedly exist alongside the living inside the home will stay quiet during the filming. Stay tuned for more on this and other hidden treasures in our beloved Holy City.

Jack tossed the paper onto my nightstand. "We'll probably get an earful from Harvey and a bunch of threats from Marc. They'll probably buy all copies of the paper to keep the crew from reading about the ghosts. I imagine if the activity reaches the levels we experienced in December, they'll all quit and Marc will claim that we're in breach of contract."

"What will we do if that happens? I asked softly.

He shrugged. "It is what it is."

It was such an un-Jack remark that I stared hard at him. "Really?"

"Really," he said matter-of-factly. "There's nothing I can do but wait and see and then deal with the fallout. And keep working on my new book."

I held my breath, waiting for him to share his new project with me, just like old times. Instead, he said, "You and I are remarkably adept at dealing with fallout, aren't we?"

"Except for one notable incident," I reminded him.

"Except for one notable incident." He studied my face. "So, what did you need to tell me? I can't imagine you'd have more to talk about than what happened yesterday at Veronica's. Although things do seem to happen a lot to people and things around you."

I grinned. "You know me so well."

He didn't return my smile. "Yes. I do."

Focusing on my coffee, I took a slow sip while I tried to compose myself. "Jolly had another one of her psychic experiences. She told Thomas that she saw the spirit of a girl who said, 'The girl is in danger.'"

"'The girl'? Not a name?"

I shook my head. "No. I guess it could be anyone—or no one, because it is Jolly—but she's had weirdly accurate predictions before. I just want us to pay attention. I'm worried about Nola. She says that the ghost with the melted face is there to protect her—although she's not sure from what. And then there's Louisa. I smell her roses every day. Like she's on alert."

He nodded slowly. "I keep wondering what the ghost was trying to show Nola when we found her at the clock." He reached for my laptop. "Maybe she's been reading the treasure-hunting blogs. I figure if ghosts can make phone calls and send texts, then going online wouldn't be beyond the realm of possibility, right?"

"Probably not, but help yourself. There's been a lot of activity on all the treasure sites."

He propped himself next to me against the headboard. "Go ahead and eat your doughnuts while I browse. I promise not to tell Nola."

With a quick glance to make sure he wasn't joking, I removed a doughnut from the bag and took a bite.

"Your Melanie self-improvement worksheet is looking a little sparse."

"Please close that. It's a work in progress. And private."

"Sorry." He clicked a button. "Wow—the college spreadsheet is pretty impressive. Have you shown it to Nola yet?"

I shook my head, then swallowed another bite of glazed doughnut. "No, because I'm not done. I need to add columns with all the deadlines for scores, applications, essays, and those kinds of things. Then she'll be able to sort by date so that she doesn't miss any deadline. And I'd also like to dress it up with fonts and shading."

A shadow of a smile crossed Jack's face. "How did we ever manage to get into college without modern technology?"

"Oh, I had a worksheet. I did it by hand in pencil. When I met a deadline, I'd make a huge check with a red marker. And I used highlighters in four different colors so that—"

"Thanks, Mellie. But that was a rhetorical question." He closed the spreadsheet, then whistled. "You've got nine tabs open in your browser and all of them are treasure-hunting blogs." His eyes met mine over the top of the computer. "You've been busy."

"I've been bored just lying here and being forced to do nothing," I said truthfully. "And since it involves us and our house, I want to know what people are saying. Which is nothing new, actually. Except that Blackbeard person keeps stirring the pot whenever the ongoing conversations begin to die down. He doesn't mention me by name, but he—or she—claims that 'someone close to the family' is using their psychic abilities to speak with the ghost of Captain Vanderhorst regarding the location of the sultan's diamond."

"Do you think Blackbeard might be Marc's online name? That would make sense—posting everywhere to get other people to do the hard part of researching the rumors for him."

Jack raised his eyebrows. "Good thinking. That's pretty much Marc's MO. Wouldn't surprise me at all."

The sudden eruption of barking from three small dogs brought us both out of the bed and to the window, from where only a portion of the backyard was visible, so the dogs and whatever they were barking at were out of view. The dogs were being kept in the kitchen during the filming, and they were very obedient to Mrs. Houlihan, who fed them and took them outside to do their business. She would never allow them to bark uncontrollably.

"Something's wrong." I threw on my heavy bathrobe and fluffy slippers and headed toward the door.

"Stay here, Mellie. You're supposed to rest in bed, remember?"

I pretended not to hear and hurried out of the room and down the stairs, Jack close behind me, nearly colliding with Mrs. Houlihan, who had just come in the front door. She wore her hat, coat, and gloves and carried her large pocketbook, which undoubtedly contained a stack of the romance novels she enjoyed reading in her off time.

"I guess the paperboy skipped our house this morning, because the newspaper wasn't at the curb."

I remembered what Beau had said about the door being opened for him and the nice lady telling him to go upstairs. And how the newspaper had been on the hall table. It had definitely not been Mrs. Houlihan who'd let him in, which left me with warm feelings about Beau's knowing that Louisa Vanderhorst had welcomed his presence in our home.

The housekeeper looked at her watch. "I'm so sorry I'm late. Traffic was horrible on the Crosstown and I had to take my husband to work because his car is in the shop."

"No worries," I said. "Take your time getting settled. We'll go see to the dogs." I met Jack's eyes as we turned in tandem and walked quickly to the kitchen, where the back door stood wide open. I followed Jack out the door toward the sound of the yapping dogs, to where they stood by the cistern, growling like three avenging cotton balls at the spot where the old kitchen house once stood. Their ears lay back, their usually plumed tails trailing between their legs. Beau stood next to them by the wrought iron fence, staring in the same direction as the dogs, his toolbox at his feet.

Jack and I reached Beau in time for me to see the long skirt and almost transparent form of a teenage girl slowly evaporate like steam over a pot, the wagging tail of an almost invisible dog soon following. I stooped to pick up General Lee, who had begun to whimper, and held him close to my chest.

"Did you see that?" I asked Beau.

He faced me, his light brown eyes cool and clear. "See what?"

I stared at him, waiting for him to tell me he was joking, because I recognized his expression. The look of denial I'd seen in my own reflection many times. "Never mind." I picked up Porgy while Jack hoisted Bess, who, despite being the same age as her brother, was a good five pounds heavier. "We'll let you get to work."

Jack and I returned to the kitchen and put the dogs down at their bowls, which Mrs. Houlihan had already filled, then headed toward the foyer to speak in private. "What was that all about?" Jack asked.

"I'm not sure. He definitely saw the same thing I did—the girl and dog Nola and I saw near the grandfather clock the other night. But he denied it."

"Should I be worried?"

I shook my head. "Louisa likes him. She opened the door for him and told him to go upstairs. I don't believe he knew he was talking to a ghost."

Jack met my eyes. "So why did he deny seeing the girl and her dog?"

"I have no idea. But I'd like to find out. I'd also like to know more about his parents. The woman with the wet footprints might be his mother, and I'd like to know why she's still here."

Jack's phone beeped and he looked at it. "It's from Desmarae. I need to take this. She probably has some more brilliant marketing strategies for me, like adding aliens or action heroes."

"And I guess I need to go back to my prison." With exaggerated slowness, I headed up the stairs.

"Mellie?"

I stopped. Turned. "Yes?"

"Earlier—upstairs in the bedroom. That might have been almost kiss number six."

"It would be. If you believed in do-overs."

"If I believed in do-overs." His phone buzzed again. "Maybe I'm starting to."

He turned around with the phone to his ear while I stared at his back and felt the old and new versions of myself play tug-of-war. Melanie Version 107 must have won, because I found myself marching down the stairs toward Jack. I reached up and pulled his head down to mine, cutting him off in midsentence, and kissed him the way I used to kiss him, the way I still did in my dreams. Jack pulled me closer, kissing me back, and I knew he was remembering, too.

I pulled away and looked into his startled eyes. "Maybe I do."

I turned around and climbed the steps in as dramatic an exit as I could muster wearing a fluffy robe and slippers.

CHAPTER 19

I staggered from my car toward the house after work the following day, in desperate need of sweet hugs and kisses from my children and a long, hot soak in the tub. Even the Tupperware container of homemade lemon bars I'd brought back from the office didn't make up for the two lucrative listings Catherine Jimenez had secured the previous day while I'd been stuck in bed. She'd managed this while also coaching her daughter's volleyball team and packing care packages for our troops with her DAR chapter. And, apparently, baking homemade lemon bars. I needed to attach a surveillance camera to her perfectly ironed lapel to see how she did it, although I was now fairly certain that she'd managed to clone herself.

I stopped in front of my house, sure I was at the right place only by the sight of Harvey's red Ferrari once again parked partially in the street and blocking the sidewalk and driveway. The yard had the appearance of a circus. People moved about furiously, shouting and talking over one another while the sprinklers spurted water and all the house lights turned on and off in sync with the loud music pulsing from somewhere inside the house. I paused a moment to appreciate the familiar chorus to ABBA's

"Dancing Queen" before returning my gaze to the front yard and trying to make sense of the pandemonium.

My attention was caught by a flash of Ashley Hall plaid near the red Ferrari. I spotted an apoplectic Harvey Beckner, his face the same shade as his car, screaming expletives at Nola and her two friends, Alston and Lindsey. Nola stood slightly in front of the other girls, taking the brunt and not just a little spittle flying from Harvey's mouth.

I ran toward them, the Tupperware acting as a possible battering ram as I approached.

"What are you doing?" I said, the lemon bars and I stepping in between Harvey and the girls.

"They vandalized my car!"

"We didn't do anything," Nola said, trying very hard to hold back tears. She wasn't a crier, nor was she used to being screamed at. "We were just watching the filming and he started screaming." The last word caught in her throat.

"Hold these, please." I handed Nola the container of lemon bars while giving her a sympathetic look so she'd understood that I believed her. Then I turned to Harvey so I could play nice. "Show me what you think they did."

With an accusing glare at the girls, he led me to the front of the car, then pointed at the windshield. Even though the temperature now hovered in the low sixties, starbursts of snowflake-shaped ice spread across the glass. Scratched into the frost were what I thought at first to be random letters.

I moved to the side of the car so I could get a better look at the windshield. I leaned forward to touch it, then jerked back at the burning sensation of frostbite and the sudden realization that the frost was on the inside.

Rubbing my hand, I looked at Harvey. "Don't you keep your car locked with the alarm on?"

"Of course I do! Do you think I'm an idiot?"

I raised my eyebrow but didn't comment. I returned to the front of the car so I could study the letters again, and I realized that they weren't gibberish but backward. "This was written in the frost from the inside of the car."

"Well, then, these three gangbangers must be experts at breaking into cars." He looked at me smugly. "And I have proof."

I was barely aware of Harvey marching to the driver's-side door and the sound of beeping as he unlocked it, as I was too busy deciphering the backward words etched across the windshield.

The girl is in danger. Watch for the tall man.

I jerked back, breath held, watching the words slowly vanish as the temperature inside the car returned to normal, each letter disappearing like vapor.

"See?" Harvey yanked open the driver's door. "I have proof!"

I hurried toward him, pausing at a loud crack from under the heel of my boot. I lifted my foot and looked down to see a large china button split into three parts and surrounded by a dozen other antique buttons. Harvey didn't seem to notice, as he was too busy cursing and pointing at something in his driver's seat.

I smelled the waft of smoke and knew what I would see before I even reached the door. Frozen Charlotte lay supine in her iron coffin, her sightless eyes staring up through the small window of the lid. Swooping down, I picked up the offending object and threw it in my tote, having no doubt who'd put it there, and it wasn't Nola or her friends.

"Was your door locked?"

He looked at me as if I'd lost my mind. "Of course it was. Do you think I'd leave a three-hundred-thousand-dollar car unlocked, especially in this neighborhood? They must have picked my pocket and taken my key and then put it back."

I let the slight about my South of Broad location pass, as well as the insinuation that my daughter and her friends were a pickpocket gang, because I was too intent on smoothing his ruffled feathers. "Look, Harvey. No harm done, see? Not even a single fingerprint or speck of dust or any damage. Maybe if you didn't park this way and block the sidewalk as well as the driveway, your car wouldn't be such a target."

He let out another loud expletive, which was thankfully blocked out by the sound of horns from all vehicles in the vicinity blaring at once. Marc appeared on the piazza, his gaze scanning the chaos from the front door, his hands held over his ears. He glared when he spotted me, and began running down the piazza steps.

I turned to Nola. "Go to the kitchen. Now. And use the back door. You're welcome to eat as many lemon bars as you like."

"Are they vegan?"

Lindsey rolled her eyes, then used both hands to push on Nola's back to get her moving in the right direction, Alston jogging along behind them.

I was relieved to see Jack had arrived and was parking the minivan behind the Ferrari. He slammed the door as he raced toward me, reaching me at the same time as Marc.

"Make it stop!" Marc screamed. "We had a deal, remember?"

Jack stood in front of Marc. "Do not yell at my wife, or a bunch of commotion on your film set will be the least of your worries."

Harvey moved to stand next to Marc, neither one of them looking very threatening. Maybe it was the fake tans and the brilliant teeth that advertised their inexperience with street brawls. Obviously, Harvey didn't get the message, because he leaned close to me and said, very loudly and succinctly, with plenty of spittle, "Make. It. Stop."

I put my hand on Jack's arm to hold him back while using my other sleeve to wipe my face. "Have you tried asking nicely?" I forced a smile if only so I wouldn't be tempted to spit back at him.

"Ask nicely?" Harvey sneered. "I shouldn't have to ask you—"

"Not me—the house."

He closed his mouth, narrowed his eyes. "I'm not stupid. I'm not going to embarrass myself by—"

Marc turned to face the house. With his hands bracketing his mouth, he shouted, "Stop it!"

The mayhem continued, the noise even louder.

"See?" Harvey pushed Marc on the shoulder. "They're just trying to make you look more idiotic than you already do."

"The lady said to ask nicely." Jack put his arm around my shoulders.

With a narrowed-eye glance at us, Marc turned around again and shouted, "Please!"

Immediately, the sprinklers stopped spewing water, the lights remained on, and the blaring music and honking horns blessedly stopped.

"See what can happen when you're polite?" Jack said. "You should try it more often."

Marc took a menacing step toward us. "We had a deal."

Jack put a hand on Marc's chest. "Yes, we did. We still do. But if you recall, Melanie made no promises about things beyond her control."

Harvey stepped into the fray. "Then how do you explain that article in the *Post and Courier*? My crew is already freaked out from what the last crew told them happened in December. If this crew deserts the set, it will set us back so far, we might not be able to recover." He stepped closer to Jack, who was a good head taller. With a buffed and manicured index finger, he poked Jack in the chest with each word. "That. Had. Better. Not. Happen."

Jack took a step closer. "Do that one more time. Please."

The menacing look on Jack's face must have convinced Harvey that he was serious.

"Melanie." Marc tried to look contrite and conciliatory, but it was clear that was a first for him and he ended up looking more like a grinning Skeletor.

"I already told you that I have no control over any of"—I waved my hand in the general direction of the house—"that." Turning to Harvey, I said, "And if you have an issue with the newspaper, I suggest calling the journalist who wrote the story. I believe her name is Suzy Dorf."

"I did," he said through gritted teeth. "She won't return my phone calls."

"How rude." I turned away, my attention redirected to a commotion at the side of the house, where Nola and her friends were crowding around a young couple and handing them pieces of paper.

"Please don't tell me . . ." Jack stopped.

"Who is that?" I asked, squinting through the growing darkness.

"That's Chelsea Gee and Jacob Reynolds." Harvey waited a moment for recognition.

The names did sound vaguely familiar—like someone Nola might have talked about. Maybe Chelsea was a classmate? I shook my head. "Just tell me already. I have no idea."

Harvey stared hard at us for a moment as if to make sure we weren't joking. "Those are the actors playing the two of you."

Jack and I looked at each other, then back at Harvey. "But they look young enough to be our children," I said.

Marc smiled smugly. "Then it's a good thing that I'm in charge and not you. Sex sells in the entertainment industry, and nobody wants to see old people having sex on the big screen."

Jack affixed on his face a smile that was neither pleasant nor friendly, but meant as a warning. "But isn't sex with minors illegal?"

"That's not funny," Harvey bit out. "They're both thirty. They just look younger."

"No, it's not funny," Marc agreed. He lowered his voice. "And if I see one more inflammatory news article about my book or this production, I'm going to consider our contract null and void."

"I don't think that's allowed," Jack said, shoving his fists into his pockets in an effort to appear casual. "Especially when everything is true. Especially the *farb* part." He chuckled, but I'd seen his jaw throbbing and knew how tightly he was holding on to his control.

"Don't test us," Harvey said, stomping back toward the house. "And keep those vandals away from my car!"

With one look back at us, Marc strode away and began shouting at the crew. "Break's over. And nobody's going home until we finish this scene."

I took hold of Jack's arm and began walking toward the house. "Let's get inside. It's almost dark and you know things always get a little weird around nightfall. Especially when Louisa sees what Marc has done to her story. Most respectable women don't like to be falsely portrayed as child-abandoning adulterers."

He looked down at me, raising an eyebrow, the familiar light in his eyes having returned. "I don't know much about respectable women, so I'll take your word on that."

I blushed, wondering if he was remembering our kiss at the bottom of the stairs, too. "Very funny."

We both stopped and turned around at the sound of another vehicle pulling up in front of the house. The too-familiar Hard Rock Foundations truck signaled the arrival of our handyman on call, Rich Kobylt, who apparently was now also on Marc's speed dial.

Jack grabbed my hand and hurried me toward the side of the house. I doubted either one of us had the energy to deal with another problem. Or the rear view of Mr. Kobylt.

We passed Harvey's Ferrari again and I backtracked, feeling light-headed. I shivered at the chill emanating from the car, the glass once again frosted from the inside. And there, on the windshield, were the same words, written backward, that I'd seen before. *The girl is in danger. Watch for the tall man.*

Jack touched the glass, then stood facing me. "It's on the inside."

"I know." Behind him I saw Harvey hurrying in our direction. Grabbing Jack's hand, I said, "Come on—I'll explain later."

We ran the rest of the way to the kitchen, trying to escape Harvey's loud and inventive cursing, the unexpected weight of my tote bag reminding me of the tiny iron coffin and its inhabitant and all the unanswered questions that taunted me almost as much as the unresolved status of my marriage.

CHAPTER 20

The following morning, I woke with a start, the words on the windshield dancing behind my eyes. *The girl is in danger. Watch for the tall man.* The Rolodex in my brain was flipping through all the men in our lives and their approximate heights. Harvey couldn't be described as tall by anyone except a small child, so he was quickly eliminated. But there were so many other contenders that I needed to make a spreadsheet. At the top of the list would be Marc Longo.

I sat up, feeling disoriented until I remembered that today was Saturday, which was why my alarms hadn't awakened me. I squinted at my bedside clock—nine twenty-two—and then at the empty cribs on the baby monitor. Even General Lee was missing, presumably fed and walked while I slept like a dead person. *Or like a very tired person,* I corrected myself. The dead didn't always sleep.

I quickly showered and dressed, then went in search of Jack and the children, assuming they'd be together since today was Jayne's day off. The crew was still filming the outside fountain scene, so I went downstairs without tiptoeing for the first time in over a week, for once not fearful of interrupting a scene or running into Marc or Harvey.

When I reached the bottom stair the distinctive sound of the grandfather clock case snapping shut caught my attention. I froze, wanting so badly to ignore it—especially if it was the specter of the girl with the melted face. But the sound was quickly followed by a very solid and very real footfall on the hardwood floor. With a deep breath, I slowly walked toward the parlor.

I almost didn't see anyone at first, only the movement of the drapery panel alerting me that I wasn't alone. I marched to the window and threw the curtain back. Marc Longo stood behind it, facing the Plexiglas wall panel I'd had installed to protect Nevin Vanderhorst's childhood growth chart made by his mother, Louisa.

"What are you doing?" I asked, although I was fairly sure I already knew the answer. "Aren't you supposed to be outside filming?"

Marc feigned surprise as he faced me. He stepped out from behind the curtain, failing again at looking contrite or conciliatory. "We're taking a break—union rules. I was curious about the growth chart, so I thought I'd take the opportunity to come check it out. I'd heard about it, but I didn't think it was important enough to put in my book."

He was lying, but I played along. "I know," I said, not bothering to disguise my disdain. "The most important part of the story of Louisa and Nevin Vanderhorst is the love between mother and son—something you completely ignored in your rendition and then twisted into an unsavory tale of adultery and child abandonment. You shouldn't be surprised that Louisa is angry with you."

His lips whitened as he tried to control his anger, his reluctance to release his true emotions letting me know that he wasn't done asking for favors. "But you can talk to her, right?"

"I already told you—"

"Not about this." He leaned forward, his voice quiet, his eyes shifting to make sure no one else was listening. "About the lost diamond."

"You know as well as I do that the news article that started all that was based purely on conjecture."

His eyes narrowed. "But there's photographic proof."

I was unable to resist rolling my eyes. "Yes, the Sultan of Brunei is wearing a large diamond on the same ribbon King Louis XIV used to wear the diamond then known as the French Blue. But besides there being a lack of evidence that the sultan's diamond is the missing half, I can assure you that there are no more diamonds hidden in that clock or anywhere else in the house. Trust me. We've looked."

"Yes, well, it wouldn't be the first time you and Jack were completely oblivious, would it?"

I wanted to slap the look of self-satisfaction off his face, but restrained myself with every ounce of self-control I possessed. I would not be the reason for the breach of contract. If it were to happen, it would have to come from Marc.

"I've heard enough. And please stop snooping around our house. Not only because you won't find anything, but because I don't want your dirty fingerprints all over everything. God only knows where your fingers have been."

I turned to leave, but Marc grabbed my elbow, an odd light in his eyes. He lowered his voice. "Everything I've read online tells me that the sultan's diamond was hidden with or near the rest of the Confederate diamonds. And we found those right here in your clock."

His thumb caressed my arm, making my stomach turn. "*We* didn't find anything—Jack and I did, despite your best efforts."

I tried to yank my arm from his grasp, but he held on, his thumb running revolting circles on my sleeve. "We used to have something, remember?"

He raised his eyebrows with insinuation, and I sincerely believed I would throw up right there on the Aubusson rug. I wrenched my arm from his grasp.

Unaware of my growing nausea, he continued. "Since you and Jack are on the outs, I say you and I put our brains together and find this treasure. We'll never have to worry about money again."

I stared at him dumbly for a long moment, waiting for him to tell me that he was joking. When he didn't, I said, "That would mean just one brain working, and I'm not referring to yours. There is no *we*. There never was and there never will be. You're forgetting that you have a wife with a baby on the way. And besides, the rumors online are just that—

rumors. Just in case nobody ever told you, don't believe everything you read online." I swallowed back the bile that had risen in my throat. "Now, why don't you get back to your crew so you can finish filming and leave us alone?"

I started to leave but paused. "By the way, how tall are you?"

He narrowed his eyes. "Why do you want to know?"

I blew out an exasperated breath. "Because I'm having a coffin made." I left the room, unable to stay in his presence for a moment longer without ruining the antique rug.

I found Jack and Nola in the rear garden, away from the actors and crew at the fountain. The twins sat in the mini swing set my father had made for them. They were wearing mismatched outfits that Jack had apparently pulled at random instead of reading the labels on the drawers. I took a deep breath and counted to ten as Jayne often suggested, focusing on how cute the twins looked despite their uncoordinated apparel. I bit back a comment about how Sophie must have dressed them while blindfolded, in an attempt not to disrupt the scene of family harmony before me.

Nola sat next to Jack on the bench pulled up in front of the swings, resting her head on his shoulder while occasionally giving a gentle push to her little sister's swing.

"Good morning," I said, handing Jack a cup of coffee, which he inexplicably drank black. I might have actually shuddered when I had set it next to mine while I added the sugar and cream into my own mug.

I kissed all three kids on the forehead and tweaked only the babies' cheeks, since Nola wouldn't allow me to tweak hers. Then I joined them on the bench, Nola in the middle.

"Thanks," Jack said, holding his mug. He smiled at me, his eyes sparkling, and I had to look away so I didn't do anything foolish or inappropriate in front of Nola and the twins.

"I finally forced myself to finish Marc's book," he said.

"I'm sorry. I wish I could have spared you the trauma, but you probably needed to see it for yourself."

He took a sip of coffee. "It's a lot like looking at Rich Kobylt's backside—there are just some things you can't unsee."

Nola sat up. "At least the sex scenes are being filmed on a sound set in LA. They're pretty graphic. Especially the scenes between 'John and Margot Trellis.' They're obviously meant to be the two of you. I mean, ew."

Jack and I stared at her.

She shrugged. "I found the book lying around, so I read it. Awkward."

We were silent for a moment before Jack said, "So, how 'bout those RiverDogs?"

Nola rolled her eyes while I scanned the garden and spotted Beau at work on the rear fence. He hadn't made much progress, due to the intricate craftsmanship and the requirement of not using modern tools (dictated by Sophie).

For the first time since inheriting the house, I was grateful for the labor- and time-intensive methods that were required to authentically preserve a house. Even if my gratitude was due completely to the delay in invoicing.

As if sensing my gaze, Beau turned and nodded his hello, then bent down to retrieve something before heading over to where we sat.

"Oh, no," Nola moaned as she crouched lower on the bench as if trying to hide.

When he got nearer, I recognized the red heart-shaped pillow in his hand. "Is this yours? Someone put it in the passenger seat of my truck while it was parked in your driveway. Can't figure out who or why, but I was hoping you might know who it belonged to." He leaned it against the bench leg next to me.

"It's mine—thanks. I must have dropped it outside and one of the crew just tossed it in the nearest vehicle."

It was an obvious lie, but Beau seemed as eager to accept the explanation as I was. The strong scent of Vanilla Musk suddenly sat heavily in the morning air. Beau turned and tilted his head back slightly, sniffing.

"Does anybody smell that?" I asked, looking closely at Beau.

Nola's nostrils flared slightly. "Smell what?"

"The perfume." The scent had become strong enough to make me feel nauseous.

Beau shook his head, his gaze focused anywhere but on my face. "No, ma'am. I thought I smelled the starburst magnolia bush, but they're not blooming yet." He leaned down to give both children a small push in their swings, eliciting squeals from both Sarah and JJ and distracting me from wondering why he wasn't telling the truth.

Sarah reached up toward Beau, her small hands opening and closing like a little lobster's claws. "Hol' me, hol' me!" she chimed sweetly.

Beau unlatched her from her swing and picked her up, giving her a little jiggle in the air and making her laugh.

"I think you have a new friend," I said, watching as Sarah pointed behind Beau's head at something—or someone—I couldn't see, and giggled.

"She sure is a happy baby, isn't she?" Beau asked, apparently smitten, as Sarah returned her focus to his head and began playing with his ears.

"She's just not very discerning," Nola said, not completely under her breath.

"Nola!" I said.

Beau settled a calm gaze on Nola. "Have you told them?"

"Told us what?" Jack asked.

Nola straightened on the bench, then lifted her chin to look at Beau. "He fired me."

"I put you on probation. There's a difference."

"Not really. My grandparents own the store. You shouldn't be able to do either one."

"Well, your grandmother apparently disagrees, which is why you're on probation for a week."

"What happened?" Jack asked slowly.

Nola's cheeks reddened, her lips pressed tightly together.

"Nola," I prompted softly.

"Should I tell them?" Beau asked, looking very adorable and not at all serious as Sarah played with his hair, spiking it so that it stood straight up.

"My friends and I were just having some fun," she blurted. "It's only a game."

"What game?" I asked.

When she didn't answer right away, I knew. I swallowed. "A Ouija board?"

She nodded once.

"You put her on probation because of a game?" Jack sounded more annoyed than concerned.

"She was supposed to be working," Beau said calmly. "There was a customer in the store wanting to ask someone about a Regency bow-fronted buffet table, but couldn't find an employee because Nola was in the back room. I happened to enter the store as the customer was about to leave and ended up making a considerable sale."

I studied Beau's face, certain that Nola's probation wasn't about her playing a game in the back room while she was supposed to be working.

Nola looked up at Beau defiantly. "Alston has been listening to your podcast and she heard the caller from Savannah ask about playing with the Ouija board. She and Lindsey brought it to the store because I told them I was bored since there hadn't been many customers. It's just a stupid game. Besides, you made it very clear to the caller that you don't believe in all that stuff."

Beau's face went rigid. "Whether I believe in it or not is irrelevant. You were on the clock. If you weren't Amelia's granddaughter, I would have fired you on the spot."

"Did you . . . have any luck?" I asked casually, feeling Beau's eyes on me. Nola knew I'd forbidden Ouija boards and why, so I tried very hard to keep my voice calm.

Nola shrugged. "I don't think so. I'm pretty sure Alston was moving the planchette. It kept spelling out the name Adele."

"Like the singer?" Jack asked.

"Yeah, spelled the same way. That's how I knew it was Alston. She's obsessed with Adele."

"And what did you do with the game after Beau found you?"

Nola sent a glaring look in Beau's direction. "He took it."

I met Beau's gaze. His face had noticeably paled; his lips were pressed together so tight, they'd gone white.

"Good," I said. "I would have done the same thing."

Nola sank a little lower on the bench. I stole another glance at Beau, whose color had begun to return, but his eyes looked wary.

Sarah began to fuss and I reached for her, but she clung to Beau. Instinctively, he patted her back and she placed her head on his shoulder, smiling again at someone standing behind him.

Nola's phone beeped with a text. She quickly read it, then looked at Jack. She was silent for a moment as if considering whether or not to say anything, but another text beeped, and this time she gritted her teeth and drew in a breath as if for courage. Nola straightened, then swallowed. Turning to Jack, she said, "There's a Mardi Gras party in a few weeks at the Bay Street Biergarten. Alston and Lindsey are going as well as a lot of other friends from school. Can I go, please? I promise to be back by curfew."

"I don't think being on probation at your job is something I want to reward. Plus you're all underage."

"Dad!" Nola protested. "My friends are all going and they serve other things besides beer. I'll be the only one not there and I'll have to hear about it for a month."

"Sorry, Nola. It's a definite no from me."

She looked at me, hoping for a second opinion.

"I have to agree with your dad, Nola." I smiled. "Staying home can be just as fun. I'll make popcorn, and then we can watch Hallmark mysteries on TV. Or silly dog videos on YouTube."

"Oh, boy," Nola said, crossing her arms. "Sounds like a lot more fun than a party."

"I know, right? And maybe your dad would like to join us."

Jack looked at me over Nola's head, his eyes sparkling. "Count me in."

"A lot of my classmates are talking about going," Beau said. "It supposedly gets pretty wild. It's definitely an older crowd."

Nola glared at him.

"Even more reason for you not to go," Jack said. "You're still in high school and should definitely not be going to college parties."

Beau shrugged, but I sensed he was enjoying torturing Nola. "I'm only going because Mardi Gras reminds me of home. I usually ride in the Bacchus parade, but I'm having to miss it this year."

"Isn't Bacchus the god of wine and fertility?" Jack asked, sounding more accusing than curious.

"Yes, sir. As well as agriculture." He gave Sarah another pat on her back before returning her to the swing and giving her a little push. "I've got to get back to work. Otherwise I'll be here until Sarah and JJ graduate from college."

"That's okay," I said. Nola kicked me. "It takes as long as it takes, right?"

"Yes, ma'am." Beau paused a moment. "By the way, how many dogs do you have?"

"Three," I said. "Why?"

He started to say something, then shook his head. "That's what I thought. I guess there's a stray that keeps coming around. Seems sweet, so nothing to worry about." He said good-bye, then walked away, turning back once while the three of us watched.

When he was out of earshot, Jack asked, "How tall do you think Beau is?"

Nola shrugged. "He's a little taller than you. Maybe six three or six four?"

My eyes shifted to Jack, and I knew we were both thinking the same thing.

"Why?" Nola asked, her gaze now focused on Beau.

"His dad was a tall guy, too. I was just wondering."

I silently high-fived Jack for successfully sidestepping the truth.

"Nola . . ." Jack began, then stopped.

"What?"

"I want you to stay away from Beau, all right? All men, actually. Especially if they're tall. And tell your friends, too."

She squinted in confusion. "No problem with Beau—trust me. It's bad enough that I have to work with him. And it's not like I'm going to any parties where I might actually meet any other guys, so I think we're safe there." With an exaggerated sigh, she stood. "Since I'm not allowed to go anywhere fun, I guess I'd better get started scrubbing the floors on my hands and knees." She started walking toward the back door, her voice carrying back to us. "Then I'll milk the cows, feed the horses, muck the stables. . . ."

"Where does she get her sarcastic sense of humor, do you think?" Jack mused as he watched the tall form of his daughter disappear into the house.

I remained silent, not sure if he was serious.

We sat quietly for a few moments, gently pushing the twins, enjoying the peacefulness of the garden, the sun shifting through the limbs of the ancient oaks and magnolias, the dormant remains of my father's garden waiting to burst into bloom at the first signal from spring.

"I've been thinking," Jack said.

My heart squeezed, and I did my best to disguise the hope his words had sparked. "Yes?"

"I remembered something you told me Yvonne had mentioned—about a portrait of Captain John Vanderhorst being in storage at the Charleston Museum."

I managed to hold on to my smile. "Right. The Charleston Museum."

"Since we can't find any information about whoever that headstone might have belonged to, I called a friend of mine at the museum to see if they might have other Vanderhorst portraits or paintings that we might be given access to study."

"Did he tell you it would take a while? I can't imagine they're easily accessible."

Jack leaned forward to push JJ, who was banging on the swing with his whisk and shouting, "More! More!" Sarah sat with her head back, contentedly contemplating the world around her.

"Actually, Mandy made an appointment to show me what they have this Wednesday afternoon at two."

"'Mandy'?"

Jack coughed, focusing on pushing the swings. "We may have dated once or twice."

"Of course you did."

"You're welcome to come, too, you know."

"I'll have to check my schedule. Two o'clock?"

"I'll even drive."

"I'll let you know." I looked down at the red heart-shaped pillow on the grass by the bench, needing to change the subject. "I caught Marc snooping in the front parlor. He's convinced that missing half of the Hope Diamond is here somewhere."

"Wouldn't that be great? If it were true. Marc must really be desperate for money if he's believing everything he reads online. We can only hope that he does something stupid so that he's the party in breach of contract."

"Or that the film crew gets spooked enough to abandon the film set."

"Either way," Jack said, "we win. I'm beginning to forget what that feels like."

I put my head on his shoulder. "Me, too," I said softly. "In the meantime, I really need to figure out who's haunting Nola and why she's sending us warnings."

Jack put his arm around my shoulders and pulled me close. "We will. We always figure it out together, don't we?"

I closed my eyes, breathing in his scent. *Almost,* I thought. *Almost.*

"I just wish Rebecca's pregnancy wasn't interfering with her ability to see things in her dreams. Her premonitions are almost worth having to claim her as a relative and be nice."

"Be careful what you wish for," Jack said under his breath right before I heard the latch on the garden gate open.

"Yoo-hoo! Anybody home?"

Jack removed his arm from around me at the same moment I spotted Rebecca, turned out in her new signature mauve maternity coat and matching ankle boots and carrying two shopping bags with pink and white tulle spilling over the tops.

"Oh, no," I groaned. "I forgot she was coming over to discuss her baby shower."

"That's my signal to leave." Jack stood and picked up both twins with record speed. "By the way"—he leaned down so he wouldn't be overheard—"I enjoyed our kiss. I miss that, too." Then he straightened and called out a brief greeting to Rebecca before heading back to the house in the opposite direction.

I picked up the red heart-shaped pillow when I stood, playing with the ruffle as I watched Rebecca approach, suddenly aware that the pillow was soaking wet. As if it had been immersed in water.

I looked back at Beau and our eyes met before he returned to his work, leaving me with no doubt as to who had placed the pillow in his truck. Or that Beau knew, too.

CHAPTER 21

I left the house early to meet Sophie in her new office at the Cigar Factory on East Bay, leaving enough time to find a parking spot and sit in my car listening to ABBA as loudly as my ears could take it. I needed at least twenty minutes of the latter before I was able to block out the black-and-white faces of the deceased factory workers who apparently still felt the need to show up for work each day, and pressed their faces against my car windows as if I were taking attendance.

Despite the extensive renovations that had transformed the old factory building into luxury lofts, restaurants, classrooms, and office space, I had to walk quickly and pass the brick walls, wood ceilings, and newly buffed floors with my head down if I hoped to get in and out before any more restless spirits noticed me.

Sophie's door—covered with posters of rainbow-colored peace signs; "shop local" reminders; no fewer than three house-hugger bumper stickers (including one that read *Historic Preservationists Make It Last Longer*); and a ubiquitous anti-cruise-ship graphic—stood partially open. I gave a brief tap before entering.

Sophie stood from behind a cluttered desk to greet me. As usual when I first saw my friend, it took a moment to absorb her ensemble. If

I'd had to guess, I'd have said her toddler, Skye, had done her hair—if judging only by the sheer number of multihued plastic barrettes that covered Sophie's curly hair like confetti—and had also selected her outfit. She wore nineteen eighties–style overalls with rainbow suspenders à la *Mork & Mindy* and matching leg warmers pulled over the cuffs and up to her knees. I wasn't surprised that her toes were swathed in rainbow knit that peeked out of her lime green Birkenstocks.

"Tenure," Sophie reminded me as she answered my unasked question of how she was allowed to dress the way she did.

"Good morning, Mrs. Trenholm."

In a corner of the room, Meghan Black straightened from a file cabinet she'd evidently been searching through, her pearls and cashmere cardigan standing out in marked contrast to Sophie's outfit. Seeing the two of them together was a bit like watching the "before" and "after" of one of those "what not to wear" reality shows.

"Hello, Meghan. It's good to see you again. Haven't seen much of you since the filming at the house began."

"I know. Dr. Wallen-Arasi has been keeping me busy researching brick mortars in the city and coming up with short- and long-term goals for brick walls that were previously 'repaired,'" she said, using air quotes around the last word. "People who didn't know better used mortar with heavy concentrations of cement. That kind of mortar is too heavy for old bricks and will crack them. It's really devastating to see."

"I bet it is," I said, attempting to sound enthusiastic.

"Mortar needs to be the sacrificial element, not the brick." She smiled at Sophie. "We should put that on a bumper sticker."

"Great idea." Sophie appeared serious and actually made a note on a pad of paper. Returning to her seat behind the desk, Sophie said, "So, what did you want to give me for safekeeping?"

I reached into my tote and pulled out the Frozen Charlotte in her coffin, the strong aroma of smoke clinging to it like a shroud. I plunked it in the middle of Sophie's desk on top of a folded newspaper. "This. Can you put it somewhere safe? Like behind a locked door." I sent a glance toward Meghan. "It keeps turning up in odd places, and I don't want it to get lost."

I actually would have *loved* for it to get lost, but I couldn't say that out loud in present company.

Sophie picked it up, studying it carefully as she turned it over in her hand. "You know," she said, returning it to her desk and opening the lid, "this reminds me. The Gibbes Museum has a new exhibition running for the next few months that you might want to see."

Sophie smiled at me with the same smile she used when thanking me for a gift card for a hair salon or nail appointment. It lacked the sincerity I was used to seeing from my friend. "It's called 'The Living Dead.'"

Meghan slammed a file drawer behind me. "Ew—you mean the Victorian postmortem photography? There is no way I'm going to go see that. It's photos of dead people propped up like they're still alive. The stuff of nightmares."

"Yeah. The stuff of nightmares," I repeated. *Or worse.* I couldn't imagine what sort of hangers-on would accompany a single postmortem photograph, much less an entire roomful. "Why do you believe I might want to go see that? I have enough trauma in my life right now, don't you think?"

"I get it. But these particular photographs were chosen because their subjects were Charlestonians. In many cases, the photographs were donated along with the personal effects of the deceased, and they are being displayed together. But I thought of you because several of the subjects are holding charm strings and at least one has a Frozen Charlotte doll."

I glanced at Meghan, whose attention was buried in a file she'd extracted from the cabinet. Returning to Sophie, I said, "If the girl who owned our Frozen Charlotte was a burn victim, surely there wouldn't be a photograph, right?" I shuddered at the thought.

"Who knows? The Victorians certainly did stranger things than photograph burn victims. But not all of the items are postmortem photographs. Besides, you're not even sure she died in the fire of 1861."

"Oh, I'm sure," I said, glancing down at the Frozen Charlotte, the intense smell of smoke nearly overwhelming.

Sophie let out an exasperated sigh. "Aren't you trying to find the identity of a teenage girl who may or may not have been buried in your backyard around 1861? You know that her first name started with an E and may or may not have been Evangeline, so at least that's a start. I know it's a long shot, but as you told me yourself, even Yvonne has reached a dead end looking for her." She grinned. "No pun intended. Like I said, it's a long shot, but what have you got to lose?"

"My mind?"

"You have three kids, Melanie. I can't imagine you have much of a brain left. I have only one child and I feel as if I'm only functioning with half a brain most days."

I heard a laugh from Meghan behind me, quickly disguised as a cough.

"Fine. I'll go. I'll find someone to go with me, because I'm not doing it alone."

Sophie picked up the Frozen Charlotte coffin and placed it in a desk drawer, then turned a key. "I'll burn some sage, too, to get rid of any toxic or negative energy."

Meghan and I shared a glance.

"Okay," I said. "Whatever you think will work. It reminds me a little of the Edison Doll we found in Jayne's house—remember?"

Sophie's eyes widened. "Oh, yes. I'm still having nightmares. This doll in her coffin is like a cuddly teddy bear compared to that." She shuddered. "I should have saged it, but I hadn't yet learned how to smudge properly then."

She picked up the newspaper that the coffin had been sitting on, and handed it to me. It had been folded to highlight a three-columned article. "I almost forgot—have you seen today's paper?"

"Not yet." I took the paper, skimming the headline. HAINTS OR HOAX? My eyes fell to the next line. *Do evil spirits threaten the living in a bid to guard a legendary diamond? Death toll is two so far—but could there be more?* I knew the byline would read *Suzy Dorf* without having to see it.

I scanned the rest of the short article—mostly a promotional blurb about the continuation of her popular Sunday series about the old houses, families, and legends of Charleston. It mentioned several other reputedly haunted structures in the historic district, including the Old Exchange Building and Poogan's Porch restaurant, so I wouldn't feel singled out.

"I'm guessing Jack hasn't seen it yet or he would have called me by now." I checked my phone to be sure, but there were no missed calls, voice mails, or texts. I felt a twinge of nervousness, but not because I thought he'd be upset at the negative publicity that might put us in breach of contract. I was more nervous that he might *not* be. Our recent conversation and his apathy regarding this same possibility had been niggling at my brain ever since, but for reasons I hadn't been able to put my finger on. Yet.

I returned the paper to Sophie's desk and glanced at my watch, then double-checked the time on my iPhone. "I should be going. I'm meeting Thomas and Veronica at Martha Lou's Kitchen, and I told Jayne I'd swing by and pick her up first."

"I've heard they're offering cholesterol-lowering drugs with every entrée and a blood-pressure cuff at every table." Sophie crossed her arms, although I was pretty sure I remembered having lunch with her at Martha Lou's before she went all vegan and healthy on me.

"Very funny. It's not like I go there every day, and sometimes a person just needs some of Martha Lou's fried chicken and corn bread. I love her collard greens, but she serves those only on Wednesday, so I guess I'll have the baked macaroni as my vegetable."

Meghan looked up from the folder she'd been reading. "Excuse me, Mrs. Trenholm. But you do know that baked macaroni isn't a vegetable, right?"

Sophie leaned her elbows on her desk, in what might have been an attempt to look menacing but failed completely because of the plastic barrettes in her hair. "Melanie thinks that because it's listed with the actual vegetable sides, it's a vegetable. Please don't try to argue with her. It's pointless. She and I have been arguing that exact point for over a decade. Although she apparently does know something, because she makes her children eat real vegetables. Even organic ones. But that could just be because I threatened to call family services."

Meghan's brows rose as she looked from Sophie to me and then back again, but she wisely remained silent.

I slung the straps of my bag over my shoulder, prepared to leave, but another gnawing thought tickled my brain. "One more thing, Meghan. Since you mentioned that you'd once dated Beau Ryan, I wanted to ask you something."

She looked wary. "Sure?"

"Beau told us that his parents disappeared during Hurricane Katrina looking for his baby sister. Did he ever tell you the circumstances?"

Her fingers played with the pearls around her neck as she contemplated her answer. "He didn't really talk about it. He'd answer my questions but would never elaborate." She paused. "I'll admit that I was curious, so I Googled their names." Meghan glanced at Sophie. "I mean, that's pretty much what everyone does these days, right?"

I wanted to deny it, to pretend I was above that sort of thing, but I remembered Googling Jack when we'd first met. I nodded absently, then scolded myself for not thinking of Googling Beau's parents before.

"Did you find anything informative?"

Meghan chewed on her bottom lip. "Not so much informative. Just . . . strange."

"How so?"

"I found an article about Jolie—Beau's baby sister. She was apparently abducted a week or so before Katrina. It's why Beau's mom didn't want to evacuate when the hurricane was coming. She didn't want to leave in case Jolie was brought back or there were any clues that might be erased. Beau was sent with his grandparents to the mountains in Alabama, where they had a house to ride out the storm and the aftermath. No one knows what happened to his parents or Jolie. None of them has been seen or heard from since."

I recalled again the wet footprints that seemed to follow Beau, and the middle-aged woman I'd seen on King Street. "How much younger was Jolie than Beau?"

"Less than two years, I think."

"So she'd be about eighteen years old now."

Meghan looked up in surprise at the sound of relief in my voice. "Yeah. She went missing when she was three."

"How tragic." Sophie pressed her hands against her heart, no doubt thinking of our own toddlers.

"It is," I agreed. "Jolie might be alive somewhere and not even know who she is or that she has a family in New Orleans. And it's even worse that her mother died without knowing what happened to her."

"Why do you think Mrs. Ryan is dead?" Meghan asked, her attention fully focused on me.

I shrugged, realizing my mistake. "Just a guess, I suppose. Maybe because I'm a mother. If I were separated from any of my children, I would do everything in my power to be with them. To be a part of their lives." *And maybe she already is.* "Since she's not, I'm assuming she's deceased. Possibly her husband as well, for the same reason."

Meghan nodded. "I think that's why Beau has his podcast. He tried for a long time to communicate with his parents using mediums and psychics—even self-proclaimed witches and fortune-tellers. He spent a lot of money and had nothing to show for it. He started his podcast to debunk all of it. I guess he wanted to save other people from throwing away their hard-earned cash."

"Yeah." I nodded emphatically. "Makes total sense. I wouldn't blame him." I smiled, a stray thought flitting around my head like a gnat that wouldn't leave me alone. "My husband actually met Beau's father when they were in the Army. His name was Beauregard Ryan, so I assume Beau's named after him. I'm curious, though. When you Googled the family, did you find any mention of his mother's name?"

"Actually, yes, and I remember it because I'm a huge fan of the singer. . . ."

"Adele," I finished, recalling the name from what Nola had told us about the Ouija board game she'd played in the back room of Trenholm Antiques.

Meghan looked at me with surprise. "How did you know?"

"Beau must have mentioned it. Thanks for answering my questions. I appreciate it." I turned back to Sophie. "And thank you for taking care of Charlotte and for letting me know about the exhibit at the Gibbes. I'll let you know if I find anything. I'll treat you to a fruit smoothie from Caviar and Bananas if I do. And you can get me a dozen doughnuts from Glazed if I don't."

I said good-bye and headed toward the door.

Sophie called after me, "Oh, you never responded to my e-mail, but I still need you to help pass out flyers this weekend about the community garden I'm starting. I have a corn husk costume and a tomato costume— I'll let you pick which one you'd prefer and I'll wear the other."

"Oh, sorry. I have a call," I said, holding my phone to my ear and pretending to listen. I waved at Sophie and left her office, closing the door behind me.

Jayne was waiting in the driveway when I drove down Tradd Street, and she was running toward the car by the time I stopped behind the red Ferrari. She was shouting something as she ran, so I put the passenger window down so I could hear.

"Keep going!" she said. "I'll catch up."

I wasn't exactly sure what she was planning on doing—perhaps she had watched too many *Jack Ryan* episodes—but when I looked behind her, I saw Harvey and Marc racing toward me, followed by Jack at a much more leisurely pace.

I reached over and unlatched the car door as I hit the button to raise the window, and she'd barely made it in and locked the door when Harvey and Marc reached us. Harvey slammed his fist on the windshield and waved a copy of the newspaper so that I didn't have to ask Jayne what they were so upset about.

We watched as Jack nonchalantly strolled up to the car. He gave me a thumbs-up and then gestured for me to leave, smiling as he casually draped an arm around Harvey's shoulders. Harvey quickly brushed him off.

I cracked my window. "Are you sure?" I shouted to Jack.

He nodded, making a shooing gesture with his hand. "Have a nice lunch. I'll probably take the twins to the park if it doesn't rain."

Both Jayne and I stared at his casual stance and his ability to ignore someone shouting in each ear.

Marc grabbed the paper from Harvey and pointed at Suzy's article. "Two of my guys quit today. I'd better not find out you're behind this!"

Jack again gave me the signal to leave, so with a quick wave in his direction, and a brief pause to make sure he wasn't going to change his mind, I pulled away from the curb, nearly hitting Marc with the car. I'm glad I didn't, because I liked my car.

"So, how has your day been?" Jayne asked.

"Very funny. You've been hanging around Jack too much." I gestured behind the car at the shouting men. "When did that start?"

"Pretty much as soon as you left this morning. I was busy with the babies, so I didn't get involved—Jack said he'd handle it."

I glanced in the rearview mirror to see Jack standing with arms folded while listening to something Marc was shouting at him. I saw him wipe his face before I turned off the street, heading toward East Bay.

"Did he seem worried at all?"

"Nope. Should he be?"

I hesitated a moment before nodding. Jack and I had shared very little about our unorthodox agreement with Marc and Harvey, not wanting friends and family to see us as pathetic as we knew ourselves to be.

"Yes," I said. "If the filming has to be stopped, the party responsible will be held in breach of contract with pretty severe ramifications."

"And what else? There's something you're not telling me."

"Why would you say that?"

Jayne sighed heavily, and I imagined she probably rolled her eyes, too. "Because I'm your sister and, just like Mother, I know when something's up with you. I feel it here." I glanced over at her in the passenger seat, where she had placed her fingers on a spot on her neck. "You know the spot that burns when you have something too sweet?"

"I don't think I've ever eaten anything too sweet, so no."

She sighed again. "Yeah, well, something's up. Does this have anything to do with our meeting with Suzy Dorf in the ladies' room at the Grocery?"

I focused my attention on avoiding jaywalking pedestrians as I turned left on East Bay. It had rained heavily the night before, leaving deep puddles on the road, but at least the road was passable, which wasn't always the case. The veritable bouquets of flowers in pots and window boxes and the almost excessive drapes of wisteria vines that dressed the Holy City during springtime almost made up for the frequent flooding.

"I'm dreading the first spring flood, aren't you? That reminds me—my rain boots have holes in them and I need a new pair."

"Melanie." My name came with an implied warning.

"Hmm?" I remained focused on the road in front of me.

"Fine. You don't have to tell me everything." She squeezed my hand where it rested on the steering wheel. "Just remember—we're stronger together."

I nodded. "I remember."

"Just stay away from cemeteries, all right? I don't think I can go through that again."

I slid her a glance, wondering if she'd been speaking to our mother. I pulled my car into the parking lot in front of the squat pink building that housed Martha Lou's Kitchen, my mouth already watering. I spotted Thomas's and Veronica's cars, which let us know they were already there and hopefully had a table, since a line had begun forming at the door.

"Are you okay?" I asked Jayne, indicating Thomas's car.

"Sure. Why wouldn't I be?"

I raised my eyebrows, then stepped to the back of the line. We placed our orders, then joined Veronica and Thomas at a four top. They were already sipping their sweet teas, their white foam plates waiting next to plastic forks and paper napkins.

Thomas dutifully stood and pulled out our chairs while Jayne smiled her thanks and said, "You have tea. It's sweet."

"Yes, it is," Thomas said as he sat, his long legs tucking awkwardly beneath the small table.

After greeting everyone and a little bit of chitchat—mostly to warm up Jayne—we all dug into our meals, knowing that once we got started it would be hard to pull our attention away from the delicious baked macaroni and okra soup.

When we'd started to slow down, Thomas pulled out his notepad from his jacket pocket. "So, are you ready for a few updates?"

I wasn't, because I was considering going back for seconds, but instead I nodded and took a sip of my sweet tea. We all sat forward, watching as Thomas flipped through the pages before pausing at one.

"I visited Lauren's parents in Florida to interview them in person. They were happy to see me and still very eager to find their daughter."

"She's been missing as long as Adrienne has been gone," Veronica said. "I imagine we're both feeling the same sort of loss."

Jayne placed her arm around Adrienne and squeezed.

"It was pretty heartbreaking," Thomas continued. "Lauren was their only child. They kept her bedroom exactly the same as when she last left it, like they were waiting for her to return at any moment." He reached into his pocket and pulled out a small stack of photographs and placed them on the table. "I took these while I was there."

Jayne studied one of the photos, her eyes narrowing as if she was trying to see more detail. "Are all of those trophies for sailing?"

Thomas nodded. "Lauren's mother said that her daughter seemed to love sailing from the moment she was born. And that Lauren was always happiest when on a sailboat."

Jayne pointed to something in the photograph and turned it to show Thomas. "This large one—it looks like the trophy in the yearbook photograph. Is it?"

"Good eye," Thomas said, making Jayne flush a deep red. "I thought the same thing."

He pulled out his phone and slid his finger across the screen a few times before turning it around for all of us to see. Veronica handed me a pair of reading glasses.

Thomas continued. "I took a photo of a page of the yearbook so I wouldn't have to bring the whole thing with me. This is the team photo with the national championship trophy. It's similar to the one in Lauren's room, but it's not the same one. I know because I checked. The actual trophy is supposed to be with all of the other sports trophies at the college in a locked display case."

"But it's not," Veronica said softly.

We all turned to her.

She looked down at her folded hands on the table. "After Adrienne died, I spent a lot of time walking around campus, needing to . . . to . . . *feel* her. As if by seeing the things she'd seen and loved, I could have a part of her back. And I suppose I was also looking for clues, anything that might tell me what it was she had tried so hard to talk to me about before she was killed."

Veronica picked up the remains of her watery sweet tea and took a sip. "I went to see the trophy because Adrienne had been as proud of it as if she'd actually been hoisting the sails herself. When I couldn't find it in the case where it was supposed to be, I asked the team coach. He said he'd allowed the captain to bring it home to show to his father, who was apparently critically ill at the time. The captain brought it back to his dorm, but before he could return it to the case, he claims it was stolen from his room."

"Any idea by whom?" I asked.

Thomas shook his head. "At the time, they thought it was a prank and that it would show up eventually. But it never did."

Veronica took Thomas's phone and studied the yearbook photograph. "That boy—the one holding the trophy. I think I remember him. He might have been one of the boys who helped move Adrienne's things when she and her roommate moved to the bigger dorm room."

"Charlie Bleekrode," Thomas said. "Sailing team captain. And Lauren's boyfriend."

The three of us turned to Thomas with expectation.

"And with a solid alibi. He was a senior, but he missed graduation to join a crew for a round-the-world sailing trip. He was somewhere around the tip of South America when Adrienne was killed and Lauren disappeared."

He flipped to another page in his notebook. "Here's where it gets interesting. I noticed that Lauren's very extensive CD collection had been kept intact at her parents' house. She had pretty eclectic taste in music. Everything from classical to reggae and pretty much anything in between. Her favorite, according to her father, was eighties electronica and avant-garde music, especially by a highly acclaimed performance and sound artist named Laurie Anderson. I'd never heard of her before I got involved in this case."

"Nobody has," I said.

Jayne shot me the nanny look she gave the children when they weren't being nice. "She had that one surprise pop hit in the early eighties, I believe. A bit of an earworm, if I'm recalling correctly."

"'O Superman.' Once you hear it you can't forget it. Unfortunately. It's eight minutes long—and if you can listen to the whole thing, you're a stronger person than I am. I guess it takes a more . . . educated ear to appreciate it." I raised an eyebrow.

Thomas cleared his throat. "Yes, well, her father said that one of the last concerts Lauren went to was in Columbia, at USC, where Anderson was performing." Thomas paused. "She told her mother that she was going with her new boyfriend. And that 'O Superman' was her new favorite song because it reminded her of him."

"Meaning not Charlie?" Veronica asked.

"Exactly. They were surprised, because Lauren hadn't mentioned that she and Charlie had broken up. And they were a little concerned when Lauren was secretive about the new relationship. She didn't even tell her parents his name because she didn't want to jinx it, and she was going to wait until she knew it was the real deal before introducing him to her mom and dad. They claimed she had a really good head on her shoulders and they trusted her judgment."

"That's so strange," I said.

Jayne looked at me. "What? That she loved 'O Superman'?"

"Well, yeah, but also that she never told her parents anything about her new boyfriend."

"And that's not all," Thomas said. "I received the handwriting analysis comparing known samples of Lauren's handwriting with both the note left in her dorm room and the notes periodically sent to her parents. They weren't a match. They were very close, and would have been enough to fool her own parents. But under the microscope, it was clear they were forgeries."

Veronica sat back in her chair, her bread pudding untouched, her fingers busily shredding her paper napkin. "Do you think this means Adrienne's murder and Lauren's disappearance are related?"

"It's certainly a possibility," Thomas said, "especially if Lauren didn't leave of her own accord. They knew each other, and Lauren disappeared around the same time Adrienne was murdered. So, yes, they could be related. Or it could just be a coincidence."

Jayne and I shared a glance. "Except there's no such thing as coincidence," she said quietly.

I eyed Veronica's bread pudding, wondering if it would be rude to ask her if she was planning on eating it. A pile of shredded napkin had begun to grow next to it. I pulled my attention back to Thomas. "So, where do we go from here?"

"I'm not sure. We're going to put new efforts into finding Lauren now that we know she didn't send those notes. A great lead would be if we could find the missing part of Adrienne's necklace. My guess would be that since we haven't found it, it's either been destroyed or hidden in a place nobody can find it. Perhaps by her killer." Thomas looked pointedly at Jayne and me. "Unless we can go to the source and ask directly."

"I agree," I said. "But there's . . . someone else. Someone who doesn't want me talking to Adrienne. The same someone who shoved me down the stairs. I think Adrienne doesn't use her strength to appear because she needs to save it. To protect us from . . . whoever that is."

Jayne sat up. "Unless there's a place where Adrienne might be alone." Turning to Veronica, she asked, "Where is Adrienne buried?"

"At Magnolia Cemetery." Veronica paused, then glanced at me. "But do you think that's a good idea?"

"We wouldn't have to go at night," Jayne suggested.

"*We* wouldn't have to go at all. At least not together. I can only imagine the parade of spirits lined up to talk to us. And I really don't like the idea of either of us going alone."

"I don't see an alternative, Melanie. Unless you want me to bring Mother."

"That's an even worse idea."

"Well, then," Jayne said, crumpling up her napkin and placing it on her foam plate, "I say start practicing your ABBA."

By the time we left the restaurant, it had started to rain again. I unlocked my car door with my remote. Then Jayne and I ran in a fruitless attempt not to get wet, and neither of us made any moves to fasten our seat belts as we stared at the splashes of rain hitting the windshield.

Finally, Jayne spoke. "I think Veronica knows more than she's telling us."

"Why? Because she shredded napkins at lunch?"

"Well, that and also because of Veronica's guilt over her belief that she let Adrienne down. Mostly, it's just a feeling. I've learned over the years to listen to my intuition. It's never wrong."

I studied my wedding ring as I gripped the steering wheel. "I've wondered about the phone calls Adrienne made to Veronica before she died. Adrienne might not have told her everything, but what if she said *something*?"

"And what could Veronica's reasoning be for not telling us?" Jayne pulled on her seat belt, pausing as she caught sight of something on the floor in front of her. She reached down, then held up the red heart pillow. "I would ask you why you're carrying this around in your car, but I have a feeling you didn't put it here."

I stared at the pillow, aware now of the faint scent of Vanilla Musk inside the car. "I didn't."

I put on my seat belt and shifted the car into reverse. We were silent as I backed out of the parking space, neither one of us speaking until I turned the car onto Morrison Drive, when both of us broke out into an impromptu and imperfect rendition of "Waterloo."

CHAPTER 22

I replaced the key in the lockbox on the front door of the Lowcountry-style home on James Island I'd just toured with Veronica and Michael, firmly affixing a smile I definitely didn't feel before I turned around. Broad front porch—check. Large eat-in kitchen—check. Pool in backyard—check. Accessible to downtown Charleston—check. Miles of marsh views—check. It had been the eighth house I'd shown the couple that day, another perfect home—according to my spreadsheet—that clicked the most boxes for both of them. Yet Veronica remained as unimpressed and undecided as Michael was enthusiastic and ready to sign on the dotted line.

Veronica looked a little startled when I turned around, and I relaxed my cheek muscles a bit to avoid looking like the Cheshire cat.

"So, what did you think?" I asked, girding myself.

"The pool was a little big," she said.

"'A little big,'" Michael repeated slowly, an edge to his voice I was becoming familiar with.

"And I'm afraid that with the marsh so close, we'll be inundated with mosquitoes."

I could almost hear Michael holding his breath and counting to ten.

I unclenched my teeth. "You know, Veronica, this is South Carolina. Mosquitoes are part of the deal. The back of this house has one of the largest screened-in porches I've ever seen in my career as a Realtor. And to get that view at this price is unheard-of. It's a brand-new listing but I guarantee this house will be gone in a day or two. I don't think we're going to find a more perfect house that the two of you will agree on. I suggest making an offer today."

She turned to look back at the house, at its pristine lawn with moss-laden oak trees and its new roof. "I'm not a fan of the front porch lights."

"Veronica . . ." Michael started.

I held up my hand. "Those are easily changed, and at this price, replacing them wouldn't be an issue." I took a deep, cleansing breath. "Look, why don't we get back into the car and drive around the neighborhood a bit so you can think? Stiles Point Plantation is one of the most sought-after neighborhoods on James Island, so not only is it a beautiful home to live in now, but it's also a great investment."

We piled back into the car, with Veronica in the passenger seat and Michael in the rear, and I began to drive slowly around the established neighborhood with older-growth trees and well-manicured lawns. I attempted to dispel the thick miasma of tension with real estate chatter.

"There's a neighborhood tennis court, a basketball court, and a five-acre park all right here. And so close to the Ravenel Bridge that Lindsey can easily make the six-mile drive to Ashley Hall in less than twenty minutes—depending on traffic, of course."

Veronica was silent as she looked out her window, although I wasn't sure she was actually seeing the scenery. Eventually, she said, "I think I want to look again in South of Broad. It's just that it's so familiar to me and I can't see moving away from it."

"But that's exactly why we're moving, Veronica," Michael said from the backseat, his anger barely concealed behind his words. "We might as well stay where we are if we're just going to move down the street!"

"Is that an option?" Veronica asked, turning her head to face her husband. "Because that's what I'd prefer to do. None of these houses, as lovely as they are, will ever be the home I grew up in and love."

"Look," I said in a last-ditch effort to dispel the tension. "Why don't you two sleep on it, talk it through, then call me in the morning? We're all tired, we've seen a lot of options today, and after a good night's rest, we can regroup."

I took their simmering quiet as an assent and headed out of the neighborhood and back toward Charleston. As I turned onto the James Island Expressway, I said, "You know, there's no need to rush this decision. Even if you sell your Queen Street house quickly—which I suspect will be the case—you can always rent somewhere. That would buy you time to figure out what you really want." I met Michael's eyes in the rearview mirror. "I think I heard Lindsey mention that you have a fishing cabin on Sullivan's Island, right?"

"No," he said abruptly. He drew in his breath. "What I meant was that it's not really suitable for a family or full-time living. I wouldn't want to force my wife and daughter to live there for any amount of time."

"He's right," Veronica said. "I've only been there once. Right after we were married. It was built in the thirties and I don't think it's been updated since. It's just one room—and no door on the bathroom." I heard the smile in her words. "He's never invited me back, and I'm okay with that. It's his man cave, I suppose."

She turned in her seat to face Michael. "I guess if worse comes to worse, you could sleep on your fishing boat and Lindsey and I could take the cabin." I could tell she was trying to lighten the mood, but Michael didn't respond.

Veronica faced forward again, her voice straining to keep it light. "He named the boat the *Omega Three* because it's a fishing boat. Get it? I thought it was pretty clever."

"Very." Trying to spare her the burden of carrying on the labored conversation, I said, "Do you two get to spend much time on the boat?"

"Oh, no." She forced a lighthearted laugh. "The *Omega Three* is an extension of Michael's man cave. I've been on it only once—that same trip when I stayed in the cabin. Let's just say that I'm happy to allow him his privacy on his fishing weekends. Maybe we should look for a house with a deepwater dock so we could keep the boat nearby and Michael can teach Lindsey and me how to fish."

Michael said nothing, and the car descended into an uncomfortable silence. I usually didn't listen to the radio with clients in the car, but I thought it necessary in this case. I turned it on and the car was immediately flooded with the mind-jarring repetitive *ha ha ha* background refrain of "O Superman."

The disconnected landline phone in my bedroom rang at three a.m., ruthlessly shaking me from a dream in which Jack and I were standing in the garden by the fountain, surrounded by friends and family. It reminded me of our wedding, except I was wearing the red dress instead of my wedding gown, and Beau was there strumming his guitar. Nola stood next to him, singing, and by the third ring of the phone, I realized she was voicing the refrain from "O Superman."

I stumbled out of bed, trailing blankets and a grumpy General Lee across the room to pick up the phone's receiver. "Hello?" I said, my frequent conversations with my deceased grandmother no longer making me feel foolish speaking into a disconnected phone.

The distant noise coming through the earpiece made me think of the black nothingness of outer space, the hollow echo the sound of stars spinning through empty inkiness.

Nola.

The sound of my grandmother's voice came through more as a breath than a word, but I understood her just the same.

"What about Nola?"

Nola, she said again, the one word dripping icicles down my back.

I closed my eyes, waiting for her to speak again, feeling myself spinning with the stars, unable to stop.

She's in danger.

I gripped the phone tighter. "From what?"

Only the occasional crackle of static came through the phone. I waited for a long moment, my knuckles hurting from my tight grasp on the receiver. I was about to hang up when I heard her again.

The tall man.

There was a click, and then a dial tone, letting me know that the phone call was over.

I quickly slipped on my robe and padded in my thick sleeping socks down to Nola's bedroom, General Lee in my wake as if he needed to check on his big sister, too.

I partially opened the door and peeked inside. Nola lay on her side, facing the door, Porgy and Bess curled up against her in spoon position. They both looked up at me as General Lee got up on his hind legs to make sure everything was all right. Nola didn't stir as I lifted the older dog onto the mattress and he snuggled in with the two pups.

Nola sighed in her sleep, a sweet smile settling on her face as she draped an arm around the three dogs. I watched her, wondering if I should head down the hallway and wake Jack to tell him about the phone call. The thought had barely crossed my mind before I dismissed it, knowing I'd be treading into dangerous territory.

Instead, I curled up in the oversized club chair Greco had insisted Nola needed, and waited until dawn broke and I knew that Nola was safe. For now.

I had a hard time staying awake as Jack drove us to the Charleston Museum on Meeting Street for our meeting with Mandy after lunch. Even the discussion of the previous night's phone call from my grandmother wasn't stimulating enough to keep me awake.

"We're here," Jack said, gently shaking my shoulder.

I glanced up to see that he'd parked in the small lot behind the brown brick museum in apparently the last remaining spot. "You are the luckiest parker in the world," I said, unclicking my seat belt.

"I usually am, but I can't take credit for this one. Mandy said she'd reserve a spot for me and left a cone in the middle of the space. You weren't aware of me leaving the car and removing because you were snoring like a chain saw."

"I don't snore."

He raised his eyebrows. "How would you know if you snored or not?"

"How would you?" I shot back, regretting the words as soon as they'd left my mouth.

"Touché," he said quietly, his smile slipping.

We exited the minivan and were met at the front door of the museum by a pretty redhead in her early thirties whom Jack introduced as Mandy Reeves. She wore a cinched-in minidress that advertised the fact that she'd never given birth to children, much less twins. Although Jayne's prescribed torture of running most days had helped me shed most of my baby weight, my waist would never be the same.

She gave us a friendly greeting, and I remembered how Jack had admitted that they had once dated. It was only when I spotted the large emerald-cut engagement ring on her left hand that I relaxed. Which was foolish, really. I'd learned in my short marriage that there was nothing and nobody that could separate us. Except me.

We followed Mandy into the lobby of the museum, then up the stairs beneath the giant whale skeleton dangling from the two-story ceiling. I heard the murmur of voices that had started almost as a faint whisper grow louder as we followed Mandy through several exhibits of old silver, Native American artifacts, and ancient weaponry. I began humming "Mamma Mia" as we neared the textiles-and-fashion exhibit, where a flurry of otherworldly activity surrounding a midnight blue beaded evening gown in a glass case vied for my attention. Instead I grasped Jack's arm and hummed even louder until Mandy unlocked a door and led us through it.

"Are you all right, Melanie?" Her green eyes looked at me with concern.

Jack patted my hand. "She gets this way sometimes when she's trying to remember an ABBA lyric. She has to hum her way through it."

Mandy laughed. "That's adorable! My mother loves ABBA, too. I'm not much of a fan. Definitely for older tastes."

She kept walking as if she was unaware that she'd just implied that I was old enough to be her mother. I tried to think of a way to let her know that I was probably only a decade older than she, but couldn't find the words. Jack pressed his hand against mine on his arm, trapping it as if he was afraid I might strike out.

"Here we go," Mandy said, opening up another door and stepping into an empty office. A group of paintings—all with cardboard protective corners on the frames—had been leaned against a wall. Four smaller portraits sat on top of the desk, facedown on Bubble Wrap.

"This should be all of the art from the Vanderhorst family found in the museum's collections. I chose an empty office so you'd have room to look through everything. Just please don't touch anything without putting on a pair of these." She indicated a box with rubber gloves. "And do not remove anything from this room or we will all be in trouble." She looked surreptitiously outside the door, then closed it softly behind her. "I'm not supposed to be doing this, so if anyone asks, tell them that you're considering a huge donation."

"Got it," Jack said with a wink.

Mandy's pale cheeks flushed a pretty pink. "I've got a meeting in five minutes, so I'm going to leave you two alone. If you're done before my meeting is over, please lock this door behind you and tell the receptionist in the lobby to let me know so I can put everything back. Feel free to take photographs, but no flash, please."

We said good-bye, and she left. I waited until the door had closed and said, "She's a bit bossy, isn't she?"

Jack gave his trademark grin. "I find it admirable when a woman isn't afraid to show she's in charge."

A flood of heat swept through me as I recalled just how admirable he found it. I put my tote bag on the ground and pulled out a pen and a notebook, along with my phone for pictures.

"Let's do this systematically," I said. "We'll move from left to right, back to front. While you hold up the portrait, I'll write down whatever is on the nameplate on the frame and then take a photo. I've already prepared a spreadsheet where we can cross-reference—"

"Mellie?" Jack interrupted.

I lifted my head from the notebook on which I'd been numbering lines. "Hmm?"

"Can we just look at the portraits and see if there's anything that might help our investigation? There're only twelve, so it shouldn't take that long. If we find something, then we can do all that other stuff. Okay?"

I looked at the portraits just begging to be organized and categorized by my methods, which were bound to be superior to any museum's. "I guess." I placed my notebook next to my bag, then grabbed two pairs of gloves from the box before squatting down next to Jack and handing him a pair.

It was a pleasant surprise to see that the paintings had been organized in chronological order with the oldest in front. It was comforting to know that if I ever got tired of selling houses, I could consider a career in museum curating. Or as a librarian.

The first four portraits showed the earliest Vanderhorsts, who predated the house on Tradd Street. Because I lived in their descendants' house and had become intimately acquainted with more than one of their family members, putting faces to the names on the family tree was a bit like discovering long-gone relatives. Except they weren't my relatives, and they weren't exactly gone.

Jack quickly passed over the next paintings, of a prized horse and of a camellia bush in full bloom; then he paused at one of a peacock, its glorious tail spread out in splendor.

"It's signed by Elizabeth Grosvenor," he said.

My throat tightened as I remembered the Revolutionary War spy who'd helped me find the rubies buried in the Gallen Hall cemetery. I lifted my phone and snapped a picture.

"At some point, we need to find a way to get this back to Gallen Hall to hang next to Eliza's portrait in the stairwell. But I'm not going to ask Anthony. It just doesn't make sense to have it here, hidden in storage."

I snapped a photo of the next painting, too, one of Carrollton Vanderhorst in a Colonial-era waistcoat and breeches—the same Carrollton who'd built the mausoleum at Gallen Hall and who'd used the old mausoleum bricks to create the cistern at our house on Tradd Street, thus causing me all sorts of problems. He'd also murdered his son, whose forgiveness and reunion with him I'd witnessed. Right before Marc had been dragged inside the mausoleum and Jack had almost died. Jack made no comment but flipped the painting forward as soon as I'd snapped the photo.

He slowly fanned through the next few paintings, reading out familiar names from the eighteenth and nineteenth centuries, then stopped. "Ah, now, here's one we should look at more closely." He moved aside the paintings we'd already examined and stood so he could hold up the painting of a Confederate officer on horseback, saber at his side, steely gray eyes staring at the viewer. "'Captain John Vanderhorst, First Regiment, South Carolina Cavalry,'" Jack read from the nameplate.

"That's the painting Yvonne said we should try to acquire since she says it belongs in the house. He's also the man behind the diamonds," I said, "and the source of lots of angst."

"Also the man responsible for saving us from financial ruin."

"True," I agreed. "But as much as I've enjoyed getting to know his granddaughter-in-law, Louisa, we could have avoided a lot of problems if he'd just appeared and talked to me, you know?"

"Maybe we need a Ouija board."

I quickly made the sign of the cross even though I wasn't Catholic. "Don't say that. Ever. Nothing good has ever come from using a Ouija board. I'm sure if Captain Vanderhorst wanted to speak to me, he would have said something by now." I narrowed my eyes at the face in the portrait, trying to read his secrets. "If there was any truth to that Hope Diamond rumor, he'd know, wouldn't he?"

Jack was already lowering the portrait to return it to the stack. "He would. But there's no truth to that story. Believe me, if I thought there was, I'd consider a Ouija board. But there isn't. I'm positive."

I opened my mouth to remind him about the dangers of Ouija boards, but he interrupted me.

"Hey, did you see this?"

He hoisted the painting back on top of the desk and pointed to the background that I'd overlooked because I'd been too drawn by the captain's face. Jack pointed to a small whitewashed structure in the distance. "I think this is where the back garden is now—see the iron fence? There was just open property behind the house back when this portrait was painted." He leaned forward, squinting. "See the smoke coming from the chimney? I bet this is the kitchen house."

Jack leaned closer to the painting. "I'm assuming Captain Vanderhorst would have commissioned the portrait. But in most commissioned paintings, the subject is eager to show off his or her accomplishments or wealth or whatever they're most fond of. Correct me if I'm wrong, but from what I remember of the Vanderhorst family tree, John died later in the war, but his widow and son, William, were still alive."

I slid on my glasses and stepped closer to the painting. "So why would he have himself painted on his horse in uniform, and then show the kitchen house instead of his actual house and family?" I leaned forward to get a closer look, focusing on what at first looked like a large brown rock on the steps of the kitchen house. My eyes widened. "It's a dog."

"Where?" Jack leaned close to me, our cheeks almost touching, his nearness almost making me forget what I was saying.

I pointed. "Here—see? You can just make out the tail and the ears." I straightened. "It's Otis."

"Otis?"

"The dog I saw in the parlor playing with the other dogs. And in the back garden. I believe he belonged to the ghost girl who's been haunting Nola. That's how we know his name is Otis. Nola said the girl told her."

"The girl with the melted face. Evangeline."

I nodded, studying the painting again. "At least we know we're talking about the right historical period since this shows Otis in 1861, apparently before the fire. I just wish I knew where to get the answers to the rest of our questions. Because every time we ask a question, we just get another one in response." I picked up my phone and snapped a close-up of the kitchen house and the dog.

Jack's voice came very close to my ear. "As I've said before, we always figure it out. That's why we make such a great team."

Our gazes met. "I'm not the one who needs convincing."

His eyes drifted down to my mouth. "I want—"

There was a brief tap on the door and a young man wearing a vest and a bow tie and with a Mohawk hairstyle opened the door. "Mandy just sent me up to see if you two needed anything. Maybe a glass of water?"

Jack stepped back. "Not for me, but thanks."

"Me, neither," I said. "We're almost done here."

"Okay. My name's Tim—so just call down to the front desk if you change your minds."

Jack had already shifted his attention to the remaining portraits by the time Tim closed the door behind him.

"Wow." Jack sat back on his heels. "This would have made a great cover for my book if it had ever gotten published." He held up a small painting, maybe three feet by two feet, in an elaborate gold filigree frame. "'Louisa Gibbes Vanderhorst, 1921.'"

I'd seen black-and-white photographs of Louisa, but this oil painting showed her beauty and grace more eloquently than any photograph. It was as if the artist had captured her spirit in the paint, evolving it into a three-dimensional depiction not available from the quick snap of a camera. I'd seen her as only a wispy filament, but this rendition of Louisa in full color brought her to life.

"I wish we had the money to buy this painting from the museum," I said. "She should be back at the house, where she belongs, not in some storage room where nobody can see her." I held up my phone and took a picture.

The remaining two paintings were watercolors of Louisa's roses in full bloom and of the oak tree that had stood sentinel in the yard for over a century. A little boy sat in the dangling swing, and even though no plaque identified its occupant, I knew it was a young Nevin Vanderhorst.

"And these, too," I said as I snapped my final photos, stepping closer to capture the boy on the swing. "They're part of our house and its history. They belong with the house." My voice caught, surprising me. I could almost hear Mr. Vanderhorst whispering in my ear. *It's a piece of history you can hold in your hand.* I had come a long way since viewing my inherited house as just bricks and mortar. Yet somehow I'd managed to let the foundation crumble. Without Jack, it no longer felt like home.

A freshly pressed handkerchief appeared in front of my blurry vision. I took it with surprise—not at the fact that Jack carried a handkerchief with him, but that I was crying.

"It's going to be all right, Mellie. I promise you. I have a good feeling that we're going to come out on top, and Marc will be the one wondering what hit him."

I wiped my eyes and nodded, wanting desperately to tell him it wasn't our finances that consumed most of my waking—and sleeping—hours.

I composed myself while Jack placed all the paintings in their original order, then followed me out of the office and back down to the museum's lobby. Mandy was still in her meeting, so we left a message at the front desk to let her know we were done. Then we exited the building in silence, both of us lost in our own thoughts. I wanted to know how he could be so certain that everything would be all right. Either he was a lot more optimistic than I realized, or he knew something that I didn't.

Jack started the engine of the van but didn't put it in gear. Instead he stared out the windshield as if the ugly brown bricks of the building were immensely fascinating. Finally, he turned to me.

"I think that would have been almost kiss number seven if you hadn't attacked me at the bottom of the stairs the other day. So now I'm wondering if we need to go back to the beginning."

"I did *not* attack you! And even if I did, you sure didn't fight back."

His wicked smile told me that he knew he'd accomplished his goal of dragging me out of my black mood. Before he could say anything else, his phone buzzed with a text.

He looked down. "It's from Mandy."

I resisted the impulse to look over his shoulder and read it myself.

"Well, that's interesting."

"What is it?"

"She was just informed by a staff member that there's a painting from the Vanderhorst collection that we didn't get to see. It's a small painting of the fountain in the Vanderhorst garden. Apparently, it was taken out on loan without her knowledge or approval."

"On loan? But who besides us would be interested in the Vander-horst . . . ?" I stopped. Felt my throat go dry.

He looked down at his phone again. "According to Mandy, it was someone who flashed his credentials as a movie director filming in the city and promised a walk-on role in return for a favor."

Jack turned to me, his expression an odd mixture of disgust and what could have been amusement. "Marc," we said in unison.

CHAPTER 23

I held up an adorable pink smocked dress with matching diaper cover to show Rebecca. We were at the children's boutique Kids on King in my last-ditch effort to convince Rebecca that her baby shower should be a brunch affair in the garden with punch and tea sandwiches and lots of frilly pink clothes for her baby girl. And not the evening adult party with lingerie gifts that Rebecca envisioned.

"*This* is the sort of thing one receives at a baby shower," I said. "I mean, you've been to a baby shower before, right?"

As usual, Rebecca was draped head to toe in mauve, her new shade of pink. She took the hanger from me and looked at the tiny dress for a brief moment before putting it back on the rack. "Of course I have. Tons. And when we met to discuss my shower, I thought that was what I wanted. But I've changed my mind. Those kinds of baby showers are for older mothers. Like you. I want something a little more . . . unique. Something younger. Besides, I want to be the one to plan what my child will be wearing—not something chosen by someone else."

I let the insult about me being an "older mother" slide, and pulled out a white eyelet sleeper with a satin ribbon threaded through the middle. "But that makes it special—remembering who bought what for your little one when you're dressing her."

Rebecca took the sleeper from my hand and put it back without even looking at it. "I'm sorry, Melanie. I've already made up my mind." She patted her slightly rounded belly. "Besides, I've bought little Peanut here everything she will be wearing for her first year of life and really don't need anything else. What I really need is some lingerie to spice things up in the bedroom." Her eyes slid away and her shoulders slumped. "Come on. Let's head to Victoria's Secret since we're downtown, but tomorrow let's go to Mt. Pleasant. I adore Bits of Lace. They always have just the right thing. I can set up registries at both places."

I followed her out of the door onto King Street's crowded sidewalk. She walked fast for a small pregnant woman and I had to run to catch up to her. I grabbed her elbow, making her stop.

"What's this all about?"

She avoided my eyes. "I don't know what you mean."

I moved us against a storefront window to avoid the jostling of pedestrians. "You said you wanted to 'spice things up in the bedroom.'" I leaned in closer so I could lower my voice. "Is Marc cheating on you again?" I'd tried to think of a more delicate way to say it, but Rebecca never understood nuance.

She pressed her hands against her mauve-draped belly. She didn't say anything, but her eyes moistened with tears, the tip of her nose reddening. Eventually, she nodded. Just once, but it was enough.

Despite our somewhat mercurial relationship and the fact that she had willingly married Marc Longo, I felt sorry for her. I wished my mother or Jayne were with us. They were so much better at this than I was.

"Rebecca, sexy lingerie isn't going to fix your marriage. You know that, right?"

She wrenched away from me. "How would *you* know how to fix a marriage? I don't see you and Jack back together, do I?"

I held my breath, if only to prevent myself from saying the first thing that came to mind, and instead summoned the new Melanie. "You're right. Jack and I still have our problems. And you might not want to listen to me. What I do know is that Jack and I love each other despite everything and that we both want things to work out so that we end up together. I also know that neither one of us would ever turn to someone outside our marriage for . . . comfort. That's not what a couple dedicated to their marriage does."

With jerky movements, she yanked a pink tissue from her purse and dabbed at her eyes. "You don't know *anything*. I love Marc. And I know he loves me. It's just that"—she looked down at her belly—"he doesn't find me attractive right now. That's why I need a sexy-lingerie shower."

Not wanting to kick her while she was down, I didn't mention that the first time Marc had cheated on her, she hadn't been pregnant. I looked around and saw a group of tourists slowing to watch the spectacle of a pregnant woman breaking down on the sidewalk, so I gently took hold of Rebecca's arm. I led her along the street to Charleston Place and a secluded bench in the lobby near a window. I smelled coffee from the nearby coffee shop, Community Perk, and knew I couldn't get through my conversation with Rebecca without sustenance.

"I'm going to go grab myself a coffee—can I get you a decaf?"

She nodded. "And a fruit cup."

I headed toward the café, but she called me back. "No, change that to a pastry. And a candy bar."

I returned with two of everything, because I didn't want Rebecca to eat alone.

I waited for her to take her first bite of croissant before I spoke. "I hate to be blunt, but somebody needs to be. If Marc were committed to you and your marriage, he wouldn't be cheating on you."

Tears filled her eyes again. "But who can blame him? I'm as big as a whale!"

I recalled how many times Jack had told me I was beautiful when I was pregnant with the twins, and I felt my own eyes begin to moisten. "First of all, you're hardly showing. Your ankles aren't even swollen."

She looked down at my legs and nodded. "Thank goodness for that. I remember how huge yours were. Like watermelons. I guess I should be thankful that's not hereditary, too."

"Thanks for remembering," I said. "But my point is that no matter what you look like, that's no reason for Marc to be cheating. You're carrying his baby. That alone should make you the most beautiful woman in the world to him." I paused, trying to find a way to soften my words, but I realized being blunt was the only way to get the point across. "Rebecca, if Marc truly loved you, he would find everything he needs with you and your baby."

Instead of more tears, a grim determination settled across her delicate features. "He's just confused. That's all. And the stress of the filming is just about killing him. Half of his film crew has quit, and several of the producers are threatening to pull out because of the delays this has caused." She glared at me. "Don't think that I don't know you and Jack are behind all of it. We had a contract, remember?"

"As I told Marc and as you know full well, I have no control over what goes on in that house. And besides a few electrical mishaps, I wasn't aware of anything else."

"Yeah, well, those 'mishaps' have caused some serious delays." She chewed furiously on her second croissant, then took a gulp of her coffee. "Marc's doing his best to keep quiet about it because he doesn't want to upset Harvey, who is already halfway out the door. Katherine Heigl just pulled out because she's on a tight schedule to start her next project and can't have any overlap, which is pretty much guaranteed at this point because they're so behind schedule. Rob Lowe is starting to make noise, too, which is giving all of the producers the jitters. Without those two big names, the whole production is at risk."

"I can't say I'm sorry. But I can say that I had nothing to do with any of that. Neither did Jack."

Rebecca began unwrapping her Snickers bar, attacking the paper with sharp pink-painted fingernails. "And those hateful articles in the paper. I met Suzy Dorf yesterday for lunch. We had a nice chat."

I kept my face neutral. Rebecca and Suzy had once worked at the paper together, so it made sense that they kept in touch. But it still made me nervous. "And what did she say?"

"She told me everything she's written has been entirely her doing, without any coercion from you or Jack." Rebecca pressed her lips together. "Not that I believe her, of course." Her mouth turned up in a half smile. "We were considering suing her for libel, except all those negative comments about his book created a real boost in sales. Buxton Books had to order three more cases to keep up with demand."

"How nice," I said, and took a sip of coffee to wash down the sour taste in my mouth. "I can only promise you that I have not put words into Suzy's mouth. We did a short interview about my family's experience during the filming so far, but the rest is from her own research."

"I could almost believe you, except . . ." She looked at me with wary, tearstained eyes. "I shouldn't be telling you this. Marc would hate me even more." She hiccupped.

I resisted the urge to tell her that if she thought her husband hated her, her marriage was in worse shape than she thought. "Look, Rebecca. We're family, right?" I almost bit my tongue saying it, but I hoped it would be the one thing to make her listen. "I'm trying to help you. I'm simply suggesting that Marc . . . maybe isn't the man you think he is. Or the husband he should be."

Fresh tears spilled from her big blue eyes. "But he is. I know he is." She shook her head as if to clear it. "And I know you're behind the rest of the stuff going on at the house. Admit it."

"Really, Rebecca. I have no idea what you're talking about."

"Yes, you do! Every time Marc or one of the film crew goes anywhere near the stairs when Jayne is up there with the twins, icy hands shove them away. The first guy who quit broke a finger when he fell, so it's not like he's imagining things."

"Maybe he's just clumsy?" I asked, feigning hopefulness.

"And the other three guys who say the same thing? They're clumsy, too?"

Before I could come up with a plausible explanation, she said, "And whatever or whoever it is won't allow Marc near the grandfather clock.

He says his hair stands on end whenever he enters the parlor, and he feels actual hands grabbing at his shirt, pulling him away, whenever he gets within five feet of the clock."

I didn't say anything, but I was sure that Louisa was protecting the children and wouldn't allow anyone she didn't know up the stairs. And she more than likely was messing with the electricity to show her displeasure at the invasion of her home. As for whoever was prohibiting Marc from getting too close to the grandfather clock, I had my theories. I couldn't help but remember the girl with the melted face and her dog, Otis. I'd seen her in the parlor before, with Nola. I just couldn't think of why.

I took a deep breath. If I wanted her to be candid, I needed to reciprocate. "First of all, Marc has no business messing with the clock. Now, I do admit to having a . . . conversation with Louisa. She's always been protective of the children, and I made it clear that she had my full approval to continue during the filming. If she got a little . . . carried away, I wasn't going to stop her. Maybe when you're a mother, you'll understand."

She sniffed and dabbed at her eyes again with her wadded napkin.

Gently, I asked, "Why hasn't Marc said anything to me if he thinks I'm responsible?"

Rebecca was quiet for a moment. "I'm not sure. I asked him the same thing. And he . . ." She stopped.

"He what?"

She looked down at the crumbs and wrapper shreds on the napkin in her lap and shook her head.

"I can't help you, Rebecca, if you don't tell me everything."

After a deep, shuddering breath, her eyes met mine. "He . . . smiled. Not his usual friendly smile."

I wanted to ask her if we were talking about the same Marc Longo, but I didn't want to interrupt her.

"He said not to worry about it, that he had everything under control and that I should go back to growing our baby. Which was kind of sweet, but I was once a journalist and I suppose I always will be, so I had to keep asking questions."

I bit my lip so I wouldn't be forced to contradict her about Marc's comment being misogynistic instead of "sweet," and remained silent, my telltale crossed leg bouncing with impatience.

Rebecca continued. "So I kept asking. He's always so proud of himself when he figures something out, so I knew it wouldn't be difficult to get him to tell me. It's too hard for him to keep it to himself. He's such a brilliant man, I can't really blame him for wanting to share some of that brilliance, you know?"

I thought my lip might start bleeding if I kept biting it. Instead I forced a smile and nodded, my leg continuing to bounce.

"Anyway, he said that he'd found some kind of proof about the existence of something valuable. Something that he said would get us out of debt and secure our financial future." She looked at me. Swallowed.

"What else did he say, Rebecca? Anything I need to know?"

I could tell she was wavering, desperately torn between her loyalty to Marc and her loyalty to her family. But only one of us was cheating on her.

"As the future godmother to Peanut and as a family member?" I hadn't meant to lower myself and play that card, but Marc and his machinations always brought out the worst in me.

She looked around the bustling lobby, at the shoppers and tourists and hotel guests strolling unhurriedly in front of us, blissfully unaware of the personal drama unfolding on the bench in the corner.

Lowering her voice, she said, "He told me that the success of the film wouldn't matter, that we wouldn't need your financial support. That we would be free from all of our debts and any obligation we'd have to you and Jack."

I sat up, the pastries I'd eaten sitting like a ball of raw cookie dough in my stomach. With a voice that sounded a lot calmer than I felt, I asked, "Did he tell you what it was?"

She shook her head. "I'm pretty sure it has something to do with an old painting that he seemed excited about, but he wouldn't tell me anything else. He put it in his office so I don't have to look at it. Maybe it's a newly discovered Rembrandt or something. I don't know and I'm tired of asking. To be honest, I'm okay with him taking charge. Growing a baby is hard work, and I'm just so exhausted, I can hardly think."

"Try growing two while working full-time," I muttered.

"I'm sorry. What did you say?"

"Nothing important. Do you think you could snap a picture of it on your phone and send it to me? Maybe I can help you figure it out."

"Seriously, Melanie? I may have pregnancy brain, but I haven't completely lost a grip on my senses. If you want to see it, you should ask Marc. But I'm pretty sure he's keeping it under wraps for a reason."

"Maybe I will." I took another sip of coffee and pretended to think. "Off topic—do you know if Marc surfs any treasure-hunting blogs or websites?"

"Oh, definitely. He says it's his favorite hobby."

"Me, too! I guess the whole diamonds-in-my-clock thing started it. It's something to do when I can't sleep. I haven't seen Marc's name, though. Does he use a handle? Like Blackbeard, maybe?"

"Blackbeard?" she said, then laughed. "No. I told him he should use a name that was uniquely him."

I ran through all the names I remembered seeing in the various blogs and chat rooms I'd been browsing over the past weeks, trying to come up with any that made me think of Marc Longo, and drew a blank. "Like what?"

"Jonathan Goldsmith."

I might have blinked a few times. "I'm sorry—who is Jonathan Goldsmith?"

"Marc picked it because it takes a person of a matched intellect to understand it."

"You mean like a third grader?" I said it before I could stop myself. There was only so much swallowing my words that I could take.

She didn't seem offended. "You and Jack just don't understand Marc.

That's why you don't get along. Marc just operates on a separate intellectual plane that's hard for others to understand."

I wondered for a moment if someone might have spiked her coffee, then settled on the explanation that love could truly be blind. "So who is Jonathan Goldsmith?"

"He's the actor who played the Most Interesting Man in the World in those beer commercials. Remember? And that is *so* Marc."

"Because he likes beer?" I ventured.

"No, Melanie, because he truly is the most interesting, fascinating man on the planet."

Hearing Marc described that way made my stomach churn, and I was glad we were only a stone's throw away from the restrooms. "Well," I said, swallowing back the rising bile, "I guess that's better than Blackbeard." I began gathering up our trash to throw it away, making a mental note to go back through all of the blogs and chat groups to find Jonathan Goldsmith to see what he'd been posting.

I took her elbow and helped her stand, then waited as she delicately brushed crumbs from her lap. "So, what are you going to do now?"

Her chin jutted toward me. "The same thing you're doing. I'm going to fix my marriage, which means I want the sexy-lingerie party. We can still have it in your garden and keep it on the same date. I'm sure Marc will be happy to adjust the filming schedule to accommodate us."

I looked closely at her just to make sure she hadn't lost her mind. Her slightly reddened eyes stared calmly back at me. "Rebecca—"

She cut me off. "As I think I've already mentioned, you're really not in the position to give anyone advice on marriage, are you? You promised you'd give me a baby shower, remember?"

"Yes, but . . ." I stopped, an idea forming in my mind. "You know, you're right," I said instead. "I did promise. And if it's all right with you, I'd like to get my mother and Jayne to help. They're so much better at parties than I am. I can do all the organizing needed, but they add the glitter."

Her eyes widened with excitement as she clapped her hands. "I love glitter! You see? I knew you'd come around to agreeing that I was right! And the more the merrier, I say. When and where should we meet to plan?"

I pulled out my multiple calendars and did a cross-check. "How about next Friday, noon, at your house? With Marc at our house all day filming, yours will be nice and quiet. I'll double-check with Jayne and Mother, and with my dad, who will need to watch the twins, but let's plan on it. And because I don't want you to lift a finger, I'll bring take-out from Rodney Scott's BBQ and we'll have lunch while we talk."

Her eyes brightened. "And doughnuts?" Her eclectic taste in food combinations confirmed our blood ties.

"Of course." Prepregnancy Rebecca had been a strictly nonpro-cessed, nonsugar, nonmeat person, and it was refreshing to know that she could be normal.

"Should I bring General Lee and the pups? Reunite the family for a playdate?"

She clapped again, her angst over Marc temporarily forgotten. "That would be so cute! I'll take lots of photos for my Insta page. I'm trying to become an influencer. I've already got two thousand followers!"

"That's great," I said, having no idea what she was talking about.

I did have an Instagram account that Catherine Jimenez had said I needed and had set up for me to post houses on the market. I actually paid Nola to do all the postings with clever little blurbs and link them to the Henderson House Realty website and my phone number. It was a win-win.

We walked together toward Rebecca's red Audi convertible, which she'd parked in the attached garage. She was headed home for a nap but would drop me off at my office on Broad Street on her way. After she'd stopped at the curb in front of Henderson House Realty, she pulled me back when I opened my door and began to exit.

Gripping the sleeve of my coat, she said, "I lied to you."

I sat down again. "About what?"

"About not having any more dreams. I haven't had any since I got pregnant, but I had one last dream right before I found out. It had nothing to do with all those dreams I was having at the time about Jack getting buried alive, so I sort of forgot about it."

I took a deep breath, preparing myself. "All right. So what was it about?"

Rebecca closed her eyes. "She was on the floor in the parlor. On her back. She was in front of the tall clock, and it was like she was trying to fit beneath it. But then . . ." Her eyes shot open. "But then there was a tall shadow. A man, I think. He was pushing on the clock. And then"— she rubbed her temples—"it fell on her. It crushed her."

I felt ice sluice through my veins. "Crushed whom, Rebecca?"

She turned to me, her eyes wide with shock. "Nola."

I sat on the piazza in a rocking chair, drinking a glass of wine helpfully provided by Mrs. Houlihan before she'd gone home. I usually drank only at parties or on special occasions, and never by myself. And definitely not sitting on my porch, where Jack might see me. He'd been sober for a long time, but he still had moments when his sobriety was challenged by stressful events. Of which there had been quite a few in recent years, up to and including—but not restricted to—the crumbling of his career and a crisis in his marriage. Thankfully, I could claim responsibility for only one of them.

But after spending nearly a full day with Rebecca and then her revelation about her dream, I'd been in need of something to settle my nerves so I could talk with Jack. And not just about what Rebecca had told me.

I sat wrapped in my coat and two blankets—one brought by Mrs. Houlihan along with the wine—as the sinking sun grabbed the warmth from the day and dragged it beneath the horizon. I breathed in the chill air, enjoying the peacefulness. It was still too early for the spring tourist season, allowing the street to fall quiet with only the faint sound of tags clinking as owners took their dogs for end-of-day walks.

Despite the quiet, I couldn't settle my thoughts. Charleston sat waiting for spring, fat buds of wisteria and jasmine poised to erupt in gardens and window boxes all over the Holy City. I felt suspended, too, waiting for . . . something. Maybe it was the key to discovering what had happened to Adrienne. Or whatever it was that Marc thought would solve his financial woes. Or the elusive insight that would help me solve the problem of Jack and me. Like the eye of a hurricane, I remained still as the world swirled around me, changing directions while I waited for landfall.

The sound of a lone car approaching made me sit up and strain my eyes to see down the street. I recognized Jack's minivan, and my blood swished through my veins a little faster. Because the film crew had already left, Jack parked his van at the bottom of the driveway. I took a slow sip of my wine as I watched him exit the van, then walk toward the house and the piazza steps. Despite it being dusk and the exterior lights not being on yet, he was as aware of my presence as I was of his. He paused to look up at me, and I once again felt that familiar electric zing as his blue eyes met mine.

"Good evening, Mrs. Trenholm."

Just the sound of his voice saying those words made me sweat. "Hello, Jack."

I listened as he ran up the wooden piazza steps, using the time before he came through the door to collect myself and to slow my heartbeat.

He walked down the piazza and sat in the rocker next to me, placing his overstuffed backpack and a small white shopping bag next to his feet. "I'm sorry I'm a little late. I lost track of time at the library doing research, and then I had to run an errand. Did I miss bath time?"

I raised my arms to lift the blankets and open my coat to show off the huge wet spot in the middle of my blouse. "Yes, but I promise you that the twins will get dirty again tomorrow, so you'll have another chance. Mrs. Houlihan put our dinners in the oven to warm so we can eat together and Nola is in her room studying for the SAT. She's getting a bit panicked."

I took another sip of my wine, aware of him watching my every move. "I bought a four-leaf-clover good-luck charm at the Pandora store to give to her for her bracelet before the test."

A slow smile lit his face. He leaned over and picked up the small shopping bag, holding it close enough for me to recognize the Pandora label. "Me, too."

A gentle warmth settled on me, and it wasn't from the wine. "I can exchange mine for another one."

"Don't."

I looked at him in surprise. "Why not?"

He scratched his chin, thinking. "So that she knows that we are at least united in how we feel about her. That despite everything else, she has both of us watching out for her."

I looked into my wineglass, blinking rapidly. "We need to keep an eye on her. Rebecca's last dream was about Nola. A tall shadow was pushing the clock down on top of her. We need to talk with her, to tell her to stay away from the clock until we can figure this out."

"Agreed."

I nodded and took another sip of my wine. "How was your day? Is your book research going well?"

"Very." He paused, and I thought for a moment he might finally tell me more. Instead, he asked, "How was your day?"

I sat back in my chair and began rocking. "I spent most of it with Rebecca, which should tell you pretty much everything you need to know. I did have an interesting conversation with her, though, and learned something that we may or may not find helpful."

I saw his raised eyebrow in the dimming light.

"Marc's online handle in the treasure-hunting chat rooms and blogs isn't Blackbeard. It's Jonathan Goldsmith."

"You mean the Most Interesting Man in the World?"

I stared at him. "How did you know that?"

He shrugged. "Doesn't everyone?"

To avoid answering, I said, "I went back through all the saved chats and read through the blogs, and he's not the most talkative of members. He never adds anything new to the topic being discussed, but he certainly asks a lot of questions. There's a definite divide between those who believe in the existence of the missing half of the Hope Diamond and those who don't. And Mr. Goldsmith, from what I could tell, seems to be on the side of the believers."

Jack didn't say anything but rocked slowly back and forth, his chair creaking like old bones against the floorboards.

"What about you, Jack? Are you starting to change your mind?"

He continued to rock silently.

"Jack?"

Startled, he turned to me. "I'm sorry. What?"

"I asked you if you'd started to change your mind. About the existence of a Hope Diamond twin."

He didn't answer right away. "I've been watching all the back-and-forth chatter online, and some of the evidence is very convincing, especially the theories that Blackbeard has talked about. All I know for sure is that you and I have thoroughly searched this house and found nothing. And I'm positive Marc did the same at Gallen Hall when looking for the rubies. We've found nothing." He shrugged. "I'd love to believe it's true, but there's just no solid evidence, and even if it once existed, it has long since disappeared into history."

I lifted my glass, surprised to find that it was already empty. "Rebecca also told me that Marc found something that he believes will solve all of their financial problems. She thinks it has something to do with a painting he brought home. I'm not even going to bother suggesting there's a coincidence there with our missing painting."

He was silent for a long moment, making me think he hadn't heard me again. I was about to repeat myself when he spoke. "I suppose anything is possible. We can't know for sure unless we can see it for ourselves."

I smiled. "Well, then, we're in luck. I've arranged for a baby-shower-planning meeting at Rebecca's house next Friday. I've invited my mother and Jayne to act as decoys—I'll ask my father to be on grandpa patrol—so I can do some snooping."

"Sounds like a plan." His face remained serious as he leaned forward with his elbows on his knees, his hands clasped in front of him.

"I thought you'd be more excited," I said.

"I guess I'm more interested than excited. Like I said, the success of this film and the happy fulfillment of our contract with Marc are becoming less and less important."

"I wish you'd tell me why, Jack. You used to tell me everything. You even said that we made a great team. What's changed?"

It was full dark now, but I felt him watching me, sensed his gaze on my face. "I wish I knew the answer, Mellie. I really do."

"Is this where you say, 'It's me, not you'?"

He stood, picked up the shopping bag and his backpack. "I'm tired," he said. "Too tired to have this conversation now. I'm going to go to bed early."

I knew better than to think that was an invitation like it had once been. Trying to buy more time, I said, "Aren't you going to eat?"

He stopped by my chair, pausing for a moment before leaning down and kissing my cheek. "You go ahead. I'm not hungry."

I pulled on his hand as he tried to straighten. "Please, Jack. What aren't you telling me? Should I be worried?"

"No, Mellie. I just need a little more time to figure things out. I'm working on something big, and I'm not ready to talk about it yet. With anybody."

His words stung. "But I'm not just anybody, Jack. I'm your wife."

He pressed his lips against mine and kissed me gently. "I know. It's not something I could forget."

He pulled away, and stood over me for a long moment before opening the front door and letting it close softly behind him.

CHAPTER 24

*M*elanie.

The following Tuesday, I sat up in bed, roused from a heavy sleep by someone calling my name. I grappled for the switch on my lamp and turned it on, then frantically looked around the room. "Jack?" I said, out of hope more than anything else because it had definitely been a woman's voice.

Melanie.

The voice had no origin, instead seeming to emanate from inside my head and in the air around me. I watched as my door creaked open, showing only empty space and the night-light-lit hallway outside. It was only then that I recognized the penetrating scent of roses, and I knew who it was.

I glanced at the baby monitor showing both JJ and Sarah sleeping soundly, their bedroom night-light illuminating Whisk firmly grasped in JJ's fist. I made a quick mental note to ask their pediatrician if this was normal, then just as quickly dismissed the thought. For our family, "normal" wasn't a word that was easily explained.

Recalling Rebecca's dream, I hurried from the bed, leaving General Lee snoring on Jack's pillow, and walked quickly down the hallway toward Nola's bedroom. Her door sat wide open, revealing Nola's empty bed with no sign of her or the two dogs.

A light shone beneath Jack's closed door, the clicking of fingers on a computer keyboard as loud as clapping in the silent house. I turned my attention to the stairs, Rebecca's words shouting in my head about the tall shadow of a man toppling the clock and crushing Nola.

I ran down the stairs, tripping on my nightgown on the last step and skidding into the parlor, nearly colliding with Nola.

"Melanie? Are you all right?"

I nodded, looking around for a tall shadow and seeing only Porgy and Bess romping with an invisible companion. Turning back to Nola, I said, "What about you? You're not supposed to be anywhere near this clock, remember? Rebecca might not be a likely candidate for a reliable source, but her dreams are usually spot-on."

"Right. I know. Stay away from tall men and the grandfather clock. But I had to come downstairs because the grandfather clock was chiming like crazy—like, about fifty times—and I wanted to see if I could stop it. Didn't you hear it?"

I shook my head. "Maybe I'm immune to it now. But hearing it chime over and over should have awakened me. How did you get it to stop?"

She lifted her shoulders beneath her ratty Vampire Weekend T-shirt. "It just . . . stopped. As soon as I walked into the room. And saw this." Nola held up an object, but I'd already smelled the ashy scent of smoke.

I broke out in a cold sweat. "Where was it?"

"She—it, I guess—was lying on the floor, faceup and sort of shoved halfway under that little space beneath the clock."

I shuddered, tasting ash in the back of my throat. "Did, um, Dr. Wallen-Arasi stop by at any time yesterday and drop this off?" I knew it was wishful thinking, but I had to try.

"Not that I know of. I haven't seen it in a while. Not until just now when I accidentally kicked it with my foot. That hurt, you know."

"I'm sure it did." I shivered in my nightgown, wishing I'd thrown on my robe. "Did you see the girl again? The one with the melted face?"

She hesitated. "Not really. I felt her, though. Like how Dad knows you're near even before he sees you."

When I didn't respond, she said, "I'm not blind. You do the same thing when Dad's around. It's not like you can hide it. Especially from me. I write music and lyrics. I'm wired to be more attuned to human nature than most people." She shrugged as if it was no big deal. "Sort of like the way you can talk to dead people. It's just the way we're made, so we might as well make the best of it."

I scrutinized her in the dim light from the windows. "Are you sure you're only sixteen?"

"And going on seventeen." She laughed at the reference to our favorite movie, which we'd watched together at least six times so far. Her face became serious. "I just wish you and Dad would get over this thing. It's like you're matching bookends or something. There aren't any substitutions and everybody knows it. Except for the two of you, it seems."

"Oh, I know it. Jack does, too. He just needs more time." I said this to be reassuring, but I wasn't sure if it was more for her benefit or mine.

She was silent for a moment, considering her words. "I've always looked to you and to my grandmother and Ginette to show me how to be a strong woman."

"I'm not . . ." I started.

"Yes, you are. We all fail sometimes. But you always come back fighting. It's pretty dank."

"What?"

"It's pretty cool," she translated. "Except . . ." She looked down at the Frozen Charlotte as if unaware that she was still holding it, and placed it on the coffee table, then wiped her hands on her T-shirt.

"Except?"

"Except now. I'm not an expert in this girl-boy thing, but it seems to me just from all that Hallmark movie watching you've made me do since I moved in that if you want to get back together, you shouldn't be letting him call all the shots. Whatever the issue is, you're both wrong. One of you has to go first, so it might as well be you. Tell him to get over it and move on. You can figure out the rest later."

"You make it sound so easy."

She tilted her head. "Isn't it, though?"

Something wet touched my leg, and when I looked down, instead of seeing Porgy or Bess, I saw only the vanishing brown tail of another dog. "Otis?"

I felt another lick and then he was gone.

Nola stooped and picked up Porgy, who showed his thanks with licks to her chin. "Why do you think Evangeline brought the Frozen Charlotte back and put it here?"

"I have no idea, but I need to find out."

Nola scratched Porgy under his chin, making him go limp in her arms. Her gaze jumped from the clock to the Frozen Charlotte and then back to me again. She took a big step away from the clock. "Rebecca's dream is a little creeptastic. What do you think it means?"

"I don't know. I'm trying to find out." I paused as an idea formed in my mind. "What do you have last period today?"

"Creative writing. We're supposed to be doing the final edits on our short stories, but I finished mine a week ago. I thought I'd use the time to work on a new song. Why?"

"How would you like to play hooky and come with me to the Gibbes Museum? I need to do some research, and maybe you can help. I'd rather not go alone." I smiled reassuringly. "I promise to have you back in plenty of time for homework and SAT prep."

She grinned and looked so much like Jack that I had to glance away. "Sure. That could be fun. I'll let Beau know I won't need a ride home and I'll tell Grandmother that I'll clean the Depression glassware tomorrow."

My eyes widened. "Excuse me?"

"You know—the glass dishes and stuff in pretty colors . . ."

"I know what Depression glass is. I was curious about the part where Beau drives you home from school. And aren't you supposed to be on probation?"

She shrugged and dropped her gaze to Porgy. "It's no big deal. Amelia cut my sentence short for good behavior. And Beau driving me just made sense since we both are now usually working at the store on Tues-

days. I told Dad that I didn't need a ride on Tuesdays. I think he assumes
Jayne is driving me, but I didn't correct him."

"I thought you didn't like Beau."

Nola made a face. "I don't. He's such a know-it-all, and he refuses to
argue even though I tell him he's wrong about stuff. And when I'm
upset or mad, he says the same thing: 'The rain always stops.'" She rolled
her eyes. "That's so lame. But he knows a lot about music, and artists,
so I just suffer through being in his company to get to the good parts."

"I see. What is it you two argue about?"

The clock chimed three times. Nola picked up Bess, tucking the
little dog under the arm not occupied with Porgy. "It's late. I should get
back to bed."

"Is it about the podcast?"

She bit her lip. "Mostly. On his podcast, he spouts all this 'evidence'
about how ghosts aren't real and all psychics and mediums are con artists
and quacks, and I simply point out where he's wrong."

"I see. Does he ever mention me specifically?"

"Nope. I think he knows better." She grinned again. "Even when
an episode is about someone who is clearly a quack, I refuse to let Beau
know he's right. I just . . . can't. He's already too full of himself and
insufferable."

"I just worry about him because, well, he's a tall man. We can't forget what Rebecca said. I think it might be a mistake if you had romantic feelings toward him."

She gave me a sour face again. "Oh, please. He occasionally drives
me to school and bosses me around at work. Otherwise, I stay clear of
him. Besides, he's no Cooper Ravenel, that's for sure."

I heard the catch in her voice. "All right—go back to bed. I'll find
someplace to put Charlotte."

"Maybe in the bottom of the cistern?" Nola suggested.

"Don't tempt me."

"Should we tell Dad what just happened?"

"I'll tell him in the morning. He's working right now and I don't
want to interrupt him, but I promise to update him later."

I listened to the creak of the stairs as Nola returned to her room and I retrieved the Frozen Charlotte from the coffee table. I stood in the feeble light coming from the window, all of the unanswered questions swirling in my head like smoke. I clutched the metal coffin and started to walk out of the room, then stopped. I returned the coffin to where I'd picked it up, the pungent scent of burning wood heavy in the room. I left it on the table and exited, knowing that even if I did toss the Frozen Charlotte into the cistern, it wouldn't remain there for long.

As Nola and I climbed the front steps of the Gibbes Museum of Art on Meeting Street, my phone buzzed with a text from Sophie. I stopped to read it.

Charlotte and her coffin are missing.

I handed my phone to Nola so I could dictate while she typed so we wouldn't be stuck outside on the steps for another fifteen minutes while I struggled to text. "Tell her, 'No, she's not. She's in my living room.' And no emojis this time, please."

Nola's thumbs flew over the screen, and then she handed me my phone. "Too late," she said with a grin.

I looked down at the string of scared-face emojis and a smiling purple devil. "Thanks," I said, tossing the phone in my bag.

We climbed to the top of the three short flights of steps and across the black-and-white square tiles to the imposing front doors. I'd already bought online tickets to the upper-floor exhibits to save time. After showing the tickets at the visitor-services desk, I headed toward the elevators. "We have to move pretty fast."

"But I'd really love to see the miniatures collection again. Did you know that this museum has the largest collection of miniatures in the country? I don't have a lot of homework tonight, so no need to rush."

I pushed the elevator button twice. "I have other reasons to go quickly." I pressed the button again for good measure.

"Right." Nola sent me a knowing look before walking past me to the stairs.

"Where are you going?"

"To the third floor, where they have the special-exhibition galleries."

"But the elevator is right here."

She kept walking. "Taking the stairs is a good way to get in exercise throughout the day." She held up her wrist with the purple fitness tracker Jayne had given her for Christmas. "I'll wait for you at the top." There might have been a sprinkle of sanctimonious piety in her voice as she began climbing the steps.

The doors of the elevator opened, forcing me to stare into its welcoming sanctuary. I let out an audible sigh before following Nola.

There were fewer people on the third floor, and it was quieter away from the busy lobby and the lecture rooms on the first level. Our footsteps on the bare wood floors seemed to invade the hushed atmosphere but didn't completely hide the murmur of whispered voices that seemed to be getting louder as we approached gallery nine.

"I think this is it," Nola said, looking up to read the bold black letters on the wall. "'The Living Dead. Charlestonians in the Victorian Age, 1837 through 1901.'"

Only an older couple was in the room, halfway down the second row of vitrines on wooden pedestals that lined the four walls of the gallery.

I didn't need to hear Nola's confirmation. The swell of disjointed voices had grown louder, like a gathering wave leaking out of the glass cases.

Nola headed to the first one. "This is so cool."

I walked slowly toward her, gritting my teeth while humming "Fernando." The couple glanced over at me before returning their gazes to the display case in front of them. I hesitated, standing behind Nola and looking over her shoulder.

"There's no picture in this one," she said, moving aside so I could stand next to her. "Not all of the cases will contain postmortem photographs. I think the purpose is to just show the way people lived in Charleston during the Victorian era by showcasing their personal effects.

You know, like how iPhones and Crocs will be displayed in one hundred years to showcase our lives. Or, in your case, spreadsheets."

I sent her a sidelong glance before turning my attention to the displayed items. Inside lay a partially open gold brooch with a jet inlay; a silver brush, comb, and mirror set; and a crystal perfume bottle with an intact stopper, the bottom cloudy with dark orange liquid.

Nola made a face. "I think that brooch has hair inside it. It must be mourning jewelry."

I didn't need to read the sign on the case to tell that she was right. The specter of the old woman wearing heavy black widow's weeds standing next to us told me Nola was right. After making sure there was nothing about the Vanderhorsts inside the case, I dragged Nola to the next one, which contained a gold pocket watch, a man's silk embroidered waistcoat, and an engraved snuffbox. A framed sepia portrait of a middle-aged man sitting on a sofa and smoking a pipe sat amid the detritus of his life, the man identified by the plaque on the front of the case. *Henry Pinckney Middleton.* I didn't have time to figure out any family connection, as I was aware of the growing number of dead Victorians now following our progress around the room.

I moved quickly to the next case, forcibly moving Nola with me and humming loudly enough now to make the older couple surreptitiously exit the exhibit room. I stopped humming long enough to shout out, "I'm sorry!" before resuming, the growing murmur now like that of a boisterous theater audience after the curtain has closed.

I heard a baby crying before we'd looked through the glass of the next case, preparing me ahead of time for what I would see. I heard Nola's intake of breath and knew it was too late to warn her. Behind the glass sat an elaborate silver frame containing a sepia photograph of a young girl propped up on a sofa, a toddler girl in her lap, the eyes of both unnaturally closed. On either side of the girls sat two younger boys, perhaps brothers, in a macabre final family photo. A charm string sat draped over the frame, matching the one wrapped around the girl's hands in the photo.

Nola leaned down to read the plaque. "'Anne Fraser Heyward, age twelve years, nine months, and Eliza Drayton Heyward, age two years, six months. Victims of diphtheria outbreak.'" She straightened, her gaze fixed on the photograph. "That's so sad."

I nodded, my throat too tight to speak. The bright buttons threaded on the charm string winked under the bright overhead lights. I was almost glad that I didn't have time to linger, so I wouldn't have to contemplate the meaning of an unfinished charm string. I shifted my gaze to the front of the case, where a monogrammed sterling silver baby's cup sat next to a gold ring, the inlay made of fine blond hair. I was about to ask Nola if she knew if people actually wore mourning jewelry or if it was just something to have and remember when I felt a tap on my back. I eagerly dragged Nola with me to the next case, the rustling of long skirts brushing the wood floors and the heavy scent of pipe smoke following closely.

I kept hold of Nola's arm to keep us moving, glancing into each case long enough only to see if there might be anything inside related to the Vanderhorst family. Nola yanked me back to the last vitrine on the second wall. "Look—it's a Frozen Charlotte."

I stopped briefly to see the naked and very pale three-inch ivory doll with rouged cheeks and blond hair. "Lucky for her, she came without her coffin accessory." I kept hold of Nola's arm as we moved to the next wall. "Didn't Beau say that his grandmother collects Frozen Charlottes? I can't imagine why."

Nola was silent as we moved quickly past the first vitrine; then she jerked me back at the next. "Evangeline," she said, loudly enough for me to hear over my humming, which had changed from "Fernando" to "Honey, Honey."

I stopped at the name, returned to the case I'd just passed, and looked inside. A large unframed photograph had been put behind plain Plexiglas and displayed in the back of the case. Most likely taken from the vantage point of one of the city's many church steeples, the picture showed a large swath of burned Charleston city blocks, blackened debris the only evidence of the structures that had once stood. Puffs of white sat suspended like final breaths, frozen atop rubble piles. The acrid scent of smoke filled my nostrils, constricting my airway.

"Oh, my gosh," Nola said, pointing toward the far-right edge of the photograph. "That's the back of our house, isn't it? The garden's not there, but I recognize the back door and the windows." She leaned closer. "And I'm pretty sure that's the cistern, right?" She pressed her finger against the glass and slid it to the right. "Making that"—she tapped her short nail twice—"the kitchen house. Or what was the kitchen house."

She was right. Even though only a rear-view sliver of the main house was visible in the photograph, I recognized it. I felt like a mother distinguishing the top of her child's head in a crowd, and my heart leapt with recognition. My gaze slid past the backyard to what had once been the kitchen house. All that remained were the brick steps, the same steps seen in the portrait of Captain John Vanderhorst, with the brown dog sitting at the bottom.

Nola leaned down to read the plaque on the front of the vitrine. "'The north side of Tradd Street following the great fire of 1861. Artifacts recovered during rebuilding the area now known as Ford Alley.'"

Feeling the press of the growing crowd behind me, their shouts erupting into a cacophony of indecipherable words, I began humming more loudly as my gaze scanned the contents of the case, my eyes immediately alighting on a nearly completed embroidery sampler, dirt spots smearing the white linen, a blue thread dangling from a half-sewn capital letter Z at the end of the alphabet.

With precise stiches across the top of the sampler was the single name *Evangeline* followed by *1860*. A border stretched across the top, its repeating pattern a recognizable one. The face of a brown dog with pink tongue followed by an angular gold-embroidered design lolled against the top border, the last dog face singed by flames.

I took out my phone, and after making sure that the flash was off, I began snapping pictures of the plaque, the old photograph, and the sampler, eventually moving to the rest of the artifacts, which I hadn't noticed before. A blackened soup ladle that might have once been silver, a cast-iron pan missing its presumed wooden handle, and what appeared to be a very old and very bent wire whisk. This last item made me draw in my breath. I had just snapped the last photo when Nola jostled my arm, turning my attention to the woman standing in front of us, a name badge on her blouse identifying her as Dorothy.

She had a perfect helmet of blond hair and a kind face, ideal for dealing with excitable groups of schoolchildren and the occasional obnoxious tourist. "Excuse me, ma'am. Is everything all right?"

I smiled at her. "Yes, thank you."

She smiled patiently, reminding me of my third-grade teacher, Miss Blumberg, when I asked to go to the little girls' room for the third time during math. "We've had some complaints from other patrons about loud singing. . . ."

"I wasn't singing. I was humming." I considered telling her about the old man wearing a Clemson baseball hat currently standing behind her and wanting to tell her something, but I didn't think this was the time or place.

Nola tugged on my arm, pulling me toward the exit. "No worries. Sorry for any disruption—my stepmother gets carried away sometimes when looking at historical artifacts. We'll go now."

She didn't let go of my arm until she'd led me down the two flights of stairs, through the lobby, and out onto the front steps. I leaned against one of the handrails, catching my breath and keeping an eye on the front doors to see if we'd been followed by anyone—living or dead.

"Wow," Nola said. "I've never been asked to leave a museum before."

"She didn't ask us to leave," I corrected her, although it wouldn't have been my first time. "Besides, I think we saw enough."

"That was her, wasn't it? Evangeline."

"It's possible. But we don't have any concrete proof."

"I don't think that's possible, do you? I mean, we know a cook at the house on Tradd Street had a daughter named Evangeline who was born in 1847. That sampler was found in the rubble of what used to be our backyard and kitchen house, which is where Evangeline's mother worked. We know the kitchen burned from that photo and because it doesn't exist anymore, and we know that Evangeline had a brown dog."

"We're just guessing that the girl with the dog is Evangeline. We can't be positive."

"Come on, Melanie. It's not a coincidence." She held up her hand and began counting off, using her thumb first, just like Jack did. "One, the gravestone found in our garden had the letter E on it. Two, the sampler shows fire damage, and three, the dog face in the sampler looks a lot like Otis."

"I wouldn't know. I've never seen his face—just his rear end. But even if it is the cook's daughter, Evangeline, why is she coming to see you and warn you?"

"I wish I knew. I'm always a little freaked out to open my eyes when I wake up at night."

"I know the feeling." I looked at my watch. "We need to get home so you can start your homework."

We started walking toward the parked car, Nola's long dark ponytail swinging. She no longer had the purple streak weaving through it, but she hadn't lost the California spunkiness she'd brought with her when she'd first shown up on my doorstep. I loved this about Nola, her ability to blend into new surroundings and morph into someone different, creating a new version of herself that was still unique and awesomely her.

Looking down at the sidewalk, she said, "Can you ask Dad something for me?"

"Why can't you ask him yourself?"

"Because he never tells you no." She gave me her most charming smile.

I didn't correct her by mentioning the one glaring omission. "I'm not promising anything, but what is it?"

"Lindsey wants to have Alston and me over for a slumber party for her birthday."

"That sounds reasonable. When is it?"

"March third—it's the Saturday we take our SATs, so we can hang out together and celebrate being done, too."

"That's the night of Rebecca's baby shower."

Nola wrinkled her nose. "I thought it was changed to a lingerie shower."

"Yeah, well, it's a long story, but it will officially be a baby shower. And it's probably a good idea that you not be there. Both the Farrells and the Ravenels will be at the party, but if it's okay with Lindsey's mother, I don't have a problem with it."

She beamed. "Great. So I don't need to ask Dad, right?"

"I doubt he'll have any issues, but I'll check with him just in case."

"Thanks." She pulled out her phone and I watched with envy as she walked on the sidewalk while avoiding other pedestrians, her fingers flying on her screen. "Done," she said. "Just needed to let Lindsey and Alston know I'm in."

I slid her a glance. "Why couldn't you ask your dad yourself? There won't be boys at Alston's, right?"

She screwed up her nose again. "Of course not. It's just that Dad's so . . . prickly lately. I didn't want to take the chance of him saying no because I caught him at a bad time."

I couldn't argue with her. More often than not lately, the light shone under Jack's door through the night, the ceaseless sound of his typing making me feel guilty for sleeping. I knew this only because I'd begun checking on Nola each night during my frequent trips to the bathroom. Dark circles sat beneath his eyes, and he'd begun to have that faraway look that I recognized from when he was deep into his work. Except this seemed different somehow. Beyond his insistence on not talking to me about it, he appeared almost furtive. He'd been locking his door when he left the room, and he never took any of his calls inside the house. It made sense that he was trying to hide his project from Marc. But I couldn't help but wonder why he was also hiding it from me.

As I pulled out of the parking spot, Nola said, "Did you notice how all of the other samplers we saw in different cases had the stitchers' first and last names? Or at least their three initials. Why would Evangeline just stitch her first name?"

I considered her question for a moment. "Good point. I hadn't thought about that. Maybe your dad will have an idea. The only thing I know for sure is that it would be a whole lot easier to find her if we did have a last name."

Nola nodded, then bent her head to her phone, leaving me for the short trip home to wonder again about Jack's silence and why a girl who'd died more than one hundred and fifty years before had left relics of her life behind, but not a last name.

CHAPTER 25

Two days later, I was surprised to find Jack waiting for me in the kitchen when I came down for breakfast. He was freshly shaven and wearing a clean shirt, his hair still damp on the ends from a recent shower. My heart did its usual thump upon my seeing him, then settled quickly when I thought about what his reason for being there might be. Either someone had ratted on me about the hidden doughnuts, or there was something else he needed to discuss.

"Good morning, Mellie," he said, raising an eyebrow Rhett Butler–like as he sipped from his *Best Daddy in the World* mug decorated with tiny thumbprints.

"Good morning." I went to open the cabinet, but Jack held up my steaming mug.

"Fixed the way you like it. More sugar than salt in the Dead Sea and more cream than coffee."

"Perfect," I said, smiling as I took the mug. "Feeling better?"

He suspended his mug halfway to his mouth. "I wasn't aware that I was ill."

"You haven't been . . . yourself. This book seems to be taking a little more out of you than usual."

He took a long sip of coffee, his eyes never leaving my face. "Really?" He placed his mug on the counter and crossed his arms, looking at me with an expression I didn't recognize. "Have you been in my room when I'm not there?"

I almost spit out my coffee. "Absolutely not! Except for that one time when you went out at night and I was worried about you, I haven't been inside. I haven't been invited."

His eyes brightened.

"I mean, to talk. Or sit. Not to lie down. Or . . ." I made an incomprehensible movement with my hand, making the coffee slosh perilously close to the rim. "What I mean is, no, I haven't. Mrs. Houlihan has been in there to change the sheets and vacuum, but that's always when you're there. Why do you ask?"

"Because someone has been fiddling with the lock. I used the old Boy Scout method of paper in the keyhole, and it had been knocked on the floor. They didn't get in, though. The paper I'd placed between the door and doorframe was still there. But someone did try."

"Very sophisticated."

"Thank you." He relaxed against the counter. "I think it was Marc. He's still looking for that diamond. Jonathan Goldsmith has been very vocal lately online. Asking questions about legal ownership of lost treasures. I'm positive he thinks the legendary diamond is not only real, but in our house, and he's trying to avoid what happened with the rubies when they were found on property belonging to us."

"If we can prove it was him trying to sneak into your room, he's in breach of contract and we can throw him out now." I looked at Jack carefully. "But only if you want to. We know there's no diamond to find, so he'll still be strapped for cash and need our financial help. Which means he'll be contractually bound to help you. I know it's important to you. To us."

I held my breath. Everything I'd said was true. But I couldn't help but hope that his answer was no. Because if we stopped the filming, Jack wouldn't have a reason for staying in the house. We'd made little progress toward mending our marriage, other than the fact that we were now on speaking terms, but at least with both of us under the same roof, we stood a greater chance of making it happen.

Jack surprised me with a grin. "Oh, I think I'm having too much fun with this. The filming is annoying, but Harvey is paying us as promised, and I think we're sort of used to the mayhem at this point. They're way behind schedule, and I'm enjoying watching Marc self-implode. That alone makes up for a lot of the inconvenience. Assuming you're okay with that?"

I nodded, then took a long sip from my mug to hide just how okay I was.

The kitchen door opened and Jayne came in, holding the twins, who were dressed in sweaters and hats, ready for outside. Their sweaters and their hats didn't match each other's and I chewed on my lip so I wouldn't say anything even though I distinctly remembered laying out their outfits that morning after I'd taken them out of their cribs.

"We're ready for GiGi's house!" Jayne bounced the twins in her arms.

Sarah clapped her hands while JJ waved his whisk. Jayne put the children down and of course they both ran to Jack. I convinced myself it was because they'd already seen me.

Jack bent down to lift both children, loudly smooching their cheeks. "Great, we can drop them off on our way."

"Our way?" I asked.

"To Magnolia Cemetery. Jayne mentioned your plans to visit while we were attempting to have a civilized lunch in the kitchen with the twins yesterday. I figured I'd tag along if that's all right."

"Of course it is. But are you sure?" I asked slowly, certain we were all remembering the last time the three of us had been in a cemetery together.

"I am. I need to do this. Isn't that the best way to face our fears— stare at them head-on? Besides, I can pretend that you need me to be there. It will be good for my ego." His voice held a forced lightness.

"Yeah," Jayne agreed. "But maybe you should ease your way into it? Going to another cemetery with the two of us might not be the best way to reacclimate yourself."

"At least it's not at night," Jack said, looking at me. "And I've loaded my iTunes library with marching band music, so you don't have to hum. Nola said you were asked to leave the Gibbes."

"I wasn't asked to leave," I said smugly. "I left before they had the chance."

Both Jayne and Jack looked at me blankly.

"So," I said, heading for the door, "let's get this over with. It's supposed to rain later and the only thing I dislike as much as a cemetery at night is a cemetery in the rain."

The kitchen door burst open and Marc Longo entered, his reddened face sweating profusely. He held up his hand and I noticed his previously manicured fingernails were now bitten to the quick. "I have had enough of you." He pointed an accusatory finger in my direction.

JJ used that moment for a loud and malodorous passing of gas, making him giggle. Just the sight of Marc had a similar effect on the children as the sound of running water did on most people with full bladders. It was as funny as it was appreciated by everyone except Marc.

"What are you talking about?" Jack asked, stepping between Marc and me.

"I'm talking about every single wire and cord that was ripped out of outlets and knotted so tightly, it's going to take all day to straighten them out while I pay the actors and film crew to do nothing but sit around! And it's *her* fault." He stepped around Jack and stabbed his finger at me again.

"Now, hold on just a minute," Jack said, his voice still pleasant but now holding a menacing note. "My wife had nothing to do with that."

My blood warmed at Jack saying *my wife*.

"Right," Marc said, sneering. "And I'm the pope. We all know what's going on around here, and she needs to tell her little Casper friends to knock it off."

"You know, Matt," Jack said as he handed the children to me before moving toward Marc, "maybe if you were nicer to people, like your film crew, they wouldn't feel the need to play pranks to piss you off."

"My film crew is made up of professionals who would never jeopardize their jobs."

"Fine," Jack said, slipping on his jacket and zipping it up. "Tell Harvey and the other producers that a bunch of ghosts is responsible for holding up the production. Let me know what they say."

He opened the back door and allowed Jayne and me to pass through before closing it behind us, JJ letting out another explosive gas attack at the last moment. I kissed him on the cheek in thanks.

After we dropped off the twins at my parents' house, Jack drove us down Meeting Street to Cunnington Avenue and the front gates of Magnolia Cemetery. I always wondered if the nearly invisible street signage for the cemetery had been deliberately hidden to make it more difficult for tourists to find it. Despite the mosquitoes and the hard-to-find street signs, the thirty thousand burials—including many famous and infamous interred, and a real treasure trove of architectural monuments, natural vistas, and wildlife—made Magnolia Cemetery popular mostly with relatives of the deceased, taphophiles, and ghost hunters. And people like me who didn't fall technically into any of those categories but who were dragged into the cemetery by people who did.

A smattering of rain sprinkled the windshield as we drove through the gates. I was almost glad for the rain, because it meant nobody was out walking who could hear the beat of the marching band drums from our cranked-up car stereo.

I kept my head down, looking at the map Veronica had drawn for me, thankful that I didn't have to see some of the curious residents standing by their funerary statuary and the famed architectural beauty the cemetery was known for. Or peering at us from beneath the drapes of moss hanging from the outstretched limbs of the thick-trunked live oaks that shaded the dead in their sometimes restless slumber.

I leaned forward to show Jack where to go. "Veer right here on the main road past the Large Lagoon and head toward Mausoleum Road. Veronica says the plot isn't far from the *Hunley* crew graves, so you can follow the signs. She'll meet us there, so look for her car."

My phone pinged with a text from Nola. Charlotte under clock again. Marc found her. Not happy. This was followed by an angry-face emoji blowing steam from its nose.

Ywo olsu? I didn't bother to correct the typos since Nola was now an expert in translating my texts.

Fine. Beau here to pick me up. Same height so they had stare down.
GL bit Marc and ended it. Good boy.

"It's from Nola. Apparently General Lee bit Marc when he got a little feisty about finding the Frozen Charlotte. Not that I blame him."

Jack looked at me. "You don't blame Marc for being angry or General Lee for biting him?"

I grinned. "Both." I read the text out loud to Jack and Jayne.

"Please tell Nola to let Beau know that I'm available for the rest of the year to drive her to school," Jack said.

I put my phone down. "That's a lot for me to type. Why don't you just tell her yourself when you see her?"

He sent me a sidelong glance, then returned his attention to the narrow road heading toward the river, with the Ravenel Bridge visible in the distance. We spotted Veronica's car pulled over to the side of the asphalt path and Jack slid into the space behind it. A blue egret stood in the marsh grass, unblinking in the rain that had begun to fall in earnest. Despite it being almost March, the mosquitoes were out in force, their numbers most likely matching those of the spectral inhabitants who were moving toward us from behind headstones and rising from the ground.

"Can you keep the music on?" I asked hopefully.

"I doubt Veronica would appreciate it." Jack looked back at Jayne. "If anybody forgot bug spray, I have some in the glove box."

"I'm good," I said, remembering dousing myself with almost an entire can after I'd finished my shower.

"Same," Jayne said, scooting over toward the car door. She reached over the back of my seat and squeezed my shoulder. "If it gets too much, let me know. I'm better than you at blocking out the noise. I just don't want to do it now in case Adrienne has something to say."

I nodded, smiling my appreciation.

Jack held a large black umbrella over Jayne as she exited the van, helping her stay dry until she raised her own umbrella. When he approached my side of the van, he said, "My umbrella is big enough for both of us, if that's all right."

I smiled up at him, smelling his aftershave and soap, and feeling much happier than any person standing in a cemetery in the rain had a right to feel. My smile slipped slightly when I saw Michael exit the car with Veronica. It wasn't that I disliked him. It was just that I felt a resentment toward him because of his impatience with Veronica about her unwillingness to move on. I suspected he'd never lost a loved one, which would account for his inability to understand, but in my opinion, he'd been married to her long enough to have learned how.

After we greeted one another, I turned to Michael. "I didn't expect to see you here."

He put his arm around Veronica beneath their shared umbrella. "I hope it's all right. It was sort of a last-minute thing." He squeezed his wife's shoulders. "I thought we'd kill two birds with one stone." He let out a forced chuckle. "Am I allowed to say that in a cemetery? Anyway, we've decided to put in an offer on that house on James Island, if it's still available."

I focused my gaze on Veronica, who smiled back at me, her face unreadable.

"That's fabulous news," Jayne said. "I'm so happy for you. I can't wait to come see it."

"As of last night, it was still available," I said. "After I leave here, I'll go straight to my office, look at the comps, and give you a call so we can come up with a strong offer."

"Great," Veronica said. She took a step forward, out of the protection of the umbrella, making me wonder if she'd forgotten Michael was holding it. "Adrienne's over here," she said, walking across the drive to an area of the cemetery that my father would have called "gently manicured," which I knew was a euphemism for "being allowed to return to nature." A term synonymous with "laziness" in his dictionary.

Veronica stopped at a rectangle of cleared grass, a white stone cross planted at the top. A mature rosebush, identifiable to me only because of the thorns, clustered at the bottom of the cross, pregnant with buds waiting for spring. A sprinkling of pebbles sat at the apex of the cross, evidence of visitors.

Veronica smiled softly. "My mother planted the rosebush and would tend it. Now that she's not able, Lindsey and I come at least once a week to trim the grass and deadhead the roses. Adrienne preferred orchids, but they're not compatible with this environment."

We stood in a semicircle at the foot of the grave, a strong river breeze blowing rain and the salty scent of the marsh in our faces. I closed my eyes, focusing on the voices surrounding us, trying hard just to listen and not to allow my mind to open enough to invite anyone in accidentally.

"Hear anything?" Michael asked.

I glanced at Jayne and we both shook our heads. "No," I said. "Give us a few more minutes."

I concentrated, trying to separate one voice out of the jumble of words that seemed more like a tangled clump of wires. Jayne reached for my hand and I held it tightly as I clenched my eyes shut, listening closely to the indecipherable muddle of voices. The beginnings of a headache throbbed at my temples, but I continued to cling to Jayne's hand, straining to hear Adrienne's voice long after I knew it wasn't there.

"Anything yet?" Michael asked with a note of impatience.

Jayne dropped my hand. "Nothing. Nothing at all."

"What does that mean?" Veronica asked.

"It happens a lot," Jayne explained. "Spirits usually hang out in places that were important to them or wherever they have unfinished business. But if you think about it, people don't usually have strong feelings about where they're buried, because it's an unfamiliar place. Cemetery ghosts are usually there because they either don't want to be dead or don't know that they are." She gave Veronica a gentle smile. "I'm sorry. I'd hoped Adrienne might put in an appearance here."

Veronica appeared to melt, her face and shoulders slackening. "That's why she's at the house."

"Veronica." Michael squeezed her shoulders gently. "We've made our decision. We're going to make an offer on the new house. This doesn't change anything."

Veronica gave me a pleading look. "But there's still some time until we sell our house, isn't there?"

I hesitated, remembering the other spirit in their attic, the one who'd pushed me down the stairs and sent threatening texts. The main reason why we'd come to the cemetery was so I could speak with Adrienne alone.

"Of course," Jayne said.

I sent her a look of warning that she ignored.

"We still have time," she continued. "My sister and I will figure out a way. Won't we, Melanie?"

It took me a moment to form the word. "Sure." I swallowed. Forcing a smile, I said, "The renovations are almost done, but they will hopefully give us enough time." As if that was the only thing standing in our way of getting me back into the attic to ask questions.

"But not too much," Michael said. "We've got a beautiful new home to look forward to settling into." He kept his arm around Veronica's shoulders, his smile more like a grimace. "Thanks for trying." Glancing at his watch, he said, "I've got to get back to work. Come on, Veronica." Looking at me, he said, "I'll look forward to talking with you about the offer later today."

They said their good-byes and headed back to their car, Michael's hand on his wife's back guiding her to the passenger door as if he was afraid she might change her mind and stay. Her pale face stared at us through the window as they passed us, making her look like a ghost.

"Are you two okay?" Jack asked.

We both nodded. "Just tired." The rain had stopped, so I reluctantly stepped out from under Jack's umbrella so he could close it.

Jack peered at us carefully, as if making sure. "The Vanderhorst mausoleum is just around the curve. If you two want to wait in the van with the music blaring, I'd like to go take another look while we're here."

"For your current project?" I wasn't completely successful in hiding the note of hopefulness in my voice.

"Partly," he said. "I thought I'd also see if I could find anything with Evangeline's name that might have been missed in the public records."

"I'm coming with you," I said, walking toward him.

"Me, too," Jayne said, quickly catching up to us.

The Vanderhorst mausoleum was hard to miss. Even before I'd been forcibly schooled in architectural styles, courtesy of Dr. Sophie Wallen-Arasi, I'd recognized that there was nothing ordinary about this particular mausoleum.

I cleared my throat as we approached. "It was built in the Egyptian Revival style. Notice how there aren't any arches? Instead, Egyptians set their walls at seventy-degree angles to make their structures strong and sound."

"You've been Googling again, haven't you?" Jack asked, half of his mouth lifted in a grin.

"Maybe. Or maybe I just know stuff."

"Okay. What are these?" He pointed to the two stone columns flanking the inset door.

I frowned. "Columns?"

Jayne snickered softly as Jack sighed. "They're lotus columns, and the door has a cross on it so the whole structure doesn't look too pagan."

"I knew that," I said. I wasn't lying. I'm sure I'd read it somewhere the previous night while I'd been busy Googling the cemetery so I'd be prepared and know who—if anyone—to expect other than Adrienne.

Our feet sloshed with each step, forcing me to stop and look at the nice leather heels I wore. "On second thought, I'll let you walk around. The voices are getting loud again, and I'm too tired to block them out."

"Me, too," Jayne said, heading back in the direction of the van.

I'd walked only a few steps when I noticed an unusual grave marker near the Vanderhorst mausoleum, but set apart from the cluster of family graves. On the lookout for a grave that might be the final resting place of the Evangeline originally buried in our garden, I gave it a closer inspection. A marble column with a jagged edge for a capital made it appear broken off; a cluster of carved lotus leaves, matching those on the mausoleum, sat gathered on the top. No name or dates appeared on the front, only the dial of a clock showing the time of six thirty in Roman numerals.

"That's strange," Jayne said. "I wonder what the clock means. Maybe time of death? Maybe there's a name on the back."

I looked down at my shoes and then at the muddy ground between the asphalt path where I stood and the marker.

"I'll go," Jack said. "I'm already muddy." He paused to look at the monument. "You know what it means when the column is broken like that, right?"

"Sure," I said, not being completely untruthful. I did remember Sophie droning on and on about cemetery statuary at some point, but I'd blocked out most of it. "But you go ahead and tell us."

His smile could have been construed as a smirk. "It means that the person's life was cut short. Usually, broken columns indicate a young person is buried there."

I nodded somberly as Jack headed toward the rear of the monument. When he didn't say anything, I said, "Can you read the name and dates out loud?"

He didn't answer right away. Then, "I would if I could. There's just an odd symbol—nothing I've seen before. No name. No date." He walked around the monument, studying it from top to bottom to see if he'd missed anything.

"Nope. Nada." He pulled his phone from his back pocket and began taking photos. "I'll AirDrop to you and Jayne. See if you have any guesses. Could just be a decorative element, but since we're dealing with the Vanderhorsts, who knows?"

"True," I said. "And take a picture of the front, too."

My phone binged with the photos. I opened my phone and used my fingers to enlarge the photo of the rear of the monument on my screen. "At first glance I thought it might be Egyptian hieroglyphics, but it's not." I looked up at Jack and Jayne with embarrassment, remembering an earlier confession about how as a lonely child I'd taught myself how to read hieroglyphics.

We'd stopped in front of the van, the three of us bent over our phones, studying the strange carvings.

"It's very pretty," Jayne said, "which makes me think it's just decoration, but I'm not sure. It's just odd that there's no name or dates, just this weird symbol and a clockface."

I studied the picture again, enlarging it as much as I could. The design consisted of a deliberate pattern of elegant lines and curves that at first glance appeared recognizable, but after considerable study, I decided it was just random marks.

"Any guesses?" Jack asked.

Jayne and I shook our heads. I looked up, and when I glanced back at my screen, a small tingle of familiarity struck me. "I feel like I've seen it somewhere before. I just can't think of where."

"We should show it to Yvonne," Jack and I said in unison, grinning at each other in goofy surprise.

Jayne rolled her eyes. "Seriously, you two? Get a room." She slid open the back door of the van and climbed in.

I opened the passenger-side door and stared at the red pillow on the seat. I held it up for Jayne and Jack to see. "It looks like Adrienne was here after all. Maybe she just wasn't in the mood to talk."

I buckled my seat belt, resting the pillow in my lap while a dozen questions darted around my head, none of them with answers. My phone dinged with a text. I pulled it out of my bag and stared at the screen, my blood freezing in my veins.

"Everything all right?" Jack asked.

"No," I said.

I turned the phone so that he and Jayne could read the text. THE END IS NEAR COME JOIN ME IN HELL.

"We need to go back to the attic, don't we?" Jayne asked softly.

The throbbing in my temples intensified. "Yes," I reluctantly agreed. "But only after Rebecca's shower. Although, to be honest, I couldn't tell you which one I dread more."

CHAPTER 26

The dim glow from my bedside lamp was enough light for me to see my labeling gun and the open dresser drawer in front of me. The staccato click of the gun was better than therapy, even when mixed with General Lee's wheezing snore. I'd been awake since one thirty, reorganizing my drawers and replacing labels. I had just completed the third drawer with no sign yet of sleepiness and the oblivion that I needed to erase that last text from my brain as easily as it had disappeared from my phone.

My phone dinged with a text. I sat frozen, afraid to look at it in the dark. Not wanting to disturb General Lee, I took my phone to the bathroom, flipping on every light and making it as bright as day. I sat down on the edge of the tub, took a deep breath, and looked down at the screen.

U up?

Cold relief swept over me. With shaking fingers I typed Ued. I waited a moment for my phone to ring. There was only so much of my texting that Yvonne could endure. The opening bars to "Mamma Mia" echoed off the marble floors and I quickly slid my thumb over the screen to answer the call.

"Hello, Melanie. I'm so glad you're awake. I know it's a bit early, but I'm just too excited to wait before sharing what I've discovered."

"Is it about the sampler in the museum?"

"Yes. And no."

I waited for her to say more, but of course she was waiting for me to drag it out of her. I wondered if it would be impolite to shout or to threaten her, but I decided I wouldn't be able to live with myself, so instead I said, "All right. Let's start with the 'yes' part. What did you find out about the sampler?"

"Well, judging by the name and dates, I would bet my grandmama's strand of pearls that it's *our* Evangeline. Assuming I was a betting woman, which I am not. Going on that assumption and knowing her mother's name was Lucille, I did a little more digging in places most people wouldn't think to dig. But I'm a little better at this than most, I think."

After a long pause, I realized she was waiting for me to respond. "Absolutely. You're better at this than the IRS is at squeezing a drop from our last penny."

When she didn't respond, I said, "That's a compliment. Nobody knows how to dig through historical archives like you do."

"Thank you, Melanie. As I was saying, we've already dug through the family tree and records from Gallen Hall, which is how we know Lucille was married before she came to work at the Tradd Street home. Which is why we naturally assumed that the baby she was carrying was her husband's."

I sat up so suddenly that I dropped my phone in the tub. After scrambling for a moment, I held it back to my ear. "And it wasn't?"

"No. And I'm ninety-nine percent sure I know who the father is."

I wanted to ask her to skip the dramatic retelling of her brilliant researching and just tell me, but that would have been like asking a thundercloud to stop raining. I sighed with resignation. "So who is it, and how did you find out?" I sat on the floor, stretching my legs out in front as I leaned against the side of the tub, getting settled for the long haul.

She continued. "Just the fact that poor Evangeline was buried in the back garden got me thinking. Her mother was born into slavery, but John Vanderhorst freed her after he moved her to Charleston. Maybe the family needed a cook right then, but I had a little gnawing thought that there might be more. I couldn't find anything in the private records, so I had to think of a source of information that we hadn't considered yet."

I could almost hear her held breath as she waited for me to ask.

"And what was that, Yvonne?"

"Real estate! I thought you of all people would guess that. I started with property owned by the Vanderhorst family, including the Tradd Street house and Gallen Hall and a few businesses on Meeting and Broad streets. They didn't operate them of course, just leased them, but at one point they owned a gentlemen's hat boutique and a confectioner's shop. I thought you'd appreciate that last one."

She paused, waking me up from my stupor in time for me to say, "Yes, definitely. So interesting. So, besides discovering that the Vanderhorsts had their fingers in various enterprises, what else did you find?"

"I thought you'd never ask! Well, since Lucille was born into slavery but then manumitted, I decided to look into that a bit. I was able to find her manumission certificate, which only states that she was of sound mind and body and able to support herself. No motives are given, of course, but sometimes a researcher can infer certain things just from circumstances. Like why Lucille's daughter would have been buried in the back garden. I wondered why, knowing it was a piece of the puzzle. And of course I had to question why Lucille was manumitted in the first place. After 1820, a new law made manumission more difficult, requiring it to be allowed only by an act of the legislature."

I sat up straighter, tiny threads beginning to weave themselves together in my brain. "Go on."

"I decided to start examining real estate transactions beginning with 1847, the year Evangeline was born. And that's when I found it!"

When she didn't continue, I said, "What did you find?"

"No need to shout, Melanie. My hearing is just fine."

"I'm sorry, Yvonne. I got a little excited." I bit my lip and took a few deep breaths. "What did you find?"

"A deed to a house on Henrietta Street, listing the owner as Lucille Gallen."

"Gallen? Like the plantation?"

"Exactly. Frequently, a manumitted enslaved person would take their previous owner's last name, but Lucille chose not to. I can't say for sure, but I think I know why. What I do know is that there was a reason why she didn't choose the Vanderhorst name."

I sat up, the threads winding tighter and tighter. "But where would she have gotten the money to buy the house?"

"I thought the same thing. I had to do some digging, but I found the original deed and the transfer documents. And guess who bought the house and then sold it for a single dollar to Lucille."

"I have no idea. Who was it?"

"John Vanderhorst! Although, really, there is no need to shout. I can hear you just fine."

I blinked, trying to unspool some of the threads. "But what does this have to do with the sampler?"

"Well, Lucille may have had her reasons for not using the Vanderhorst name, but she made sure her daughter knew about her parentage, although for reasons I'm sure you can figure out on your own, she wasn't allowed to advertise it."

My hand flew to my mouth. "John was Evangeline's father! Oh, my gosh. Why did it take so long for us to figure that out?"

"'Us'?"

I blinked. "Sorry. You. You figured it out."

Yvonne cleared her throat. "As I was saying, I'm certain Evangeline knew who her father was, just as I'm certain by studying the sampler that she knew she couldn't advertise it. That's why she was clever about hiding her initials in her embroidery."

"Wait. What? Where?" I put Yvonne on speaker and flipped through my photos on my phone, stopping on the sampler, then using my fingers to get a close-up. "I don't see them. Where are you looking?"

"The gold-embroidered symbol between the dog faces in the border. It's the inverted letters E and V, done in a spindly nineteenth-century textura font known as Cuneiform. It was very popular with the Victorians. It's difficult to read right side up and almost impossible upside down unless one knows what one is looking at."

I made the picture even larger, and unsuccessfully turned my phone to view the photo upside down before giving up and tilting my head instead. "Oh, my gosh. You're right." I straightened. "It's—"

"The same symbol on the grave marker you saw yesterday at Magnolia Cemetery. You said you thought it looked familiar, and now we know why."

I stood and began pacing, the marble floor cold under my bare feet. "So that's where her father must have moved her body. Close to the Vanderhorsts, but not too close."

"Sad but true," Yvonne said.

"What about the clock dial? Were you able to make any sense out of that?"

"I'm afraid not. I'll keep looking, but I'm afraid I've hit a dead end with that one."

I was wide-awake now with no hope of going back to sleep. I looked at the three clocks I had placed around the bathroom, all set precisely seven minutes fast, and saw it was nearly four o'clock. "I'm dying to tell Jack what you've discovered, but I don't want to bother him."

"Melanie, may I give you some advice?"

"About research?"

"About marriage. Forgive me if I'm overstepping, but I've spent too many years analyzing research and studying human behavior not to have learned a thing or two. I've known Jack long enough to know that he's conflicted right now, and you're both at a loss as to what to do." She paused. "Sometimes all it takes is acceptance that you're both wrong. And then hold your breath and take a leap of faith."

I looked down at my phone, not sure how to respond, remembering Nola telling me pretty much the same thing.

"And one more thing," Yvonne continued. "I doubt that you waking Jack up in the wee hours of the morning will bother him at all."

I peeked into Nola's bedroom, where I found her sleeping on her side, Porgy and Bess spooning against her chest. A faint scent of ash mixed with roses floated past me, evaporating as soon as I detected it. Either the Frozen Charlotte had returned to Nola's bedroom or Evangeline had. Either way, I wasn't afraid. Not of Evangeline or Louisa, anyway.

A strip of light shone under Jack's door, but for once his keyboard was silent. I tapped gently on the door and waited a moment. With no response, I tapped again. "Jack? Are you in there?"

The air seemed suddenly saturated with the heady sent of fresh roses just as the latch clicked and the door slowly moved inward. I stuck my head in the opening. "Jack?"

I looked behind the door, then allowed my gaze to travel around the room until it settled on the large bed and the shirtless man sprawled on top of it, facedown, his laptop still open and sitting precariously near the edge of the bed.

I tiptoed across the room as quickly as I could, avoiding stacks of books and notepads, and lifted the computer, my only intention to place it on his desk. Instead, my gaze was drawn to the rotating album of family photos he used as his screen saver. I stood in the middle of the room smiling at the photos of our children and of our intact family, which included me. He'd removed the photos of the children from his office when he'd left the house to live in an apartment, leaving behind all photos of me. This display gave me a sparkle of hope, a glimmer of light the new Melanie tried to extinguish with the thought that the screen saver was old and forgotten, since nobody really looked at their screen savers anyway.

My thumb accidentally brushed the computer's trackpad, replacing the photos with a full page of text. My gaze automatically traveled to the header. POWER, GREED, AND DIRTY DEEDS: THE HOAX THAT FELLED A CRIMINAL FAMILY DYNASTY.

"Can I help you?" Jack stood in front of me, his pantherlike stealth-iness a reminder of his having been in the Army. His eyes blazed as he took the laptop from me and shut the lid, almost pinching my fingers. With deliberate movements, he placed the computer on the far edge of his desk, out of my reach.

"I wasn't . . . I mean, I didn't . . ." I swallowed, mobilized the new Melanie, and took a deep breath. "I just spoke with Yvonne and learned something interesting. She said you wouldn't mind if I woke you. I was just moving your computer so it wouldn't fall on the floor."

The shadow of a smile graced his face. "Did she, now?"

I nodded, surreptitiously appreciating his shirtless status and how the shadow of his unshaven beard summoned unwholesome thoughts of his pirate ancestor. He watched me swallow again as I attempted to ease my dry throat.

"We're pretty sure we know who Evangeline was. It's a lot of con-jecture and coincidence, but everything points to John Vanderhorst as her father. Because . . ."

". . . there's no such thing as coincidence," we said, finishing the sentence together.

He didn't say anything else, allowing the room to settle into an odd quiet, making me improbably nervous with the need to fill it. As if I no longer knew how I should behave in a darkened bedroom with my half-naked husband. As if I was afraid of what would happen next if I didn't fill the silence.

I began to jabber, barely pausing long enough to take a breath. Afraid to stop. "So it's not about Evangeline not having a last name. It's about her not being able to use it. Remember Nola telling us about the sense she had that the girl who'd appeared in her bedroom didn't want to show her face? I wonder if it had less to do with it being burned and more to do with being taught to be ashamed of her parentage. She didn't want Nola to see her face more from habit than not wanting Nola to see the scars.

"I'm glad we found Evangeline's final resting place, and at least now we know what that symbol is, although we have no idea what the clockface means—but Yvonne is still digging. I'm thinking we should bury Evangeline's toys with her and the dog bones. Maybe that will put a stop to Frozen Charlotte showing up every time I turn around. But I can't stop wondering why she's visiting Nola and why Nola thinks Evangeline is there to protect her from the tall man, although I have no idea whom she's referring to."

I took a deep breath and waited for him to speak, for the serious look on his face to transform into anything else. Finally, he said, "Yvonne was right."

"About which part?"

"About how I wouldn't mind if you woke me up."

I swallowed, the sound ridiculously loud. "I'll let her know."

He smiled his trademark grin, which always did funny things to my heart and turned my bones to the consistency of warm grits. He reached up and pulled something out of my hair, then held it up to reveal a lone Cheerio. "You're the only woman I've ever known who could make flannel and cereal sexy."

His hand dropped, the Cheerio making an audible click as it hit the wood floor. He tilted his head. "Do you remember that kiss you gave me in the foyer downstairs while I was attempting to speak with Desmarae on the phone?"

I nodded dumbly, ashamed to admit that I could barely think of anything else.

"That wasn't an almost kiss, was it?"

I shook my head.

"That was the real deal. The kind of kiss that almost makes me believe in do-overs." Jack stepped closer, his eyes studying my face while his hands cupped my head, his thumbs stroking my cheeks. "What is it about you, Mellie, that I can't resist even when I'm at the end of my rope and I'm blaming you for putting me there? I've been using these long weeks to try to work it out in my head, trying to think of how to move past everything. But I keep hitting mental roadblocks."

I watched him, not daring to move or to close my eyes. "Yvonne said something else."

Jack's eyebrows rose.

"She said we should accept that we're both wrong, then take a leap of faith."

We stared at each other for a long moment until he lowered his head and brought his lips to mine gently, like a person testing water in a tub. He pulled back, his eyes looking into mine as if he was gauging my reaction. I wanted to reach behind his neck and pull him closer, but I couldn't. I was already halfway there. I just needed him to meet me in the middle.

He moved forward, pressing me against the side of the bed. "Say no and I'll stop. No regrets."

I managed to find my voice. "I don't have a single regret where we're concerned, Jack. I've never done anything but love you."

He exhaled, his lips following the trail of his warm breath down the side of my neck, sending goose bumps—the good kind—up and down my body. Then he kissed me again—a real kiss this time—as we tumbled onto the rumpled sheets, where the last thing on my mind was regret.

I awoke in Jack's bed, the gray light of dawn beginning to erase the shadows, with what sounded like a marching band playing a celebratory piece in my head, complete with sliding trombones and clashing cymbals. I opened my eyes, surprised to find myself smiling, remembering all the reasons why.

My smile slipped when I felt the absence of a warm body next to mine. I sat up, the covers that someone had neatly tucked around me falling off. Jack wasn't in the bed or anywhere in the room. His running shoes were thrown in a corner, and his laptop was missing. I placed my hand on Jack's pillow, any residual warmth long gone in the chill of morning.

Scrambling to the other side of the bed, I picked up the bedside clock and held it within two inches of my face so I could read it. Six thirty. A part of me was relieved that it was still early enough for me to return to my room undetected to dress, but the largest part of me wondered why Jack had gone.

I slid from the bed, shivering as I searched the room for my nightgown before I found it draped over a lampshade. I threw it on, then headed for the door, stopping before I reached it. On the floor right inside the room lay a piece of notepaper, folded in half, that appeared to have been slipped beneath the door.

Eagerly, I bent to pick it up, hesitating briefly to contain my excitement.

Mellie, I'm so sorry. I shouldn't have allowed that to happen last night. I'm completely at fault and ashamed of myself. Things are still so unsettled between us, and I don't want to give false hope. I do love you. I just need more time. Jack

I felt light-headed for a moment, and when the blood flowed back to my head and extremities, it was accompanied by a strong dose of motivating anger. I remembered what my mother had said about me being her warrior daughter, who knew how to fight for what she wanted.

I crumpled the note and threw it on the bed before storming out the door. My mother might have been right about me knowing how to fight, but she'd also mentioned that I had a forgiving heart. And that was something I was no longer sure was true.

CHAPTER 27

Later that morning, I piled into my car with my mother and Jayne. My father had arrived with my mother to watch the twins; he had brought child-sized plastic gardening implements with grand plans to begin teaching JJ and Sarah about gardening. Beau was back at the fence doing the laborious task of repairing it, the sound of an old-fashioned cash register clanging in my head each time I spotted him.

I buckled my seat belt, then pulled my car onto Tradd Street, trying to unclench my jaw at my thoughts of Jack and the note.

"Why is Mrs. Houlihan so upset with you?" my mother asked as she settled her gloved hands in her lap.

"Because I rearranged the kitchen drawers and relabeled everything. I mean, I might not know how to use any of the appliances, but it *is* my kitchen. I had a lot of pent-up energy this morning and I decided to do something useful with it."

"You should have gone for a run," Jayne suggested from the backseat.

"I said I needed to release energy, not torture myself."

"Don't be so hard on yourself," my mother added. "You do know how to use the microwave, refrigerator, and coffeemaker."

I shot her a narrow-eyed glance. "Thanks, Mother."

"Where's Jack?" Jayne asked. "I saw his room was empty when I went upstairs to dress the twins."

With as casual a tone as I could muster, I said, "I'm not sure. He left early this morning before I woke up and didn't tell me where he was going."

I felt both sets of eyes on me. "He's deep in a book right now. I'm assuming he's either doing research in a library somewhere or at his apartment."

They didn't say anything, but I felt their probing looks. My phone dinged with a text, and before I could recall that it was in the purse I'd tossed on the floor of the passenger side, my mother had pulled it out.

"It's from Jack," she said. "Do you want me to read it?"

I swerved onto the on-ramp to the Ravenel Bridge. "No, that's—"

"The part I can see says to 'read before visit to Rebecca's house.'"

"Oh," I said, feeling a bit deflated. Not that I'd really been expecting an apology or an invitation for more discussion about the previous night, but still . . . "Okay. My security code is—"

"One-two-two-one," Jayne and Ginette said simultaneously.

"You really should change that," Jayne said. "Not only is it easy to guess, but you've used it for every single password in your life. Thomas says that's just asking for trouble."

"You're seeing Thomas?" I glanced at my sister, watching her cheeks pinken.

"Go ahead and read the text, Mother," Jayne said.

"I like the size of your font, Mellie. I can actually read it without my glasses. So can Martians from space, I'd guess." She cleared her throat. "'Mandy said the missing painting is a small one and shows the fountain in the garden. So you'll know what to look for.'"

"The fountain?" Jayne leaned forward from the backseat. "Why would Marc have chosen that one to take? Assuming he's trying to prevent us from discovering something, that just seems like a strange subject. He knows that the fountain has been taken apart and reassembled and nothing was found, right? Well, besides the two skeletons."

I barely heard her. "That's it? Jack didn't mention anything about last night?" I bit my lip, too late realizing what I'd just said and in front of whom.

"No," my mother said. "That's it. Do you want me to text him back and ask?"

"No!" I shouted, making both of my passengers turn to stare at me. "I mean, I'll ask him later." I turned up the volume on the radio to prevent further discussion for the remainder of the short drive.

Rebecca had moved into Marc's beachfront home on the Isle of Palms when they'd married. I'd been there only once, with Marc when we were dating, and I wasn't looking forward to a repeat visit. The yellow stucco raised McMansion was new construction, undoubtedly built on the foundation of a modest home that had once held a generation of a family's memories. Marc had told me proudly that he'd designed the house, culminating in an odd mixture of Craftsman, Greek Revival, and medieval castle. Judging by his forays into writing and movie directing, Marc wasn't of the belief that one had to have extensive training or talent for any endeavor one chose to dive into. Or, in Marc's case, make a huge belly flop.

"Wow," Jayne said as we climbed out of the car, our heels crunching on the crushed-shell driveway. "I'm glad Sophie isn't here. She'd have a few things to say about those crenellations encircling the roof deck. Doesn't really say 'beach,' does it?"

I popped the trunk open and grabbed the two bags of food from Rodney Scott's that my mother had picked up earlier as well as the requested doughnuts from Glazed, and handed one to Jayne. "Oh, just wait until you see the inside."

"Be nice, girls," our mother warned. "We should feel nothing but compassion for Rebecca right now."

"Because she's pregnant?" I asked as we climbed the long flight of tabby front steps, feeling winded by the time I reached the top.

"Because she's married to Marc Longo," she whispered, indicating the security camera above the front door.

I pressed the doorbell and listened as we were serenaded with chimes ringing out Gershwin's "Summertime."

"Is that . . . ?" Jayne began.

"It is. I haven't been inside since Rebecca redecorated it, but from what she's told me, the chime will probably be the most tasteful thing in the house, so prepare yourself."

Rebecca opened the door swathed in mauve silk disguised as a dressing gown. "Good morning, girls!" She greeted us all with air kisses, then closed the door behind us. "I'm sorry we couldn't have our doggy play-date, but our groomer had a last-minute cancellation and you know how hard it is to get an appointment with a good groomer. We were desperate because I wanted Pucci to look her best for the shower and her fur is always at its fluffiest perfection after a couple of weeks. Not to mention the color rinse. It's always too fuchsia at first, and it takes a while before it fades to the perfect shade of pink. And we want her to look her best for the party, don't we?"

My mother's knuckle prodded me from behind. "Of course. And no worries. We'll do it next time." I didn't mention that I could have sworn all three dogs looked relieved when I told them they weren't going to see Pucci.

Rebecca looked at the paper bags Jayne and I held and sniffed. "Perfect timing. I'm famished. Follow me, ladies."

Rebecca led us behind a double-winged staircase with wide brass banisters and across pink marble floors. My eyes blurred from the sheer quantity of rose-hued furniture on our way to the enormous rear patio. It overlooked the ocean and an infinity pool, but I don't think any of us really noticed either one, as we were too busy taking in all the cushions, rugs, and tableware in every shade of pink imaginable. The pièce de résistance was a blush-colored stone statue of a mermaid, with two starfish placed strategically on the tips of her pendulous breasts, that protruded over the built-in grill.

Rebecca slid open the glass doors, folding them until they disappeared into the wall, then swept past us, her silk hem swishing over the marble. "The weather is just perfect right now, so I thought we'd eat outside." She indicated chairs for us to sit around a large distressed-wood table stained a pale rose.

"It is lovely," I agreed, thankful we had the open water to look at while eating. Jayne and I began taking the food out of the bags, my stomach rumbling loudly at the tangy sweet smell of the renowned barbecue sauce.

Rebecca picked up a glass pitcher of sweet tea and began pouring it into glasses already on the table. "It will be perfect for my shower in less than a week!"

"That's not really a lot of time, Rebecca. I've been wondering if I might have a couple more weeks. I've got a lot going on, and I want to make sure that I have enough time to make this shower special." Which was only partially true. Mostly, I was hoping that given more time she'd change her mind about the theme completely.

"Not to worry, Melanie. I've done all the work for you." She picked up an accordion file sitting on a side table and helpfully placed it in my tote bag. "I've got the menu all set, the name of the caterer, and my plans for party decor. I wanted to hire your designer, Greco, but after I told him my plans, he realized that he was already booked for another job that night. Such a shame. And then, after looking around my house here, I realized that I didn't actually need anyone else's ideas." She giggled.

I shared surreptitious looks with my mother and sister as I transferred individual food orders onto rose-decorated china plates.

"We thought this was supposed to be a planning session," Mother said as she carefully took off her gloves to prepare to eat.

Rebecca's expression grew serious. "Well, yes, but then I got to thinking that my tastes are a little more . . . refined than most people's, so I decided to just go ahead and do it all myself. Besides, I didn't get the impression that Melanie was completely on board with my shower theme, so I thought it best to take charge so I can be assured it will be the party I want. Not to mention the time crunch, of course. Luckily, I have a natural knack for design and entertaining, which allows me to come up with something brilliant with very little time." She smiled brightly as she began slathering a hush puppy with honey butter. "But I'm glad you're here, because there's something else I wanted to talk about."

"Yes?" I said, poking my fork into my Pig Out Salad, the compromise I'd made with Jayne for my lunch choice. She'd said that with all the bacon, cheese, and dressing it didn't count as healthy. I'd had to point out that it was under the menu heading "Greens," and therefore it did.

"Did you have another dream that you forgot to tell us about?" I asked.

"No," Rebecca said primly. "It's about Marc. I'm worried about him."

I glanced at Jayne and our mother, who wore identical expressions of hesitant concern. Seeing as how they had evidently put me in charge, I said, "And why is that?"

Rebecca picked up a crinkle fry and dipped it into the honey butter, obviously unconcerned about the salt or calories or about double-dipping in our communal butter. "I've been following all those treasure sites and blogs to try to figure out what's going on. And don't try to deny it, Melanie. I know that you and Jack do, too. You're obviously DonutGirl and Jack's JT, although neither one of you ever posts anything. You just eavesdrop."

"It's not called eavesdropping, Rebecca. I think it's best not to post anything in a public forum peopled by experts if I don't have anything to add to the conversation. Unlike some people," I said, a veiled reference to her husband and other amateurs like him who happily shared conspiracy stories that linked the Hope Diamond to the assassination of President Kennedy and Prince Philip's death. I didn't need to ask what Rebecca's online persona was, having long ago recognized her as PUCCISMOM. At least she didn't post much, just the occasional random question regarding weather and fashion in various corners of the world when a contributor mentioned their location.

"Yes, well, as you know, Marc is very well-informed and is a vital part of the online treasure-hunting community. It's just that recently he seems to be the victim of online bullying from that Blackbeard guy."

I knew which posts she was referring to. "Unless I'm missing something, Rebecca, I don't think that another contributor expressing a different opinion is considered bullying. All Blackbeard said is that if Marc couldn't show whatever proof he's claiming to have regarding the existence of the other half of the Hope Diamond, then the other members have no other choice but to assume he's not telling the truth."

"She's right," Jayne said. "Was he threatened?"

Rebecca took another fry, dipped it in the butter, then licked the salt from her fingers, evidently forgetting that she wasn't alone. "Not in so many words. He accused Marc of trying to pull a hoax. So he basically called Marc a liar."

I wanted to point out that sometimes the truth hurt, but felt my mother's knuckle jabbing into my ribs. There were times when I really resented her mother's intuition.

"Rebecca, honey," Ginny said, pushing a glass of sweet tea closer to Rebecca, "do you know for certain that Marc does have evidence?"

She stared at her plate for a long moment, then nodded. "I told Melanie. It's an old painting he borrowed from the museum." I was amazed she didn't use air quotes around the word "borrowed," because I certainly would have. "I didn't see it. He just brought it into the house and put it in his office without showing it to me."

"How do you know it's evidence, then?" asked Jayne.

Rebecca looked up, her jaw jutting out defiantly. "Because he told me. He said with the proof he discovered, it won't matter if the film gets canceled because we won't need the money. It's why he's stopped complaining to me about the spooky stuff going on in the house that's making the film crew leave."

Her lower lip wobbled as she attempted a sip of her sweet tea, and some of it dribbled down her chin without her noticing.

Jayne picked up a cloth napkin and gently dabbed Rebecca's face. "There, there," she said, her inner nanny kicking in.

"Maybe you can show us?" I suggested. "That way I can go online and back Marc up."

Her eyes met mine, and I knew she was remembering our conversation at Charleston Place over coffee, when I'd asked to see the painting and she accused me of trying to take advantage of a woman with pregnancy brain.

"Is that the best you can do, Melanie? I'm sure Jack would give his eyeteeth to learn what Marc has discovered. He's that desperate to get back at Marc."

A wave of righteous anger swept through me, making me forget Rebecca's pregnant state despite my mother's calming hand on my arm. "Can you blame him?" I asked, my voice louder than I'd planned. "Marc has tried over and over to ruin Jack's life and I'm sure he finds it irritating that Jack is still alive and kicking. And if Marc is stupid enough to believe the rumors that a giant diamond exists somewhere in our house, then he deserves to be called out in a public forum. From my experience, if Marc told me the sky was blue, I'd call him a liar."

The table fell silent as everyone looked at me. I took a sip of my tea, my appetite completely gone even though we hadn't had dessert yet. I felt my mother watching me, prodding me to apologize, but I couldn't. Because every single word was true.

Instead of rebuking me, Rebecca looked down at her lap as she twisted the dusty rose linen napkin between her hands. "He's still seeing that . . . woman. And there's another one, too. A blonde. I saw them walking into the Spectator Hotel."

"Did you ask him about it?" Jayne said, using her soothing nanny voice. "She could be a business associate and they were going for drinks. They do have a wonderful bar."

Rebecca looked up and let out a sniffle, almost making me feel sorry for her. Almost. "Except it was eleven in the morning, and they were holding hands and kissing before walking inside." She began to sob, and Jayne put a comforting arm around her shoulders.

"I'm so sorry," Jayne said. "You don't deserve that."

Rebecca looked up, her eyes and the tip of her nose a matching shade of dark pink. "I think the lingerie shower will do the trick. Don't you think so? He'll see me as sexy again and remember all the good times. He won't want to look at anyone else."

Again the table fell silent. "Rebecca," Ginny said softly, "regardless of what Marc thinks, it doesn't erase his actions, which are inexcusable, hurtful, and solid grounds for divorce. I know you think you love him and want to hold on to him, and that's your decision. But whatever you decide, remember that we're your family, and we'll help you through whatever happens."

"And maybe even plan a little revenge," Jayne suggested.

I nodded eagerly while our mother sent us a warning glance.

Rebecca remained silent except for a sniffle as she placed her twisted napkin on the table and slid her chair back. "I'm tired. I think I'll go take a nap now if you don't mind seeing yourselves out. Just leave the doughnuts on the table—I'm sure I'll be hungry later."

Without looking directly at us, she said, "If any of you would like to powder your nose before you head back, the powder room is down the hall to the right of the door where you came in." She paused a moment. "Right next to Marc's office. He was in a rush this morning, so I don't think he had time to lock the painting in his safe. He thinks I'm too stupid to be curious about what he's up to, which makes him careless."

She swept past us into the house, the sound of swishing silk following her as she headed for the stairs. We looked at one another and then, without a word, walked in the direction of Marc's office.

This room had apparently been off-limits to Rebecca's decorating skills, meaning it wasn't pink, but neither had anyone with any knowledge of design touched any part of it. It resembled a college dorm room rather than the office of a successful businessman, with a mishmash of furniture and with random pictures hanging on the walls. A tall file cabinet stood between the windows next to an antique partners desk; the file drawers were locked, as were the desk drawers. A large safe sat on the other side of the desk, its door solid and very, very locked.

"So, we're looking for a painting?" Ginny asked.

"Yes. A small one of the fountain in my garden. I don't think it's tiny, so it shouldn't be too hard to find. I'm thinking a thick gilded frame since all the other paintings we saw at the museum had the same frames."

"Like this?" Jayne asked, reaching into the space between the desk and file cabinet where a small painting had been casually placed on the floor. "If this is the right one, Marc is either incredibly lazy or just plain stupid."

"Do I have to pick just one?" I asked, feeling my mother's disappointed gaze on me.

I looked at the painting, recognizing my garden and trying to see what Marc had found so important. It showed the fountain and the area around it in the glow of early morning, heavy dewdrops sitting atop grass blades and rose petals and even on the nose and extremities of the perpetually peeing boy in the fountain. The sun reflected off of the myriad drops, creating pinpoints of light throughout the scene in what appeared to be a nod toward promise and hope. Definitely not something I would have assumed would attract the attention of someone like Marc Longo.

"I don't get it," Jayne said. "What's so special about the painting?"

"Maybe it is a hoax," I said, the word sounding oddly familiar. "Shake it and see if anything rattles."

She gave it a gentle shake, then pressed her fingers carefully along the back. "If a big diamond was hidden inside this painting, it's not there anymore."

The sound of movement from upstairs startled us. "We need to go," I whispered. "I don't want Rebecca to find us in here."

"She practically gave us permission," Jayne said.

"Yes, but if she finds us, then she'll have to lie to Marc, and that's what she was trying to avoid."

"Okay." Jayne drew out the word in a perfect imitation of Nola. "Let's take the painting with us, then."

I shook my head. "Absolutely not. We don't want Marc to know we've seen it, so make sure you put it back exactly where you found it."

The clack of low-heeled slippers crossed the wood floor somewhere upstairs. Ginny moved to the door. "Quick, Jayne, hold up the painting. I think it would be a good idea for Mellie to take pictures. I'll play decoy and make lots of noise in the powder room."

She disappeared into the hallway while I shared a moment of surprise with Jayne at the incongruity of our elegant mother playing decoy in a bathroom.

Jayne did as she'd been told while I took photos from every angle, with and without flash, in bursts—as Nola had shown me how to do—and in panorama. I even did a slow-motion video just to be thorough.

Ginny appeared in the doorway. "Hurry, girls. Did you get what you needed?"

I nodded as we followed her out into the hallway. As we passed the powder room, she dashed inside and did a quick flush of the toilet and ran the tap before turning on the light. "I'll leave it on so she knows we were in there," she said conspiratorially.

"I'll meet you at the car," I said. "I just want to grab something."

Jayne took hold of my arm and led me to the front door. "Rebecca said to leave the doughnuts there. Would you deprive a pregnant woman?"

I wasn't allowed to answer as I was practically dragged out the door.

We'd piled into the car and were headed back to Highway 17 to return to Charleston when my phone rang. Ginny pulled the phone out of my purse and looked at the screen before I could tell her not to.

"It's Beau Ryan. Do you want me to answer it?"

I shook my head and pressed the phone button on my steering wheel, which was the extent of my knowledge concerning all the high-tech items apparently loaded into my car. Otherwise I was blissfully unaware of them.

"Hi, Beau. Please don't tell me you're done with the fencing already." I was already planning how to ask him if I could pay in installments when his words caught my attention. "I'm sorry. What did you say?"

"There's been an accident."

I braked suddenly, making the driver behind me blare his horn as he swerved his car around me. "What? Is anybody hurt?" My mind immediately flooded with pictures of the twins poking each other's eyes out with plastic rakes. And of a car accident involving Nola. My hands gripped the steering wheel as I braced myself.

"No, thankfully. It's just Marc Longo."

"Oh, thank goodness." I looked over at my mother giving me an admonishing stare. "I mean, is he all right?"

"Well, it looks to me like he might have a broken foot. I called nine-one-one and Mrs. Longo. Her phone went right to voice mail, so she might have turned it off. The ambulance is already here and EMTs are stabilizing him before taking him to the hospital."

"Did you see it happen?"

"Yes, ma'am. I'd gone inside for a drink of water in the kitchen—Mrs. Houlihan always leaves me a pitcher and a couple of cookies. I heard noises from the front parlor that sounded like clock chimes being knocked together, so I went to investigate. Marc was standing on one of the dining room chairs—"

"With his shoes on?" I asked, getting a knuckle prod from both my mother and Jayne.

"Actually, no. I think his foot is hurt more than it might have been if he'd been wearing shoes. Anyway, it looked like he was trying to pull the pineapple finial off the top of the clock. I might have surprised him, because he sort of jerked back and lost his balance and fell off the chair. He would have stuck his landing if his foot hadn't landed on a pile of old buttons lying on the ground. I'm thinking he must have hung on to that finial and pulled the clock forward so that the clock landed on his leg when they both fell."

"Buttons?" Jayne asked from the backseat.

"Yes, ma'am. A pretty big pile. I haven't had time to really look, but I did see a tattered string on the floor, so they might be from an antique charm string. Not sure what they're doing on the floor, though." He paused as if waiting for someone to offer an explanation.

The three of us glanced at one another inside the car but remained silent.

"Must have been a ghost," he said, then laughed. "If there were such a thing. Anyway, Marc's lucky the clock didn't land on his head—that thing is heavy. Jack and I tried to lift it, but it wouldn't budge. Solid mahogany is my guess. Doesn't look like the glass broke, which is surprising, but I imagine that the inner workings will need some repair. The ones in old clocks are very delicate. I'll be happy to recommend some experts my grandmother works with."

The phantom sound of the cash register rang again in the back of my brain. "I'll let you know. And you can take the rest of the day off," I said hopefully. "I'm sure it's all been pretty traumatic for you."

"That's very nice of you to offer, but I'll keep going. I'll keep trying to reach Mrs. Longo if you like."

"No. Thanks, Beau, but I think I need to be the one to tell her." I didn't mention that I wanted to suggest calling off the baby shower since Marc was injured.

"One more thing. Do you know anything about a filming hiatus? Chelsea Gee and Jacob Reynolds just stopped by to pick up a few things, saying they were flying back to LA. Not that it's any of my business. Just curious."

"I have no idea. Is Jack still there? Maybe he knows."

"Actually, he just left."

I frowned. "Did he say when he'd return?"

There was a long pause accompanied by the feeling of my stomach sinking. "No, ma'am. I mean, Melanie. But it might be a while. He put a couple of suitcases in the trunk before he left."

"I suppose it's too much to hope that Harvey Beckner is in one of them." I forced a laugh just so I wouldn't cry.

"I believe Harvey's in LA," Beau said.

"Right." I swallowed thickly. "I'll be home in about fifteen minutes. See you then."

I clicked the steering wheel button and disconnected the call, then tried twice to reach Rebecca, the call going to voice mail each time. I slammed my hands against the steering wheel in frustration.

"Are you okay, Mellie?" My mother's soft voice was almost more than I could take.

"I'm fine. Just fine." I pressed down the accelerator as we headed toward the East Bay exit ramp, slowing down only when I saw my mother brace her hands against the dashboard.

"What are you going to do?" Jayne asked quietly.

I took a deep breath. "I'm going to drop Mother off at her house and bring you back to mine so you can rescue Dad from the twins, who are most likely covered in dirt and in desperate need of a bath. Then I'm going to survey the damage in the parlor and try to figure out how to put the clock back on its feet so I can see how bad it is—although I'm seriously wondering if I can just leave a broken clock in my parlor and pretend it just needs winding." I took a deep breath. "And then I'm going to start planning the most amazing and unique baby/lingerie shower this city has ever seen. I'll think about everything else tomorrow."

CHAPTER 28

Unfortunately, I didn't have the luxury of waiting until the next day before the rest of my life interrupted my plans. It's hard to keep calm and carry on when a nearly eight-foot-tall antique grandfather clock is lying prostrate on one's parlor floor. Right next to a pile of antique buttons.

I stopped only long enough to survey the damage before running upstairs to Jack's room, knowing what I'd see before I spotted the neatly made bed, the empty closet, and all traces of him removed. I wanted to lie down on the bed and press my face into the pillow. But that was the old Melanie. The new Melanie backed out of the room and walked calmly down the hallway, returning a moment later to shut the door.

I left Mrs. Houlihan in the parlor to fret about how the clock was ruining the antique rug and worrying about cleaning the bloodstains, and joined my father in the garden. He sat on the bench, staring at the remains of all of his hard work. His grin told me he was already planning the reconstruction in his head, eager to start over and get his hands in the dirt.

I sat down next to him and rested my head on his shoulder, narrowing my eyes to blur my vision, hoping to see what he was seeing. He clasped my hand in his, allowing them to rest on the bench between us.

"I think I'm going to start all over and redesign your garden as a classic Romantic Garden."

"I've never heard of that. What are they?"

I heard the smile in his voice. "They're also called Extravagant Liars."

I lifted my head to look at him. "I've never heard of those, either. Why are they called that?"

His chest swelled as he took a deep breath, and I saw he was in his element, sharing his love for gardens with me, and I felt that connection with him, one that I had once thought irrevocably broken.

"So," he said, "Romantic Gardens became popular during the Industrial Revolution as a kind of nod toward the empowerment of the common man. When he came home from working in the factories, he wanted a completely different scene to make him forget about the dreary realities of his workday. There's no symmetry, or plan, with a surprise around every corner. Sometimes there are small vignettes tucked away into little alcoves, and meandering paths that lead nowhere. The gardens are meant to bring the viewer where emotion takes precedence over reason, and appeal directly to the soul."

Sitting back, I stared in front of us at the swath of fake grass stretched over the cistern and the plastic flowers used for the film production. "And you can see beyond this mess to envision it?"

He nodded slowly. "To a point. I'll have to sketch it out, but that's part of the joy for me. Not to always know what's next, but to trust that I'll figure it out as I go along, changing things as needed. Just because I start with a plan doesn't mean I can't stray from it if my heart pulls me in another direction."

An unexpected thickness filled my throat and it was a moment before I could speak. "I just don't know how you do it. I see only a complete wreck of all your hard work, and if it were me, I would rather go inside and forget the entire backyard exists than start all over."

He squeezed my hand. "Sure. Me, too. But then you lick your wounds, pull yourself up, and get to work fixing things because it's not in us to live with a mess. We know that no matter how bad things look, we always figure out how we can fix them." I rested my head on his shoulder again and he kissed the top of my head. "You inherited that bullheadedness from both your mother and me, so you got a double dose. And I consider that a good thing. The world is full of people who are either afraid to fail or too afraid to try again once they do. The rest of the people are like us—too bullheaded to throw in the towel."

I took a deep, shuddering breath. "Jack left."

"I know. I had a few words with him when he came to kiss the twins good-bye."

I grinned against his shirt, imagining that exchange. "Thanks, Dad. I'm glad you have my back."

"Of course I do. We all do. I just wish I knew what was going on in Jack's head, but he wouldn't tell me. I just think . . ." He stopped. "Never mind. I don't want to butt in where I'm not needed."

"I'm really out of options here, Dad, so if you want to butt in, please do."

He hesitated a moment before speaking. "Like I said, your mother and I are both pretty bullheaded—or strong-willed, depending on whose point of view it is." He grinned down at me. "Since meeting Ginny, I have never been under the illusion that women are the weaker sex. Some men—and Jack is one of them—appreciate strong women. But sometimes, when their male ego gets bruised, it knocks them down and makes them feel as if they need to prove their worth."

"You make Jack sound like a caveman going off to find the biggest woolly mammoth to drag home for dinner."

Dad chuckled, his shoulder rumbling under my cheek. "Well, it's pretty much the same thing. I don't know what he's up to, but my bet is on him trying to prove himself to you. To make himself worthy of you, if that makes any sense."

"It doesn't. But I'm willing to try to understand it, because I don't really have a choice. I'm just so angry with him right now for not telling me what's going on. But I refuse to wallow. I've got my children, my career, a baby shower to prepare for, and a broken antique grandfather clock in my parlor that I have to deal with. I've got work to do and I don't have time to wallow."

"Exactly. And he knows that's what you're going to do because that's what strong women do."

"It just hurts so much," I said, unable to hide the tears in my voice.

He squeezed my shoulders, holding me tight while he kissed the top of my head. "I know, peanut. I know."

We sat like that for a long time, staring at what was left of the garden, both of us imagining possibilities. I eventually sat up and wiped my eyes with a clean tissue my father handed me.

"Feel better?" he asked.

I nodded. "A little. Thank you."

Smiling, he asked, "Did you girls have a productive meeting with Rebecca?"

My heart warmed at "you girls," the mere words illustrating how far we had all come in a few short years in our relationships with one another. "Yes and no. We learned that we actually have very little planning to do for the shower because Rebecca was kind enough to provide me with a folder of her ideas, caterer selections, and places to shop where she has already put items on hold for me to pick up. And pay for, of course."

"I'm guessing that's the 'no' part. What's the 'yes' part?"

"Remember that painting I told you about, the one that Marc Longo 'borrowed' from the Vanderhorst collection at the Charleston Museum? I saw it at their house today and took about a dozen photos. Rebecca seems to think that something about that painting holds all the answers Marc is looking for—including financial freedom. But neither Jayne, Mother, nor I saw a thing. And we checked the frame and backing, too, in case some big diamond was hiding there, but didn't find anything. We're wondering if this is just another one of Marc's hoaxes."

"Hoaxes? Now that's not a word we hear every day."

I shook my head, remembering thinking the same thing, trying to recall where I'd seen it written recently. "No, it's not. But it fits." I pulled out my phone and opened it to the pictures I'd taken earlier. I scrutinized the up-close shot I'd taken of the cherub's face, the starbursts of light dotting the stone.

"Let me see that." Dad took his glasses from his pocket and put them on as I handed him my phone. He scrolled through the various photos, his finger moving back and forth across the screen. "That's a beautiful painting, isn't it? I love the garden all covered in dew—we gardeners call those angel kisses."

I smiled. "That's sweet. I used to think of dewy grass as something to avoid unless I wanted to ruin my shoes."

"And you don't anymore?"

"Maybe a little. But now I'll think of it as angel kisses."

He continued to move between photos, bringing the screen close to his face. "So, what exactly am I supposed to be looking for?"

"That's a very good question. Just something valuable. But all we could see was the fountain and the dew. And the peeing statue."

"And the dog."

"What?" I leaned in to get a closer look. "Where?"

He expanded the screen and with a green-stained finger pointed to a small brown figure sitting at attention in the grass next to the fountain, blending perfectly into the shadows of the bushes behind him. I blinked, just to make sure he didn't go away.

"It's like an optical illusion. But once you spot him, you can't not see him. I wonder if that was intended by the artist."

Dad adjusted and minimized the photo. "Whoever the artist was, he or she didn't sign it. Assuming it was a commissioned piece, I'm confident that the inclusion was intentional. We've certainly learned over the years that the Vanderhorsts love their puzzles." He moved through the photos again, stopping on a close-up I'd taken of the bushes, where the dog was clearly visible now that I knew what to look for.

"Nola thinks his name is Otis," I said, squinting to see better.

"I'm not going to ask why she thinks that." He brought the phone closer to his face, blocking my view. "Maybe it's on his collar." He stayed poised that way for a long moment before sitting back, an odd expression on his face. "Well," he said.

"Well, what? Is his name on the collar?"

"No," he said slowly. "But those bright spots on his neck that look like giant dewdrops? I'm pretty sure they're not."

I unceremoniously grabbed the phone out of his hands and brought it closer to my eyes. I focused my gaze on the dog's furry face, moving slowly down to its short, thick neck. "I don't . . ." I began.

"Here." Dad handed me his reading glasses.

I put them on and stared at the brown spot in the picture. It was the first time I'd seen Otis's front end—assuming it was the right dog. Jack was always telling me how I shouldn't assume, but in this case, I thought I had enough reasonable evidence. A thick black collar appeared to be studded with three large stones of equal size sparkling like dew. They were set into the collar, and at first glance I would have thought them to be cut crystal. Except for the fact that we were looking for a missing diamond, I would have settled with that thought.

I met my father's gaze. "I never even thought about the possibility that the diamond was cut again. It would have made it easier to hide, wouldn't it?"

A wide grin crossed his face. "In today's dollars, the diamonds would still be very valuable, not just because of their provenance, but also because the Hope Diamond is a rare blue diamond. And Marc Longo apparently believes they're hidden in your clock."

I sat back against the iron bench, my thoughts stopping and starting, jumping from one thing to the next. "But they're not," I said. "And since they're not, where are they?"

My father stood, offering me his hand to help pull me up. "It's anyone's guess. But I sincerely hope you find them before Marc Longo does."

CHAPTER 29

I awakened the following morning from a fitful sleep to find a dozen missed calls from Jack. I'd put my phone in do-not-disturb mode not out of spite but because I needed time to think and absorb what my father had said to me in the garden. It was most important because my heartsickness had morphed into a red-hot anger. Remembering my promise to be a better version of myself, I quickly turned off the do-not-disturb mode.

The voice mail icon alerted me to a waiting message, but instead of listening to it right away, I sent an obligatory text to Rebecca asking about Marc—broken foot, pins in bones, he'd survive—then went into the bathroom to start my shower. I needed to be dressed and in full makeup first, feeling like I was suiting myself up in armor before heading out to battle. Not that I thought of my marriage as a battleground, but if my parents thought I was a warrior woman, I needed to dress the part so I could pretend they were right.

I sat down at my dressing table, put my phone on speaker, and listened to the voice mail. At the sound of Jack's voice, I closed my eyes, wanting at least to imagine that he was in the room with me.

"I don't blame you for turning off your phone. I can't blame you. I just wanted to tell you that I'm sorry, Mellie. For everything. For that night especially. That shouldn't have happened—not when everything is so unsettled between us. It just felt right at the time, and I gave in to it. Delayed gratification isn't something I'm good at. At least not where you're concerned."

I found myself leaning forward, as if Jack were standing in front of me and I could touch him. My hurt and anger could never mask how much I loved him and what the mere sound of his voice did to my heart.

"Anyway, I know we need to talk. Face-to-face. I have a lot to tell you. I had to catch a flight last night to DC to do some research, so I couldn't wait until you returned from Rebecca's. I moved my things back to my apartment since it appears the filming has stopped—at least for now.

"Please give Sarah, JJ, and Nola a kiss from me and tell them I love them and I will be back tomorrow. I love you, Mellie. Never forget that. I'll see you soon."

I stayed where I was for a long time, replaying the entire message over and over, sending myself into emotional whiplash. I might have sat there all day if the alarm on my phone hadn't gone off, letting me know it was time to leave for my appointment with Veronica and Michael to sign the offer papers for the home on James Island.

Catherine Jimenez's van was already in the parking lot behind Henderson House Realty, in the space that the business's owner, Dave Henderson, had recently designated as reserved for the month's top seller. As if seeing her name at the top of the leaderboard each month where my name used to be wasn't hard enough.

Catherine was in the lobby with Jolly when I walked in, and I tried to sneak by behind them without notice. I'd nearly reached the hallway when Jolly called my name.

"Good morning, Melanie. No messages for you, but as a reminder, you have your meeting at nine o'clock with Mr. and Mrs. Farrell."

"Thanks, Jolly. And good morning, Catherine." I took a step toward my office, but Catherine called me back.

"Good morning to you, too, Melanie," she said cheerfully, with the kind of enthusiasm I could muster only after four cups of coffee. "Last night was craft night in our house and the kids and I made friendship bracelets. I thought I'd make some for my office friends."

She held out a neon green macramé bracelet with dangling tie strings. I stared at it before I realized that I was meant to take it.

Jolly held up her hand, where a matching bright blue bracelet sat on her wrist. "I have one, too. Isn't it gorgeous?"

It took me a moment to respond, my brain still caught on "craft night." "It is. Thank you, Catherine. I'll look forward to wearing it."

"Would you like me to tie it on your wrist?"

"Um, maybe later. I'm afraid it will clash with my outfit."

"Got it! Have a great day! And congrats on finding a house for the Farrells." She smiled her friendly and genuine smile, which made it very hard to dislike her as much as I wanted to.

"Thanks. You have a great day, too. And, Jolly, please just send the Farrells back when they arrive—I'll be ready for them."

I hurried to my office to prepare for the meeting, placing the bracelet on the top of the desk, neatly lined up against the edge. I didn't own anything neon green, but I'd have to wear it at some point. Maybe it would give me some of her pep and optimism. But I had a strong feeling there was only one thing that could do that, and he had just moved back to his apartment and flown to DC to do research on a project I knew nothing about.

I had barely sat down and flipped on my computer before Veronica and Michael arrived, a good ten minutes early.

"I'm so sorry," Veronica said. "Michael was so excited about making the offer official that he practically dragged me here. Excuse my hair— I don't think I had time to brush it yet."

I waited for them to remove their coats and take the two seats in front of the desk. "No worries," I said. I indicated the papers facing them, which I'd e-mailed to Jolly and asked her to prepare and leave in my office prior to our scheduled meeting. "We're all set. I just need your signatures where I have the yellow stickies with the red arrows."

Michael slid the pile toward himself and began flipping through the pages, signing where indicated.

"Aren't you going to read what you're signing?" Veronica asked.

Michael didn't even look up as he signed another page. "Nah. No need. I trust Melanie. Don't you?"

"It's not that, Michael. I just want you to read over all the details to make sure you're okay with everything."

"I am okay with everything. Now that we've made a decision, I'm eager to see it through." He slid the papers and the pen to Veronica. "And because the renovations are taking much longer than they should be, I've decided to work from home until they're done. I figure if I'm there keeping an eye on the workers, they'll hustle more and maybe not take so many breaks. Now that we've found a new place, the renovations are the only thing holding us back."

"Well," I said, "we haven't put the house on the market yet. We need to wait until all the renovations are done. And I was thinking about new landscaping—"

"No." He cut me off. "No more delays. I'm giving them until March third to be done, and then they're out of there. No extensions. If I have to put duct tape on the walls to hide unfinished work, so be it."

"But that's the date of Melanie's party for Rebecca," Veronica protested. "Lindsey, Nola, and Alston will be having a slumber party. I don't want the workmen to still be here working overtime if they're not done. Can't we move it to—"

"No, Veronica. We can't. Someone has to put their foot down to end this nonsense, and I've realized that has to be me since no one else is stepping up to the plate." He looked pointedly at the still-empty signature line above Veronica's name. "Go ahead and sign, and then we'll be able to put this all behind us."

She looked at her husband for an extended beat, then briefly glanced at me before lifting the pen and scribbling her signature.

"Great," I said, stacking the papers. "I'll get this in today and let you know as soon as I hear anything. It's a strong offer, so I don't think we'll have problems getting your dream house."

I hadn't meant to say that to Veronica. It was what I usually said to clients at these meetings, but none of them had her reasons to stay in their current houses or had been as reluctant to move as Veronica.

I sent her a look of apology, then stood. "I'll go ahead and get started on this. If you need to use the restrooms, they're down the hall to the right."

I hoped Veronica would get my hint and stay. We needed to talk about how I was supposed to have another meeting with Adrienne in her attic if Michael was working from home. Of course, my plan would work only if Michael excused himself, which he did not.

Instead, he stood and pulled out Veronica's chair. "I think we're good. We're headed home anyway, aren't we, Veronica?"

Before she could respond, Jolly's voice came over the phone's speaker. "Detective Thomas Riley is here to see you. Should I send him in?"

I pushed the button to respond, but Thomas appeared in my doorway before I could say anything. "Sorry—I hope I'm not intruding. Hello, Veronica, Michael." He nodded in their direction. "I was headed your way after I spoke with Melanie, but since everyone's here, I'll let you all know that I have new information about Adrienne's case."

Veronica's hand went to her throat while Michael put his hand on her shoulder. I stood and came around to the front of the desk. The gold chain that I wore around my neck for safekeeping heated my skin and sent an electric jolt down my spine. Almost as if it were alive.

Thomas reached into his jacket pocket and pulled out a photograph. "Lauren's parents sent me this. It was taken on her last visit home before she disappeared, over Christmas break."

He handed it to Veronica, and I moved next to her to get a closer look, with Michael standing behind us, tall enough to lean over us. An Olan Mills photography studio stamp embossed in gold sat at the bottom right of the professional headshot. It showed an attractive blonde with sun-bleached hair and a suntanned face against a typical speckled blue studio background.

Veronica narrowed her eyes at the photograph. "That's Lauren, isn't it? We saw her picture in Adrienne's yearbook."

Thomas pointed at something in the photo, directing our attention to the necklace the girl wore, partially hidden by her collar: a thin gold chain and dangling Greek letters. The skin on my neck began to pulse with heat.

Thomas looked at Veronica, his voice gentle. "It looks like the necklace we found with Adrienne's things, doesn't it?"

Veronica nodded. "Although I can't say for sure it belonged to her. I don't think I ever saw Adrienne wear it, but she loved jewelry and clothes, so she had a lot of both. I think because of a lack of funds, she and her friends did a lot of borrowing to stretch their wardrobes." She looked away from the picture and shook her head. "Adrienne was living at the dorm, so I didn't see her every day. I'm afraid I just don't know if the necklace belonged to Adrienne or not. All I know is that it was found in the box of her belongings in the attic."

"Would you mind if I borrowed it too?" Thomas asked. "I promise to keep it safe and return it to you."

"Sure. If you think it will help. But Melanie has it. I thought she could use her"—Veronica glanced nervously at Michael before continuing—"her intuition to hopefully find out more."

I reached behind my neck to undo the safety pin I'd used to replace the broken clasp, then handed the chain to Thomas. "Were Lauren and Adrienne both members of Omega Chi?"

Thomas nodded. "And all of the items we looked through in your attic came from Adrienne's dorm room after she died?"

"All of it," Veronica said. "I know because Michael and I packed it up ourselves. It was too hard for my parents. I think we all just forgot it was there. It was easier that way."

"And no one else has been up there in all this time? No roof repairman or pest control? Anybody who might have taken a partial gold charm and a CD?"

Veronica shook her head. "No. No one. Just you and Melanie and me. And Michael, of course. We keep our Christmas decorations in the attic, so we have to go up twice a year."

Thomas nodded slowly. "I see." He held up the necklace. "I'll get this back to you as soon as I can."

A shudder went through me as I recalled what had happened when my mother had touched it. The dark voice that had erupted from my mother's mouth. *You. Don't. Want. To. Know. The. Truth.* An icy chill chased the blood through my veins as I watched the gold chain dangle between Thomas's fingers before he placed it into his coat pocket.

"What do you think this means?" Michael asked.

"I'm not sure," Thomas said. "If I can find the missing half of this necklace, I think a lot of questions will be answered."

"Well, then," Michael said, steering Veronica toward my office door. "I guess we need to keep looking. Right now let's go home and change clothes. Then we'll go somewhere nice to celebrate our big step forward. And tomorrow we're going to be sorting through all the junk that has accumulated in the house over the years and start getting rid of some things. It's the only way for a fresh start, right, honey?"

Michael smiled broadly, but Veronica's attempt seemed pulled by a puppeteer's strings. "Text me day or night," Michael said to me, holding up his phone. "I want to know when it's official."

They said good-bye, and I returned to my seat behind my desk, but Thomas lingered, looking uncomfortable. "There was something you wanted to see me about?"

He shoved his hands into his pants pockets and smiled shyly. "There is. It's, um, about your sister."

"Jayne?"

"Do you have more than one?"

"Not that I know of." I smiled, trying to put him at ease. "What about Jayne?"

"You may or may not recall, but she and I stopped seeing each other because I thought the two of you shouldn't go public with your . . . gifts. And then Anthony Longo came along and we've had trouble reconnecting since then. I, ah, still have feelings for her, and I sense that she reciprocates those feelings. But getting her to talk to me is like trying to get ahold of a greased pig at the county fair, you know?"

"Did you just compare my sister to a greased pig?"

He shook his head. "Sorry. It's just an expression my sisters and I have used ever since they took me to the state fair and I tried to catch a squealing piglet. The piglet won."

"Got it," I said, trying not to smile. "And what would you like me to do?"

"Well, she seems to do better when you're around—at least until she's comfortable with me again. I've already told her that whatever you two decide about making your gifts public is up to you. I think we just need to spend more time together. I was thinking maybe we could arrange a double date with you and Jack?"

He must have seen something in my expression. "Oh, right. Sorry. I thought that since you and Jack were living under the same roof again . . ." His words faltered.

"Not anymore," I said, forcing a smile. "But I'm sure we can still double-date with you and Jayne."

"Great," he said, his eyes suddenly serious. "And maybe we can all have a talk together about the two of you teaming up and helping me with my cold cases. We could keep it anonymous for your safety. When I think about all the people you could help find answers about missing loved ones . . ." He stopped. "Well, let's just say that I've seen what you and Jayne can do, and I'd like you both to consider it."

"I promise to think about it and to have a discussion with Jayne. But I'm pretty sure that after I'm done helping Veronica, I'm done. I want my old life back."

He studied me, digesting my words. "I guess I can understand that. All I'm asking right now is for you to consider it." He moved toward the door. "I'll get back to you with dates and ideas for our double date, all right?"

"Sounds good," I said, happy for Jayne and for all the promise and optimism of a new romance. And if I was being honest with myself, a little bit jealous, too.

Thomas turned back at the door. "One more thing. If you don't mind me asking, how well do you know Michael Farrell?"

I was surprised at the question. "Not very well. I've only reconnected with Veronica recently, and of course our daughters are best friends, so we see them at school functions. But I definitely know Veronica much better than Michael." An ugly thought hit me as I rolled over the implications of his question in my mind. I stood and walked toward him. "You don't think that . . ."

Thomas held up his hand. "That he had anything to do with Adrienne's murder? He has a solid alibi verified and confirmed by Veronica. They were together at the time of Adrienne's death, so he's never been considered a suspect." He was thoughtful for a moment. "I was just curious, I guess. I would never have picked out Michael and Veronica in a crowd as being a couple, that's all."

I'd often thought the same thing, but was reluctant to admit it out loud, trying to be loyal to my friend. "Yes, well, sometimes opposites do attract, I suppose."

We said our good-byes, and Thomas left, leaving me standing in my office, staring at the door, the scent of Vanilla Musk creeping around me. I felt unsettled, as if someone had just given me an answer to a question I'd already forgotten.

I returned to my desk, not surprised at all to find the red heart-shaped felt ruffled pillow in my chair, sitting up at attention, waiting for me to do something. I picked it up and held it against my chest, wishing I knew the answer to just one of all the questions swirling inside my head.

CHAPTER 30

I set my laptop on the garden bench, opened to my latest worksheet. It sat next to Nola's iPad, which was displaying the weather forecast for the weekend. I'd already placed the hourly expected temperatures in the correct worksheet columns, as well as the amount of sunlight versus shade throughout Saturday and the chance of precipitation. I'd just realized that I needed to add more columns for the phase of the moon and the exact times of sunrise and sunset since Rebecca's shower would start before sunset and continue into the evening.

I felt back in my element, experiencing a rare but much-needed realignment in a familiar place where I felt in control and, above all else, organized. It's what had gotten me through a difficult childhood and other challenging periods in my life. I'd been feeling like a car with unbalanced tires tugging it in different directions, none of them where I wanted to go.

Beau had just left, having worked on the fence for most of the afternoon except when I'd distracted him with requests to hold one end of a tape measure or to give his opinion on various seating arrangements for an outdoor baby/lingerie shower. I'd be lying if I said delaying him wasn't an added bonus to receiving his help.

I straightened while typing the "average daily rainfall" number into the spreadsheet, the back of my scalp tingling, my pulse tripping. "Jack?"

"If I didn't know you so well, I'd guess you were working with NASA to plan the next rocket launch. But since you're Mellie, I'm thinking you're planning Rebecca's shower."

I didn't turn around, needing more time before I saw his face. Remembering the last time I'd seen him. "I'm just trying to find the right places for the food table and seating arrangements. And figure out how many outdoor heaters and glitter blasters we'll need." I saved my work and closed my laptop, taking a deep breath before turning to face him. "So, you're back."

"I said I'd be back today. Didn't you listen to my voice mail?"

"I did. But I assumed you'd go to your apartment, since that's where you live now."

Jack walked toward me, stopping only a few feet away, his deep blue eyes searching mine. "I came straight here from the airport."

I didn't move, resisting the magnetic pull that seemed to exist between us. "Why? Did you forget something?"

"No. Because I wanted to see you. To talk with you face-to-face." His features tightened as if he was fighting an emotion he didn't want me to see. "I miss you, Mellie. I miss you when we're apart, even if we're just down the hallway from each other. I miss you when you're at work and I'm here. I miss you when I close my eyes."

I reached out to collect Nola's iPad, unable to look at Jack anymore if I had any hope of clinging to my resolve not to allow my feelings for him to overtake my righteous anger over him leaving me. Again. I completely believed that the punishment he'd delivered far exceeded whatever crime he believed I'd committed.

When I didn't say anything, he said, "Can we talk?" He sat down on the bench.

"I thought we were."

"I have some things I need to tell you. They might be hard to hear."

I managed to keep breathing despite the sensation of my heart flying into my throat before sinking into my stomach. "All right." I sat down next to him, placing the computer and iPad in the middle to physically distance myself from him. Despite everything, I wasn't sure I could fully trust myself now that Jack was close enough to touch.

"You're probably wondering why I was in DC."

I gave him the look Nola gave me when asked if she'd left the size nine running shoes in the middle of the foyer. "Yes. That and about a dozen other things. But that's a good place to start."

"I went to meet an old Army friend of mine, Bobby Hannican. He's a freelance journalist now as well as an author of a couple of books about well-known hoaxes and conspiracy theories. He's the one who wrote the story in *USA Today* about the Hope Diamond and its possible twin." He took a deep breath. "I was the one who fed him the idea."

"Okay," I said slowly, the recollection of where I'd seen the word "hoax" stealing my breath for a moment. It was in the title of whatever Jack was working on, which I'd seen on his laptop. *Power, Greed, and Dirty Deeds: The Hoax That Felled a Criminal Family Dynasty.* I sat up straighter. "And?"

"I needed to make sure that there really was no firm evidence to support the existence of such a diamond. That all the online chatter and theories are a lot like the Kennedy assassination conspiracy theories. Interesting to think about but with no basis in reality."

"And what did Bobby say?"

"He said there was a ninety-nine percent certainty that such a thing doesn't exist."

"But what about those people who do believe there's another half of the Hope Diamond hidden somewhere? Like Blackbeard. Where are they getting their information?"

He rested his elbows on his knees and looked down at the ground. "That's the thing, Mellie." He drew in a deep breath before meeting my eyes. "I'm Blackbeard."

I waited a full minute before saying anything, either for him to tell me he was joking or for any of it to make any sense. Finally, I said, "But why? I don't understand. . . ."

He sat up, his eyes steady as he regarded me. "Can't you guess?"

"No, Jack. I really can't. Because you've been basically lying to me all this time—not to mention to all those people in those forums who seem to hang on Blackbeard's every word."

"Like Marc Longo."

He paused as if expecting everything to suddenly make sense. But my anger pushed all of my brain cells aside, nearly erasing any coherent thought. "He's an imbecile. Now tell me something I don't already know."

He took a deep breath. "I've been waiting a long time to exact my revenge for everything that he's done to me. To us. It blinded me to everything else in my life. I thought if I could bring him down by not just exposing his grandfather's seedy and murderous past in a book, but also by exposing Marc and making him look like a fool for falling for a hoax manufactured by me, it would be the perfect revenge. At least until I realized the toll it was taking on you. And me. On our marriage."

I stood, attempting to catch my breath, then sat back down, realizing that my legs were shaking. "I get lying to Marc. He deserves it. But why me, Jack? Why couldn't you let me in on the secret?"

He rubbed his hands on his pants and sat up straight, avoiding my gaze. "Because . . ." He paused, considering his words. "Because I wanted to do this on my own, without your help. Without anyone's help. I wanted to work on a project completely on my own to prove to myself that I still could, that I hadn't lost that 'special sauce for success' that I'd once had." I watched as his jaw worked beneath the beard stubble, grinding on the words. "I needed you to be proud of me."

I sucked in my breath, any compassion, understanding, and love quickly overshadowed by a flash of red heat. Even though my father had told me almost the exact same thing, I still couldn't believe that Jack had just dragged us both through hell because of his bruised male ego.

I looked at Jack, my mouth moving as I searched for any words that might come close to expressing how I felt. I closed my eyes so I could concentrate and find the right response, the precise thing I needed to say to explain an emotion that was like disbelief wrapped tightly around abject fury, but nothing seemed to fit. Remembering my bouts with therapy, I took four or five deep and calming breaths. Finally, I settled on the first thing that had come to me when he finished speaking. "You're an idiot, Jack."

He sat up, his look of surprise slowly fading into appreciation. "Do I get points for agreeing?" He gave me the grin that almost made me lose my resolve.

"A few," I conceded. "How could you even think that I'm not proud of you, regardless of what you consider your successes and failures? I love you. And that means I support you through all the ups and downs of your career. I thought we were a team."

I was too close to tears to continue speaking. He reached his hand over to cover mine, but I shook it off, too bewildered and angry to allow him to touch me and dilute everything I was feeling.

Very softly, he said, "We are a team. That's why you've been feeding Suzy Dorf with ideas for her column to antagonize Marc. We've apparently been working with the same goal in mind. Just separately."

"How . . . ?"

"Suzy told me. I approached her to ask for help with some of the research for the book I'm writing about the Longos. That's the project I've been working on."

"The hoax that felled a criminal dynasty," I said quietly. "I accidentally saw the title on your computer. I should have guessed. But then we . . ." I flushed, remembering what had happened right after I'd seen it.

"Anyway," Jack continued, "after two meetings with Suzy, she confessed that she was working with you to bring Marc down, too. She said she couldn't stand to see the two of us at cross-purposes without at least one of us knowing."

We sat in silence while I tried to figure out what to do next. I recalled what Yvonne had said. *Sometimes all it takes is acceptance that you're both wrong. And then hold your breath and take a leap of faith.* Nola had said almost the same thing, yet the old Melanie refused to go away and allow me to admit that I might have been wrong, too.

The one thing I knew for sure was that we were on the brink of getting Marc out of our lives forever, and the only way to do that was to work together. After a shuddering exhale, I said, "There's something you need to see." I pulled out my phone and opened it to the close-up of the fountain that showed the dog and his studded collar. "We found the painting Marc took from the museum when we visited Rebecca. I took these pictures of it."

He held the phone and looked at it closely. "I see a painting of our fountain covered in dew. Am I missing something?"

I pointed to the brown blob. "Here."

"It's a dog," he said with surprise. "He's so hidden that—" Jack stopped abruptly. "That's not dew, is it?" He zoomed in as close as he could get, blurring the sparkling stones on the dog's collar. He sat back. "I can't . . . I mean, I didn't think . . ." He shook his head. "Maybe that's why Bobby is convinced the rumors are false, because nobody has seen the diamond since that picture of the sultan in the eighteen sixties. It's not inconceivable that it would have been cut into smaller diamonds, but . . ." He stopped again.

"And the stones in the collar might not be diamonds. Or, if they are, they might not be connected with the sultan's diamonds at all. It could just be coincidence that the dog in the painting belonged to the daughter of the man who'd hidden the sultan's other diamonds in his grandfather clock."

"Except there's no such thing as coincidence," we said in unison.

He looked down at the photo again. "I guess this explains why Marc was trying to get into the clock. He probably thought he'd won the lottery when he saw that painting."

"And he will if he finds them before we do. Assuming they weren't buried in fire or earthquake debris in the last one hundred and fifty years. At least we know they're not in the cistern, because we would have found them. So that's a start."

Jack was slowly shaking his head, staring at the photo. "I had no idea whether the diamond actually existed when I started this. But if we do find the diamonds, imagine the book that would make. Humiliating Marc *and* finding a lost treasure. It's almost too good to be true."

"I just hope it was worth damaging our marriage for." I stood, too angry at both of us to remain sitting, and needing to physically distance myself from Jack. I picked up the computer and iPad and took a step back. "I may have acted rashly in speaking with Suzy, but I wanted to fix what Marc had done. Thinking that maybe if I did you would forgive whatever flaw you saw in me you couldn't live with." I was close to tears, but wouldn't give in to them.

He stood, too, but had the sense to stay where he was. "You know that's not it, don't you? I made a mistake—a huge one. I have no excuse except that the possibility of revenge blinded me. Blinded *us*."

I knew he was giving me an opening to admit my own culpability, but the old Melanie kept nudging me, telling me that what I had done seemed so small in comparison. I studied the big Apple emblem on the cover of my laptop. "I can't think about this now. I need to get through the party first. Then we'll figure out us."

"That's fair. We can at least work on finding the diamonds in the meantime. The one thing we can agree on now is that we need to find them before Marc Longo does."

"Or everything we've just gone through will have been for nothing."

Jack nodded, his face serious. "I'll be at the apartment if you need me." He paused, and for a wild moment I thought he might be waiting for an invitation to stay. I kept my gaze averted so I wouldn't change my mind. But then he turned and let himself out of the garden gate.

I sat down on the bench again and stayed there for a long while, staring at my father's defunct garden while trying to see it as he did, with the grass green, the garish splashes of brilliant blooms filling the now-fallow ground and lining the weedy paths. Yet all I could see was the bare ugliness of how it was now, as if all of my hurt and confusion were clouding my perception of what might be.

I immersed myself in the planning for the party, my dream of going off script plundered by Rebecca's need to control every detail and micromanage everything from the number of helium balloons to the way the napkins should be folded. One morning, while I was laying out the matching socks for the twins' outfits, I mentioned to my mother and Jayne how annoying Rebecca was being, and all they did was stare back at me without blinking.

Fortunately, my irritation and my busyness with both work and the party planning meant I didn't have too much time to think about Jack and me, and I was too tired at night to do anything but fall into a dreamless sleep. Jack spent most of his days at the library or online researching everything he could find about the sultan, the diamonds, the oddest sites around the world where buried treasure had been found, and even dog collar manufacturers from the nineteenth century. (That swiftly resulted in a solid dead end.)

When he wasn't doing that, he was tapping on walls to check for hollow spaces, pulling up rugs to look for any loose floorboards we might have missed while sanding and restaining the hardwood, and studying cornices and ceiling medallions for any crevice or crack that might indicate a hiding space. Despite all of this, the most productive part of his week was finding someone to lift the clock, although they couldn't show up until the morning of the party.

When I wasn't arguing with Rebecca, I explored Nevin Vanderhorst's library, searching for hollowed-out books, and examined each crystal drop on every chandelier with a magnifying glass. Jack and I even put Yvonne on the scent, but so far she hadn't turned up anything new.

As if by unspoken agreement, the only time Jack and I spent together was each night at the dining table with the children, since we both thought it important for us to show a united front to them. But after we'd bathed the twins and put them to bed, and Jack had said good night to Nola, he left for his apartment. Sometimes he hesitated, as if waiting for me to invite him to stay, but I clung to my resolve, knowing how easy it would be to give in. And that would solve absolutely nothing.

The filming had been put on hold indefinitely, until Marc had recovered from his surgery to repair the smashed bones in his foot and ankle, and I could once again enjoy the run of my house at all hours of the day. We consulted with Mr. Zerbe, our lawyer, about the contract implications, and he said to wait and see. Jack and I were fine with this, knowing that a waiting period gave us time to find the three diamonds. Which, at this point, seemed highly doubtful, but I held out hope.

The Thursday before the party, Nola found me in the back garden arranging pots full of plastic baby bottles designed to look like sprouting flowers, and stringing a clothesline between two trees.

"Need help?" she asked, taking one end of the black nylon rope.

She still wore her school uniform, so I was immediately suspicious of her offer. She usually changed first and put her headphones on so she couldn't hear me ask her to come set the table.

"Thanks. Go stand over by the oak tree so I can make sure it's long enough."

"What's it for?" she asked as she dragged the rope across the grass.

"It's where we're going to hang the lingerie gifts as they're opened. I bought some nice padded lingerie hangers in bordello red and pink to go with the party's theme. Don't worry. I've made sure that they won't be visible from the street or by our neighbors. They've already suffered enough."

"Good plan. And just hope none of them gets close enough with their phones to video it or I guarantee you'll be an Internet sensation in less than an hour."

"Well, don't give Rebecca any ideas. She wants to be an Internet influencer and would love the publicity."

Nola made a face. "I think I just threw up in the back of my mouth."

Not that I disagreed, but I had to be the mother and forced myself not to laugh. "Be nice, Nola. I can only hope that Rebecca was dropped on her head at some point in her childhood to account for her sense of style and taste. Otherwise, I'm going to worry about JJ and Sarah."

"Same," she said, reaching up to loop the rope through the metal hook I'd already screwed into the temporary wooden arbor under which Rebecca would hold court while opening her gifts.

"So, what did you need to ask me?"

"What makes you . . ." She stopped. "You're a little too good at this mom thing, you know. It's okay if you slack off a bit. At least until JJ and Sarah are teenagers."

"Thank you. I think. So what is it?"

"Well, since you asked, I wanted to know if I could go with Lindsey and Alston to see a movie before the sleepover Saturday. It's the new Emma Stone flick and it's PG-13, so I can go. We promise to come right home after the movie. Lindsey's and Alston's parents have already said yes."

"Have you asked your father?" I asked, knotting my end of the rope on a lower limb of the live oak. I imagined it sighing in resignation at being so sorely abused and was absurdly glad there was no such agency as the ASPCT.

"No. I mean, that's your job, right? I know he's not sleeping here at night, but you're still talking. So I figured you could ask him. After you told me yes, of course."

"I don't know, Nola. I'm still worried about Rebecca's dream and my grandmother's phone call."

"It's fine, don't you think? I mean, the grandfather clock can't fall on me now, can it? And the tall man is obviously Marc Longo, so I'm safe."

I put my hands on my hips, agreeing with what she'd said but still unsure.

"I'll be with Alston and Lindsey. And Mr. Farrell said he'd be happy to drive us there and pick us up at the end of the movie before coming back to the party."

"That's very nice of him, but still—"

"Please?" she begged. "I've been working so hard, studying for the SATs. It will be fun to have something to look forward to afterward. And I promise to be extra careful and keep my head on a swivel."

I recognized her last remark as the ending phrase Beau used on his podcast.

I sighed. "I guess. I'll check with your father to be sure. And I'll expect you to text me when you leave the theater and when you get to Lindsey's house."

She ran toward me and surprised me with an embrace. "Thanks, Melanie." She stepped back. "I'll need a new dress. Do you think you'll have time to take me shopping?"

"Why do you need a new dress to see a movie?"

She shrugged. "No reason. But Lindsey and Alston are going shopping with their moms, so I thought it would be nice if you and I did, too. I'll even pay for my own dress." She grinned her Jack grin, which she probably knew I couldn't resist.

"Sure. Most everything is already set for the party. So tomorrow after lacrosse practice? I'll pick you up. Unless you'd rather go with Rebecca."

She made a gagging noise. "Please. I'd rather go shopping with Grandpa and end up with overalls and a straw hat."

"You'd still look cute," I said, giving in to the impulse to rumple her hair.

Nola pretended to be annoyed and stepped back. "I've got to do my homework and more SAT prep. I don't think I'll have time to set the table."

"Right. Hey, quick question before you leave. If you were to hide something valuable, where would you hide it?"

She thought for a moment. "In the most obvious place, I think. It's always the last place people look."

With a quick wave, she walked back to the house, her solid gray uniform skirt swaying.

I went back to arranging potted baby bottles, trying to ignore the unsettled feeling I'd been carrying with me since Jack's return. I'd been able to compartmentalize the issue of our marriage and place it into a box to be opened later. My unease felt more like fear, as if I had my hand on the doorknob of a darkened closet and I was unable to see inside. Too busy with life, work, and the party preparations, I reverted to the old Melanie—at least for now. Because doing so meant I could make myself believe that if I ignored it long enough, it would go away on its own.

CHAPTER 31

On the day of the shower, Rebecca and Pucci arrived early—and thankfully alone. Marc's foot was completely immobilized and he was confined to a wheelchair for the time being, and Rebecca's pregnancy prevented her from helping him down the stairs or into a car. I was doubtful that Marc would make an appearance at all, but Rebecca assured me that Marc would show up. Any normal person—a category that didn't include Marc—wouldn't have the gall to show up at the same house where he'd vandalized a valuable antique clock hunting for a treasure that didn't belong to him, but Marc continued to insist that the clock had simply fallen on him when he'd stopped to admire it. I'm sure if Marc could find a way, he'd be here, prepared to snoop from his wheelchair.

"Maybe you should go home and stay with him in case he needs anything," I suggested. "The party doesn't start for another six hours and I've got everything set up here and ready to go—"

"I'm sure you think you do," she said while pushing a blush-stained Pucci in a doggie stroller, its three wheels bumping over the grass in the backyard. If it got stuck, I wasn't going to help her pull it out. She stopped in front of the glitter cannon. "Where are the other five I asked for?"

I smiled patiently. "The man at the party rental store assured me that one is more than sufficient for the space. Besides, I'm not sure how environmentally safe the glitter is, and we have lots of birds and squirrels in the backyard who probably shouldn't be eating it, not to mention two toddlers."

"Maybe you should teach them not to eat off the ground."

"The animals or the children?" I asked, my voice laden with sarcasm, which always winged its way over Rebecca's head.

"Both."

I bit back a thousand comments, knowing that revenge would be sweet when I said the same thing to her in about eighteen months' time.

Rebecca pushed the stroller forward toward the arbor canopy, where she'd be opening her presents. My father and his gardening club had covered it with beautiful puffs of pink and white carnations entwined with pink mesh and white lace. It had turned out so well that they'd taken pictures of it to be entered into an upcoming gardening competition.

Rebecca's face fell. "But I wanted roses! I specifically said roses."

I clenched my hands behind my back so I wouldn't be tempted to strike her. I didn't want hitting a pregnant woman to appear anywhere on my permanent record.

"Yes, you did. But since I'm paying for it, I had to find something more economical. And they did such a beautiful job, don't you think?"

"They're still not roses." She sniffed. "Didn't you read everything in the folder I gave you? Or listen during our dozens of phone calls?"

"Of course I did. Some things just weren't . . . practical. But I used your caterer and menu—including wiener roll-ups to look like babies in blankets and bra-shaped sugar cookies." I needed to make sure that no one gave me credit for the latter.

"And I have the two spotlights you requested in alternating red and pink to be trained on you while you open your presents. My dad will be the technical expert tonight, making sure the glitter cannon and colored lights operate as planned."

She looked slightly mollified. "At least *something* will look right."

I was saved by the back door opening and Nola coming out into the garden with Lindsey and Lindsey's new white husky, Ghost. Lindsey carried a corrugated box, the flaps tucked into each other to keep it closed.

Ghost did his puppy lope toward us while Rebecca shrieked and picked up Pucci, holding him high.

"Oh, Ghost wouldn't hurt Pucci, Mrs. Longo," Nola soothed as Lindsey placed her box on the patio table. "He's much too sweet."

Rebecca's expression made it clear she didn't believe Nola.

"How did it go, girls?" I asked, referring to the SATs.

"Don't ask," Nola said. "I felt prepared, but it's too hard to tell. I'm glad I had these for luck." She held up her arm and jangled the two new four-leaf-clover charms, making my heart expand. "Lindsey and I finished early, but Alston was there until the last minute. She was crying when she finally left. I think her mom's taking her shopping to help her feel better. But I think I aced the essay."

"Well, you are your father's daughter," I said, making her blush.

Lindsey turned to me. "Do you think Mrs. Jimenez will mind watching Ghost with your dogs tonight? He's still basically a puppy and not used to being left alone. With us at the movies, I don't want him to get lonely."

Rebecca pursed her lips. "Do you think that's safe? Your dogs are just little morsels to a big beast like that."

"They'll be fine," Lindsey assured her. "Ghost is really an angel. And he loves other dogs and small children."

"For breakfast, maybe," Rebecca said, hoisting Pucci up a little higher on her chest.

Ignoring Rebecca, I said, "Probably not, but you'll have to call Mrs. Jimenez and ask her yourself. They have a huge fenced-in backyard because she does agility training in her spare time."

"Wow," Nola said. She's like Super—"

"Stop now. Unless you want me to rescind permission to go tonight."

She made the motion of zipping her lips and throwing away the key. "Are JJ and Sarah ready to go to Grandma and Grandpa's sleepaway camp? I haven't seen Amelia this excited since we sold that Chippendale sofa with the missing leg."

"Your dad's getting them ready now. I already packed their bags, so please do not allow him to remove or add anything." I gave her a stern look so she'd understand the seriousness of mismatched outfits. I indicated the box Lindsey had just dumped on the patio table. "And whatever that is, could you please remove it? I'm having a party here tonight, remember? I'll need the table for food."

"Sorry, Mrs. Trenholm." Lindsey pulled up the flaps. "My mom told me to bring some of the boxes she's been packing up to see if you might want any of it. Mostly old books and a bunch of nice shoes that she's hardly ever worn. She remembers from college that you wear the same size." She removed a thick stack of brown packing paper from the top and her face fell. "Oops. I think I brought one of Dad's boxes instead." She exhaled an exaggerated sigh. "I'll bring this one back and my mom can bring the right one when she comes for the party."

She picked up the paper to close up the box and Nola stopped her. "Hang on—there's a bunch of old CDs here." She held up a stack of discs in their cases and a few loose ones on top and turned to me. "Maybe your dad can use some of these for tonight, because I'm sure only ABBA is on the playlist right now. Isn't he the music-and-light guy for the party?"

Rebecca turned to me, her voice almost a shriek. "You didn't hire the DJ I recommended? I had to pull a lot of strings to get him to agree!"

"Yes, well, the one string you didn't pull was your purse string, so I had to work on my budget and not yours. And my dad fit the budget perfectly. There's nothing high-tech beyond a CD player and speakers, but it will work. It's just background music anyway."

"You mean, no dancing?" Rebecca's expression was probably as horrified as mine had been when I'd read that part of her plan in the folder she'd given me. "There was supposed to be dancing on a dance floor made to look like a Victoria's Secret fashion show runway. I even had pictures to show your carpenter! When we spoke earlier this week, you said you were working on it."

"Yes, but then when I realized how many guests you'd invited and how much more seating we'd need, there just wasn't room. But my dad is setting up a big screen behind his DJ station to keep old Victoria's Secret shows on a continuous loop."

I didn't wait to hear her response before turning back to Nola and taking the CDs she was holding. "Not that there's anything wrong with playing my ABBA CDs, but a little variety might not hurt."

"And prevent a mass stampede as everyone tries to leave at once." Nola grinned innocently. "We'll be right back after dropping off JJ and Sarah at the store, so be thinking of what you want us to do first."

"I thought Amelia was going to pick them up here."

"But it's such a nice day, I thought we'd use the jogging stroller. It's not that far, and I'll get to spend a little time with them. I've been so busy studying that I really haven't had a chance." Nola smiled brightly while Lindsey nodded in agreement.

"That's very sweet of you. I'm sure the twins will like that." I was a little suspicious of Nola's good mood and eagerness to help, but I chalked it up to her having gotten the SATs over with. "When you return, I'd like you to help your dad string the twinkling lights in all the trees and around the DJ and gift tables. Just keep all the wires away from the firepit. Maybe after the movie, you can ask Mr. Farrell to drive you here first to have some s'mores."

Lindsey and Nola looked at each other. "Maybe. Depends on how tired we are," Nola said. "It's been a long day."

"I'm sure it has been. I'll see you girls in a little bit, then. But please put Ghost in the kitchen for now. He's making Pucci nervous."

Lindsey took Ghost by the collar and followed Nola into the house. I took a fortifying breath and returned my attention to Rebecca, expecting to see her still sulking. Instead she had moved with Pucci to the flower-draped arbor, apparently after noticing her chair for the first time. It was an obnoxiously gilded throne Sophie had helped me procure from the College of Charleston's drama department; it had been used in a recent production of *Beauty and the Beast*. Jayne and I had worked hard festooning it with pink and red balloons and Vegas-worthy feathers, almost hiding the gilt but not completely. Glimmers of gold shone through to alert viewers of the true horror of what they were seeing.

"This is the most beautiful thing I've ever seen." Rebecca sounded as if she might cry. "At least you haven't erased all of my personality from my own party." She sniffed, and because she was pregnant, I didn't point out that the entire format of a baby/lingerie shower was all the evidence of her personality that was needed.

The back door opened and Jack stepped out. "Mellie, can you come here, please? I think you need to see this."

"I'll be right there!" With a stab of worry, I turned to Rebecca to see if she'd be okay if I left her for a few moments, but she had already seated herself in her throne and appeared to be getting comfortable.

"You go on—I'll be here practicing opening gifts."

"You do that. I'll be right back."

I jogged across the yard to the back door, skirting the cistern, which my father had judiciously encircled with caution tape and parking cones he'd painted pink and red, and entered the kitchen. Jack had already left, so after a quick pat on the head for Ghost, I ran through to the dining room, calling Jack's name.

"In here," he said from the direction of the front parlor.

I skidded to a stop in the foyer on the threshold of the parlor, the sight of Rich Kobylt leaning over the prostrate grandfather clock forcing me to clench my eyes, although I was sure I'd seen enough to give me nightmares for weeks. A young man I recognized as his son, Brian, greeted me, causing his father to mercifully straighten. Rich turned to face me, allowing me to read his T-shirt. *That's what I do, I drink beer, smoke cigars, and know things.*

"Hello there, Miz Trenholm. I'm afraid I've got some bad news."

My gaze flicked up to Jack as I realized that the professional he'd hired to move the clock was our jack-of-all-trades, Rich Kobylt. Not that I didn't like Rich, or thought he didn't do a good job. I'd just hoped Jack would find someone cheaper. Or at least someone who wouldn't discover some waiting catastrophe that needed fixing, too.

"What's wrong?" I asked.

"Well, my boy, Brian, here and me tried to lift up the clock, but it won't budge. It's the strangest thing, too. I don't think it weighs more than three hundred pounds, but it feels like an elephant is sitting on top of it. I'm afraid we're going to need to bring in some special equipment."

"Of course you are," I muttered, looking at the six-inch drag marks on the hardwood floor.

Brian spoke up. "We did manage to slide it out from the wall enough so that a person can stand at the base, but that messed up the floors a bit, and we don't want to do any more damage. Besides, we can't get it over the lip of the rug, and if we damage that, well, gosh, it will probably have to go back to France for reweaving. Anyway, we're going to have to resand and polish the floor as it is, and didn't want to have to replace boards, too."

"Definitely not." I might have shouted the words, because all three men were looking at me with concern. "Sorry," I said. "I was just thinking out loud." My only consolation was that I might be able to get Marc to pay for the damage since he was the one who'd caused it, regardless of what he said. A grandfather clock didn't just fall over without provocation.

Rich adjusted his pants. "I'll give you a call next week to discuss when I can come back here with the proper equipment."

"Wait—so you're going to leave it like this? I've got a party tonight. Not that anyone will need to come in here, but still . . . it just looks so . . . wrong."

"Yes, ma'am, I understand. But there's nothing I can do about it. I don't own the equipment, so I have to borrow it from a buddy of mine and I need to make sure he doesn't need it right now. It could be a couple of weeks or more."

Jack gently took hold of my arm, apparently sensing my misplaced anger and growing frustration. "Thanks, guys, for coming out. Just give me a call when you can come back to take care of it."

"Yes, sir." Rich and Brian headed toward the front door, but Rich held back. "Uh, one thing, if you don't mind me saying. I know you've got little ones here, but I don't think they should be playing with an antique like that."

"What do you mean?" I gritted my teeth, preparing for the worst.

"There's a baby doll inside the case there and a bunch of buttons—which, to be honest, is a choking hazard for the little ones."

"And that baby doll's a little creepy," Brian said with a small shudder. "I'm not really sure any kid should be playing with it."

Jack squeezed my arm to keep me from saying anything I might regret. "Yes, you're both right. We'll take care of it. Thanks again for coming out."

Jack walked them to the door as I bent over the casement and saw the face of Frozen Charlotte staring up at me. I glanced over to the coffee table, where her coffin remained, the lid ominously open.

Jack returned to stand next to me. "I'll put caution tape across the doorway to prevent people from coming in. I'll stick balloons on it to go with the theme. Maybe borrow some of your bras and panties, too? I'd hang a few of your nightgowns instead, but they're all flannel. Not the same vibe, you know?"

"Very funny," I said, resisting a smile.

Jack's face became serious. "I haven't forgotten, Mellie."

I looked up at him. "About the twinkling lights?"

"No. Not that. You said you'd be able to talk about us when you were done planning the party, and the party is tonight. What time do you want me here in the morning? Or I could sleep in the guest room so I'm ready when you are."

I flushed, remembering what had happened the last night he'd spent in the guest room. I was tempted to ask for a few extra days, as if somehow all of our troubles would solve themselves if we gave them just a little more time. Yet, regardless of how unfinished the new Melanie worksheet was, I had learned something in the last few months. Things rarely worked themselves out, and no matter how many things I pushed off until tomorrow, tomorrow always arrived, carrying its own baggage.

I met his gaze. *I miss you when I close my eyes.* Even though I was still hurt and confused, I couldn't forget that he'd said that. And that my love for him hadn't diminished despite everything. "As soon as you want to get here. I'm an early riser."

"I remember, Mellie. It hasn't been that long."

I nodded, then retrieved poor Charlotte from the clock and returned her to her coffin before closing the lid. "I'm going to assume Evangeline put the doll in there, because no one I know would voluntarily touch her. I only wish I knew why."

We heard the back door open and Rebecca call out. "Is there anything for lunch? I'm starving."

Ghost let out a bark, followed by Rebecca screeching, and I was tempted to head out the front door and pretend I hadn't heard her.

"Just a few more hours, Mellie," Jack said as he pushed me in the direction of the kitchen. "You can do it."

When he headed in the opposite direction, I said, "Where are you going? Aren't you going to run interference?"

"I wish I could. But I've got to hang the twinkling lights. And milk the cow, feed the hogs, mow the back nine . . ."

He continued until the shutting of the front door silenced him before I could.

CHAPTER 32

Despite last-minute glitches—a broken ice machine, a plastic T. rex belatedly discovered post-flush in the downstairs toilet, and a brief appearance by two rough-looking "associates" of Marc's who'd driven Marc in a black Navigator with tinted windows and then carried him and the wheelchair to the back garden—the shower was in full swing by five thirty. The guests seemed to be enjoying themselves, the steady hum of conversation filling the garden and mixing with the strains of music filtering from the hidden speakers. My dad was doing a wonderful job of mixing ABBA with other music from the seventies and eighties, along with the various nursery songs sprinkled in at Rebecca's request.

The juxtaposition of the constantly running lingerie fashion show behind the DJ table against the nursery music had an admittedly artistic yet bizarre vibe, and it was probably one of the main reasons for the quick depletion of our champagne supply. Either that or the need for guests to soften the sight of the guest of honor herself, wearing a sparkling tiara on top of her blond head and a voluminous red silk peignoir set with a white fur stole around her bare shoulders. It wouldn't have been so awful except that Pucci wore a matching outfit. Rebecca had plopped the poor dog in the lap of Marc, who sat in his wheelchair next to her throne, unable to move away, which might have been the source of his malevolent stares directed at Jack and me.

I stood nearby talking to Lindsey's and Alston's parents when Jack walked up to Marc.

"Having a good time, Matt? Anything I can get you? I don't know if the caterer brought any humble pie, but I can ask if you like."

"Go to hell, Jack. You've lost again, but you don't know it yet, do you? As usual, you're oblivious. And I'm not talking about that stupid contract, either. Screw the contract. I've got bigger and better things I'm working on."

There was a long silence, and I strained my neck to hear what Jack said.

"Did you know that stealing art from a museum is a federal crime? I imagine it's hard to run when you're in a wheelchair."

"What?"

Marc's shout of outrage turned heads, but Jack ignored him, instead joining our conversation circle, where we continued our chat about our girls and the SATs and lacrosse. I was just beginning to relax and enjoy the party when I found myself actively listening to the sound playing over the speakers.

Alston's mother, Cecily, started laughing. "Oh, my goodness. What is that?"

"'O Superman,'" Veronica said, her smile strained.

"Yeah. That's it." Michael shoved his hands into his pants pockets.

"I've never heard of it. Is that supposed to be music?" Cecily asked.

"It's, um, performance art," I said. "I don't remember putting that in the playlist. Will you excuse me for a moment? I need to speak with my dad about what music to play for present opening." I looked at my watch. "Which should commence in approximately twenty-three minutes and"—I lifted my other hand, in which I held another watch, with a second hand—"fourteen seconds."

I hurried across to where my father stood behind his DJ table, wearing a Hawaiian shirt, sunglasses, and a flower lei that he'd procured on his own. I didn't ask if he'd chosen a DJ name, because I was afraid to hear the answer.

"Hey, Dad, you doing okay?"

He gave me a peace sign in response.

"Wrong era, but I'll go with it. Can I get you more water?"

"Your mother just brought me cold seltzer with lemon, so I'm good—but thanks. And, yes, I'm aware that I need to change the playlist for the gift portion of the party. The three alarm clocks you've set up in my booth will let me know in plenty of time." He smiled, but it didn't seem as sincere as it should have.

"Quick question: Where did you get that last song from? I don't remember having that CD in my collection."

"The Laurie Anderson song? That came from the collection of CDs Nola brought to me. Lots of cool stuff in there. Why?"

"What collection?" And then I remembered the box Alston had mistakenly brought from her house. The box of things her father had packed up to get rid of in preparation for their move. I looked at my father, feeling a little light-headed. "Was it in a case?"

He looked down at a pile of CDs. "Not that one—no. There are actually quite a few without cases. You shouldn't store them that way, you know. They scratch easily."

"Right," I said. "Thanks." I began to walk away, then turned abruptly. "Can I have that, please?"

"I promise I won't play it again."

"No, it's not that. I just . . . I need to show it to Thomas." There. I'd said it. I'd given voice to a nagging thought that wouldn't go away, no matter how hard I tried to push it down.

"If you insist." He carefully picked up the disc with his thumb and middle finger and placed it in an empty case. "Here you go. And if you don't mind, I'd like to have it back when you're done with it. I want to listen to the whole album. It's a bit strange, but fascinating in a train-wreck kind of way."

I nodded distractedly, clutching the case while searching through the crowd for Thomas. I assumed he'd be with Jayne, but I couldn't find her, either. Needing to escape for a moment to think, I walked around the house to the front door to avoid the caterers in the kitchen.

As I climbed the steps of the piazza, I nearly choked on the saturated scent of Vanilla Musk, the overpowering aroma descending as suddenly as a storm cloud. I began walking toward the door, but I stopped suddenly when I kicked something soft. I knew before I bent to pick it up that I would find Adrienne's pillow. I studied the fine stitching that connected the ruffle to the body of the pillow, recalling Veronica saying how Adrienne had wanted to be a fashion designer. I clutched the pillow to my chest, feeling an overwhelming sadness.

"What are you trying to tell me?" I whispered. I paused expectantly, waiting for a reply that wouldn't come.

I considered sitting in one of the rocking chairs for a few moments while the party stragglers were being rounded up by my mother to take their seats for the gift opening, but I was afraid that if I did, I'd never want to leave. I just needed a few moments of peace and quiet to get my thoughts together.

I heard arguing as soon as I opened the front door, the voices coming from the dining room. I recognized Veronica's voice, although I'd never heard it raised before.

"You should have told me, Michael! Or at least given it to Detective Riley. I don't care how innocent you are; it looks really bad, don't you think? Especially since you were planning to throw it away!"

As I approached them, I hid the case behind Adrienne's pillow. They both looked up when they saw me. I didn't pretend that I hadn't overheard them. "I was just wondering the same thing, Michael. What were you doing with the Laurie Anderson CD?"

His face looked like a road map of mottled red and white. "I already told Veronica; how many times do I have to repeat it? It was my CD and Adrienne borrowed it. I happen to like Laurie Anderson—her stuff is really different. When the police returned the CD player in the box, I took the CD back. It's not like they hadn't already seen it."

"That doesn't explain why you didn't tell Detective Riley when we were searching for the CD." Veronica seemed close to tears.

Michael took a deep breath. With a lowered voice and clear and concise words, as if speaking to a kindergartner, he said, "Because the CD belonged to me. I didn't tell Thomas because I knew the CD wasn't important or relevant to the case. And if you want to know, I'm a little embarrassed for people to know that it was mine."

With a low, shaky voice I'd never heard before, Veronica said, "But what about Adrienne's phone calls, Michael? She said it was urgent that she speak to me. And I refuse to believe that you have no idea what it was about!"

Michael let out a groan of frustration, then glanced at his watch. "Perfect timing. I have to go pick up the girls and take them to the movie theater. I'm considering this conversation closed." He brushed past me, and I felt the radiating heat of his body as he passed.

The front door slammed, but I didn't turn around. I was too focused on Veronica and how she looked as if a strong wind might blow her over. "Do you need to sit down? Can I get you something to drink?"

She shook her head. "No. I just need some time to think."

I pulled two chairs from the dining room table and ordered her to sit while I took the seat next to her. "Is there something you haven't told me? Something I should know?"

Veronica stared down at her hands, her fingers looking pale and small splayed on the dark wood of the table. "Yes," she said, her voice so quiet, I had to lean close to hear her. "When I said that Adrienne was trying to reach me, to tell me something important, there was one detail I left out."

I didn't move or prompt her, not wanting her to reconsider. I watched as her throat worked, forcing out the words.

"In those phone calls to me before she died"—Veronica took a deep, shuddering breath—"she told me that what she needed to tell me was about Michael." Her voice caught.

I sat back. "Why didn't you tell this to the police?"

The tortured expression on her face told me that she'd run through this over and over again since her sister's death. "Because I knew Michael didn't have anything to do with Adrienne's death. He was with me when she was killed, so I had no doubts. I didn't want to cause him any needless trouble."

"Until now," I said matter-of-factly. "Because we found the missing CD in his things."

Her eyes met mine, our thoughts running in tandem. "I'm sorry, Veronica. I don't know what any of this means, but we need to tell Detective Riley."

"I'll tell him," she said, her voice soft but laced with steel. "But I want Michael to be with me. As soon as he gets back from dropping off the girls, we'll go talk with Thomas." Her gaze fell on the pillow, which I'd placed next to the CD on the table. "Why is that here?"

"That's a good question. I tripped on it on the front porch."

Veronica picked up the pillow and began playing with the fringe. "I just wish I knew what she was trying to tell us."

"Me, too."

A loud gong sounded—Rebecca's idea—announcing the gift-opening portion of the evening, and letting everyone know it was time to find a seat. We left the pillow on the table but stuck the CD in a drawer in the breakfront for safekeeping as we hurried outside. I walked toward the throne to assume my position on a tiny footstool at Rebecca's feet, where I would be in charge of listing the gifts and the gift givers for future thank-you notes, grateful to be on the other side of Rebecca so I wouldn't have to look at Marc. I'd already set up my worksheet, and my laptop was waiting by the stool. At least there was one thing about the party I could get excited about.

Because it was early March, dusk had already begun to settle, allowing the twinkling lights to masquerade as stars against the purpling sky while the glow from the firepit and the portable heaters warmed the night.

I felt the side of my face heat, and I knew Jack was watching me. I turned my head, spotting him immediately in the crowd like a compass finding true north. He smiled, then pointed to his wrist, and I knew he was thinking about the party being over, and then it would be morning, when it would be time for us to talk. I felt almost dizzy with the rush of opposing thoughts that flooded through me, and I was unable to fully comprehend any of them. I gave him a brief smile and looked away, eager to open my laptop and to confront the easy and familiar.

The hubbub of conversation had begun to die down when I felt a sharp tap on my shoulder. I didn't turn around, assuming it was Louisa or another otherworldly guest and not wanting anyone to notice me speaking to an empty space. The entire shower had already made most of our guests question my sanity, and I didn't want to confirm their doubts.

"Melanie?" This time the tap was accompanied by a familiar voice.

My head whipped around. "Beau? What are you doing here?" He was dressed in khakis and a collared golf shirt; instead of his usual sneakers, he wore loafers.

He saw me looking and said, "Sorry—I'm not crashing the party; I just wanted to check to see if Nola made it home."

Tiny alarm bells began jangling in the back of my head. "What do you mean? She's at the movies with Lindsey and Alston."

"She wasn't when I saw her about an hour ago. She was at the Mardi Gras party at the Bay Street Biergarten."

I stood, barely catching my laptop before it slid to the ground. "She what? Were her friends with her?"

"No, ma'am. Alston bailed and called her brother, Cooper, to come get her, and Lindsey went with them. Cooper said he was driving them back to the Ravenels' so he could keep an eye on them until their parents got back. Lindsey begged him not to call her mom or dad because they would be extra mad if they had to leave a party, and he agreed to wait."

"But what about Nola? Why didn't she go with them?"

"She refused. I told Cooper I'd keep a close eye on her and make sure she got home safely. She, uh, she'd been drinking pretty heavily. She was drinking from a can of Coke, so I didn't think anything of it. But it must have been mostly rum."

"Why didn't you call me?"

"I did. And Jack, too, but nobody answered. I texted and left messages. I figured you didn't have your phones on, so I decided to drive here. Nola told me she wanted to go to Lindsey's house to pick up her guitar and then meet up with her friends at Alston's, but I told her I was going to bring her home because she was too wasted." He swallowed. "That might have been the wrong thing to say. She said she needed to use the ladies' room first. I think she must have bolted and taken an Uber, because no one saw her after that."

My mother had approached and I thrust the laptop at her, grateful she was wearing evening gloves. "Can you please take care of this for me? I have a little issue I need to deal with right now."

"Of course. Anything I can do?"

"Yes, please. If you could just take over the party for a bit, that would be great. And call me if you see Nola."

She looked at me with a worried expression, and I knew we were both thinking of my grandmother's phone call. "It'll be all right, Mother. It will." I had no idea if that was true, but I had to say it so that I could believe it.

I began walking away, Beau following. I heard my mother soothe Rebecca's protests as Jack approached, his gaze worried.

"What's wrong?"

"Nola's missing," I said quietly, and began walking around the house to the front piazza, aware that Marc was watching us closely. Beau repeated what he'd already told me as we entered the foyer.

"Okay. Has anyone tried her cell phone?" Jack asked, pulling his own out of his pocket and flicking the switch on the side to turn it off silent mode.

"Yes, sir," Beau said. "Multiple times. She's not picking up."

"And no texts from her on my phone." Jack pressed his screen, then held his phone to his ear.

I could hear a ringing sound while he waited, our gazes meeting. Eventually we heard Nola's voice in her recorded message before Jack clicked off.

"Let me check my phone—hang on." I ran to Jack's office, where I'd left my phone plugged in and charging, not thinking I'd need it. I opened the screen as I raced back to the foyer.

"I have a text from Nola," I announced, then read it out loud.

We got another ride to theater and back. Lindsey already texted her dad to stay and enjoy party. Have fun and see you tomorrow.

I looked up. "Something's not right."

"What is it?" Jack asked.

"Well, according to the time stamp, Nola sent the text almost two hours ago. Assuming Lindsey's text was sent to her father at the same time, Michael knew the girls wouldn't be waiting for him when he told Veronica and me that he was going to pick them up."

We looked at each other, somehow managing to suppress the growing panic.

"I'll drive," Beau said as if reading our minds. "My truck's in the driveway behind the caterer's."

"I'm right behind you. I just need to grab my coat."

I ran toward the back hall closet, coming to a skidding stop when I spotted the red pillow on the floor in front of the closet door, neatly stabbed in the middle by a carving knife I'd last seen in the breakfront drawer in the dining room with the rest of the sterling silverware. I picked up the pillow to move it out of the way, and the knife fell, barely missing my foot, and exposing a two-inch gash in the red felt, revealing white stuffing. And something else, which reflected the overhead light.

Vanilla Musk saturated the air, compelling me to stick my finger inside the pillow and pull out whatever it was Adrienne needed me to see right then. A gold charm emerged, the hook that had once held it on a chain lying open, the word "THREE" in bold letters, the T sitting to the right of a manufactured jagged edge of gold.

I couldn't breathe. I couldn't scream, or cry, or run, or do any of the things I needed to do. Because at that moment I had no doubt that if I matched the necklace to the one I'd given to Thomas, it would complete the charm: OMEGA CHI intersecting with OMEGA THREE. The name of Michael's boat. And I knew without a doubt whom the necklace belonged to and why Adrienne had hidden it.

CHAPTER 33

Jack and Beau had already left by the time I made it outside, but Jack had called Thomas, and he, Jayne, and Veronica were waiting for me outside in Thomas's car, the emergency light on the roof flashing at the same rate as my racing pulse.

I sat in the front seat, the gold charm hot against my palm. I held it up by the broken clasp, highlighting it with my phone's light. "I found the missing half of the charm in Adrienne's pillow."

"What does it say?" Thomas asked, not risking a better look as he sped down darkened Charleston streets.

Jayne took the charm and held it up. "It reads 'three.'"

Thomas frowned. "So if we put the two pieces together, they'd spell—"

"Omega Three," Veronica choked out. "That's the name of Michael's boat."

I could see Thomas's eyes narrowing as he filed through all the information we knew and reached the same conclusion as I had. "It's Lauren Dempsey's. It's the necklace she was wearing in the photo her parents gave me."

Jayne leaned forward from the backseat. "But why would it be in Adrienne's pillow?"

I waited for Veronica to say it, unwilling to make her see the truth before she understood it herself.

"Adrienne put it there. She stitched it inside to keep anyone from finding it. Because she knew what it meant." Veronica stopped, unable to continue.

"That Lauren and Michael were having an affair," Jayne said gently. "He must have given it to her."

"I can't figure out why the two pieces would have been separated," I said.

"I've been wondering the same thing," Thomas said. "I think the chain had somehow broken and fallen off of Lauren's neck and Adrienne found it. Maybe she returned part of the necklace to Lauren under the pretense that the remainder of the charm was lost so Lauren wouldn't guess that Adrienne knew her secret."

"Except Lauren somehow found out. Maybe she overheard Adrienne on the phone saying to me how she had something important to tell me. There was that public pay phone in Adrienne's dorm. It would have been easy to overhear." Veronica paused, and I could almost hear her mind racing, the wheels spinning as the cogs finally slipped into place. "But if Michael didn't kill Adrienne, then . . ." She stopped, her realization temporarily stealing her voice.

"Lauren did." Thomas's voice was matter-of-fact, which was oddly reassuring. "Because she knew Adrienne was going to tell you about the affair. I believe that Lauren continued to wear the partial charm on the chain, but it got yanked off in the struggle with Adrienne in Adrienne's dorm room. That's why it was found with Adrienne's belongings."

"But how . . . ?" Veronica couldn't say the words out loud.

More gently than before, Thomas said, "I think I figured out something else. Adrienne was killed by a blow to the head. Remember the missing sailing trophy? I bet that Lauren had taken it from her old boyfriend's room—the sailing team captain—as a prank or just because she wanted it in her room. She may or may not have intended to kill Adrienne, but if they were arguing about Adrienne telling Veronica about the affair and there was a struggle, Lauren might have picked up the first thing she could find to subdue Adrienne. Unfortunately, she chose the trophy."

"And when Michael found out that Lauren had killed Adrienne, he strangled her." I touched my throat, remembering the press of icy hands. "He wanted to punish Lauren because he knew how much your sister meant to you."

Veronica gave a choking laugh. "As if he cared enough to try to avenge my feelings." She shook her head. "He . . . Michael travels a lot for work." Veronica's voice sounded stronger now, as if focusing on the details helped blur the truth of what her husband had done. "He could have sent those postcards in from Lauren." Veronica paused. "They must have spent a lot of time in his fishing cabin and on the *Omega Three*, because of the necklace he gave her. Knowing him, he buried her body at sea so she wouldn't be found."

Thomas took a sharp turn onto Queen Street. I faced the backseat. "I'm sorry, Veronica."

"Don't be. There's consolation in knowing that Adrienne can rest in peace now." With a lifted chin, she added, "And in that we know who is responsible and can bring him to justice." She didn't say Michael's name, but her words trembled with anger and hurt.

Thomas pulled up to the curb in front of Veronica's house, shutting off the engine but leaving the lights on. "If he's here, he's either looking for the other half of the charm so he can destroy the evidence, or he's packing. Or he's already done both and is long gone."

We scrambled out of the car. "Right now I just need to find Nola."

I felt Thomas looking at me but didn't meet his gaze. Because if I did, I'd have to acknowledge that Nola might be in the house with Michael, and if he felt threatened, I didn't know what he might do.

The house sat in total darkness, its roof angles and pointed turret peaks like retracted claws against the full moon. Milky light highlighted the dormers and reflected off of the windows, lending the house the appearance of an old man peering out at us with foggy spectacles. We clustered together in the driveway while Thomas pulled a flashlight from his car and let its beam flood the front yard, illuminating Beau's truck parked halfway into the grass, the front passenger door left ajar, and Michael's car pulled up close to the house. The front door of the house stood wide open, exposing empty darkness inside.

Veronica's voice was unusually high-pitched. "The workmen were dealing with an electrical wiring issue today. The lights weren't working when we left, although they promised me the lights would be operational by the time we got home."

"Either they were wrong," Thomas said, "or someone has cut the power. Melanie, can you reach Jack on his cell?"

I'd been hitting his number over and over, but the call kept going immediately to voice mail. "No—he must have turned it off."

Thomas nodded grimly, then briefly returned to his car, where he called for backup, making the situation seem suddenly more real. Without stopping as he walked past us, he said, "Stay here. I'm armed, and it's dark, and I don't want anyone getting hurt." Before we could protest, he ran toward the house and disappeared inside.

I tried Jack's and Nola's phone numbers again, but both calls went straight to voice mail.

Veronica began to cry. "I'm so sorry. I didn't mean for it to end this way. I didn't want anybody getting hurt. Especially not Nola."

She'd just put my fear into words, and I began to shiver beneath my coat.

Jayne's voice remained calm. "Nobody said anyone was getting hurt. If Nola is in there, I imagine she's passed out on a couch or a bed and has no idea we're looking for her or that Michael is in there, too."

I looked at Jayne, needing reassurance that she was right, but her gaze was focused behind me at the house. "There's a light . . ." she started to say, pointing toward the high attic window.

We all turned as a piercing female scream shattered the silence. Without waiting to see if anyone followed, I took off at a fast run, losing both shoes before I'd reached the front steps. I stopped abruptly inside the door, causing Jayne and Veronica to bump into me. Nola's guitar sat in its case in the middle of the floor, its meaning unclear. Either Nola had been too impaired to do anything but find a bed to fall into, or she'd been interrupted while trying to leave. Before I could weigh the implications, another scream followed by scuffling feet from above steered us toward the staircase, all of us flipping on our phone flashlights, the beams bouncing along the newly painted walls as we hurried to the second floor. The scent of Vanilla Musk enveloped us, growing stronger with each step, reassuring me that we weren't alone.

We paused in the upstairs hallway, shining our lights into doorways, hoping to find Nola in one of the beds or discover the source of the scream, praying they weren't connected. More movement sounded from the attic above, and then a man's voice. *Jack.* I ran toward the attic steps and looked up to see a light flickering from the space beneath the door.

Before I could take my first step, Veronica pulled me back. "Shouldn't we wait for backup?" she whispered. "We don't know what's going on, and we might make things worse."

I looked at Jayne. My one consolation amid the agony of worrying about Nola was knowing that if she was in the attic, Jack, Thomas, and Beau were in there with her.

After a brief hesitation, she nodded. "She's right. And Adrienne is here."

"But so is Lauren."

I'd sensed the heavy presence at the same time I'd smelled Adrienne's perfume, feeling a growing force field as we got closer to the attic. I recalled being shoved down the stairs and was wavering about what we should do when the sound of Nola whimpering came from behind the closed door.

Instinct took over, and I raced up the stairs, the attic door flying open with sudden violence that sent it crashing into the wall behind it before I'd even reached the top step. It took a moment to register the scene in front of me: the lit glass hurricane lamp sitting on the windowsill, the red pillar candle inside it still decorated with pine boughs from a long-forgotten Christmas; Beau, Thomas, and Jack standing in a semicircle near the door with their backs to us and facing the corner; and Michael and Nola huddling in that corner near Adrienne's box of belongings, which had been upended, the contents scattered across the attic floor. He towered over her like a menacing shadow. *The tall man.* I gritted my teeth at my stupidity, my obliviousness. The light from our phones reflected off of something long and shiny at Nola's throat.

"Melanie," Nola said with slurred words, her eyes glassy with fear as her head lolled back against Michael's shoulder.

"Put the knife down, Michael." Veronica stepped forward slowly, her voice decisive and strong. She held up a small object, the gold winking in the candlelight as it swayed from her upheld fingers. "We found Lauren's charm. We know you killed her. She killed Adrienne, didn't she? Because my sweet sister found out that you were having an affair and Lauren didn't want me to know." She took another small step forward. "Let Nola go, Michael. There's no place you can hide. Don't make it any worse."

A cold breath blew on the back of my neck, and I saw Jayne touching her own neck at the same time. *Lauren.*

Thomas stayed where he was as he spoke. "She's right, Michael. You're only making things worse. Drop the knife and no one else gets hurt."

Veronica took another step toward him, but Michael raised the knife. "Don't come any closer, or I will cut her throat. We all know that without a hostage I won't make it out of this room a free man. She's my only chance."

"Then take me," I said. I felt Jack's eyes on me, but I didn't turn my head. "Nola's drunk and can't run as fast as you right now. But I can."

He responded by squeezing Nola tighter and making her whimper.

"Please, don't do this, Michael." Veronica's voice broke. "Haven't you hurt me enough? And have you thought about what you're doing now and how it will hurt our daughter?"

His gaze flicked over his wife, the knife shaking, hinting at hesitation. "Don't you see?" He half shouted, half sobbed out the words. "It doesn't matter anymore. I've got to get away—to start over. You and Lindsey don't need me. Just. Let. Me. Go."

"Michael, listen . . ." Jack began.

"Shut up! Everybody—move away from the door and press yourselves face forward against the wall. If I see anyone turn around, I'll kill her."

"Please, Michael," Veronica sobbed. "What are you doing?"

"Shut up!" he shouted again. "And do as I say. One more word out of you, and it's all over."

We formed a line against the wall, Jayne on my left side and Jack on my right.

"Jack," I whispered, my voice thick with fear.

"I'm here," he whispered back.

And in that moment, all the uncertainty and confusion that had surrounded us for the last months rubbed away like tarnish, leaving behind the solid foundation that had always been Jack and me. Despite the direness of the situation, I felt a surge of confidence. We had yet to fail at overcoming a problem as long as we had been together.

I felt Jayne's fingers touching mine, and slowly I took hold of her hand as we silently chanted the words our mother had taught us. *We are stronger together.*

The sounds of shuffling movement and Nola's soft crying came from behind us as Michael dragged her toward the open door. Her feet bumped down the steps before an icy wind swept through the room, slamming the door with a deafening crash. We collectively rushed toward the door as Thomas tried to turn the now-immovable knob. A wobbling noise redirected my attention to the window, where the hurricane lamp teetered on its base, rocking back and forth as if in the middle of a tempest.

Everything seemed to move in slow motion, my shouts slurred and my feet leaden as if I was running in a dream. Before I reached the window, the lamp tilted one last time before crashing to the floor, shattered glass hitting me in the legs, and the lit candle falling on a pile of old newspapers. The paper ignited with a loud *poof*, tall flames erupting and reaching toward the ceiling like groping fingers.

Jayne grabbed my hand and dragged me toward the door. "Adrienne! Help us!"

The cold wind continued to whip at our faces and at the fire, feeding the hungry flames. Jayne squeezed my hand, giving me the courage to speak.

"Lauren—don't do this! He's not worth it—he took your life because you hurt his wife. His *wife*. You were a fling and nothing more. Why are you helping him now? Why are you ruining your one chance at redemption?"

LIES. The word rebounded inside my head, the single syllable a low growl that ricocheted off the walls of the attic.

The flames grew fiercer, creeping toward us as we all huddled by the door, the icy wind continuing to spin like a whirlwind, a tornado of fire twisting in the middle of the room. We pressed ourselves against the door, feeling the heat on our faces, choking on the smoke as the three men worked on opening the door, their shouts of frustration mixing with the roar of the flames.

The scent of Vanilla Musk ebbed and flowed as if Lauren and Adrienne were locked in battle. I fell back against Jack as the flames neared and he pressed himself against Jayne and me, his back to the flames.

"Please, Lauren," I cried out. "You don't have to do this. We know what Michael did. You don't need to protect him anymore." The wind picked up, the flames exploding toward the ceiling. My blouse stuck to my heated skin, saturated with sweat and the possibility of defeat.

Beau's voice bellowed over the roar of the fire and the pounding on the door, an indecipherable sound like a cross between a wounded howl and an ancient curse. The wind stilled for a moment, and then a large chest of drawers scraped its way across the room, creating a temporary barrier between us and the fire.

Beau turned toward us, his face dripping sweat. "Open the door. Now!"

Jack and I grabbed the handle together, and it twisted under our hands. He stepped back and gently shoved me forward down the stairs. I grabbed the banister as I felt the press of people behind me, propelling me downward. I waited for Jayne, watching as everyone else ran down the stairs. Then I took hold of her hand.

We began chanting loudly. *We are stronger together.* I felt Lauren's cold hands on my back pushing me forward, but I didn't stop, even as I stumbled. I would have fallen down the rest of the stairs, but Jack caught me and held on.

Jayne's voice rang out in the stairway as she faced the inferno in the attic. "You're forgiven, Lauren. Do you understand? You're forgiven. You don't need to hold on anymore. It's over."

The direction of the wind changed, the scent of perfume now stronger. I lifted my face and spoke toward the flames. "Head toward the light, Lauren. It's okay to leave. You are forgiven. Leave now so Adrienne can also find peace."

A loud moan mixed with the wind whipped around our heads before the wind suddenly stopped, the cold and the oppressive force dwindling until all that was left were the roar of the fire and the sound of sirens outside.

"Nola," I said. "We have to get Nola." We hurried down the stairs to join the others, choking and coughing, as desperate to get away from the flames as we were to find our daughter.

We raced out into the yard to find pandemonium, with firemen, policeman, and neighbors congregating in the small yard. Thomas had apparently caught up to Michael, and he was in the process of cuffing him when Jack ran across the lawn and began shaking Michael hard enough that it made my own teeth hurt.

"Where is Nola? Where is she?"

"She's fine, Jack," Thomas said. "She's in the back of Michael's car, but she's unharmed."

Jack shook Michael one last time and then the two of us headed toward the car, realizing before we reached it that the backseat was empty. We looked up in confusion, searching the sea of people in the yard for Nola. I started to panic at the sight of the house, where flames and smoke were now pouring out of the upstairs windows, and my ears pounded with the sounds of shattering glass and splintering wood.

And there, climbing the front steps in a zigzag motion, was Nola. We stared in numb horror as she waved at us.

"I need to get my guitar," she shouted, her voice barely audible over all the noise. She turned, swaying as she made her way through the open front door.

"Nola!" Beau shouted, but she didn't reappear.

We had barely begun moving forward when Beau sprinted past us and disappeared inside the house behind her. Not two seconds later, a loud crash came from inside, followed by a billow of smoke and fire from the doorway. I screamed, falling to my knees as Jack ran toward the front door, only to be pulled back by a fireman who refused to let go no matter how much Jack struggled or cursed at him.

I ran to Jack and we clung to each other, neither one of us willing to accept what we had just seen. Veronica and Jayne came to stand with us, all of us sobbing, deaf to the pleas of the fireman, who urged us to step away from the flying sparks and growing flames as the fire consumed the house.

A great roar arose from the gathered crowd at the sound of a window smashing. The roar was quickly replaced with loud applause. We turned to watch as Beau threw a chair through the large library bay window, then carried Nola through it, pivoting on the windowsill before jumping down with her in his arms.

We ran toward them, the crowd parting. Then we showered both Nola and Beau with indiscriminate hugs and kisses, and I knew that, with the exception of my wedding day and the day the twins were born, this was undoubtedly the happiest day of my life.

CHAPTER 34

It was nearly five in the morning when we returned home from the hospital with Nola, who was remarkably unscathed despite her ordeal. I imagined that healing mentally would take longer and probably require professional help, but for now she was safe and sound and tucked in her own bed.

We had all thankfully suffered few effects from the smoke. Unfortunately for Nola, this gave Jack a clear enough head to begin working on a very long and very arduous punishment that meant no friends, no phone, and no free time. Not that she didn't deserve it, but I felt the need to mitigate some of it. At points in every parent's career, it's necessary to take turns being either the mean parent or the nice parent, and I was choosing now to play nice. We had come so close to losing her, and my gratitude at having her back made me never want to let her out of my sight again.

The whole ride back from the hospital, she'd been complaining about the loss of her guitar and how if Beau had just waited a little longer, she could have saved it. Her reasoning was completely irrational, but we were oddly reassured that she was going to be fine.

We stood in Nola's bedroom watching her sleep, and I wasn't planning on leaving until she awoke. I kept touching her, as if to make sure she wasn't missing any parts, until Jack gently pulled me from the room, afraid I would wake her.

"I'm too wired to sleep right now," he said, "and I'm thinking you probably are, too. This would be a good time for us to talk. No one else is here, and Nola will most likely sleep all day."

I already knew what I wanted, and I would have been happy to skip past any discussion and just lay my cards on the table. But that was solidly "old version of Melanie" territory, and we'd come too far for me to slide backward.

"Sure. Can I make you some coffee?"

"Only if it's decaf. I'm afraid I'll start flying on my own if I add to the adrenaline still pumping through me. And we'll both need sleep when it wears off."

My original look of horror at the word "decaf" was replaced with one of resignation. "I know Mrs. Houlihan keeps her own stash of beans in the pantry. Why don't you wait for me in the parlor? Just don't trip over the clock."

My fingers shook, from either residual shock or nervousness or both, as I went through the motions of grinding beans and making the coffee, using our favorite mugs, which had been decorated by our children. I poured a hefty amount of cream in my coffee, followed by four teaspoons of sugar. I placed it next to Jack's plain black coffee on a small tray and carried it into the parlor, the mugs clanking together as my hands shook.

Jack took the tray so I could step over the clock, and he set it down on the coffee table. We had both taken a seat on the sofa when Jack popped up again and walked across the room. He picked something up from the floor next to the grandfather clock, and I saw that he was holding Frozen Charlotte's coffin with as few fingers as he could manage.

"What is this doing here? After her most recent escape, I put her in her little coffin and stuck it in the closet in my office behind a case of copier paper."

I frowned. "Maybe Evangeline is just pointing out that she tried to warn us that Nola was in danger from the tall man and we didn't heed her warning?" A shudder went through me as a brief picture of what had happened in the attic flashed through my brain. "I shouldn't have assumed she was referring to Marc just because he was the easiest candidate—especially after the clock broke his foot. I'm so angry with myself. I've been given this gift, and yet I still managed to mess things up. And because of that, we almost lost Nola."

An unexpected sob rose from my throat, shaking my entire body. Jack placed the small coffin on the coffee table before taking my cup from me and wrapping me in his arms. "Don't, Mellie. Please don't. You did nothing wrong. The only person at fault is Michael Farrell. The rest of us would have died if it hadn't been for you and Jayne."

"And Beau," I sobbed.

At some point I would need to dissect what had happened in the attic and Beau's part in getting us out. But not now. I had more important things to work through first.

"And Beau," Jack agreed. "But you didn't mess anything up. You couldn't. You have never done anything where the motive wasn't based on the love you have for those around you. You have quirky ways of doing things for sure, but that's you. And I can't change it."

I sat up to look at him, wiping my eyes with the backs of my hands. "What are you saying?"

"I'm saying you need to delete your 'new Melanie' spreadsheet."

My chest constricted, my heart shrinking. "Why?" I asked, even though I knew. Whether I was the new or old Melanie didn't matter. He had found the flaw he couldn't live with.

"Because I shouldn't expect you to change."

Anger yanked away my hurt and confusion, propelling me to stand and face Jack. As usual, the words poured out of me before I had a chance to check them. Everything that I'd bottled up over the past months erupted from my mouth uncensored. I no longer cared if it was spoken by the new or old version of me—it simply came from Melanie, the woman I was now.

"You know, Jack, I shouldn't be the only one trying to change. You have to meet me halfway. Because did it ever occur to you that you're at fault, too? That it's unrealistic if not downright cruel to believe that all of my insecurities should be banished just because you said you loved me? Maybe I just needed a little more understanding. A little more help. I agree that I need to stop pushing everything unpleasant under the carpet and to confide in you more. But changing my stripes is hard all by myself. Maybe I shouldn't have to change all of my stripes anyway. Needing to be organized and having an independent nature aren't things that need to be fixed. They're not addictions that need to be cured."

He opened his mouth to say something, but I barely drew a breath before continuing. "And one more thing. You left me because you said you couldn't trust me because I'd gone off on my own to figure out where those rubies were hidden. Because you had the *flu*, for crying out loud! But even still, you said it was an issue of trust. Sure, I probably should have let you know what I was doing, and I've learned from that. And yet here you are, creating a whole scenario about a missing half of the Hope Diamond with an assumed identity and not telling me *anything*. Talk about lack of trust. And, sure, I understand that your male ego has been sorely damaged by everything that's happened in your career. You have nothing to prove to me. You've already shown me what love is between a husband and wife and what an amazing father you are. That's all I have ever needed. I'm just sorry you don't feel the same way."

He stared at me without saying anything.

"And, yes, you're right. I was wr—" I paused, trying to form the unfamiliar word. "I was . . . wrong to talk to Suzy without telling you. I'm sorry."

I stood there, my chest heaving, waiting for him to stand and leave. And take my heart with him.

Instead, a small twitch appeared at the side of his mouth. "You're right, Mellie."

"About being wrong?"

"Well, that, but about the other stuff, too. I've been a complete idiot. Everything you've just said is true. All of it. We're equally to blame for everything that's happened in our marriage. What is it that Yvonne said we should do? Admit it and then take a leap of faith?"

I stared at him, my words of protest dying on my lips. I blinked. "What?"

He stood as well, facing me. "I don't want a do-over. Unless we can re-create exactly the happiest years of my life so far. And I don't need or want a new version of you. You're my Mellie. You're perfect the way you are—quirks and all—and I don't want to change a thing."

"Even my labeling habit?"

"Especially that. I've come to realize that a house isn't a home without the constant clicking of a labeling gun."

I gave him a wobbly smile. "Then maybe we take that leap of faith and see where we land."

He pulled me toward him and kissed me the way he used to, and I felt as if I'd been away for a long time and finally found my way home.

I lifted my head. "Do you really think we're going to be okay?"

He kissed me again, gently this time. "I do. No matter what. As long as we're together, we're going to be okay."

The grandfather clock began to chime, the sound muffled against the carpet. Our eyes widened in mutual surprise before we both turned toward the clock.

"I thought it was broken," I said.

"Well, it hasn't chimed or ticked since it fell, so that was my assumption." Jack looked at his watch. "It's six thirty. Why would it be chiming now?"

We stood next to the clock, looking down at it, feeling the vibrations from the chimes beneath our feet. I counted ten more chimes as we stood there. "I don't think it's going to stop. Maybe we should call Rich and beg him to try again to lift it without the special equipment? Maybe with us helping that would be enough?"

Jack nodded slowly, his brow furrowing. He glanced at Charlotte's coffin lying on the coffee table. "There has to be a reason why Evangeline is still here and why the clock is chiming now when it hasn't made a sound since it fell."

I looked at my phone, confirming that it was now six thirty-two, and then at my watch, noting that the big hand and little hand were both pointed near the six. I jerked my head up. "Wait a minute. Evangeline's grave marker. The clockface on the front. It showed six thirty."

Jack met my gaze, a slow smile making its way across his face. "Or the hands are arrows pointing downward."

I followed his gaze toward the clock, remembering how each time we'd found the Frozen Charlotte, she'd been faceup halfway under the clock's base. "I think there's something on the bottom of the clock we're supposed to see." We moved behind the clock where it had been pulled away from the wall by Rich and his son, Brian. Etched on the pale wood on the bottom of the clock case were faint lines that had been dug into the surface with a sharp instrument. We could barely make them out.

"Wow. We searched the entire clock for more diamonds but never thought to look here." Jack squatted closer to better see the indistinct scratches.

"Hang on. I have lead pencils and tracing paper in my craft drawer in the kitchen. I'll be right back."

"Of course you do," Jack said as I stepped over the clock and ran toward the kitchen, returning in less than a minute as the clock continued to chime.

"For the record," I said, handing him the supplies, "being organized can sometimes come in handy."

"I never said it can't." Jack held the paper over the scratches, gently rubbing the pencil on it until enough of an image had been revealed. He stood, holding the paper so we both could see.

"I don't understand." I leaned in closer. "It's a drawing of the clockface on the gravestone."

Jack sat back on his haunches. "So, if I were a captain in the Confederacy and I came into possession of a legendary diamond, I'd want to hide it in a separate location just in case the first stash was found. But he chose not to hide it and instead put the cut gems on full display in a collar for a dog belonging to his illegitimate daughter."

"Maybe he meant for them to be her legacy, and that was the cleverest way to hide them from both sides and ensure she remained in possession of them."

"But she died before he did. In the fire of 1861." Our eyes met as we reached the same conclusion. Jack spoke rapidly as if trying to keep pace with his thoughts. "So he hid them in her monument, not expecting to be killed before he could retrieve them after the war."

"If all of this is correct, there's no guarantee they're still there," I said. "If John told someone, or someone followed the clues he left behind like us, they could be long gone."

"Or not," Jack said, his eyes sparkling. With a sudden shout, he picked me up and spun me around. "Either way, it's one heck of a way to end my book, don't you think?"

I nodded as we both became aware that the clock had finally stopped chiming and the Frozen Charlotte and her coffin were gone.

CHAPTER 35

Jack and I sat on the garden bench under a blanket, pushing the bundled-up twins in their newer and bigger swings. They had grown so much over the past eight months that my father decided that, as part of the garden refurbishment, he'd gift JJ and Sarah with swings that should take them at least through their preschool years. I hated to think of them growing up that quickly, but as Nola began her senior year at Ashley Hall, we'd come to accept the inevitable.

Two things that hadn't changed were JJ's attachment to his whisk, currently clutched in his hand, and Sarah's constant chattering even when she was by herself. I wasn't sure how, or if, either thing mattered to their futures, but I wasn't going to worry about it. Jack and I would take it in stride together.

My phone beeped and I looked down to see another text from Rebecca. Despite her hopes that the shower would change her marriage, it had not. She blamed it on my desertion, as if I'd planned Nola's abduction by a murderer and the ensuing house fire. Still, she texted me several times a day from her new house on Kiawah Island, asking me for advice on mothering her infant daughter, Tiffani. I'd tried to dissuade her from saddling her daughter with that name and spelling, but like everything

Rebecca, she wanted to do it her way. Including her sensational divorce, in which she'd taken Marc for everything that hadn't been confiscated by the Feds when he'd been arrested in a surprise Sunday morning take-down the week after the shower. Jack and I had happily lent Rebecca the funds needed to hire the best lawyers. It was the least we could do, I told her. Because we were family. I put my phone on silent, not wanting to spoil this perfect morning with Jack and our children.

"Hello? Anybody out here?" Suzy Dorf came through the garden gate, latching it behind her. My stomach no longer clenched when I saw a text from her, and now I even considered her a friend. Although still overly inquisitive and sometimes downright nosy, she'd proven to be a strong ally in our battle with Marc Longo.

Jack stood, offering his seat on the bench, but she refused. "Really, Jack, sit back down. I only wanted to stop by for a minute to give you this." Suzy handed us a copy of the morning paper. "I thought you two should be the first to see it."

I leaned over Jack's shoulder and read the bold-faced headline.

LOCAL BUSINESSMAN MARC LONGO
FOUND GUILTY OF RACKETEERING,
TAX EVASION, AND ART THEFT

I looked up, unable to stop smiling. Marc deserved everything he had coming to him, and I couldn't find a scrap of sympathy for him.

"It's been a long time coming," Suzy said. "If you hadn't made the introduction with Anthony Longo, I would never have had the access to other insiders and documents. It turned out to be a much bigger case than I'd originally thought. Marc's going to get a lot of years behind bars, that's for sure. And to think I was only out for a little revenge for my baby brother when this all started."

Suzy reached into her tote and pulled out a stack of newspapers and handed them to Jack. "I thought you might like extras to give to friends. Or wallpaper your office." She grinned. "By the way, I really loved the *Today* show piece they did on you. The video clip of you two finding the diamonds at Magnolia Cemetery was fascinating, and the scene where the dog bones and children's toys were added to Evangeline's grave was a nice touch. Great promo for your appearance on *Treasure Hunters*, too. I just hope that Marc has a TV in his jail cell so he can watch it."

"We can only hope," I said, giving both children's swings a little push.

Her expression changed to one of concern. "By the way, I've been meaning to ask: How's Nola doing?"

"Surprisingly well," I said. "Her grades are great, and she's excited about participating in the Ashley Hall Christmas play. She misses her friend Lindsey, who's taking a year off from school to take a sailboat voyage around the world with her mother. They both needed to get away. There's a full crew and they're learning to sail. We've received a few postcards, and they sound like they're having a blast."

"Even better," Jack said, "Dr. Wallen-Arasi is so busy with rebuilding their house while they're gone that she's leaving us alone. She's doing her best to incorporate what the fire didn't destroy into the new build, so I'm sure it will be a wonderful home for Veronica and Lindsey when they return. In the meantime, I'm enjoying the temporary reprieve from constant construction." He smiled with satisfaction.

Suzy nodded. "So, this is completely off-the-record, but that boy who saved Nola, Beau—did the fire forge a relationship between them?"

"Yes," I said.

"No," Jack said at the same time.

We shared a glance before I tried to explain. "Jack and I think Nola's constant bickering with Beau Ryan is helping her refocus. We're starting to think that he irritates her on purpose just for this reason. It doesn't help that she blames him for the loss of her guitar. It belonged to her mother, and I'm sure it's made Nola grieve for her all over again. We replaced it with a brand-new one that she picked out herself, but she says it's hard for her to write music with it because she can't feel her mother's presence."

Jack frowned. "Yes, well, I think Beau is enjoying the bickering. It's a way some guys show they're interested. As long as it doesn't go any further than that, I'm fine with it."

"What's wrong with Beau?" Suzy asked, the gleam of a journalist's curiosity twinkling in her eye. We'd given her exclusive access for interviews with us and Nola following the fire, which most likely accounted for her continued interest.

Jack and I shared a glance, both of us remembering the bizarre moment in the attic before the door opened. In the intervening eight months, we'd asked Beau about it more than once, but he never strayed from his assertion that he'd shouted out only in frustration, which must have coincided with Michael opening the front door, creating enough of a draft to push open the attic door.

That didn't explain the chest of drawers sliding across the attic floor, but I wanted to believe that Jayne and I had given Adrienne enough strength to do that and thus buy us a few precious minutes before the flames could reach the door.

Jack shifted uncomfortably. "Beau is a nice guy. But just not the right guy for Nola. Besides, she's too young for any kind of a relationship."

"Yes, well, she heads to college next fall, right?"

Jack groaned. "Yes. Despite acceptances to the College of Charleston, Clemson, and the University of South Carolina, she's decided on Tulane in New Orleans. She insists it has nothing to do with Beau, who will be returning to New Orleans after his graduation from the American College of the Building Arts."

"Interesting," Suzy said. "I can't wait to hear about how Nola enjoys New Orleans. It's very similar to Charleston, but I've heard several Charlestonians refer to the Crescent City as Charleston's slightly younger and more tawdry sister. At least she'll be used to the heat and humidity and the flying palmetto bugs. Except in New Orleans they don't sugarcoat it—they just call them flying cockroaches."

She saw my expression and hoisted her tote higher on her shoulder. "I guess I should be going. Sorry—I didn't mean to stay so long. You ready for tomorrow, Melanie?"

"As ready as I'll ever be."

As promised, I was allowing Suzy to interview me. My mother and Jayne would be joining me to share our experiences communicating with the dearly departed and to tell how helping the loved ones they've left behind find closure had given us new insight on how to view our gift.

My biggest trepidation had been about how it would affect my career, so I'd met with my boss, David Henderson. Instead of the pushback I thought he'd give me, he congratulated me on my new promo gimmick to attract more buyers of historic real estate to our agency to work with me. Jolly had also approved, asking if Suzy would like to interview her, too. I told her I would let her know.

Jack stood. "Thanks for stopping by, Suzy." He surprised us both by embracing the diminutive reporter. "I really can't tell you how much I appreciate everything you've done. I just wish you'd told me years ago that your oldest brother was the publisher for Mapson and Webber. It would have saved me a lot of foaming at the mouth over my career—not to mention from having to do a shirtless photo shoot."

Suzy grinned. "Yeah, but then you would have disappointed all of your female fans. I say, all's well that ends well. Even a year out from being published, I hear the buzz for *Power, Greed, and Dirty Deeds* is already the biggest thing in publishing since the last installment of *Harry Potter*. And Hollywood buzz, too. Maybe your house will have another chance to star in a movie."

The words were barely out of her mouth when every light in the house flashed off and on several times. Suzy turned back toward us with wide eyes. "Or not."

"So, Suzy," Jack said, walking her to the gate, "one more thing. That unnamed source and those anonymous letters you received about our house that you wrote about in some of your articles—who really sent them?"

She looked back with genuine surprise. "They really were anonymous. They'd arrive on my desk with my name on the front of the envelope and nothing else. Nobody ever saw who put them there." She tilted her head. "I always assumed they were from you."

"From me? Why would you say that?"

"Because you're a writer. Aren't writers always looking for a good story? And publicity doesn't hurt, either."

"All true—but I didn't send them."

Jack and Suzy looked at me.

"And I definitely didn't. I've only ever wanted to live in my house in peace. Digging up bodies was never part of the plan."

"Well, then," Suzy said, a sparkle in her eyes, "I guess it's a mystery."

We said good-bye; then Jack joined me back on the bench, pulling the blanket over us again. I put my head on his shoulder and sighed with contentment.

"I really love what your dad did with the garden," Jack said. "What is it he calls this type of design?"

"A Romantic Garden." I frowned. "I'm not so sure I like it. It seems so . . . unplanned. None of the paths have right angles or straight lines. And he's placed tall plantings so that it's impossible to see what's around the next turn. I find it . . . unsettling."

Jack chuckled, his hand reaching for mine under the blanket. "That's sort of like life, though, don't you think? As long as you have a partner to walk with, you won't get lost."

I nuzzled my nose into his neck. "True. And I think the garden will make a beautiful backdrop for Thomas and Jayne's wedding."

"What? They're engaged?"

"Not yet. But Mother and I see it coming. I've already started planning the matching wedding outfits for Sarah, JJ, and Nola."

Jack gave me a sideways glance but was smart enough not to comment. Instead, he said, "Have you decided what you want for Christmas?" He leaned forward to kiss the tip of Sarah's nose before giving her swing a push.

I thought for a moment. "To be honest, there's not a single thing on this earth that I need. Everything I need in my life is right here in this house."

"Me, too."

Our lips met, and I lingered there, too content to move. In just a few short years since I'd unwillingly inherited my house on Tradd Street, so much had changed in my life—a husband, children, dogs, a sister, and a renewed relationship with my parents. But so much remained the same. The old house still stood proudly, its windows peering out at the same street it had been facing for more than one hundred and seventy years. Her cornices were no longer cracked, and her new windows sparkled beneath the eaves and columns wearing fresh coats of paint.

The shuffling feet of an old man had been replaced by the running footsteps of toddlers and the bounding energy of a teenager. Mr. Vanderhorst had been right when he'd told me that a person couldn't really own an old house like ours, but merely acted as guardian for future generations. I closed my eyes, remembering my first meeting with Nevin Vanderhorst, when I'd hoped to get the listing to sell his house. I had seen his mother, Louisa, in the garden by the rope swing, and that was all he'd needed to know that I would be its next guardian. And I would never forget what he had told me.

This house is more than brick, mortar, and lumber. It's a connection to the past and those who have gone before us. It's memories and belonging. It's a home that on the inside has seen the birth of children and the death of the old folks, and the changing of the world from the outside. It's a piece of history you can hold in your hands.

"Do you remember what you said to me when we got married?" I asked.

Jack smiled against my lips. "I do. We were standing in this very garden and I told you that I intended to live here with you forever. And maybe even longer than that."

"Then let's make that happen," I said, and sealed my words with a kiss.

The sound of rope against wood drifted across the garden from the ancient oak that had stood sentinel for as long as the house had been there, the tree's long branches reaching over the yard in a maternal embrace. And above the sounds of the rope and our babbling children, I imagined I heard the applause of a multitude of unseen hands and an unspoken chorus of a single word reverberating inside my head. *Home.*

NOTE TO MY READERS

When *The House on Tradd Street* was published in 2008, it was supposed to be the first book in a two-book series. I was busily working on the second book when the first book was published, and the love readers showed for Melanie, Jack, and the city of Charleston made it clear to both my publisher and to me that my wonderful readers wouldn't be satisfied with just two books.

So then came *The Girl on Legare Street* (2009), followed by *The Strangers on Montagu Street* (2011) and *Return to Tradd Street* (2014). By the time I'd finished *Return to Tradd Street* it had become clear that my readers were as attached to these characters as I was. In what I thought was the final book in the series, I wrote an epilogue that would open up the possibility of more books if my readers wanted more. And they did.

The Guests on South Battery was published in 2017 and was followed by *The Christmas Spirits on Tradd Street* in 2019. Knowing it was the penultimate book in the series, I realized that the latter couldn't have the tidy ending my readers might have been expecting. But I'd never ended any of these books with a *true* ending where everything is cleared up, and *The Christmas Spirits on Tradd Street* would be no different. Especially since I knew there would be one more book.

And so here we are at the end of the series, with the seventh and final (really!) book, *The Attic on Queen Street*. I am confident that I have tied up any loose ends and answered any lingering questions. I am also hopeful that I have whetted my readers' appetites for more with the introduction of Beau Ryan as well as the beautiful city of New Orleans for the next chapter in the lives of Nola Trenholm and the extended family we have all grown to love.

Because I knew I couldn't completely leave behind my beloved Tradd Street series, I have started writing a spin-off series set in New Orleans, featuring Nola and a new cast of characters (and the appearance of old ones). The first in the series, *The Shop on Royal Street*, will be out in 2022, with a second one to follow in 2023. And if readers love this new series as much as they loved the first, then be prepared to join me on this next journey.

So thank you, dear readers, for your extraordinary support and enthusiasm for all of my books, but especially for my little series that was meant to last for only two books. I've said it before and I will say it again—my readers are THE BEST, and I will continue writing as long as you continue reading.